CHRISTINA'S CUPBOARD

ANITA KLINE PLISEVICH

Christina's Cupboard

© 2024 Anita Kline Plisevich—Independently Published.

For information about this title, contact the publisher:
Anita Kline Plisevich
anitaklineplisevich@gmail.com

ISBN: 979-8-9895779-1-0 (eBook)
ISBN: 979-8-9895779-0-3 (Softcover)
ISBN: 979-8-9895779-2-7 (Hardcover)

Printed in the United States of America
Cover and Interior Design: 1106 Design

I dreamed of someday taking on the challenge of writing a novel. However, my life had this funny way of throwing out interruptions that gave me the excuse to say, "Now is not the time."

I retired after thirty-five years as a marketing manager and suddenly found loads of free time to sit at the computer and start writing.

This novel-in-stories is historical fiction, and I hope you enjoy reading it as much as I in writing it.

This book is dedicated to my biggest supporter, my husband, Harry. He never lost interest as I read him every edited chapter — over and over.

A very special thank you to my granddaughter, Sydney, for being so encouraging and one of the first to read my early attempts at writing these stories. I'm also appreciative to Cathy, Linda, Marge, and Rochelle for reading my first draft and offering their comments, suggestions, and honest opinions.

"It is only a novel … or, in short, only some work in which the greatest powers of the mind are displayed, in which the most thorough knowledge of human nature, the happiest delineation of its varieties, the liveliest effusions of wit and humour, are conveyed to the world in the best-chosen language."

Jane Austen, *Northanger Abbey*

THE WADE FAMILY TREE

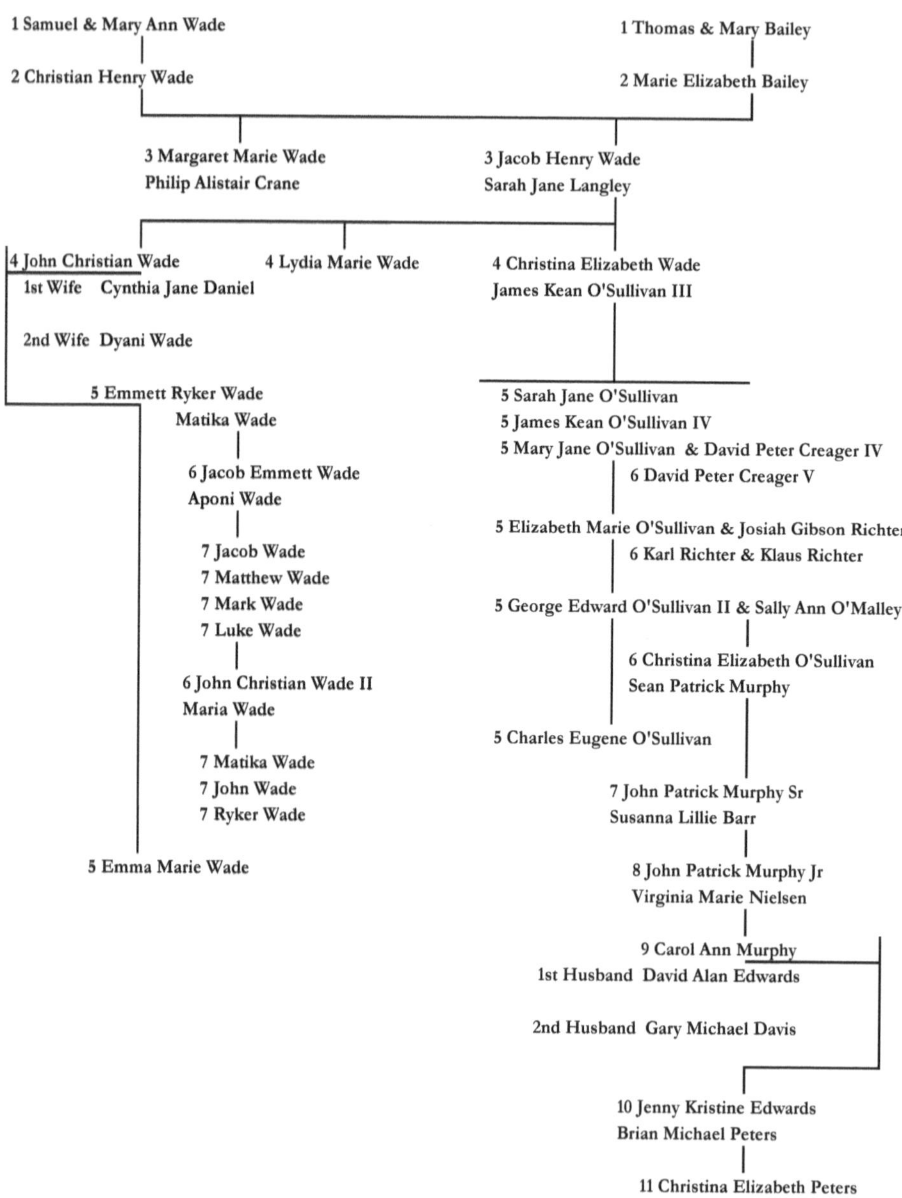

PROLOGUE

"You must learn some of my philosophy.
Think only of the past as its remembrance gives you pleasure."

Jane Austen, *Pride and Prejudice*

*B*orn in Dayton, Ohio, in 1916, my father, John Patrick Murphy Jr., was raised on a farm in the small town of Christiansburg, Ohio. Christiansburg was named after an early ancestor of ours, Christian Wade, who emigrated from England to America in 1791, bringing his wife, adult children, as well as his children's spouses. Dad wanted to learn more about the Wades, as well as other family members with the surnames Bailey, Crane, Langley, Daniel, Creager, O'Sullivan, Richter, O'Malley, Barr, Nielsen, Kraus, and our own, Murphy.

He didn't want to know just the birth and death dates of our ancestors; my father wanted to know how they met their spouse, how and where they lived, what they ate, what they did for fun, and lastly, their cause of death. He wasn't content to merely post names and dates on a family tree; he wanted to become better acquainted with the people in his lineage on a more personal level.

In 1980, my parents took the first of several trips to Salt Lake City, Utah, so Dad could study at the Family History Department of the LDS Church. He said he actually enjoyed sitting for hours viewing microfiche records and poring over dozens of old manuscripts. During his research, he discovered ancestors from England, Ireland, Scotland, Germany, Austria, and Denmark.

Dad visited graveyards and cemeteries to inspect old headstones and monuments. He used a tape recorder to interview our many cousins. He researched the validity of tales told by my grandfather and my great-grandmother.

Looking for additional clues, he painstakingly searched through the trunks and boxes in our attic. There, he found personal letters, newspaper clippings, business ledgers, diaries, and scrapbooks. My parents traveled to Maryland to look for remnants of the old mill where the Wades lived before moving to Ohio. Over the years, they also took several vacations to Europe to visit the cities and towns where our ancestors originated.

When I was ten, my great-grandmother revealed that she had taken a long train trip out West with her father when she was not much older than me. She was able to recount the details of the entire trip as if it had happened yesterday. Dad ultimately found old letters written by family members who had moved to Idaho in 1842 and whose descendants still live there today.

This wasn't just a hobby; it was a labor of love. He wanted to leave a legacy for future generations. However, despite all his research, my dad found most of his inspiration from the items in the massive cupboard that still stands in the library of our old house in Christiansburg. It is difficult for me to fathom how much effort it must have taken for the Wade family to transport that large, beautiful cupboard from England to America. We still refer to it as "Christina's Cupboard," as it was my great-grandmother, Christina Elizabeth O'Sullivan Murphy's, pride and joy.

The cupboard was handcrafted in 1766 from the wood of a Wych elm by Thomas Bailey, Christian Wade's father-in-law. Mr. Bailey gifted it to his daughter, Marie, on the day of her marriage to Christian. The cupboard holds the Wade Bible, as well as personal journals dating back to the 1700s, along with dozens of old books. Even the cookbooks and recipe cards my father found in that cupboard gave him insight into how our early ancestors lived.

This old cupboard, while extraordinary, is neither magical nor mystical. Whether someone is looking for a game to play, a spice to bake a cake, or a good book to read, it merely stands quietly at attention, serving ten generations of my family for over two hundred and fifty years.

The things Dad found in the cupboard helped him fill the voids in his research and gave him the human-interest stories he longed to uncover. He then documented his findings on his manual Underwood typewriter. Mom said she enjoyed curling up in Dad's comfy leather chair in their library room and listen to him read what he had written that day. He appreciated her constructive feedback.

So began Dad's journey of writing the stories about our family. I am honored that the first story he wrote was about me, Carol Ann Murphy Edwards Davis.

I moved back to Christiansburg from Florida to care for my aging parents. But I was also homesick for the life I'd left behind at just twenty-two years old. No sooner had I moved back than Dad began sharing his manuscripts with me. I then began the painstaking task of keying into my computer what he had lovingly typed on his typewriter or written out in longhand. At ninety-five, Dad knew his days on this Earth were numbered, so a day didn't go by that he and I didn't work on his project. He died a year later. But before he passed my father gave me specific instructions on how he wanted the stories he'd written assembled: "Carol, I want you to organize the eighteen stories I've written about our family by starting with the ones of the living family members."

So I placed the story my father had written about me first, followed by my daughter Jenny's story. The third was my granddaughter Lizzy's story, which he started writing the year he died. I finished it after his death. I followed these first three stories with the one he had written about our ancestor and founder of Christiansburg, Christian Wade. The saga continued with Christian's descendants.

The last story was the one my father had written about himself, modestly, in the third person. This brought Dad's endeavor full circle. His idea was that as family members passed, they would be moved to the end, with stories of future family members added to the beginning.

I'm optimistic that his wishes will be followed, and that future generations will read, appreciate, and add their own stories to the legacy my father worked so hard to begin.

CAROL ANN MURPHY EDWARDS
1980

"The more I know of the world, the more I am convinced that I shall never see a man whom I can really love. I require so much!"

Jane Austen, *Sense and Sensibility*

*M*ost days, Carol's daughter, Jenny, proved a polite, well-behaved little girl. But on the first day of third grade, her attitude changed completely.

Jenny was frantically running around the house; her hair was a stringy mess, and she was still wearing her Holly Hobbie nightgown. Hopefully, Carol assumed, this morning's tantrum was merely Jenny's anxiety over starting at a new school. The stress of setting up their new life in Chicago was challenging to both mother and daughter.

"I miss my daddy!" Jenny screamed.

Carol had met Jenny's father, David Edwards, during their senior year at The Ohio State University. They married in 1969, a few months after graduation, and moved to Cleveland so David could start law school. Carol graduated with a marketing degree and found a position as an advertising executive with a regional ad agency. Counting their time together at college, they'd remained a couple for almost twelve years before their divorce was finalized in June.

"Jenny, please use your inside voice," Carol admonished her. "The windows are open, and our neighbors will think I'm murdering you."

"I'm not going to that stupid old school," Jenny cried.

Carol's new house stood a few blocks from St. Michael School. The school, for students in grades K-8, sat on the corner next to St. Michael Catholic Church. Carol hadn't planned on sending Jenny to a parochial school. But it was an excellent school with a better teacher-to-student ratio than the local public school. The good news for Carol was that Jenny's father paid the substantial tuition.

The screaming stopped just long enough for Carol to attempt to braid Jenny's long hair.

"Mrs. Kessler will pick you up from school today," Carol said. "After school, she's taking you and Heather to the park, and I'll see you when I get home after work."

Carol had loved her job in Cleveland, but when a headhunter contacted her about an opening for an ad exec position with the Williams-Nelson Advertising Agency, she escaped to Chicago. Williams-Nelson was considered one of the top ad agencies in the Midwest, and Carol felt she needed a break from her life in Ohio. Fortunately, David didn't object to her taking Jenny to Chicago, as he'd already started his new life with Marlene.

"Now, let's put on your pretty new dress we bought on Saturday at Marshall Field's and see if Heather is ready to walk to school with us," Carol said in her most persuasive Mommy voice.

Typically, the children wore their school uniforms, but they were allowed to wear something special on the first day.

Jenny had eaten only a few bites of oatmeal when there came a quiet knock on the front door. Carol opened it, and a small tow-haired girl rushed inside. The two young girls held a long embrace. Heather's parents, Barb and Dan Kessler, stood on Carol's porch, smiling. The Kesslers lived three doors down, and Heather was the same age as Jenny. They were such nice people. Carol was thankful she and Jenny had both made such good friends so soon after leaving Ohio.

"My, you look so pretty, Jenny!" Barb exclaimed. "Your strawberry blonde braids look lovely against your new green dress. Are you ready for your big day?"

Barb Kessler was the first person Carol met when she and Jenny moved to Hinsdale, Illinois, a small town just twenty miles southwest of downtown Chicago. Barb had graciously offered to walk the girls to and from school and to watch Jenny at her house every evening until Carol returned home from work.

"I thought we were only going to school," Jenny quipped to Mrs. Kessler. "And you didn't say anything about my new shoes. Mom always says a girl needs pretty new shoes if she's going on an adventure."

The morning's drama finally passed, and Jenny cheerfully found her way to the third grade.

Once the girls were safely settled into Miss Weber's room, the three adults walked to a small neighborhood pastry shop for some much needed coffee. It was a sunny September day, and even with the morning's drama, Carol had a crazy premonition that today could be a good day.

Carol had lost a lot of weight when she and David went through their divorce, so today she indulged herself with a cherry Danish. She justified the Danish by planning to grab a salad for lunch from the little cafe near work in Water Tower Place. She could afford a few extra calories now but knew she needed to start watching her diet since she hadn't always been this thin. Besides, the coffee and pastry should give her a little boost before boarding the train into the city.

"I wish I could eat that luscious looking glazed donut," Barb whined as she stared into the display case. "I still need to lose ten pounds."

"Go ahead, babe, you look great," Dan told her, squeezing her around the waist. "Besides, with all the running around you do with the children, you'll lose it soon."

Dan worked as a commodities trader at The Chicago Mercantile Exchange, or "The Merc," as he called it. Carol was not exactly sure what a commodities trader did, but it appeared to Carol that Dan made a decent living. Carol worried she might lose her amazing neighbors if the Kesslers ever sold their brick Colonial to buy one of those million-dollar homes just a few miles away on Hillcrest. She selfishly hoped the Kessler family would never move away.

Carol envied the couple their relationship. They seemed very much in love, and Barb appeared more than happy to be a stay-at-home mom. Besides Heather, Dan and Barb shared Matt, their precocious two-year-old, and the baby, three-month-old Eric. Barb's mom, Lillie, who lived across the street from Barb and Dan, always made herself available to help with the kids. More than likely, Lillie was with the babies so the three could go for coffee.

At times, Carol wished her parents lived across the street. But remembering how rarely she and her mother saw eye-to-eye, she quickly dismissed the thought.

Most of the houses in the small village of Hinsdale were large, older family homes. Loads of children could be seen riding their bikes, jumping rope, or roller skating down the sidewalks.

The moment she saw the 1930s two-story Dutch Colonial on North Grant, Carol fell in love with it. With its three bedrooms and two full baths it was a little out of Carol's price range, so Carol's parents generously gifted her the money for the down payment.

A wrought iron fence encircled the property. The previous owners had painted the house's exterior traditional colonial blue with white shutters and a white front door. There was a pretty yellow Dutch door that led to a sunny back porch; the split door was a prominent feature of traditional Dutch Colonial homes.

Next spring, when her parents came to visit, Carol planned to ask her father to help her build some window boxes. Luckily, Carol came from a long line of furniture makers, carpenters, and home builders. Of course, Carol's mother would choose the flowers. Carol didn't mind, as she had no gardening skills whatsoever. In contrast, her mother's gardens in Ohio were pure perfection.

She won ribbons whenever she entered her prized roses at their local county fair.

Conveniently, a small powder room stood off the kitchen. Unfortunately, the kitchen needed some work, as the white cabinets looked as if they'd been painted a few times. The old appliances in the kitchen matched, and they all still worked great. Carol found an art deco kitchen table with a red-and-white porcelain top and four white chairs at an antique store in nearby downtown La Grange. It fit perfectly in her large kitchen with its black-and-white checkerboard linoleum floor. A butler's pantry off the kitchen boasted a funny little door to the outside. Carol's realtor explained this was a "milk box." In earlier times, it allowed the milkman to deliver the bottles of milk and cream without having to interact with the housewife.

Carol's favorite room was the dining room. Its bronze chandelier with five vintage glass slip shades threw a lovely amber glow onto her dining table. Two sconces on either side of a built-in hutch against the room's back wall matched the chandelier. Carol was delighted that the previous owners kept all the period light fixtures during the home's last renovation and refinished the house's beautiful white oak hardwood floors.

The two large bedrooms on the second floor shared an adjoining bathroom. Carol's room faced the backyard. A small wooden balcony was just big enough to hold the little wicker rocker she'd brought from Cleveland.

Jenny's room faced the street and had the sweetest window seat. When they moved to Chicago, Carol's parents gave Jenny a white canopy bed with a matching dresser, like the canopy bed in Carol's childhood bedroom in Ohio.

The third bedroom was in a remodeled attic on the top floor with an ensuite bathroom. Perhaps when Jenny was a little older, she might want the attic room for her bedroom.

An old unused coal chute still existed in the basement, and Carol placed an antique Rookwood vase in the vintage phone niche in the hallway. All the rooms were exceptionally large, and with their double or triple aspect, the whole house was quite light and airy.

Aside from the house, what Carol liked most about Hinsdale was its shady tree-lined streets that made this community quite different from the one where Carol spent her childhood.

Carol grew up on a farm in a spacious Greek Revival-style house in Christiansburg, Ohio, built by her early ancestors, the Wades. But by the time Carol was a teenager her family had pretty much stopped all farming activities on their large homestead.

When the Wade family arrived in Ohio in 1810, they built two tiny log homes. In 1815, they built a larger, two-story log home. In 1839, Greek Revivals were in vogue, so the Wades demolished the large log home and built the Greek Revival in its place.

Named after Carol's fifth-great-grandfather, Christian Wade, Christiansburg sat high above the river valley and the larger city of Dayton. Christian and his son purchased the land, and it was passed down through the generations to its present-day owners, John and Virginia Murphy, Carol's parents. Growing up, Carol lived with her parents, her grandfather, John Murphy Sr, and her great-grandmother, Christina Elizabeth O'Sullivan Murphy.

Carol's grandfather was thirty-six when he secured sole ownership of the O'Sullivan Building Company after the death of his grandfather, George O'Sullivan. He then changed the company's name to the Murphy Construction Company. Regrettably, her grandfather was seventy-five when he suffered a broken hip and died of a heart attack a few days after surgery. His death occurred a month before Carol started her third year of college. His wife, Carol's grandmother, Susanna, died several years before Carol was born.

Carol's great-grandmother, Christina, graduated from Oberlin College in 1888. Christina taught Latin and English Literature, rare for a woman born in 1866. Carol enjoyed fond memories of sitting in her great-grandmother Christina's bedroom, watching her sew on an old treadle sewing machine. Sadly, Christina died just before Thanksgiving in 1958 at ninety-two years old. Although Carol was just eleven when Christina died, she still thought of her with great admiration.

Carol never knew her mother's parents, William Nielsen and Hannah Kraus. Born in Austria, Hannah died shortly after Carol's mother's third birthday. Carol's grandfather, William Nielsen, lived a full life but died a few years after Carol's birth, so she was too young to remember him.

William Nielsen's parents immigrated to America from Denmark, and Carol's mother cooked many tasty Danish dishes that had been passed down from William's sister, Carol's great-aunt Edith, who helped William raise his daughter, Virginia, after Hannah's death.

Seven years younger than her husband, Carol's mother kept relatively active. She had her natural blond hair fixed every week at the local beauty shop, along with a fresh manicure. She played bridge once a month with her many "lady friends." A local Junior League chapter member, she often volunteered at the YWCA for their children's program. Virginia was an excellent cook, always busy planning a lavish dinner party for their close friends. She aptly called them her "monthly soirées."

After World War II, Carol's father and grandfather took advantage of the housing boom. They developed nearly one thousand acres of their land into a community of large, expensive, modern homes, naming the development Wade Estates. A decade later, they continued to develop a good portion of their land when they built Wade Plaza, a quaint shopping area with gift boutiques and antique shops.

A successful home builder and real estate developer, Carol's father was now retired, having sold his company several years earlier. Because of injuries John sustained fighting in World War II, he found it harder and harder to maneuver the many stairs in their home. So last year he commissioned to have an addition built onto the back of the house and moved their main bedroom downstairs; with a large adjoining bath and equally generous dressing room. He also added a small sunroom next to the kitchen. John was turning sixty-five next year, so Carol and her mother were making plans for a grand birthday party, inviting John's many friends.

Growing up, Carol received everything a little girl could ever want, but to keep her grounded, Carol's dad emphasized that she must never take her material possessions for granted. John was a smart, gentle, kind man, and a great listener. During her teenage years, Carol usually confided only in her dad about any problems in school, much to her mother's aggravation.

Carol's parents presented her with a pony on her eleventh birthday and a beautiful bay gelding when she turned fourteen. Sadly, Carol's little pony died last year. Unfortunately, since no one rode the big bay, her parents decided they needed to sell him. Carol knew it was time, but she still cried when they told her he had been sold.

Lately, Carol had been attempting to persuade her parents to sell their house and move somewhere warm; however, John said he wasn't leaving until they carried him out. Besides, what would they ever do with Carol's great-grandmother Christina's old cupboard the Wade ancestors had brought over from England? That old antique cupboard belonged in the house.

The last time Carol spoke with her parents on the phone, they complained about how much they missed good friends who had recently moved to Tampa. Before Carol could say anything, her mom groused, "We traveled there this past spring, and it's too humid for me."

"Like Ohio isn't humid, Mom?"

Virginia hung up without saying goodbye.

It was almost noon by the time Carol crammed herself into one of the few open window seats for the train ride into downtown Chicago. She sat lost in her thoughts, paying little attention to those around her.

That past Saturday, she and David would have celebrated their eleventh wedding anniversary. Since they'd separated earlier that year, she surprised herself by feeling somewhat melancholy, but she knew their breakup was for the best. When David called Saturday night to wish Jenny good luck with school, for one moment, Carol pondered why they weren't still together, celebrating. She wondered if he even remembered their anniversary. What happened to the young couple who seemed to have it all?

If the trains ran on schedule, Carol had an hour to travel from the train station in Hinsdale to Union Station in Chicago. Once Carol arrived at Union Station, she hailed a taxi for the final leg of her journey. The cab was well worth the extra money; otherwise, it would take another forty-five minutes to walk to her office—in high heels.

Carol turned thirty-three in July. As a birthday treat, she visited a new salon in Hinsdale where they permed her thick auburn hair. She could tell her now "big" hair had gone airborne. She hoped no one saw her until she could get to the ladies' room to smooth it down.

"Why is it always so windy in this otherwise fabulous city?"

Did Carol shout that question out loud to no one in particular? If she did, no one crossing Michigan Avenue responded to it.

The offices of Williams-Nelson were located on the twenty-first floor of the John Hancock Center. Entering the lobby, she found it packed with people streaming out of the elevators and heading for lunch. Carol was famished but knew there wasn't time to stop for a salad. As she walked toward the elevators, she saw their receptionist, Amy, walking toward her.

"Hey, Carol," Amy shouted above the crowd noise. "I'm headed over to Park Grille for sandwiches for Mr. Williams and Mr. Nelson's meeting. Do you want me to get you anything?"

"You're a lifesaver. I skipped lunch and could use one of their big house salads with their house dressing. I'll pay you when you get back."

"No worries," Amy chuckled. "Mister Big is buying."

Robert Nelson stood at least six foot five, but the employees never called him Mister Big to his face. He'd played football while studying at Northwestern University and looked to be in his early fifties. About the same age, his partner, Jonathan Williams, was short, round, and a little bald on top; he definitely had not played football in college. The college roommates started their first ad agency in Evanston, while still undergrads. They advertised frat parties and helped promote campus events. Until they landed their first big client and moved downtown, their office was in Mr. Nelson's former home in Rockford.

Right after starting at Williams-Nelson, Carol noticed how all the employees addressed Misters Williams and Nelson by their first names. Brought up to never address someone in authority by their first name, Carol found it difficult to call her new bosses Bob and Jon; she wasn't sure she could ever get used to doing so.

Both partners' families lived in Chicago's Gold Coast area. Replete with stately old homes and brand-new high-rise apartment buildings, the Gold Coast bordered Lake Michigan. If you were looking for upscale shopping or dining, you could find it on North Rush Street.

Jon Williams lived on North Astor in a three-story classic Greystone with his wife and teenage daughter. When he heard that Carol lived in an older home in Hinsdale, he disclosed that his house had been built before the turn of the century, in 1893.

Bob Nelson and his wife lived in a new high-rise apartment building. Those fortunate enough to be invited to their home claimed it was quite opulent, with a breathtaking view of Lake Michigan.

When they first arrived in Chicago, Carol and Jenny walked along the tree-lined streets of the Gold Coast. As they walked, Carol fantasized about someday living on East Oak or maybe even iconic North Astor. As they passed the renowned Astor Tower Hotel, she noticed it had gone condo. She wondered if someone had restored the swanky Maxim's de Paris restaurant in the hotel's basement, which had been a disco in the '60s and '70s and pretty popular with Chicago's social elite.

As she stepped off the elevator and opened the large glass doors into the agency's lobby, Carol bumped into Jim Ferguson, head of their graphics department.

"Sorry, Carol," he gasped. "I put those ad layouts we worked on last week on your desk."

Jim was an extremely handsome man, and their little collision left Carol a bit shaken; she silently mimed, *Thanks*.

Back in Cleveland, Carol had worked at the ad agency for almost ten years as an ad exec for a large regional restaurant chain. Here in Chicago, she was considered only a junior ad exec. Carol received a downgrade on her title but made considerably more money working in Chicago.

The advertising field was still considered a male-dominated world. Because Carol was a woman and a single mom, she remained an anomaly. Her current client was Sheffield's Grocery, a regional grocery store chain based in Chicago. The client utilized print ads, billboards, and radio. It was an easy assignment, with no travel required.

As Carol walked past the conference room, she saw Misters Williams and Nelson through the glass windows sitting at the table with her boss, Gary Davis. Never married, Gary looked to be in his late thirties. He dressed as if he had just stepped off Fifth Avenue in New York City. Miles Peters was also in the room; she and Miles shared a secretary.

Miles had started at Williams-Nelson five years earlier, and she figured him to be close to her age. She couldn't see who the other two men were, as they were facing the opposite direction; they were most likely new clients.

As she approached her office, she noticed the new nameplate on the door with her name, "Carol Edwards," in gold letters. The plaque made it official: she now lived and worked in the city she'd always enjoyed visiting.

Her office had a door she could close for privacy, but it had no large windows looking out onto Lake Michigan. In fact, there were no windows at all. *Maybe someday,* Carol thought, *I'll sit in one of those large corner offices with the wraparound windows and have my own secretary.* For now, she shared Martha with Miles, and Martha sat right outside Carol's office.

"Hi, Martha. Do I have any messages?"

Martha looked up and smiled, "Oh hi, Carol. I put a couple of phone messages on your desk; there's one from your dad. How'd it go dropping off Jenny for her first day at school?"

"No major issues, but I'm pretty certain I'll hear all about it tonight."

Carol's daughter could talk your ear off if you let her. It was when Jenny turned quiet that Carol started to worry.

Carol's first phone message was from her client. She quickly called to say she planned to send the new ad layouts by courier for their approval. Before she could call her dad, Martha stuck her head around the corner.

"Mr. Nelson asks if you could come to the conference room to meet some potential clients," Martha said.

Carol grabbed a yellow legal pad and a Bic pen and hurried down the hall, still wondering how her hair looked.

As Carol walked into the conference room, all six men stood up.

"Good afternoon, Carol," Bob said. "I think you already know these two gentlemen."

At precisely the same time, both men turned around. Surprised, Carol saw her former clients from Cleveland, Jerry and Tim Bailey, standing before her. The brothers owned Bailey's Steakhouse, a Midwest regional restaurant chain.

"What are you doing in Chicago?" was all she could think to say to her former clients.

"We've expanded so much in the past few years that Tim and I both felt we needed a bigger agency to handle our advertising," Jerry said. "We've been in talks with Williams-Nelson for several months now and decided to finally come to Chicago to see if this agency was right for our growing company."

"As we talked about our current agency, your name came up," Tim added. "We explained to your bosses that if we hired Williams-Nelson, we'd want you as our ad exec."

Carol was confident she had mentioned her move to Chicago to them, so she was flattered to think they may have considered hiring Williams-Nelson because of her.

As they talked, Carol noticed Miles looked a bit miffed. Perhaps they'd initially tapped Miles to work the Bailey account, and he felt he had been passed over by someone with less seniority. She knew little about Miles, but Martha did tell Carol she believed he might be married because he talked about having a son. With different clients and schedules, Carol and Miles didn't interact much, usually just a brief hello in the morning.

Suddenly, Carol realized that if the Baileys did hire Williams-Nelson, she would be required to travel. She wondered if she earned enough to hire a nanny. She needed a solution, and she needed one quickly; she couldn't pass up this opportunity.

"Well, I do know your business," she teased. "I guess we can just pick up where we left off."

Carol felt she might faint from hunger when Amy finally walked in, pushing a cart with salads, sandwiches, and drinks. After eating, Carol excused herself to the ladies' room. She glanced into the mirror to check her new hairdo and smiled at the strange woman looking back. No matter how badly the day started, Carol's premonition was coming true: today was turning out to be a very good day.

When Carol returned, Gary and Miles had left the conference room. Miles also reported to Gary and would probably gain Carol's grocery chain account. He may have been excited about potentially landing a big client like Bailey's. Hopefully, he didn't take it personally, but Carol couldn't worry about Miles. The five continued to talk for another hour. When the meeting broke, Carol was pleased to hear they planned to return the next day to meet the rest of the staff.

As they left the conference room, Bob pulled Carol aside and asked, "I know you have a little girl, but can you arrange for someone to watch her tomorrow night? We're planning to take Jerry and Tim to Gene & Georgetti for dinner, and we hope you can join us. Don't worry about getting home. I'll ask Martha to hire a car to take you to Hinsdale. Oh, and thank you, Carol, for accepting our offer to join the agency; I think you will be happy here for a long time."

Remembering her father had called earlier that morning, once back in her office, she dialed her parents' number. Her father answered; he sounded out of breath.

"Hi Dad, what's up?"

"Hello Carol. I've been outside pruning your mother's hydrangeas."

"You called earlier. Is anything wrong?"

"No, nothing's wrong. I wanted to let you know that your mother and I are traveling to Salt Lake City tomorrow and also to ask how Jenny did on her first day of school."

"Why Salt Lake?"

"I've been researching our family's history, and I heard the Genealogy Society allows you use of their library."

"Jenny had a rough start but it turned out fine. Should I have her call you tonight?"

"That sounds great! And we'll call you once we get to Salt Lake. We fly TWA out of Dayton with a layover in St. Louis. I made reservations at Hotel Utah. Do you remember when we went skiing in Park City fifteen years ago?"

"I do remember; it was a fun trip. I'll talk to you tonight; I have good news!"

Carol caught the train to Hinsdale. Once settled in her seat, she started to worry about her new assignment and how it might affect Jenny. She was excited about working with the Baileys again but couldn't continue to take advantage of Barb and Dan; she needed a better plan.

It was already getting dark when Carol reached the Hinsdale train station. She glanced at her watch. It was past seven o'clock, and she still had another ten-minute walk to her house.

Living in Cleveland for eleven years, she had grown used to the cold and snow. Now she began to worry about the coming months. It wasn't the cold and snow she worried about; it was more about how dark it would be when she arrived in Hinsdale each night. Carol decided that starting the next day, she would drive to the train station and park in its lot.

Carol's parents had gifted her a red 1969 Mustang convertible when she graduated college; she loved that car. But after Jenny's birth she traded her snazzy Mustang for a sensible Subaru: the silver four-door station wagon had little style and no pizzazz. *Maybe someday I can afford to buy myself another little red sports car,* Carol imagined.

Carol reached Dan and Barb's house and rang the bell. Jenny opened the door and gave her mother a big hug. "Mommy! I thought you'd never get home," she squealed. "I have so much to tell you."

"OK, baby," Carol said, kissing Jenny's cheek. "After I talk to Mr. and Mrs. Kessler, we'll go home and get you into a nice bubble bath and you can tell me all about your day."

After Carol gave Dan and Barb a quick rundown on the day's events, she said she needed a better plan for Jenny. She appreciated them caring for her daughter but didn't want to continue to impose on their already busy lives. She explained about the dinner the next night and asked if they knew someone who could come and stay with Jenny.

Lillie, Barb's mom, was sitting in the living room. "I'd love to come and stay with Jenny tomorrow night," she said. "I can pick her up after dinner, take her to your house for her bath, then put her to bed before you get home."

"That is so kind of you. I'll leave my spare key with Barb tomorrow morning."

Carol and Jenny walked the short distance home, and Carol put her daughter into a warm bubble bath. Jenny couldn't stop talking about her first day of school. Because she still had so much to say, Carol let Jenny call her grandparents before she put her into bed.

Before she hung up the phone, Carol told her dad her news.

"The Bailey brothers came to the agency today," Carol said. "Needless to say, I was extremely surprised. They are switching agencies and I'm now back working on their account. By the way, did you ever determine if we are distant relatives with them through Marie Bailey, my fifth-great-grandmother?"

"I don't think we are related," her dad said. "Our Bailey ancestors are from Chawton, England. When I met the Bailey brothers last year, they told me their family is from Scotland."

After talking with her parents, Carol fell into bed, totally drained.

The following day, Miles and Carol sat in Gary's office to review the details of her passing the Sheffield account back to Miles.

Early that morning, the Baileys confirmed hiring Williams-Nelson as their new agency; Carol landed back in familiar territory. The conference call with her current client went well. Miles had worked on the Sheffield account before Carol started, so she felt confident the transition would be seamless.

As Carol and Miles left Gary's office, Miles explained, "I can't lie," he said. "I was disappointed when I didn't get the new restaurant account. But I understand, and I'm totally on board with you getting the assignment. Besides, I'm hungry; let's go to lunch and celebrate your good fortune."

Surprised by his lunch offer, she said yes but didn't want to read too much into it. With Lou Malnati's a mere ten-minute walk, they decided on pizza.

Remembering her dinner plans, Carol chose their Malnati Salad.

"Salad two days in a row for lunch; I feel I'm turning into a rabbit."

Before taking that first bite of his luscious-looking deep-dish pizza slice, Miles said, "I understand you're going out to dinner tonight with the big guys and the new clients."

"Yes, I can't wait. I've heard so much about Gene & Georgetti."

"I've been in Chicago for five years now and haven't eaten there yet," Miles added.

Carol wondered if he felt a bit jealous.

"Well, you should take your wife there for a date night," Carol suggested.

"Oh, my wife and I divorced a couple of years ago. Brenda got the house in Oak Park, and we share custody of our eight-year-old son, Brian." Without taking a breath, he continued, "You need to order a juicy ribeye tonight to get you past this salad phase. Maybe you'll get to sit in Sinatra's booth."

Maybe I will, Carol thought.

When Miles and Carol returned from lunch, she directed the Baileys through the office, introducing them to the key players who would create the advertising campaigns for their business.

Jerry and Tim had started their company with just one unit in Cleveland. They now owned forty-eight restaurants throughout the Midwest. Carol knew they wanted to expand their reach, so they talked about creating some local television spots. They currently ran radio ads, but television would be a new venture. They discussed their current billboards, four-color inserts in the Sunday newspaper supplement, and the print ads in the coupon section of the Wednesday shopper's edition of the local newspapers. The Bailey brothers also revealed their plan to start franchising their concept.

Most everyone had left for the day by the time a limo picked up the six in front of the office and drove to Chicago's River North neighborhood.

Gene & Georgetti retained that classic old-time Chicago club atmosphere. Carol noticed it sat directly under the "L," and she could hear the trains as they rumbled overhead. The restaurant staff greeted everyone like family and guided the group to a large table. Carol laughed to herself: *I wonder if this is Frank Sinatra's table.*

Carol chose the veal parmigiana, and the men ordered gorgeous-looking steaks. They talked a little business, and Carol's bosses seemed impressed at how highly Jerry and Tim spoke of her during her time in Cleveland. She felt included and comfortable. They treated her like an equal.

After dinner, the driver dropped the Baileys off at the Whitehall Hotel and Bob, Jon, and Gary at the office. It was after eleven o'clock when he finally dropped Carol off at her home.

Carol hurried inside to find Lillie up and watching TV.

"Oh, you're home," Lillie said drowsily. "I love Tuesday night television: *Happy Days*, *Lavern & Shirley*, and *Three's Company*. I'm anxious for *Dallas* to return in November to find out who shot J.R. Ewing. How was your dinner?"

"Fantastic! Thank you so much for watching Jenny."

"I can watch her anytime, but I wanted to talk to you about my niece, Linda. She starts college in a few weeks and plans on living with me. She'll be attending Elmhurst College; it's only eight miles from Hinsdale. My brother and his wife, Linda's parents, live in Janesville, which is too far to commute, and they don't have the money to pay for her to live in the dorm. How do you feel about her living with you? She could stay with Jenny while you're at work or on a business trip."

"That might be the perfect solution!" Carol exclaimed. "I could offer her room and board and pay a small salary. Do you think she'd be okay with seventy dollars a week?"

"I'll call her tomorrow and let you know her decision," Lillie said. "She has orientation at school next Monday, so she's coming over on Sunday to spend the night. Why don't you and Jenny join us for dinner on Sunday? You can meet Linda, and she can meet you and Jenny."

After Lillie went home, Carol climbed into bed feeling anxious about starting her new assignment. At the same time, she felt optimistic that she'd found someone to stay with Jenny. Her thoughts were spinning, but she finally drifted off.

Pleasantly surprised, Carol answered the phone the following evening to find Lillie's niece calling.

"Hello, this is Linda Miller. Is this Mrs. Edwards?"

"Yes, but please call me Carol."

"My aunt told me about your generous offer to live with you and take care of Jenny. You may not remember, but I met you several weeks ago at my cousin Barb's house."

"Oh my gosh, I do remember! You were outside playing with Heather."

"Well, I'm ready to say yes if you are," Linda said.

"It's a deal. I have a feeling that both of us will benefit from this arrangement. Thanks for calling, Linda. Jenny and I will see you Sunday."

That Saturday, Carol started cleaning out the attic bedroom.

"Do you want to help Mommy clean?" she asked Jenny. "With Mrs. Kessler's cousin coming to live at our house, we must move all these boxes and furniture."

"It will be exciting to have Miss Linda living with us," Jenny said.

Dan came over and helped move the heavier boxes to the garage. Once the room was cleared of all the boxes and clutter, Carol washed the windows while Jenny swept the hardwood floors. Dan helped

Carol move a bed, small dresser, side table, desk, chair, area rug, and two small table lamps into the room. Now they just needed curtains, sheets, towels, and a new bedspread.

"Sears at Oakbrook Center is having a sale," Carol told Jenny. "Let's go buy some pretty things for Miss Linda's new bedroom. Then we can catch that Peanuts movie you've been wanting to see."

Once they finished their shopping Carol and Jenny walked to the small theater at the back of the mall. Carol ordered a large box of popcorn from the concession stand, and the two settled into some seats in the back row. It felt so nice to be together for one whole day and not worry about rushing off to school or work. The move to Chicago no longer felt challenging. It felt more like a fantastic beginning to the rest of their lives.

JENNY KRISTINE EDWARDS PETERS
1998

"Life seems but a quick succession of busy nothings."

Jane Austen, *Mansfield Park*

*J*enny's mother, Carol, left the house early that morning to pick up Jenny's grandparents from Chicago's O'Hare Airport. It was the weekend of Jenny's wedding. In a mere seventy-two hours, Jenny would marry the love of her life, her high school sweetheart, Brian Peters. She had already made plans to sign this year's Christmas cards from Dr. and Mrs. Brian Michael Peters. Jenny was very proud of Brian.

Jenny was born in Cleveland on May 26, 1972. However, Jenny's mother and father divorced when Jenny was eight, and she moved with her mother to Hinsdale, Illinois. Jenny's father, David, and his new wife, Marlene, married shortly after he and Jenny's mom divorced. As a youngster, she would visit her dad and stepmom in Cleveland, but those visits were rare.

Before her mother and father divorced, Jenny and her parents would travel to Christiansburg from their home in Cleveland for an occasional weekend visit with her grandparents. One of the highlights of those visits was when Jenny's mother led her to the old black barn behind her grandparents' house to visit her mother's two horses. When Jenny was no more than four or five years old, her mother sat her upon the little pony named Lightning that Carol's parents gave Carol when she was eleven. Carol named the pony Lightning after a book her father used to read to her titled *A Pony Called Lightning* by Miriam E. Mason.

When Carol was fourteen, her parents gifted her a second horse; a big bay she named Sugar-N-Spice. A gentle giant and an excellent jumper, everyone called the horse by his nickname, Sweetie.

Grandmother Virginia was seventy-five and Grandfather John was eighty-two, and they still lived in their rather imposing house in the now sprawling city of Christiansburg, where Jenny's grandfather had lived all his life.

With its expansive front porch and four large pillars, the house looked out over a manicured lawn. In neat beds at the front of the house, Jenny's grandmother's award-winning roses bloomed in a profusion of red, yellow, pink, and white. Along the back and sides of the house, peonies, lilacs, hydrangeas, and forsythia bloomed in the spring. In the summer, an abundance of daylilies encircled the large pond. A long lane led out to the road and at the end of the lane was an old sign. The sign read: *The Wade Homestead Est. 1810.*

It had been over one hundred years since anyone named Wade lived in the present house. Jenny's fourth great-grandmother, Christina Wade O'Sullivan, died in 1889. Christina's father, Jacob Wade, and her husband, Jamie O'Sullivan, built the house in 1839, replacing an old two-story log home the family built just after the end of the War of 1812.

When Jenny's ancestors, the Wades, first arrived in Ohio, they built two small log cabins. Those log cabins still existed in the woods near the current house. Jenny's grandfather declared that as long as he was alive he would never allow anyone to tear down those cabins. Looking back, Jenny never fully appreciated that her playhouses during her visits to Ohio were homes where her ancestors lived years ago.

The Wade family came from England in 1791, first immigrating to Maryland before settling in Ohio almost twenty years later. When Christian and his son, Jacob, brought their families to Ohio, they purchased two thousand acres of pristine woodland. They left most of the land as forest, from which they sold the timber for additional income. After clearing some of the land, the early Wades farmed nearly two hundred acres. Because Jenny's grandfather and great-grandfather developed a large portion of those original two thousand acres into Wade Estates and Wade Plaza, the large white house now sat on the remaining fifty acres of mostly woods.

Jenny adored her grandparents. When she turned nine, Jenny started spending her annual school summer vacation with them in Christiansburg. One of the best parts of those summers in Ohio was the grand Fourth of July celebration. Christiansburg sponsored a parade and fireworks, and families enjoyed picnics near the park's old gazebo. Never lonely or homesick during those summer visits, Jenny boasted as many lifelong Ohio friends as she did friends from Illinois.

Decades earlier, the Wades planted a small apple orchard behind the barn. Only one old apple tree still grew where the orchard once flourished. On those sweltering, humid Ohio summer afternoons, Jenny sat under the old apple tree, drank a glass of her grandmother's refreshing lemonade, and listened to Grandpa John as he told her stories about their ancestors.

Jenny frequently found her grandfather in his library, writing in his journal, typing on the old typewriter, or reading a book on genealogy. A large cupboard stood in the library. It held dozens of old books from as far back as the early 1700s. The Wades brought those books and the large cupboard from England when they came to America. During one of the home's many renovations, John and Virginia needed to move the cupboard. Surprisingly, they found an inscription burned into the back: *I, Thomas Bailey, built this cupboard for my daughter Marie's marriage to Christian Wade 6 September 1766 Alton England.*

Many of the books in the old cupboard belonged to Christiansburg's first schoolmaster, Philip Crane. Philip was Christian Wade's son-in-law and lived in Christiansburg until his death in 1838. Professor Crane was instrumental in building a one-room log schoolhouse; opening the first school in Christiansburg in 1815. A second, larger schoolhouse was built in 1825—the town had outgrown the first. When Wade Plaza was built, Grandpa John sold those two old schoolhouses. The larger one became a quaint antique store, and the smaller one a museum owned by the city and managed by volunteers.

Reading the books in the cupboard didn't interest Jenny. It was the old board games her grandmother stored at the bottom of the cupboard that Jenny loved the most. Grandpa John particularly enjoyed allowing her to beat him at checkers. One day, Grandma Virginia pulled down an antique toy tea set from off the very top shelf.

A night wouldn't go by that Grandpa John might call out, "Where's our cookies and milk, Virginia?"

Virginia would fill the tiny teacups with milk, and Jenny and her grandfather would eat her grandmother's legendary chocolate chip cookies off the tea set's tiny plates. Her grandmother baked luscious pies, cakes, and cookies like a professional.

Virginia loved to cook and proudly owned all Julia Child's cookbooks. Jenny likely developed her love for cooking and baking from watching her grandmother. A typical Sunday dinner consisted of Chicken Cordon Bleu or Leg of Lamb. But on most weeknights, she fixed one of the many Danish dishes her Aunt Edith taught Virginia to make. Jenny loved when her grandmother fried pork belly with apples for supper, served on fresh rye bread. Virginia allowed Jenny to stand on a stool to watch her cook—or sometimes let her measure out the ingredients.

Jenny's grandmother also baked a scrumptious chocolate cake with apricot jam, a torte recipe Virginia's mother, Hannah, brought from Austria. Hannah made the torte for her daughter and husband to serve after their Shabbat lunch of potato kugel and chicken soup. Virginia's mother died not long after Virginia turned three years old. Sadly, Jenny's grandmother only vaguely remembered her young mother and her outstanding meals. Hannah's recipe box was one of Virginia's most cherished possessions.

Almost ten years ago, Bob Nelson, the co-founder of Williams-Nelson Advertising Agency, retired after his partner, Jon Williams, died. Bob then sold the agency to Carol's boss, Gary Davis. Carol was promoted and moved into that much-sought-after corner office with the wraparound windows.

A year after Mr. Williams's death, his wife decided to sell her Chicago home and move to Charleston, North Carolina. Carol gave her a full-price offer, and Mrs. Williams gratefully accepted.

Carol quickly sold their big Dutch Colonial home in Hinsdale and moved to Chicago's exclusive Gold Coast neighborhood. It was the same year Jenny left for her first year at Northwestern University.

The classic old three-story Greystone on North Astor contained four bedrooms and four bathrooms. It featured the original cove moldings, six-panel doors, lovely marble bathrooms, and wood-burning fireplaces in the living room and library. Someone had converted the fireplaces in each bedroom to gas years ago.

Jenny knew the one thing her mother loved most about the new house was the attached two-car garage where Carol parked her little red Alfa Romeo Spider. Jenny loved the private rooftop deck with a peek at Lake Michigan.

Jenny and Brian graduated from Northwestern University in 1994. Jenny earned her BSBA with a major in general management. The summer after graduation, she started a six-month course at the Culinary Institute in Chicago. It was Virginia's idea. After Brian graduated, he began his studies at Northwestern University Feinberg School of Medicine.

Growing up, Brian Peters lived in Oak Park with his mom. Brian and Jenny had known each other since they were eight when Brian's dad, Miles, and Jenny's mother briefly dated. Sometimes, all four went to the zoo or Miles and Carol allowed the kids to tag along on a movie or dinner date.

Miles and Carol worked together and started dating not long after Carol began working at Williams-Nelson. They stopped dating when Miles left the agency to work at the corporate office of Sheffield's Grocery. Brian and Jenny lost touch but reconnected at a high school football game. Brian looked very different from the gawky eight-year-old Jenny remembered. The Hinsdale Central High cheerleader and one of the Oak Park football team's star linebackers found each other again.

Today, while Jenny awaited her grandparents' arrival, she arranged a vase of flowers to brighten up the bedroom where they would be staying the weekend.

Suddenly, the front door opened, and Jenny heard her grandmother's laughter. Jenny ran down the stairs and gave her grandparents a giant hug.

"Grandma, you look fabulous. I love your dress. How was your flight from Dayton?"

"Slow down, girl, and let me catch my breath. The flight was tolerable. The drive from the airport took longer than the actual flight. I enjoyed a mimosa in first class, which put me right to sleep.

And this dress is old but comfortable for travel. Wait until you see the dress I picked up at Rike's department store for the wedding; it's perfect."

"Mom, you mean Lazarus," Carol interjected. "It hasn't been Rike's since 1982."

"It will always be Rike's to me," Virginia said.

A man of few words, Jenny's grandfather stood back and smiled while the ladies excitedly greeted each other. It was as if they hadn't seen each other for years; yet it had been just two months ago when Carol and Jenny visited Christiansburg for Carol's birthday.

"You two are welcome to lie down; we have hours before we leave for the restaurant," Carol told her parents.

"Your offer sounds tempting; I am a little tired," Virginia said.

"I think I'll go sit outside on your deck," John replied.

"Jenny, please help your grandfather take the suitcases upstairs and hang their clothes in the closet. I'll make some sandwiches and bring you three a sandwich and a glass of iced tea."

"I don't want to spoil my dinner. I hear you're serving lots of good food tonight," Virginia said.

"Chicken salad on a small croissant shouldn't spoil your dinner," Carol replied.

As Jenny began hanging her grandparents' clothes in the closet, Virginia reclined on the chaise lounge in front of the window in the large guest bedroom.

"Jenny, your mother told me you and Brian will be living here after you return from your honeymoon, and he starts his first year of residency at Memorial Hospital. You must explain how this arrangement works for the three of you."

"There's plenty of room, Grandma. With all three of us being so busy, it should work out fine. Remind me to take you and Grandpa downstairs tomorrow and show you how I've decorated the apartment where Brian and I will live."

Carol called the small apartment an English basement. It sat partially below and partially above ground level with a separate entrance. It contained a comfortable living room, a small dining area, a galley kitchen, and a spacious bedroom with an adjoining bath.

"How many guests will be at dinner tonight?" Virginia asked.

"Counting Brian and me, forty people have been invited to the rehearsal dinner. In addition to you, Grandpa, and Mom, are our hosts: Brian's mom, Brenda; his dad, Miles; and Miles's wife, Judy," Jenny explained.

Miles began dating Brian's stepmom, Judy, after he left Williams-Nelson and started working as the VP of Marketing at Sheffield's Grocery. Miles and Judy married in 1983 and moved into a large old home in Edgebrook. Judy, the owner's daughter, inherited all thirty of Sheffield's grocery stores, becoming the company's president and CEO when her father died unexpectedly.

"Of course, my dad, Marlene, and my four brothers will be there tonight," Jenny said.

Because she was his only daughter, Jenny's dad, a prominent Cleveland attorney, planned to cover all the costs for the wedding and reception. He could afford to spare no expense. Jenny asked her four half-brothers to be wedding ushers: seventeen-year-old David Jr., fifteen-year-old Alan, and thirteen-year-old twins Lucas and Liam. They seemed excited, but you can never tell what teenage boys think when asked to be part of a wedding party. Jenny always assumed Marlene kept trying for a girl, and after four boys, she figured it was futile.

"Another important person invited to dinner tonight is Mr. Davis, Mom's partner at the ad agency," Jenny continued. "They've known each other for eighteen years, and I think they are dating, but Mom has never confirmed my suspicion; don't tell her I told you that."

Never married, Gary Davis lived in a condo in Astor Tower and owned a home in Palm Beach.

"Of course," Jenny continued, "the wedding party and their significant others are also invited. We chose ten close friends for our wedding party. You know Heather and Linda."

Jenny chose Heather Kessler, now Heather Taylor, as her matron of honor. They had been friends since the third grade. They stayed friends after high school when they became roommates at Northwestern. Jenny served as Maid of Honor and Brian as Best Man when Heather married Bill Taylor at St. Michael Catholic Church last spring. Of course, Brian chose Bill to be his best man. The couples still called themselves the Fab Four. They doubled-dated, studied together, and even made a pact to name each other as godparents to their future children.

Linda Miller, now Linda Parker, was another important person Jenny wanted as one of her bridesmaids. Jenny even chose Linda's two small children as her ring bearer and flower girl. Linda lived with Jenny and her mom for four years while Jenny attended elementary school and Linda commuted to college in Elmhurst.

Linda cared for Jenny when Carol worked late or went out of town on business. She walked Jenny to school and back home after school was over, fixed her dinner and even helped with her homework.

"I can't wait to see the church," Virginia said.

Although Jenny was baptized Lutheran, Carol sent Jenny to St. Michael Catholic School when they moved to Chicago. By high school, Jenny decided to convert to Catholicism, so she chose Chicago's Grace Cathedral for the wedding ceremony. Destroyed by the Great Chicago Fire, it was rebuilt in 1875. Cardinal Mahony would perform Jenny and Brian's Nuptial Mass, assisted by Father Francis.

"I started attending Mass at Grace four years ago, and the first time I walked through the front door and into the nave, its beauty stole my breath away."

Later that afternoon, Jenny and her mom drove to Grace for the rehearsal. Jenny's grandparents stayed home so Grandma Virginia could dress for dinner at her leisure. Mr. Davis graciously volunteered to pick up Carol's parents and drive them to the restaurant.

Jenny invited Heather's parents, Barb and Dan Kessler, to the rehearsal dinner, along with their two sons, Matt, now twenty, and Eric, now eighteen. The Kesslers had lived three houses down from them in Hinsdale. They'd all remained close friends, even after Carol moved to Chicago's Gold Coast neighborhood. Lillie, Heather's grandmother, who'd always treated Jenny and Carol as family, would also be in attendance. Unfortunately, Jenny had no grandparents on her father's side. They'd died in a car accident a few years after Jenny was born. Jenny's father grieved for years after their untimely death.

Jenny's wedding planner, Kay, greeted Jenny and her mom when they entered the church.

"Hello, Carol and Jenny; everyone is here, so let's start. We'll begin with practicing the processional."

Kay was an expert in getting everyone organized. The rehearsal was concluded in no time.

"You all did great," Kay said. "Some of you must have done this before. I look forward to seeing you all on Saturday."

The group hailed several taxis and arrived at the restaurant hungry and ready to celebrate.

River Side American Tavern had hired Jenny as their sous-chef after she finished culinary school. Located on LaSalle, right on the Chicago River, they promoted her to chef de cuisine last year. It was logical that Jenny would reserve the private room at the restaurant where she worked for her rehearsal dinner.

The dinner started with roasted tomato and sweet pepper soup garnished with grilled cherry tomatoes. For the main course, the guests could choose either lollipop lamb chops pan-seared in rosemary and garlic butter alongside roasted red-skinned potatoes or free-range chicken oven-baked in a mushroom and white wine sauce, served with sweet potato pancakes. The dessert choices included dark chocolate sponge pudding with chocolate sauce or glazed lemon tart with citrus syrup. The wine steward chose the perfect wine to complement each course.

As soon as dinner concluded, Jenny went into the kitchen. "I want to thank everyone for the tremendous job you did tonight," she told the crew. "Our guests are still raving about this fabulous evening."

Some guests lingered over a glass of port while others chose a Brandy Alexander.

After dinner, Brian and Gary came back to the house. Once the six settled in the library, Carol brought in mugs and a carafe of decaf coffee. It had been a busy day, and it was now time to relax.

"Thanks to the three of you for the generous gift you gave to Jenny and me," Brian said to Jenny's mother and grandparents. "Our honeymoon in Paris and Venice will be amazing and a much-needed vacation from school and work."

"Yes," Jenny added. "How did you decide on such an amazing honeymoon as our wedding gift?"

"Many years ago, your grandfather and I went on this wonderful vacation to Paris and Venice," Virginia said. "We loved it so much, your mother and I felt you and Brian might like it too. First, you'll fly to Paris, where you'll stay at Hotel Mayfair, a romantic little boutique hotel near Tuileries Garden. The next week, you board the Orient Express for an overnight train trip to Venice. There, you'll stay at Hotel Londra Palace, which overlooks the San Marco basin. By the way, what are you wearing for the wedding, Brian?"

Brian grinned. "Absolutely no idea. What am I wearing, Jenny?"

"For the wedding ceremony, you're wearing a gray cutaway coat with gray waistcoat and gray striped trousers. For the reception, you're changing into a traditional black tuxedo."

"My, my, how handsome you will look," Virginia teased.

"And thank you, Mr. Davis, for the champagne flutes from Tiffany," Jenny said. "They're exceptionally beautiful."

"You are more than welcome," Gary replied.

"How big is this shindig?" Virginia asked her daughter. "Is handsome Mr. Nelson coming?"

"We've invited two hundred, and almost everyone has confirmed they plan to attend," Carol said. "And, yes, Mr. Nelson and his wife will be at the wedding."

Before Brian returned to his dad's house, he reminded Jenny of the men's golf outing the following day. "I'll pick you up tomorrow morning at seven o'clock, Mr. Murphy," Brian said. "Jenny, I'll have him back in time for us to leave for our get-together tomorrow night. Gary, our tee time is seven-thirty. We'll see you at the country club bright and early."

The next night, Jenny and Brian planned to host a gathering for wedding guests who wanted to greet the wedding party. They reserved a restaurant on the fortieth floor of the Chicago Board of Trade building and ordered plenty of hors d'oeuvres, beer, and wine.

Once Brian left, Jenny and her grandmother excused themselves and went upstairs to Carol's bedroom while her grandfather stayed in the library with his daughter and Gary.

"You ladies go talk wedding particulars," her grandfather said. "I'll be down here reading the *Tribune*. Let me know when it's safe to come upstairs."

"As soon as I say goodnight to Gary, I'll make some hot chocolate," Carol said. "Mom, put on your nightgown, and I'll bring the tray to your room."

"Here is my wedding dress," Jenny said. "What do you think, Grandma?"

"Oh my!" Virginia exclaimed. "It's gorgeous, and I love the long lace sleeves."

"Actually it's a lace jacket over the dress I can remove for the reception. The tulle skirt with its train also comes off, and voilà la, it's a whole new dress."

It was almost midnight by the time Carol came upstairs.

"Do you remember your wedding dress, Carol?" Virginia asked as Carol set down steaming cups of hot chocolate on the small table beside the bed.

"Yes, I remember it. White satin with those horrible puffy sleeves and all that bling. Did I tell you, Mom, Jenny is wearing our tiara?"

"How does it go? Something old, something new, something borrowed, something blue, and a sixpence in your left shoe?" Virginia recited.

"Well, I guess you could call my dress is my something new," Jenny said. "I'm borrowing Mom's pearl necklace that Dad gave her on their wedding day. The tiara you and Mom wore at your weddings is my something old. My something blue will be the blue sapphire earrings worn by every bride in our family since way before my time."

"The tiara is old, but I don't know exactly how old," Virginia said. "My grandfather gave it to my grandmother on their wedding day, so it must be over one hundred years old. He owned a jewelry store in Vienna, and I believe he designed and created the tiara himself. My mother brought the tiara from Austria when she immigrated to America in 1914. Those earrings have been in our family for well over two hundred years."

"Tell me about your wedding, Grandma," Jenny asked.

"Your grandfather and I will be married fifty-seven years next April. Your grandfather was raised Catholic, but we started attending the Lutheran church in downtown Dayton after we married. We tied the knot right before he left for Europe. Did you know he was a pilot during World War II? While waiting for John to return from the war, I worked at Delco Products, assembling shock absorbers for tanks and trucks."

"So, Grandma, did they call you 'Rosie the Riveter?'"

Virginia merely smiled.

"Was your wedding a big affair, Grandma?" Jenny asked.

"John's grandmother made my dress, and I think it's still in an old trunk in our attic. It was made from white taffeta, using a McCall's sewing pattern. It was very form-fitting, with long sleeves and a flowing train. I never met my grandmother, the one who lived in New York. My other grandmother died back in Vienna. John's grandmother became the grandmother I never had."

Carol said, "Jenny, the lady who made your grandmother's wedding dress lived with us when I was young. She died around the time I turned eleven. I was heartbroken, which is probably why your grandparents gave me my pony," she added. "I guess they hoped it would ease my sadness. Christina Elizabeth Murphy was the dearest, sweetest great-grandmother a girl could ask for."

"What a beautiful name, Christina Elizabeth!" Jenny exclaimed. "Is that why we call the big cupboard in the library at your house in Christiansburg, Christina's Cupboard?"

"Why, yes, I guess it is."

"How did you meet Grandpa?"

"Riding a roller coaster when I was fifteen, but that's a story for another time. So, what's on the agenda for tomorrow?" Virginia asked.

"I'm meeting our wedding planner at the hotel to ensure the gift baskets for our out-of-town guests are distributed before they arrive. Afterward, my bridesmaids and I will enjoy a spa day with manicures and pedicures. I also want to check out the ballroom to ensure it's properly set up."

"Tell me everything!" Virginia exclaimed.

"The bridesmaids are wearing long cornflower blue chiffon dresses with ruffled sleeves and carrying white hydrangeas. My bouquet has white cabbage roses and blue hydrangeas."

"Aren't hydrangeas a spring or summer flower?"

"Grandma, you can buy any flower these days; they might just cost a little more."

"Most likely, Grandma and I will be gone before you wake up, as we also have manicures scheduled for early tomorrow morning," Carol said. "Gary has arranged to take us to L'Auberge for dinner tomorrow night. Dan, Barb, and Lillie are also invited."

"Oh, a French restaurant," Virginia exclaimed. "Your father and I used to go to a lovely French restaurant near Salt Lake City. I think its name was La Caille. I wonder if it is still there. John and I ate there every time we went to Salt Lake for him to do more research on his family tree. I guess it's safe to tell John he can now come up to bed."

The next morning, Jenny slept in. When she came downstairs, Carol and Virginia had left for their manicure appointments and Brian had picked up her grandfather for their golf outing. She grabbed a leftover muffin and drove to the hotel.

Jenny and Brian booked a suite for two nights. She planned to stay there that night; she and Brian would also spend their wedding night there. Saturday morning, the ladies in the wedding party arranged to meet at Jenny's suite to have their hair and make-up done. So, Jenny packed her wedding dress and everything she needed for the party that night, the wedding the next day, the reception, and finally, the breakfast for the wedding party at the hotel on Sunday.

The historic Drake Hotel on East Walton Place still possessed plenty of its classy nineteenth-century charm. The Drake boasted that the size of its ballroom was the same as the ballroom within Buckingham Palace. Along with its impressive views of Lake Michigan, it epitomized the perfect choice for Jenny and Brian's lavish reception.

As Jenny prepared to unload her car, Kay saw her struggling with the bags and dresses and came to help. The bellman placed everything on a luggage cart and wheeled it to Jenny's suite.

"Let's go in, and I'll show you the gift baskets the hotel staff will deliver to your out-of-town guests," Kay said.

Jenny wanted to be sure the baskets contained several Chicago souvenirs; Frango mints, a small tin of Garrett Popcorn, Fanny May chocolates, and French macarons in a dupioni silk bag from La Pâtisserie. They also included two mini bottles of Prosecco, along with two champagne flutes engraved with their monogram and wedding date. Happy with how the baskets turned out, Jenny approved the distribution to the wedding guests' rooms.

"Can I see the ballroom before I go upstairs?" Jenny asked excitedly.

In the ballroom, they found a large crew of workers setting up the tables, the dance floor, and the area for the band.

"Let's go into the kitchen and talk to the chef," Kay said. "I want to reconfirm the reception menu."

Before they entered the kitchen, they noticed that Ashely's Bakery had delivered two impressive cakes earlier that morning. The first was a four-tiered wedding cake, covered with white icing and decorated with blue sugar hydrangeas, which cascaded down and around the sides. It had been placed on a large round table covered with a white tablecloth. The second cake was a chocolate groom's cake. It was decorated with white fondant to look like the front of a doctor's white coat with a piped stethoscope draped around the collar. The bakery wrote Brian's name in chocolate script lettering on the pocket.

"For your reception," Chef Marc explained, "the first course is tomato-basil crab bisque followed by a garden salad of baby head lettuce with champagne vinaigrette. Before the next course, the guests will be served a small bowl of lemon sorbet. Your response card gave your guests their choice from four entrées: lobster thermidor, prime rib with baked potato, sautéed rosemary chicken breast with mushroom sauce, or butternut squash ravioli. All the entrees come with sautéed asparagus with Hollandaise sauce. We offer the hotel's signature red and white wines throughout the meal. Finally, dessert will be crème brûlée. Of course, we will serve the champagne and cut your wedding cake later in the evening."

Kay added, "While you are having photographs taken, hors d'oeuvres will be available for your guests outside the ballroom for the two hours before dinner is served. You chose to feature a fresh oyster bar, along with tuna tartare cones, prosciutto-wrapped persimmons with goat cheese, and shrimp cocktail shooters. We plan to place two charcuterie boards, cracker baskets, and vegetable and fruit platters on the buffet table. We've also commissioned two swan ice sculptures to be placed at the center of the main hors d'oeuvres table and set them facing each other so their necks form a heart."

"And the open bar?" Jenny asked.

"Two bars will be set up, one in each of the two back corners of the room," Kay replied.

Everything looked perfect. Jenny couldn't wait for all the festivities to begin so she could happily share this weekend with all her family and friends. She hoped she could keep her composure during the ceremony. If there were any tears tomorrow, Jenny was confident that the tears would be happy ones.

September 19, 1998, finally arrived! Jenny held tightly to her father's arm while standing in the cathedral's vestibule. Her bridesmaids had already walked down the center aisle and awaited Jenny's entry. Jenny could see her handsome groom standing in front of the altar. The afternoon sun streamed through the twelve round stained-glass windows while a piano and cello performed Pachelbel's *Canon in D.*

After the ceremony, Brian, Jenny, and the wedding party walked back up the aisle as the cathedral's massive pipe organ played Mendelssohn's *Wedding March*.

After greeting their quests, the happy couple walked down the church's granite steps to a shower of rice. The six bronze bells in the cathedral's tower pealed loudly. No doubt, they could be heard all over Chicago.

CHRISTINA ELIZABETH "LIZZY" PETERS
1999 – 2018

"Till this moment I never knew myself."

Jane Austen, *Pride and Prejudice*

*I*t was almost a year to the day after Brian and Jenny were married that Jenny's mom left for a weekend with Gary Davis. Once home, Carol called her daughter and son-in-law into the library to tell them her news.

"Gary surprised me with a long weekend in Paris, which I must say is beautiful in September. Immediately after we checked into the Ritz, we hailed a taxi to the Eiffel Tower, or as the French say, *La dame de fer.* We rode to the very top, where he presented me with this beautiful ring and asked me to marry him."

"Mother!" Jenny squealed. "That's the biggest diamond I've ever seen! It's about time! You and Gary have known each other for over twenty years."

"We have no immediate plans for a wedding, but Gary has asked me to move into his condo, so I plan to sell the house. Are you two interested in buying it? It only makes sense since you've been living here while Brian's been finishing his medical training."

"What do you think, Brian? Are you ready to move out of the basement?" Jenny teased.

"Yes, I suppose I am!"

"Well, Mom, we have some news of our own," Jenny said. "We're expecting a baby late next March!"

Brian and Jenny's daughter was born on March 25, 2000. They named her Christina Elizabeth after their daughter's third-great-grandmother, Christina Elizabeth O'Sullivan Murphy.

"Christina Elizabeth is such a big name for such a tiny girl," Jenny said to Brian. "Let's call her Lizzy."

On May 19, 2002, Lizzy's Grandma Carol married her longtime friend and business partner, Gary Davis. The wedding ceremony took place on the beach, mere steps from their seaside home in Palm Beach. Carol wore a gorgeous white Oscar de le Renta lace gown.

"Mother, you look fabulous!" Jenny squealed.

"I brought the diamond tiara and the blue sapphire earrings that have been worn by brides in our family for generations," Virginia told her daughter. "It's a good thing the tiara is tiny and delicate, so as not to look too garish on a woman of your age."

Carol let the comment slide. Virginia would never change from the frank and outspoken person she'd always known her to be. Carol was just happy that her parents were both still healthy and active in their eighties.

At just two years old, Lizzy served as her grandma's flower girl. Unfortunately, she didn't remember anything about that day, which is why she always loved looking through the album of pictures her dad had taken.

After they were married, and while still running the ad agency, Gary and Carol traveled back and forth between their Chicago condo and their home in Florida. The commute between Chicago and Palm Beach was growing tiresome, so they decided to retire. Three short years after they were married, they sold the agency and their condo and moved to Palm Beach permanently.

The year Lizzy turned six, Gary and Carol invited her to spend her summer vacation with them in Florida. Their white Mediterranean-style house featured an orange terra-cotta tile roof and had five bedrooms, five bathrooms, and a fantastic infinity pool.

Lizzy and Carol walked the beach every morning and swam in the pool every afternoon. They bought fish from the local fishmonger and visited the farmer's market every Saturday. An excellent cook, Gary always let Lizzy help him in the kitchen when preparing their meals.

Lizzy spent only four summers in Florida. In September 2009, doctors discovered Gary had developed pancreatic cancer. He died four months later at the young age of sixty-eight. Grief-stricken, Carol stayed in Florida another year. In the end, she decided to sell the house in Florida and move back to Ohio.

In 2011, Carol's mother was turning eighty-eight and her father was turning ninety-five. If they wanted to stay in their home, they were going to need assistance. Happily, John and Virginia welcomed their daughter home with open arms. This turned out to be the best thing for all of them. When Carol was a young girl, she and Virginia butted heads about how most things should be done. Strangely, after Carol moved home, they soon became more like friends than mother and daughter. Carol also relished the time spent collaborating with her father on his genealogy research; she helped him write their family's stories.

Lizzy was eleven the year Carol moved back to Ohio, so she began spending her summer vacations in Christiansburg. Lizzy stayed in the bedroom where her Grandma Carol slept as a child. Sleeping in her grandmother's big canopy bed with the white ruffles, she felt like a princess.

Lizzy, Grandma Carol, Great-grandma Virginia, and Great-grandpa John often took a picnic lunch to the park to listen to a concert at the band shell. Or the four would sit behind the barn under the old apple tree drinking tall glasses of cold lemonade.

"Every year for your grandma's birthday, I made her a pie from the apples off of this old tree," Lizzy's great-grandmother revealed.

Whenever Lizzy and Carol walked down to the barn, she heard remarkable stories about the horses, Lightning and Sweetie. Hanging on her grandma's bedroom wall were pictures of Grandma Carol with her horses. The shelves contained oodles of ribbons and trophies Lizzy's grandma won with Sweetie. For Carol's birthday, Lizzy bought her grandma a miniature ceramic horse. Carol, of course, declared it to be the most excellent birthday gift she'd ever received.

Sadly, Lizzy's second summer in Christiansburg was the year her great-grandfather died; he was ninety-six.

After his passing, Lizzy could often be found in the one room in the house she loved the most, the library. It reminded her of Great-grandpa John. The room was lined with shelves of books. His large oak desk sat under the window that looked out over the woods; on top of the desk sat his old Underwood typewriter.

Lizzy thought of her great-grandfather as she sat in his oversized green leather chair. The dark, cool library evoked a wonderful smell: a combination of leather, old books, and pipe tobacco. At the far end of the room sat a massive old cupboard.

That summer, Lizzy found the first four of Jane Austen's novels in that old cupboard. These first four novels had each been published in three-volume sets. Lizzy found it fascinating that the novels were published anonymously. Printed on the front of each book, "By A

Lady" was revealed as the author. Even more remarkable, Lizzy found Jane Austen's signature on the title page of each book.

Each three-volume set had been tied with a dark green satin ribbon. One of Lizzy's ancestors had slipped a note card under the ribbon. When Lizzy held the card to her nose, she faintly smelled the ink used by whomever wrote the message. Lizzy realized the books must have been given to a young girl on her birthday, and *Sense & Sensibility* was the first book this young girl received. Written in the grandest handwriting with these large arching letters, the first card read: *To my niece on her eleventh birthday from Uncle Philip 18 October 1815.* Attached to the four sets of books were four note cards revealing that each collection of books had been given to the same young girl. Great-grandpa John found through his research that Philip Crane had given these books to his niece, who just happened to also be named Christina. Lizzy now realized she'd been named after two ancestors: her third and her fifth great-grandmothers.

Because those old first editions were so fragile, Grandma Carol took Lizzy to Christiansburg's library to check out copies for her to read. Over the years, she read them all: *Sense & Sensibility, Pride & Prejudice, Mansfield Park,* and *Emma.*

Some days, Carol and Lizzy walked the mile down the road to the Red Brick Schoolhouse Antique Shop—once the school Philip Crane helped to build in 1825. A smaller log building sat next to the antique store. Now a museum, the smaller building was the first schoolhouse built by Philip and the Wades in 1815.

Lizzy loved these spur-of-the-moment outings with her grandma.

The following summer, Lizzy found two more of Jane Austen's novels, *Northanger Abbey* and *Persuasion.* These two novels had been published together as a four-volume set and were published posthumously in 1818, as Miss Austen died in the summer of 1817. They also were bound with ribbon and contained a note that the books had been given to young Christina by her Uncle Philip. Amazingly, the first pages of Miss Austen's last two novels contained a biographical notice about the author. Jane Austen appeared to no longer be anonymous. Lizzy found many other old books in the cupboard, including old textbooks. But devoted to Jane Austen, she mainly read her books. Every summer, when she came for her visit, she read (or reread) at least one Jane Austen novel.

That same summer, Lizzy found in the old cupboard a 1925 publication of Miss Austen's last unfinished novel, *Fragment of a Novel.* Great-grandma Virginia told Lizzy her husband John found it in a London bookstore during World War II. He sent it back to his mother as a gift for her birthday. Miss Austen originally titled this unfinished novel *The Brothers.* She wrote eleven chapters and part of a twelfth when she stopped writing a few months before her death.

On Lizzy's sixteenth birthday, her grandma Carol gave her a copy of a book published in 1975 titled *Sanditon.* The modern author changed the name of Jane Austen's incomplete (but now completed) story from *The Brothers* to *Sanditon* and did so under the name "Another Lady."

Lizzy's dad was a well-respected cardiologist in Chicago. Her parents also owned a popular steakhouse. Lizzy's mom had worked as the chef de cuisine at this restaurant for eight years, when it was called River Side American Tavern. When the original owners retired, they sold it to Jenny and Brian, who renovated it and renamed it LaSalle Chop House.

Lizzy often spent her afternoons after school at the restaurant. She loved watching her mom work in the restaurant's kitchen. But Lizzy didn't want to watch her mom cook; she wanted her to move aside so Lizzy could do the cooking.

Lizzy dreamed of attending culinary school after high school, but her parents wanted her to attend Notre Dame University and perhaps become a doctor like her dad. Lizzy received excellent grades in school and could have readily been accepted to any university. But Lizzy wanted to cook and someday own a restaurant like her mom. After much begging and pleading, they agreed that Lizzy could attend culinary school. Once she graduated high school, she would start her classes at Le Cordon Bleu College of Culinary Arts in Chicago, finishing her studies in under two years with her associate's degree.

Carol planned to take Lizzy to Europe for three months as her high school graduation gift from her grandma and great-grandma. But first, Carol and Virginia invited Lizzy to return to Ohio for a few weeks. Lizzy couldn't contain her excitement to spend three months in Europe with her grandma, but she was also excited to start her culinary training once they returned.

Carol explained to Jenny and Lizzy that she'd hired a caregiver to live with Virginia while she and Lizzy vacationed in Europe. Lizzy's great-grandma initially balked at the idea, but once she met the young lady from the home care service, she gave the impression that the arrangements suited her.

Lizzy's Grandma Carol was a hale and hearty seventy-one-year-old. She needed no aid to travel from Dayton for Lizzy's graduation and the after-party at her daughter's restaurant. At ninety-three, Virginia was not strong enough to make the trip. So Carol asked one of their friends and neighbors, Mrs. Slater, to stay with her for the week Carol visited Chicago.

When Jenny's phone rang, she asked Lizzy, "Who could be calling our landline at seven o'clock on a Sunday morning?"

Brian had left for his morning rounds at the hospital, and Jenny and Lizzy were preparing to leave for Mass. Carol planned to stay home and relax after yesterday's hectic schedule, what with all the graduation festivities.

"Hello? Yes, this is Jenny Peters. Oh, hi, Mrs. Slater. Hold on while I call her to the phone."

"Lizzy, please go upstairs and tell your grandma Mrs. Slater is on the phone."

Lizzy's grandma usually kept her cell phone turned off. Lizzy couldn't count how often she tried to call her and how worried she'd become when her grandma didn't answer. Carol finally limped down the stairs and entered the kitchen.

"This dang knee," Carol complained. "I can barely make it down the steps without excruciating pain. I'm anxious about my knee replacement surgery when I return to Ohio. I'm thankful Lizzy will be with me to play nurse."

"Mom," Jenny said, "it's Nellie Slater on the phone. Isn't she the lady staying with Grandma? She said she tried calling you earlier but couldn't get through. How many times have I asked you to keep your phone turned on? It could be an emergency, and I might need to reach you immediately someday."

"That phone is a nuisance," Carol said. "I like it when it goes to voice mail. I wish I still owned my old answering machine. If you want me, call and leave a message, and I might call you back."

Jenny casually handed her mother the phone. Lizzy immediately knew it was bad news when Carol sat down hard and closed her eyes.

"Yes, I understand," she whispered into the phone. "My granddaughter and I were scheduled to come back tomorrow. I'll see if we can book a flight today."

When she hung up, she had big tears and could barely speak.

"My mom's suffered a stroke. They've taken her to the hospital. Jenny, could you find a flight for me and Lizzy to get us back to Dayton today?"

"Sure, Mom. Don't worry; I'll start checking for flights on my computer."

By late morning, Carol and Lizzy were in the air to Dayton. Once they landed, they drove to the hospital. The two cautiously entered Virginia's room. The lights had been dimmed, and Virginia appeared to be sleeping.

"Hello, ladies; I'm Sydney, Virginia's nurse. You must be her daughter, Carol."

"Yes, I'm her daughter, and this is her great-granddaughter, Lizzy. How is my mother doing?"

"Your mother suffered an intracerebral hemorrhage. Dr. Bright was in to see her earlier. After consulting with the neurosurgeon, they decided not to attempt to repair the bleed. At her age, they feel she would not survive the procedure."

Lizzy left the room, allowing her grandmother to grieve privately, and entered the waiting room. Lizzy had never seen anyone as sick as her great-grandma. She texted her mom to have her and her dad come to Dayton as quickly as possible. Her mom immediately called her back. As soon as Lizzy answered the phone, she heard, "Is it bad?"

"Yes, Mom, the doctor told her nurse he doesn't think she'll last the night. Grandma is with her now."

"Your dad and I are taking the late flight. Tell your grandma we will be there tonight."

On June 4, 2018, Virginia Marie Nielsen Murphy died peacefully, surrounded by her loving family.

"It's all my fault," Lizzy cried. "Grandma, if you hadn't come to Chicago you would have been home and could have saved her."

"Your great-grandma lived a long and happy life," Carol told Lizzy. "You are definitely not to blame."

The next day, Lizzy and her dad stayed at the house while Jenny and Carol made the arrangements at the funeral home.

"It's going to seem so strange with Great-grandma Virginia no longer here to tell me stories or bake me her yummy chocolate cake."

"You'll be a comfort for your grandma this summer," Brian replied.

"Dad, I want to wait a year before I start school. I want to stay with Grandma for a while after returning from Europe. What do you think?"

"Let's talk it over with your mom and your grandma. I don't have a problem with the idea, and it might do you both good."

They held the funeral three days later. Virginia was laid to rest at Woodland Cemetery in Dayton beside her husband, John Patrick Murphy Jr.

John was born in 1916 and died in 2012. Beside him lay John's father, also named John Patrick Murphy, who was born in 1892 and died in 1967. Next to his father lay John's mother, Susanna Lillie Barr Murphy, who was born in 1895 and died in 1944.

They were all buried in the Barr-Becker family plot with Susanna's parents, who died in 1911, and Mr. and Mrs. Becker. Mrs. Becker died in 1947, and Mr. Becker died in 1950. Mr. Becker's will instructed that a forty-foot obelisk be erected in the family plot to perpetuate his and his wife's memory and those of the Barrs and the Murphys.

As Lizzy stood at the gravesite during her great-grandmother's burial, she asked Carol, "Who are the Beckers, and where are the rest of the family buried?"

"Mr. Becker co-owned a beer brewery here in Dayton with Susanna's father and adopted Susanna after her parents died in a car accident. The brewery went out of business when Mr. Becker died, and your great-grandmother's father-in-law, John Murphy Sr., received a large inheritance as Mr. Becker had no children," Carol explained. "The O'Malleys are buried in the Catholic cemetery downtown, while some of your Creager, Richter, and Murphy cousins are buried here in Woodlawn. But most of your descendants, I believe nineteen, are buried in the old graveyard by the small church in Christiansburg, Christ Episcopal. The first was Sarah Langley Wade in 1813, and the last was my great-grandmother Christina O'Sullivan Murphy in 1958. My father pieced together much of his family research project by visiting that old graveyard in Christiansburg. Maybe while you're here, we could visit them all."

"Thanks, Grandma. I'd like that."

Carol and Lizzy delayed their trip to Europe until August so Carol could have her knee surgery. After surgery, Carol spent only one night in the hospital and returned home the following day. With Lizzy staying at the house, Carol didn't need to enter a short-term convalescent home. Lizzy drove Carol to her physical therapy sessions, and as the time neared for them to leave for Europe, Carol walked effortlessly with minimal pain. A few weeks before their trip, Lizzy noticed Carol had lost a few pounds.

"I think you need a few new outfits to take with us on our trip," Lizzy told her. "We should go to that trendy new dress shop in Wade Plaza. We need formal dresses for the transatlantic cruise home and we also need new shoes. You always said a girl can't go on an adventure until she buys herself a new pair of pretty shoes."

Carol asked her friend and neighbor Nellie Slater if she could pick up the mail and water the plants while she and Lizzy were away. About the same age as Carol, Nellie lived less than a mile from Carol's house in one of the mid-century modern homes Lizzy's great-grandpa's construction company built in the early 1950s. You could easily walk to Nellie's home by taking the path through the woods.

After her husband passed, Nellie's brother, Earl, came to live with his sister. Carol and Virginia often played euchre with Nellie and Earl, or one invited the others over for an impromptu dinner party. Carol could depend on Earl Whitmer to help with any issues involving her house or property.

Before they left, Carol and Lizzy invited Nellie for lunch to thank her for watching the house while they were away.

"Grandma, do you want to serve lunch outside on the patio or inside?"

"Let's eat inside; it's way too hot out today. Set the small table in the morning room with my good white china."

The morning room off Carol's kitchen suited her style. She had it painted a soft yellow and accented the room with floral wallpaper in muted tones of greens and blues. The small round table with four white chairs completed the "shabby chic" look. The French doors opened out to the patio with a view of the woods. On one side, the pasture and the big barn were visible; on the other, all the large mid-century modern homes in the valley could be seen.

The Little Miami River ran along the back of the property. A large pond near the house allowed the family to enjoy swimming in the summer and ice skating in the winter. A creek ran through the property. On a hot summer day, it was possible to gather crawfish from the creek as bait to catch the bluegill in the pond.

"I'm so glad great-grandfather kept the dense woods surrounding the two log cabins," Lizzy said. "When I walk through the woods, I can almost imagine how it might have looked back in the early 1800s."

"Originally, it was almost two thousand acres of dense forest. The early Wades cleared over two hundred to establish their farm," Carol replied. "By the old barn, you can still see remnants of a large vegetable garden someone tended years ago."

A few minutes later, Lizzy and Carol heard Mrs. Slater call through the open kitchen door. "Hello!" she exclaimed. "Is anybody home?"

"Come in, Nellie," Carol said. "We're in the morning room."

Nellie stood, at most, five feet tall. Her silver-gray hair and sweet natural curls framed her small round face. Wearing capris and a long tunic top, Nellie appeared much shorter than her five-foot frame suggested.

"Mrs. Slater, you look lovely today."

"Oh, Lizzy, you are too kind. What's for lunch? Something smells good."

"In honor of our trip, we planned a traditional English afternoon tea," Lizzy responded. "You probably smell the scones Grandma just popped into the oven. Can I pour you a glass of Prosecco, or can we offer you a cold lemonade?"

"I'll take the lemonade. Oh, those little sandwiches look adorable."

Lizzy and Carol had spent the morning making little tea sandwiches. They cut some sandwiches into various shapes and placed them on a silver tray. There was cucumber with cream cheese and fresh dill on rye, egg salad on white, chicken salad on mini croissants, and ham with brie and apple on a small, sliced baguette.

After the sandwiches, they ate the scones, fresh from the oven, with strawberry jam and clotted cream. For the finale, Carol served a generous slice of her famous Hummingbird Cake, a cake she'd been baking ever since she saw the recipe in the February 1978 issue of *Southern Living* magazine. Carol also brewed plenty of Earl Grey tea.

"I need to hear all about your trip," Mrs. Slater said.

"For the first two weeks, we've booked the same itinerary Lizzy's mom and dad traveled on their honeymoon. We fly to Paris for a week; then we take the Orient Express to Venice for a second week."

"Oh, I've heard the Orient Express is very expensive."

"It is a little expensive for one night," Carol responded. "But you dress for dinner; the dining car is sumptuous. In the morning, we're served breakfast in our compartment. Lunch will be in the dining car, and finally, they serve tea and scones in the afternoon before we arrive in Venice."

"I'm so envious," Mrs. Slater said. "Can I hide in one of your suitcases? Where do you go after Venice?"

Carol continued, "After Venice, we take the high-speed train to Vienna for a few days. Hannah, my mother's mother, was born in Vienna. She arrived in America with her father when she was fourteen. Unfortunately, Hannah and her father died when my mother was a toddler. That's how her Aunt Edith came to live with her in Sandusky. Oh, the stories mother told about her Aunt Edith. Lizzy and I talked about taking a side trip to Denmark to visit Virginia's father's homeland, but we may have to save it for our next trip."

"I remember Virginia talking about her parents," Nellie said.

"After Vienna, we fly to Shannon, Ireland," Lizzy said. "We're renting a car and driving the Ring of Kerry. I'm not sure how I'll ever get the hang of driving on the left side of the road, but I'll need to learn quickly."

"Lizzy and I want to see all the places where our ancestors originated. The Murphys hail from Cork, and the O'Sullivans from Kildare and Killarney. Besides several B&Bs, we have reservations to stay in two castles; one in Tralee and one in Dublin."

"Next, we fly to London where we rented a flat for two months. Lizzy added. "One of our side trips is to take the train to Bath. We made a reservation at a B&B in Bath. Jane Austen lived there, and we'll stay in the Lizzy Bennet suite. I'm so excited!"

"Many of our ancestors came from Alton and Chawton, so we definitely plan to visit those two towns, as well," Carol added.

"Yes!" Lizzy exclaimed. "Jane Austen also lived in Chawton."

"It sounds like you must be a Jane Austen fan," said Mrs. Slater.

"What was your first clue?" Lizzy teased. "When I read *Pride & Prejudice* and found the main character is a girl named Elizabeth Bennet and her friends called her Lizzy, I was hooked. Grandma calls me an Austenite."

"Is Elizabeth Bennet your favorite character?" Mrs. Slater asked.

"No, Charlotte Heywood in *Sanditon* is my favorite," Lizzy said. She continued, "Finally, we are taking the leisurely way home aboard the *Queen Mary 2*. It's a seven-day voyage across the Atlantic, and we're staying in one of their Princess Suites."

"My husband and I booked the same crossing back in 1985 on the *QE2*," Mrs. Slater said. "It was quite romantic, with excellent food, too."

Carol sent two pieces of cake home with Mrs. Slater to share with her brother. After Carol and Lizzy cleaned the kitchen, they sat in the library to rest before they had to think about dinner. Lizzy took an old book off a shelf in the cupboard and began to read.

"Grandma, did you ever look at this old cookbook? Maybe we can find something in here to cook for dinner."

"Oh, my dad read a few of those recipes to Mom and me," Carol said.

"Grandma, they published this cookbook in 1758, and on the first page is written, *To Marie From Mother, 6 September 1766.* It's the same date and name on the back of the old cupboard."

"I know," Carol said. "Isn't it mindboggling?"

"The title is *The Art of Cookery Made Plain and Easy* authored 'By A Lady.' Grandma that's exactly what Jane Austen's first four novels give as the author! Did she write this cookbook?"

"Writing as a profession was considered an activity unsuitable for women. So many published their writing anonymously. Your great grandpa researched the cookbook and found a woman named Hannah Glasse wrote it."

"Grandma, these recipes are written in an old English style— they're hysterical. Chapter 12 talks about Hogs Puddings and Sausages. Here's a recipe for Trifle, except it requires Naples biskets. Do you think they mean biscuits? Where can we find Naples biskets? Another one is for a sauce for roast Lark."

"Lark, like the songbird?" Carol laughed. "How in the world do you cook a Lark?"

"Here's a scary one. 'Take your Hare when it was cas'd, and make a pudding'. We won't be cooking anything out of this cookbook for dinner tonight. Maybe we could call Earl and see if he could catch us a hare."

Lizzy and Carol laughed until they cried, imagining Earl, looking much like Elmer J. Fudd, trying to catch a hare.

The pair decided to go out for dinner at a small Italian restaurant near downtown Dayton. It would take twenty minutes to reach the restaurant, so to pass the time while she drove, Lizzy started a casual conversation with a bit of a revelation.

"I've been thinking, Grandma," Lizzy said. "You should open a restaurant in Christiansburg."

"Well, Lizzy, once you're done with culinary school, maybe you can come back, and you and I can open one."

"Maybe I don't need to go to school. I've learned everything I need to know from cooking with Mom."

"Lizzy, why would you want to live in Christiansburg when the world awaits you?"

"Grandma, I've lived in Chicago all my life, but I'm never happier than when I stay here with you in Ohio. Maybe I'm meant to be a small-town girl. Have you ever considered selling the house and coming back to Chicago to live?"

"I'm like you, Lizzy. I lived in Chicago far too long to want to go back to that rat race. I'm pretty content here in Ohio. With the sale of my business and the inheritance from my mom, I can live a quiet, contented life with no real worries. Maybe I'll travel a little to visit places I've never been."

Back home after dinner, Lizzy and Carol sat in the kitchen and continued talking until well past midnight.

"My dad told me the Wade family owned a mill in Alton that we must visit," Carol said. "There's also an estate in Chawton where the Baileys lived."

"Do you mean the Baileys, as in the builder of the cupboard Baileys?" Lizzy asked.

"Yes, Lizzy," Carol said. "And I can tell you right now, the cupboard you've always loved will be yours someday."

"Oh, Grandma, I will cherish our old cupboard forever."

"First, we take the train down to Hampshire," Carol continued. "Once we arrive, we hire a car and driver to help locate the mill and the Bailey's estate and visit all the quaint old churches. I also can't wait to see Alton and stay in one of the B&Bs there. I've heard it's a fascinating little market town with many pubs and shops."

"And once in Chawton, we can see where Jane Austen lived," Lizzy added. "Her house is now a museum."

"Lizzy, I finished the stories my dad started years ago. He typed everything on the old typewriter on his desk in the library, which required me to type everything into my computer. I've put a copy of the entire document onto my iPad. I'll bring it to Europe so we can refer to it during our trip. I want you to start reading these stories before we leave so you know everything there is to know about our family. Start with Christian Wade's story, the founder of Christiansburg."

Lizzy clutched her grandmother's iPad, mounted the stairs, and climbed into bed. Once she started to read, the stories transported her to places she never knew and people she'd only heard about.

CHRISTIAN HENRY WADE
1747 – 1791

"The distance is nothing when one has a motive."

Jane Austen, *Pride and Prejudice*

*A*rchibald Wade built a water mill southwest of London, near the market town of Alton in the East Hampshire district of Hampshire, England, in 1663. The three-story millhouse, with its undershot wheel, stood along the River Wey, a tributary of the River Thames.

Constructed of fieldstone with a foundation of large river rocks, the single-story house sat on a small rise sixty feet from the water mill. In addition to the mill and the house, the family owned sixty-five acres of pristine forest of oak, beech, and elm. Near the low ground, a lush meadow overflowed with large willow trees, corn-cockle, bluebells, ramsons, and columbine.

Archibald's wife planted a formal garden near the house using rambling rose, peony, hollyhocks, and lavender. Behind the house, Mrs. Wade kept a large kitchen garden full of herbs and vegetables for cooking and baking.

Archibald was hopeful the apple trees he planted would soon bear fruit. After three years the Wades were able to sit under the arbors and enjoy the sweet floral scent of their prized apple trees when they blossomed in the early spring.

Due to the river freezing in the winter and the silt collecting in the summer, the mill needed to be repaired many times over the years. Nevertheless, the Wade family lived quite comfortably off the toll the farmers paid to have their wheat crop ground into flour and middlings. For additional income, they cut and sold timber from their land to local furniture makers and builders.

The mill stayed busy six months out of the year, from early spring into late autumn. The farmers planted their winter wheat in the fall and harvested it the following spring. The wheat sown in the early spring was harvested in late fall. Anyone happening along the road to Alton from April to October could hear the wheel creak and groan as the river's flowing water pushed its blades.

In 1727, the then current Wades built a second story onto the house using brick and flint. They added dark green shutters at the now nine windows across the front, two windows on either side of the center front door, and five across the new second story.

In 1745, Samuel Wade inherited the mill from his father, just as sons had done for generations. Samuel lived in the house with his young wife, Mary Ann, and his two spinster sisters, Emma and Charlotte.

Samuel hired a local young man, Tom Thompson, to live in the house and help him work the mill. Tom brought along his wife, Sadie. Tom and Sadie slept in a downstairs room off of the kitchen. While Tom worked in the mill, Sadie cooked, cleaned, and washed clothes. She also dried herbs and preserved fruits and vegetables for use during the winter.

This morning, as Sadie chased the chickens into the garden so they could scratch in the snow for grubs and beetles, she took unusual care, as the old rooster would attack anyone who came near the henhouse.

"Shoo, George Augustus," Sadie shouted. "You may be King here in the run, but if you are not kind to me, I'll cook you for dinner tonight. Mistress Wade's babe is due any day, and she might enjoy some hot chicken broth after the child is finally here."

Little did Sadie know that today might be the day. Her husband was waiting at the kitchen door when she returned with the eggs.

"I must go for the midwife," Tom said. "See if you can stoke up the fires to try and warm the house."

The house stayed cold and damp as the young mother labored for nearly two days. As cold as it was outside, Sadie's attempts to keep the bedroom warm were met with much difficulty. Samuel's sisters, Emma and Charlotte, stayed close to Mary Ann's bed, attempting to encourage her to stay strong.

Christian Henry Wade gasped his first breath on a frosty morning, 27 February 1747. The midwife frantically attempted to stop Mary Ann's bleeding. Sadly, the young mother died, never to hold her baby in her arms. Christian's hungry wails could be heard throughout the large house, and his father's pain and grief appeared unbearable. The front door of the house stayed draped in black crepe for an entire year. Not until the daffodils bloomed in the garden the following spring did Samuel allow the crepe ribbon to be removed.

When Christian turned seven, Samuel sent him to a boarding school in Basingstoke. While at school, Christian studied reading, writing,

arithmetic, geometry, Latin, and Greek history. When Christian was home for his summer breaks his father took the time to instruct his young son in the running of the mill.

By the time Christian turned sixteen, he had left school to assist his father at the mill full-time. His two aunts had died the previous year, and his father had been unwell for many months. The extremely harsh winter of 1763 lasted well into February. Samuel developed pleurisy and died a week before Christian's birthday. At seventeen, Christian inherited the mill and his father's sizeable estate.

Early in the summer of 1765, Christian attended a meeting with his solicitor in Alton when he met, by chance, Thomas Bailey, the squire of Hawthorne Hall.

Squire Bailey inherited a large Elizabethan stone manor house, built in 1595, that sat on two thousand acres near the village of Chawton. In addition to running his large estate, he owned a Georgian townhouse in Mayfair near Hyde Park and was a successful cabinetmaker with a reputable shop in central London. As Squire Bailey entered the solicitor's office, he immediately saw young Christian.

"Mr. Wade, sir, my condolences on your father's death. I knew your father as an honorable man. How are you faring?"

"I am well, thank you for asking. As I remember, you and your wife brought your daughter Marie and your four sons to our fête the year before my father died. Your son Ronnie and I attended school together. How is Ronnie?"

"Ronald is doing well; he matriculates to Balliol College, Oxford, this fall."

"I'm wondering if you may allow me to call on your daughter, Marie?" Christian asked.

"Of course. I am sure my daughter would be quite pleased."

The morning after meeting Mr. Bailey in Alton, Christian mounted his horse, Farleigh, and rode to the Bailey's estate.

Christian owned three New Forest ponies, but Farleigh was his favorite. Christian and his father had attended a horse race in New Forest near Brockenhurst six years earlier, and Christian planned to participate someday, confident Farleigh would win.

On his second knock, one of the Bailey's footmen opened the front door and Christian passed through the entry porch. He set his calling card on the silver plate the footman was holding and followed him past an elaborate mix of classical columns and ornate decorations to the long back hall. Once they turned right and entered the living area, the footman announced: "Mr. Christian Wade, to see Mistress Marie."

He found Marie's mother, Mary, sitting on a green velvet settee, reading a book of poems. Marie sat next to her mother in front of a large tambour frame.

"Please sit down," Mary said as she motioned Christian toward a gold brocade armchair. "Marie is just finishing an embroidery project she started before she left school."

When living in London, Marie attended Mrs. Bennet's Day School for Young Girls, where she studied French, music, dancing, drawing, and needlework.

Christian presented himself at Marie's home every Sunday afternoon that summer. Sometimes Marie played the harpsichord and sang or read him a chapter from the novel *The Adventures of Arabella* by Charlotte Lennox. Some days, Mrs. Bailey permitted Christian to escort Marie on a carriage ride along the river or bring a basket into the countryside for a picnic—but only if she accompanied the couple as their chaperone.

"Tom," Christian announced one morning in early September. "I'll be spending the day in Alton; don't expect me home until late this evening. Make sure Masie is comfortable."

Christian owned two English Water Spaniels, Masie and Maston. Born three weeks earlier, Masie's second litter of pups appeared strong and healthy: four males and two females.

As soon as he arrived in Alton, Christian proceeded to the home of Monsieur Dubois, a portrait painter. Christian had been sitting for a miniature portrait to give to Marie before she left for London.

"Ah, good morning, sir. Your portrait is ready."

Monsieur Dubois painted Christian's portrait in watercolors on ivory. Christian acquired a delicate gold locket to hold his miniature. Marie had already given Christian her miniature, which he fastened inside the cover of the pocket watch he'd inherited from his father.

Every year, as far back as Christian could remember, the Wades held an annual festival to celebrate the September equinox. They invited the farmers who used their mill to grind their wheat, officials from Alton and Chawton, and the surrounding estate owners and their families. This year it fell on a Sunday, so they moved the fête to Saturday, 21 September, so as not to interfere with the Sabbath. This would be the first festival in the two years since Christian's father's death.

During the fête, the Wades allowed the locals to set up their own stalls, out of which they sold their homemade jams, preserves, pickles, garden produce, or bakery items, and the Wades always hosted a fine dinner in the evening. Some of the local women presented their delicious freshly baked scones, selling a proper cream tea for two farthings. Given her own marquee, Sadie planned to sell her apple butter made from the Wade's apples. Busy in the kitchen most of the day, Sadie asked her young niece to work the stall for her.

Tom dug a large pit beside the barn. Over the hole, he placed a forged iron frame with a crank for turning the pig he planned to slaughter early the morning of the fête. Tom also set up tents and tables in the expansive garden in front of the house.

"Place the large striped tea tent near the house," Christian ordered. "It will allow the ladies easy access to the kitchen."

The morning of the festival was cold, but as the sun rose and burned off the fog, it looked like it would turn into a glorious day.

Tom awoke before sunup to start the fire and put the hog on the spit. He scored the hog's skin and fat to ensure plenty of the savory cracklins were available for all to enjoy. He enlisted several young lads from a neighboring farm to keep the fire hot and the spit turning for twelve hours.

Christian released the horses to graze in the meadow as Tom set up chairs in the barn, where the men would later gather to drink the cider he and Tom bottled and corked the year before.

Sadie remained in the kitchen preparing boiled potatoes and onions, garden peas simmered with mint, and stewed pompions for the dinner Christian would host later that evening. The farmers' wives baked dozens of loaves of bread to complement the meal. Several local women baked their best fruit pies. Much to the delight of the festivalgoers, after the pies were judged and the prizes awarded, the pies would be served with the evening meal.

Squire Bailey arrived midday in an open carriage with his wife and daughter; his four sons had ridden over on horseback earlier that morning. When Christian saw Marie, he was stunned by her beauty. She wore an emerald green frock over layers of white petticoats. She positioned a matching green silk calash bonnet on her head with a gauzy, light green stole draped over her arms. Christian suddenly felt he couldn't measure up to her higher social status and worried it might hurt their relationship.

The farmers' wives wore simple linen skirts covered by aprons. Sheer scarves were draped casually over their jackets, which hung loosely around their shoulders for modesty. The ladies pinned their scarves at the front, with the ends tucked into the stomachers in the front of their dresses. They covered their hair under small white caps. For the festival, some replaced the cap's simple tie with a colorful ribbon secured at the top of their head.

Once most guests arrived, the town's Morris dancers began their exhibition. Fourteen men danced in pairs. Another four men played the pipe and tabor. The bells on their pants and the sticks they beat in time to the music mesmerized the crowd. They started with the waltz, *Hey Johnnie Dee,* and finished their demonstration with *On the Banks of the Wey.*

The children played games on the lawn throughout the day, such as ring toss, leapfrog, tag, hide-and-seek, and blind man's buff. Shortly before dinner, the winners of the pie contest and dog show were announced. Mrs. Hughes won the blue ribbon for her buttered apple pie with cinnamon and rose water. Christian's dog, Maston, won the grand prize at the dog show.

Many of the locals made and donated dozens of raffle prizes: hand-painted plates; bottles of home-brewed ale; handmade willow baskets; crocheted doilies; jars of spiced apples or jam; hair ribbons; and one hand-carved toy horse and cart Squire Bailey crafted from sycamore. This year they planned to contribute all money raised to the Church of St Lawrence.

Christian was pleased that Marie had offered to help tend the raffle tent with several local ladies. While under the tent, Marie folded her bonnet back to reveal her golden curls.

Following dinner, Christian walked Marie through the formal garden. As they entered the orchard, he presented Marie with the gold locket.

"May I put this locket around your neck?" Christian asked. "My miniature portrait is hidden inside."

"Oh, Christian!" Marie exclaimed. "I will never take it off."

As he leaned in closer, they kissed for the first time. At sixteen, Marie would be returning to school in London by early October.

The Baileys invited Christian to London for the Christmas season, to arrive on 5 December and depart the day following Twelfth Night. Christian's family had never celebrated Christmas with much elaboration. Christian didn't want Marie to think him a humbug, so with some reluctance, he accepted their kind invitation.

As the carriage passed Hyde Park and turned onto Park Lane, Christian recalled a trip to London with his father ten years prior. He was only nine years old, but he remembered it as if it were yesterday.

The coach he now hired was a little more sumptuous than the one from ten years earlier. His trip from Alton proved uneventful until they reached London, when the weather suddenly turned bitter cold. Christian arrived at the Bailey's townhouse in Mayfair in the late afternoon. Greeted at the front door, Christian recognized the Bailey's butler from Chawton, Mr. Withers.

"Good day, Mr. Wade," Mr. Withers said. "Mistress Marie is in the drawing room with her mother and brothers. Let me take your cloak. James will take your travel bags to your room and will act as your valet whilst you are here at Somerset House."

Christian had wrapped the gifts he purchased for the Baileys in colorful ribbons and safely hid them in his smaller travel bag. Tomorrow was Saint Nicholas Day, and he planned to bring the packages down that evening. For Marie's mother, he bought a box of lace handkerchiefs embroidered with her monogram and a sterling silver riding crop wrapped in leather for Squire Bailey. For Marie, Christian procured an agate and gold scent bottle and a copy of *La Henriade* by Voltaire. Christian wrote on the book's title page: *To my darling, Marie. From, Christian. Merry Christmas, 1765.*

Christian packed in his larger travel bag the two new formal outfits he had a tailor in Alton make several weeks before leaving for London. One outfit was made of dark green velvet and the other of brown silk brocade. Christian packed his wig for any formal evening events, as most Englishmen had stopped wearing their wigs during the day. He also ordered a new day outfit; a three-piece set of coat, waistcoat, and breeches, all made from fine brown wool.

The footman carried his bags upstairs while Mr. Withers led Christian into the drawing room. Because it was considered bad luck to decorate before Christmas, the house lacked any Christmas embellishments. However, by Christmas Eve there would be holly and evergreen boughs in every room of Somerset House.

Christian stood close to the large fireplace with its roaring fire. It had been almost three months since Christian had seen Marie, and he longed to take her in his arms. Knowing it improper, he merely nodded in her direction.

"Mr. Wade, it is so good to see you," Mary Bailey said. "Squire Bailey is at his club but should be home before dinner; we eat at eight. Withers, pour Mr. Wade a brandy; he must be chilled to the bone."

The Christmas season in London included a series of endless parties and dinners. Over those first few weeks, Christian attended several parties at the homes of the Bailey's friends, and the Baileys hosted several formal dinners at Somerset House. One evening, they saw a new comedy play at the Theatre Royal, Drury Lane, in Covent Garden.

Squire Bailey hired two carriages to escort the family to Westminster Abbey for Christmas Eve Mass. Several street ragamuffins approached the Squire's carriage as it passed St. Margaret's Church, and Mr. Bailey tossed each a halfpenny.

It was well past midnight when the family arrived back at Somerset to find the staff had transformed the house into a proverbial Christmas wonderland. They used holly to create centerpieces on the dining table, including apples, oranges, candles, cinnamon sticks, and ribbons. They hung evergreen garlands on the stair banisters, balustrades, and every fireplace mantel.

Christian observed kissing balls of ivy, mistletoe, and rosemary hung in the doorways. Standing under one, he held out his hand to Marie, then kissed her gently on her cheek.

James, the footman, brought a large silver bowl filled with eggnog into the drawing room. Next, he lit the large oak Yule log wrapped in hazel twigs using a piece from last year's log. They would burn the Yule log every evening over the next twelve nights. After drinking the celebratory eggnog, the family retired for the night.

The following day, before the family traveled to St Paul's Cathedral for the early morning Christmas service, they ate a hasty breakfast of spiced porridge topped with cherries and apples. Later, four of the Bailey's London friends joined them at Somerset House for dinner.

Christmas dinner included a large roast goose with chestnut stuffing, roasted root vegetables, almond blancmange, brandy-soaked peaches, and spiced cranberries. The highlight sat in the center of the table: a Christmas pie filled with turkey, goose, partridge, and pigeon covered with a thick crust. Silver platters of fruit, cheese tarts, minced pies, and bowls of nuts and raisins rested on the sideboard. The butler, Mr. Withers, poured each guest a glass of Port or Madeira. Finally, the footman brought the flaming plum pudding to the table.

January 6, Twelfth Night, signaled the end of the Christmas season, and the Baileys hosted a Twelfth Night party for twenty guests. They ate, drank, danced, and played games like "bob apple" and "snapdragon." Spiced and sweetened brandy was served from a large silver bowl.

The Black Swan Bakery created Mrs. Bailey's Twelfth Night cake, an extravagantly decorated and rich fruit cake. The baker used cochineal to color the icing a bright pink, while white gum paste decorations pressed from the confectioner's board adorned the large cake. A bean and a pea were baked inside, and two gold paper crowns sat perched on top. Squire Bailey found the bean and was declared King Bean for the night. Mrs. Walker found the pea and was therefore crowned Queen Pea.

By late May, the Baileys closed their house in London and returned to Chawton for the summer. For Marie's seventeenth birthday, they planned to hold a formal dress masquerade ball for their many friends and neighbors.

When Christian heard the Baileys had arrived safely back in Chawton, he saddled Farleigh and rode to their estate. He had decided to ask for Marie's hand in marriage. He found the squire outside the stables, ready for his morning ride.

"Squire Bailey, sir, I must speak with you regarding a very pressing matter. May I ride with you this morning?"

"I'm fairly certain I know why you have come. Do you understand how pampered my Marie is? Do you think she will be content living at the mill?"

"The living quarters of the house have been recently refurbished to a very high standard, and Marie can certainly add her own feminine touches. I know we can make it suitable for a young lady of Marie's upbringing."

"I'm not certain you and Marie are ready for marriage. You are both so young."

"I promise I will take special care of Marie," Christian said. "You have my word."

"With Marie being my only daughter, her dowry is monetarily sizable, but she receives no claim to my estate. My property is being left to my eldest son, Ronald. If you agree, you have my permission to marry my daughter."

On the evening of Marie's birthday, the Bailey's Chawton estate looked like a mythical fairyland. Mrs. Bailey wore a white silk domino cloak with a gold mask. She wore the cloak over a blue French silk and linen dress. Squire Bailey dressed as an Ottoman Turk in a gold and silver robe with a black turban. Marie wore a white linen dress. Dressed as a shepherdess, she held a crook wrapped in blue ribbons, with matching ribbons wound around her yellow curls. Christian wore a floor-length black robe and mask. His black three-cornered hat included several plumes of black feathers. Other costumes included Roman emperors and empresses, lady's maids, jesters, sailors, nuns, and priests.

The impressive guest list included Mr. Thomas Knight, his wife, Jane, and their son, Thomas. The younger Thomas served as a member of Parliament for New Romney. The Knights owned a manor house in Chawton and came down from their estate in Godmersham. They planned to stay in Chawton for only a few more weeks.

A small orchestra played music for dancing. The Bailey's servants set several banquet tables on the lawn loaded with beef, lamb, rabbit, fish, bread, preserved fruit, gingerbread, and sugared almonds. Mr. Bailey arranged with a local man to put on a fireworks display. The man stuffed gunpowder into paper tubes. Setting them off at different times produced a dazzling fire art display. As Marie and Christian viewed the fireworks, he held her hand.

"My darling Marie," Christian said. "Will you make me a happy man and agree to be my wife?"

Christian commissioned a posey ring from a goldsmith in Alton, a delicate gold band engraved inside with "A Token of My Love." She said "Yes," and he slipped the posey ring onto her finger.

As much as Christian had tried to convince himself, he worried that Marie might find living at the mill difficult and be unable to cope, especially since she could not bring her lady's maid to the mill. And though Tom and Sadie still lived in the house, Sadie had other duties. But Christian didn't realize that for all her shyness, Marie was a plucky young woman who had grown up with four brothers and saw marriage to Christian as another exciting adventure.

At the stroke of midnight, the partygoers removed their masks to reveal their identities. The ball lasted well into the morning hours of the next day.

On a warm autumn morning, 6 September 1766, Christian Henry Wade and Marie Elizabeth Bailey were married in Chawton at St Nicholas Church.

At nineteen, Christian stood six feet, with a full head of black hair. He looked very genteel in his coat, waistcoat, and breeches as he stood at the altar awaiting his bride; his white powdered wig was pulled back with a black velvet ribbon.

Marie's mother ordered a custom-made wedding robe for her daughter. The cerulean blue silk faille gown featured delicate silver brocade flowers. Open in the front, the skirt showed off Marie's frilly petticoats edged in white lace.

A petite girl, Marie boasted a fair complexion and blond hair. The early morning sunshine reflected off her dress, causing her stunning blue eyes to nearly match the sapphire drop earrings she borrowed from her mother. A large bouquet of white lilies lay in Marie's arms while a wreath of pink rosebuds had been placed on her head. When Christian saw her enter the church, he fell even more in love with her grace and beauty.

Marie's father gave the young couple an enormous cupboard as a wedding gift. He'd crafted the piece from the wood of a stately Wych elm harvested from the Bailey's property several years earlier.

Mary wondered if Marie could cope with only Sadie to help her, so she placed in the cupboard a cookbook she found at Mrs. Ashburn's, a china shop at Fleet-Ditch, in London. As her contribution to the wedding gift, Marie's mother filled the cupboard with the homemade jams she had preserved. She included jars of dried rosemary, peppermint, and sage. Mary also gifted Marie the sapphire earrings Mr. Bailey had given Mary on their wedding day.

As the happy couple exited the church, the bell-ringers rang the six church bells of St Nicholas to announce the couple's matrimony and to bring Christian and Marie good luck in their marriage.

The Baileys spared no expense in the food prepared for the wedding breakfast held later that morning, with tents and chairs arranged on their estate's lawn for the pleasure and comfort of the many guests.

Sausages, back bacon, slices of black pudding, and boiled eggs arrived on large silver platters. They acquired from Mr. Lewis, a cheese purveyor in Chawton, several luscious cheese varieties from Cheshire, Stilton, and North Yorkshire. The baker placed jars of quince marmalade, blackberry jam, and honey on the table near the freshly baked loaves of bread. Dozens of teapots of hot black tea and stoneware crocks full of locally brewed cider and ale helped to quench the thirst of the happy wedding-goers.

To everyone's delight, the local baker, Mr. Coombs, brought out enough rich fruit cakes to serve everyone in attendance. Next to the cakes, one of the Bailey's footmen placed a large silver bowl of punch made from brandy, sweet wine, whole egg, and cream, with a crack of Mary's coveted nutmeg on top to make it even more remarkable. After they toasted the young couple, everyone danced to music that continued to play well after the wedding couple departed.

The union between Christian and Marie brought forth two children: Margaret Marie and Jacob Henry. The years passed quickly, and the children grew into fine young adults.

Margaret Marie was born on 14 August 1767. Starting at an early age, Marie taught her daughter the fine art of needlework. Margaret also spent several weeks each summer with Grandmother Bailey in Chawton, as she arranged for Margaret to receive lessons on the fortepiano and be tutored in French.

Margaret grew into a tall, slender, attractive young woman with her father's dark hair and features. Shortly after she turned eighteen, Margaret moved to Alton to live with her cousin Catherine and Catherine's husband, Harold. After a short apprenticeship, Margaret worked as a much-sought-after milliner in an exclusive shop. Women came from as far away as Winchester and Basingstoke to purchase a bonnet created by Margaret Wade.

Margaret was betrothed to Philip Crane, the schoolmaster at the Alton Grammar School. Philip was a quiet and studious young man.

Born in Deane, Hampshire, he'd become the schoolmaster five years earlier after completing his study of the classics at Winchester College. Disliking the wigs some men still wore on occasion, Philip always wore a soft cap over his natural hair, and small oval spectacles because of his constant studying and reading.

In addition to his *per annum* of £65, the town owned Red Rose Cottage, where the schoolmaster lived rent-free. The two-story terrace cottage, with its large bay window in front, sat in the middle of a row of similar redbrick houses. Downstairs, the house boasted a small workshop and a large hall (or sitting room) with a hearth for cooking. To reach the two bed chambers above, one needed to mount nine steep steps.

On either side of the white front door grew fragrant red roses that reached nearly to the roof. In the small, secluded back garden, Philip planted herbs and vegetables. Dark purple wisteria climbed the back of the house in early spring with dense fresh green leaves that turned vibrant golden-yellow in the fall. By late summer, bean-like pods ripened on the wisteria vines, lasting well into winter.

On 10 July 1790, Margaret and Philip married at the Church of St Lawrence, and Margaret moved into Red Rose Cottage.

Christian and Marie's second child, Jacob Henry, born on 23 September 1772, was now a tall, strapping young man with light brown hair and deep blue eyes. Jacob lived in his parents' house and assisted his father with the mill's daily operations. Jacob loved living at the mill and working with his father.

Marie taught her children to read and write using the many books she'd brought to the mill from her father's home in London. Although Jacob had no formal schooling, Christian taught Jacob basic arithmetic to count money and accurately weigh the flour bags. Jacob's Grandfather Bailey taught him to make small wooden jewelry boxes, which Jacob sold at the local farmer's market. By the time he turned twelve, he had saved nearly twenty shillings.

Jacob was only fifteen when his father observed an exchange between his son and Sarah Langley. It was soon apparent to Christian and Marie that Jacob was infatuated with the young girl who lived on a nearby farm. She often accompanied her father when he brought his wheat to the mill.

"Miss Langley, you look lovely today," Christian heard Jacob say.

"Thank you, Mr. Wade, but you may call me Sarah," she replied.

"Then you must call me Jacob."

Times were changing, and by 1790, many of Christian's neighbors immigrated to America, seeking a better life with more significant economic opportunities.

One crisp morning in early December, Christian and Marie drove their carriage to visit Marie's parents at their Chawton home. They found two gentlemen sitting with Mr. and Mrs. Bailey in the drawing room. Christian recognized them as Thomas Knight and his young adopted son, Edward. It had been over two years since Edward returned from a grand tour of Europe, and he was staying at the Knight's manor house in Chawton.

Once seated, Christian addressed his father-in-law: "I received a letter from our former neighbor, Matthew Foley," he said. "He lives in America and has sent me correspondence that a mill built in 1771 is for sale in Frederick Town, Maryland, near Annapolis. The mill is located north of Frederick Town, along Carroll Creek. Carroll Creek is a Monocacy River tributary draining to the Potomac. I need your perspective, sir," he concluded.

"America is just getting established after they fought for their independence," Mr. Bailey replied. "I think you are taking a big chance. You must be certain this mill is well suited for your family."

"Matthew explained in his letter that the large house with its mill are nearly twice the size as ours here," Christian said. "He assured me it will easily accommodate our large family."

"During my time abroad, I saw many marvelous sights," Edward interjected. "Not having gone to college, the experience of seeing new places truly shaped my outlook on life. I've heard America is quite a primitive place, but it sounds like a grand adventure."

"Yes, a wonderful opportunity, and Marie is in agreement with the decision to leave England," Christian said. "Do you know anyone who might be interested in buying my mill, the house, and the land?" he asked his father-in-law.

"I shall speak with Henry Eaton," Mr. Bailey said. "He has expressed to me several times his desire to expand his holdings. I'm sure he would offer a fair price."

As Christian and Marie stood to leave, young Edward approached the couple. "Please give my regards to your new son-in-law, Philip Crane. Philip and I were mates during our younger days when he lived with my family in Steventon. Please ask him to correspond with me when he arrives in Maryland. I am anxious to hear about his adventures in America. He may remember me as Neddy Austen."

Now in their seventies, Tom and Sadie left the mill to live with their nephew in Southampton. Sadie's departure required Marie to cook the meals for her family by herself, though she had little experience.

"I've prepared a savory Lumber Pye for this cold January night. I thickened the custard with the Naples biskets I procured yesterday from Baker Coombs," she told Christian.

"What a pleasing meal," Christian replied. "You are a better cook than you supposed."

"Why, thank you, husband," Marie said. "But you'll need to thank my mother for placing the cookbook in the old elm cupboard my father gave us on our wedding day. Now, tell your son our news."

Christian turned to Jacob. "You remember Matthew Foley," Christian began. "He sent a letter late last year advising me of a mill for sale in America."

"Are you saying you want to sell the mill and go to America?" Jacob asked. "I cannot go to America unless I can take Sarah. And what about Margaret and Philip?"

"Sarah Jane is perhaps all of sixteen," Christian argued. "She needs the consent of her parents to marry. Margaret and Philip seem excited at the possibility of a better life in America."

"You remember, husband," Marie said, "I was seventeen, and Jacob is the same age you were when we married."

"I will speak to her father," Christian relented.

Sarah and Jacob's marriage took place on 30 April 1791 at St Andrews Church in Farnham. The bride wore her favorite yellow frock with a nosegay of lily-of-the-valley pinned at the waist.

It was a simple service with no large reception afterward. Knowing Sarah would soon leave for America, her parents bid her a tearful goodbye after the ceremony. She then traveled with Jacob and his family to the mill.

Once home, Marie and Margaret prepared a modest wedding breakfast consisting of porridge, sausages, eggs, fresh bread, and jam for the newly married couple. Christian had procured several small fruit cakes from the local baker. After breakfast, he served each person a cake with a small glass of claret.

Christian's solicitor handled the transaction to sell the mill to Henry Eaton. With no hesitation, Christian made the arrangements to purchase the mill in Maryland.

"I must be able to take the cupboard my father made," Marie demanded. "And of course, we cannot forget to take the Wade Bible and my many books."

"Mr. Eaton and his son own four carts and have graciously offered to assist us," Christian said. "Your treasured cupboard shall not be left behind."

Over the next two weeks, the Wades packed numerous trunks with the bundles of clothes and household items they would require to start their new life in America.

"Plan to meet in Liverpool in two weeks," Christian told his son-in-law. "I'll arrange for rooms at Mere Brook Inn."

Once their belongings were loaded into the carts, Christian, Jacob, and the two Eaton men left Alton for Liverpool.

A week later, Philip hired a coach to travel with Margaret, Sarah, and Marie for the two-day trip to Southampton. Once in Southampton, the four boarded a luxury ferry for the cruise to Liverpool to meet Christian and Jacob.

On 13 June 1791, the three couples sailed from Liverpool to America aboard a large sailing vessel named *Fortitude*. It was an appropriate name, for their quest would take every ounce of strength and courage the family could muster.

"Well, it seems we are to be celebrating your birthday at sea," Christian said to Marie.

After seven long weeks aboard ship, on 3 August 1791, the travelers arrived in Annapolis, Maryland.

JACOB HENRY WADE
1791 – 1804

"I am the happiest creature in the world.
Perhaps other people have said so before, but not one with such justice."

Jane Austen, *Pride and Prejudice*

Matthew Foley and his family had immigrated to America three years earlier where he acquired a farm outside of Frederick Town, Maryland. Back in Alton, Matthew Foley had been one of the many farmers who brought his wheat to the Wade's mill to be processed. Mr. Foley and his three sons traveled to Annapolis to assist the Wade family in their move.

Jacob had grown up with the Foley brothers. Will and Jacob shared the same birth year, whereas Will's twin brothers, Robert and Richard, were five years younger. In England, when the boys weren't assisting their fathers, they spent warm summer days fishing and swimming in the River Wey or running through the forest, imagining themselves as knights-errant.

"Jacob!" Will shouted. "It's so good to see you, old man. I hear you married Sarah Langley."

"It is good to see you, too," Jacob responded, gesturing to his family, who were standing near the ship's gangway. "Sarah is next to my mother, Marie, and my father, Christian. You know my sister, Margaret, and her husband, my brother-in-law, Philip Crane. Please come and say hello."

The four Foley men raised their caps to the ladies and greeted the men with hearty handshakes. Soon, they set about the task at hand.

"Do be careful with the large cupboard," Marie pleaded. "It is my prized possession."

The unloaded trunks were stacked into two large wagons, including Marie's treasured cupboard and her collection of books. Mr. Foley's strange-looking wooden wagons were painted bright blue, with high-sloped sides and red-painted running gear. Over the wagons stretched a white canvas covering to protect the contents. Several large water barrels had been secured to the sides, along with a toolbox and an extra wheel strapped to the back of each wagon.

"I've never seen anything like these back in England," Jacob said. "I'm impressed with the wide iron-rimmed wheels and the six large draft horses pulling each wagon. How did you come by these strange-looking wagons?"

"They call them Conestoga wagons, named for the Conestoga River in Pennsylvania," Mr. Foley said. "I commissioned these wagons from Henri Reich, a wagonmaker from Lancaster County, who now lives in Frederick Town. I use mine to take my grain to Baltimore, where it's processed and sold abroad. Since you will now run the mill in Frederick Town, I can transport it already processed."

"Will we need to buy wagons such as these?" Jacob asked.

"Probably not," Mr. Foley said. "Weekly, wagons come from Baltimore bringing whiskey, tobacco, and other products needed here in the West. For a small fee, they will gladly take back your processed grain."

"Why do the floors slope upward?" Jacob asked.

"That's so your possessions won't shift, causing the wagon to tip," Mr. Foley answered. "You will want to talk with Mr. Jessup, the town blacksmith; he should have a coach to sell. He also knows a reputable horse trader you might barter with for the carriage horses you'll need and a couple of saddle horses. I don't think the ladies want to walk the eighty miles to the mill. We'll likely cross some streams and perhaps even a shallow river. Some roads become quite rutted; often, they contain deep mud. Although quite sturdy, the Conestoga wagons are not built to carry passengers."

After the wagons were loaded, the group drove to a large livery stable where they could board the horses with Mr. Jessep, the owner, and store the wagons overnight. Then the two families walked to the King of France tavern for their midday meal. Dinner started with hasty pudding, followed by fresh bread, a pork stew with root vegetables, and corn fritters. They finished the meal with a slice of sweet gingerbread cake.

"Sarah," Jacob said, "this fine ale tastes as good as any we drank back in England."

Next door to the tavern sat The Maryland Inn. Christian paid for one night's lodging for four rooms. The travelers planned to begin their journey to Frederick Town early the following day.

The ladies retreated to their rooms as the men walked back to the livery, where they were to meet up with Travis Cline, the horse trader Mr. Jessup recommended. They acquired from Travis two saddle horses for Jacob and Philip. Sleek and tall, nearly sixteen hands, the stallions appeared nothing like the New Forest ponies Jacob owned back in England.

"If you don't mind, Philip, I would like to ride the grey," Jacob said. "He is truly magnificent."

"Half-Arabian, these two are," Travis said. "Got 'em from a man who told me they came off a boat from Africa just yesterday, he did."

Travis was quite the talker, but Mr. Jessup vouched for his reputation and said they need not worry about the quality of the horses. They also purchased a small and sturdy closed coach from Mr. Jessup and two carriage horses from Travis. Not as large as the draft horses but heavier than the saddle horses; the carriage horses could easily pull the coach with its four occupants. Christian would drive the coach, with the three women riding inside. The trip would be slow, what with being able to travel less than twenty miles a day. They hoped to arrive at the mill after four nights on the road.

Before they retired for the night, the families enjoyed a light supper of stewed prunes, bread, and cheese, all served by the innkeeper's daughter.

"I must say, I'm impressed so far with what I see of America," Sarah told Jacob at supper. "I hope Frederick Town is as lovely as Annapolis."

"Prepare yourselves for a somewhat arduous journey," Mr. Foley warned. "We'll need to secure provisions for about four days until we arrive in Log Town, where there is a small store. If we can't find an inn at night, we may need to sleep outside on the ground; the ladies can sleep in their coach. We brought extra blankets, but we need to procure some grain for the horses and food for us."

"The trip is well worth any discomfort; wait until you see the Catoctin Mountain range," Will added.

Jacob gently squeezed Sarah's hand as the three women showed nervous apprehension. The family spent seven long weeks aboard a ship, where early on, all of them suffered from seasickness, and now they were journeying off on another rough trip.

Jacob awakened early. After a breakfast of mush and milk, he hurried to the livery stable to check on the wagons and thoroughly inspect the new coach.

The small coach was built to hold six adults. Therefore, the three ladies would have ample legroom and be quite comfortable. The curtains at the windows could be drawn shut. The smithy had replaced the standard strap suspension with springs, which should make the ride much more pleasant. With a large storage compartment in the back and a good size rack on top, there would be plenty of room for their travel bags. The seats had been covered with woven horsehair and padded with the same.

Mr. Foley filled the large water barrels, strapping the barrels to the sides of the Conestoga wagons. He and Christian then rode to the feed mill to procure grain for the horses. After securing the grain barrels onto the wagons, the men proceeded to the mercantile. They procured enough bread, cornmeal, beans, dried meat, salted bacon, and dried fruit for their four-day journey. Christian paid the merchants with the silver coins from the money casket he'd brought from England.

"Coins are not yet being minted here in America, and the Continental paper money no longer holds any value," Mr. Foley told Christian. "People do much bartering for their supplies, but any merchant will gladly accept your gold and silver as payment."

Christian remained careful not to let the strongbox out of his possession, as it held many silver and gold coins. The most significant portion of the currency was intended to settle the acquisition of the new mill.

When they left Annapolis, the weather suddenly turned hot and humid.

"We need to rest the horses often and provide them plenty of water several times throughout the day," Will Foley announced.

"Robert and Richard plan to drive one wagon each by riding astride the left draft horse hitched nearest the wagon, known as the wheel horse," Mr. Foley explained. "Will and I intend to sit on the lazy board, which is positioned on the left side of each wagon, or we'll walk alongside for easy access to operate the wagon's brake."

They made excellent time the first day, traveling almost twenty miles, stopping before they reached Huntington City. With no inn nearby, they camped in a small clearing along the Little Patuxent River.

"Even though the night is warm, we'll need to build a fire and keep it burning all night," Mr. Foley said. "Not to scare you, but black bears are known to be in this area. So we need to secure our food in the wagon. I brought my musket. Did you bring your guns to America?"

"Yes," Jacob said. "But they are all packed away."

"We should be all right; Will also carries his flintlock pistol."

Jacob and Philip heaped grain from the barrels into the troughs attached to the back of the wagons to feed the horses, and the group sat down to eat their meal of bacon and beans.

The following day, they continued heading westward toward the Potomac River. They reached Cabin John Creek before nightfall. The men spent the second night again camped on the ground as the ladies slept inside the coach.

The men awoke early. Fishing the creek, they caught several smallmouth bass and blue catfish, which they cooked for breakfast. Mr. Foley made cornmeal cakes and fried them in the same pan as the fish. Once everyone finished breakfast, they broke camp and continued the trip, traveling north toward Log Town.

"The Brass Pig Inn here in Log Town serves a hearty supper," Mr. Foley announced. "If there are not enough rooms for all of us, we can check the Red Lion."

Luckily, the Brass Pig had just enough vacant rooms to accommodate the travelers. For a small fee, the innkeeper also allowed the horses to be stabled inside his horse barn. The men secured the wagons under a dense stand of tall oak trees.

With supper over, the party retired to their sparsely furnished rooms: a bed, a small table with one candle, a wash basin, and one straight-back wooden chair. After sleeping two nights on the hard ground, the men welcomed the large goose-down stuffed mattresses.

A storm rolled through during the night, pelting heavy rain and hail against the windows. The storm raged all night, with intense lightning followed by deafening thunderclaps and howling wind. At breakfast the next morning, everyone chatted excitedly about the storm.

"What a storm!" Sarah exclaimed. "How blessed to be here at the inn with a roof over our heads. Jacob, did the storm damage the cargo in the wagons?"

"I checked this morning, and fortunately, the canvas cover protected the contents, while the tar caulking helped to keep everything dry inside."

"I don't think there is much chance we will make good time today," Mr. Foley told the group. "The roads must be dry if we anticipate reaching Frederick Town in two more days. Between here and our destination, the road is badly eroded and uneven. With last night's rain, a muddy road is a possibility. We should make every attempt to reach Hyattsville tonight."

About one hour outside Log Town, they came upon an elderly couple looking down at a small carriage in a deep ditch off the side of the road. The gentleman explained he and his wife had been traveling from their farm, heading to Log Town, when their horse slipped in a muddy rut, causing the carriage to slide into the ditch.

Marie welcomed the wife into their coach while the men discussed freeing the small carriage.

"Thank you so much for stopping to assist us," said the woman. "My name is Elsbeth Simon. My husband Jack and I were both born here in Maryland. I do not mean to appear rude, but as I listen to your accent, you must be English."

"Yes, we arrived from England a few days ago. My name is Margaret; this is my mother, Marie, and my sister-in-law, Sarah. We are traveling to Frederick Town, where we purchased a mill."

Mrs. Simon continued, "Originally from Scotland, our parents immigrated to Ulster in Ireland. You probably know us as Ulster Scots, but they call us Scotch-Irish here in America. During the reign of King Charles I, our parents decided to immigrate to America. As Ulster Presbyterians, our parents didn't wish to join the Church of England. Here in America there is greater religious tolerance."

"I do not recognize Simon as a Scottish surname," Marie said.

"My husband's father was born into the Western Scotland MacShim clan. He changed his name to Simon when he arrived in Maryland. The Gaelic form of the name is Mac Shimidh, meaning son of Simon. My maiden name is MacMillan. Mr. Simon and I met in Philadelphia before moving to our farm here in Maryland."

"Will your children help you clean the mud from your carriage when you reach home?" Marie asked.

"Yes, our son's wife and children live with us on the farm. Unfortunately, our son, young Jack, was killed during the American War of Independence."

The ladies offered their condolences.

Jacob unhitched the couple's small mare and replaced her with one of Matthew Foley's large draft horses. Jacob led the draft horse while the Foley men pushed the carriage from behind. The men quickly extracted the carriage from the ditch, and Jacob re-hitched the couple's horse. Jacob inspected the mare and the coach and deemed both unscathed.

"It is so nice to meet you, and thank you," Elsbeth said. "Perhaps we will meet again under better circumstances."

Mrs. Simon left the coach and returned to her husband.

"Marie?" Sarah questioned. "I'm worried our neighbors in Frederick Town won't accept us. Are we now Americans? We lived in

Great Britain just two months ago, and my parents are still loyal to King George."

Assisting the Simons didn't take as long as expected, and the travelers arrived in Hyattsville just before sundown.

"This town seems very nice," Margaret said. "I see a school, a store, and a blacksmith's shop."

"And also several small houses," Marie added. "I hope we find a nice inn with enough rooms to house us all."

Jacob arranged with the blacksmith to stable the horses. Fortunately, the smithy owned a large barn to shelter the wagons and the coach. They walked to the Hyattsville Inn and arrived as the evening meal was being served. During supper, Sarah recounted the conversation with Mrs. Simon to the men.

"It's been seven years since the end of the war," Mr. Foley told the group, responding to Sarah's concerns. "The Americans quickly accepted us when we arrived here three years ago. Don't worry; you should have no problems. America is a country of immigrants, just like us."

Late afternoon of 8 August 1791, the caravan of wagons and horses arrived in Frederick Town.

"Look, Marie!" Sarah exclaimed. "Our new little town looks like a small city. I can't wait to see the house!"

"I see several taverns and inns, a butcher, and a greengrocer," Marie said. "There's even a doctor's surgery and three churches."

They continued north on Independence Road for another three miles. Independence Road ran parallel to Carroll Creek.

"There's the mill!" Jacob shouted. "It looks like we turn here into a lane past the water wheel."

The procession turned right and crossed a small bridge over Carroll Creek.

Mr. Foley visited the mill several times and attempted to explain the millhouse's scope in his correspondence with Christian. His letters didn't do it justice.

"This must be twice as big as our mill back in England," Jacob said to Philip once they pulled up in front. "It's a fine-looking house made entirely of roughly coursed fieldstone."

Christian planned to meet the owner, Mr. Marshall, and his attorney the next day to finalize the transaction. The mill's former owner had already moved out, leaving much of the furniture and household goods, per the arrangement with Christian. He also left specific instructions with their solicitor back in England, allowing the Wades to move in as soon as they arrived.

The women started their tour of the living quarters, whereas the men immediately crossed over to the wing containing the mill mechanism.

"I want my cupboard placed right here in the front room across from the fireplace," Marie said. "Let's go upstairs and inspect the bedrooms."

Once they'd searched the entire house, Margaret went to the door leading into the mill and called, "Father, if you light some lamps, Sarah and I will make up beds for everyone. Mother is in the kitchen setting out supper. Please tell Mr. Foley he and his sons must stay the night."

"Philip and I will attend to the horses," Jacob said.

The men walked out to the barn, brushed down the horses, and gave each some of the extra hay that Mr. Marshall kindly left behind.

The next morning, the men made quick work of unloading the wagons. Christian paid the Foley men well for their assistance over the past several days. By ten o'clock, Mr. Foley and his sons left for their farm a few miles farther down Independence Road.

"Jacob," Christian said, "I want you to come with me to Mr. Nelson's office. You won't be twenty-one for another two years, but I want you to meet our attorney, as they call them here in America. I was near your age when my father died, and I knew nothing about running a business. Fortunately, my father's solicitor helped me manage my affairs until I turned twenty-one."

Before the two went into town, they rode out to inspect their property.

"The wheat and rye look healthy," Jacob observed. "We should talk with Mr. Marshall about whom we can find to help us harvest the crop this fall. Perhaps we ask Mr. Foley and his sons to help."

"The land doesn't contain the dense forest like back in England," Christian said. "However, the contract states we own almost fifty acres of poplar, oak, and maple trees."

"Father, just look at those magnificent mountains. I've never seen anything like them. What a view!" Jacob added.

They circled down to the river and back up to the house. They investigated the small lean-to and the outhouses, ending back at the barn.

"The barn looks brand new; Mr. Marshall claimed he built it ten years ago. It's big enough to store grain and keep our carriages covered, with enough room left to stable our horses," Christian said before the two walked over to examine a small cottage.

"The cottage is conveniently close to the barn and mill," Jacob said. "If we hire a farm manager, he could live here."

The small, whitewashed stone two-bedroom cottage looked well-made and watertight, with a heavy red cedar door and a black slate roof. Red and yellow roses bloomed beside a small vegetable patch.

A large fireplace with a stone hearth stood along the side wall of the main room. The cottage came furnished with a table and four chairs. Each bedroom contained a bedstead and chest.

"Our old rocker might look perfect here by the fireplace," Christian said. "Perhaps we can find a spare rug for the floor."

Once in Frederick Town, they quickly found Court Street and Mr. Nelson's office.

"Good morning, Mr. Wade. And this must be your son," Mr. Nelson said. "Let me introduce you to Mr. Marshall. It is good to meet you both. I trust the journey was uneventful."

"Yes, it is good to meet you as well. This is my son, Jacob. Our trip was long and tiring, but we are glad to be here; thank you for asking."

"Let's begin. You have come to finalize the sale of Mr. Marshall's farm. Please open the packet of papers before you. Mr. Marshall owns two farms three miles north of Frederick, along Carroll Creek. One farm sits on the west side of Carroll Creek, but you are purchasing the second one on the east side. This is a 250-acre lot with a three-story fieldstone house with a water mill attached. There are five outbuildings: a small cottage, a barn, two outhouses, and a lean-to. One hundred acres are seeded in wheat and rye, in excellent order. Mr. Marshall left all furnishings, household goods, and two Stanhope gigs. Additionally, he left three pigs: two sows, and one boar. He also left one dairy cow and a flock of ten chickens. You will also find a small vegetable garden near the kitchen door, planted and ready for harvest. There are fifty acres of forest, and an established orchard next to the barn with apple and pear trees. Mr. Marshall listed everything in the letter I sent you last month. If there are no questions, we shall proceed with signing the papers and transferring the money owed."

In no time, the transaction was completed. Mr. Nelson's clerk witnessed the signing of the contract, and the money was transferred from the buyer to the seller. The Wades now owned what came to be called "The Wade Family Mill."

Sunday morning, Jacob and his family attended All Saints' Episcopal Church. They were welcomed by many of their new farm neighbors and other community members, including their attorney, Henry Nelson, and his wife.

"Good morning, friends," Henry said. "Please let me introduce you to my wife, Carolyn."

"This is my wife, Marie, and my son and his wife, Jacob and Sarah," Christian responded. "And this is my son-in-law, Philip Crane, and my daughter, Margaret. Philip graduated from Winchester College and was the schoolmaster at the Alton Grammar School in England for several years."

"Our schoolmaster, Mr. Schley, passed away last year, and we need someone to take his place," Henry said. "Philip, if you are interested, please stop by my office tomorrow, and I'll arrange for you to meet Mr. Clarke, the president of our town council."

"I would be most interested," Philip replied. "I can meet with Mr. Clarke tomorrow if he is available."

Mr. Nelson ushered the Wades to a pew up front where they could all sit together. Once the service concluded, he introduced the family to other parish members.

"I must introduce you to my good friend and partner, fellow attorney General John Key, his wife Ann, and their young family: Francis Scott, John Alfred, and their daughter, Anne. Their plantation, Terra Rubra, is near here."

"Welcome," General Key said. "We must invite you to our home very soon."

Over the years, the Wades and the Keys became close friends.

The next day, Philip and Christian planned to ride into Frederick Town together. Philip was to meet Mr. Clarke at Mr. Nelson's office while Christian planned to meet with a Mr. Swadener. Alfonso Swadener, along with his wife and son, had arrived from Philadelphia a few days earlier and needed work.

"I will ride with you into town this morning," Christian said. "We are not experienced farmers. I need to hire a man to handle the planting and harvesting of the crops. I am meeting a gentleman and his family at the Evangelical Lutheran Church on Church Street. I heard he previously owned a small farm in his homeland of Bavaria."

Philip made such a good impression with Mr. Clarke that he was immediately hired as Frederick Town's next schoolmaster. Philip planned to rent a small cottage near the school and he and Margaret would move in time for the start of the fall term.

Christian hired Alfonso Swadener as his new farm manager. The two men arranged for Alfonso to move his family into the small cottage next to the mill within the next few days. In addition to providing the cottage rent-free, Christian agreed to pay the Swadener family two dollars a day.

Jacob would teach the Swadener's fourteen-year-old son, Harry, how to work the mill. Alfonso's wife, Marta, would help Marie and Sarah in the kitchen. Marta would also be tasked with cleaning the large millhouse. Alfonso would manage the fall harvest, and once the men processed the grain into flour, Jacob and Alfonso would travel with Mr. Foley, transporting it to Baltimore.

Jacob turned twenty-one two years later, and the family planned a special birthday celebration. Christian knew of the perfect present to gift his only son—he gave him the mill.

"Jacob, your mother and I decided to move into town near Philip and Margaret. I am tired of running the mill and know nothing of farming. You, Alfonso, and Harry are doing a fine job; you don't need me. I acquired a large three-story, redbrick federal-style house at the corner of Second and Market Streets. It is a fine place, built with a hipped roof, dual dormers, and an elliptical fanlight window over the front door. Mr. Nelson will draw up the papers to establish you as the sole owner of the mill."

"Father, you can't leave the mill; it is part of you," Jacob implored. "I don't know if I can run it without you."

"Of course you can. I'll be but three miles down the road," Christian said. "Now, let's celebrate your birthday."

Marta baked Jacob's favorite spice cake and prepared enough food and drink for the dozens of neighbors and friends assembled on the lawn.

Mr. Marshall, the neighbor who sold the Wades their mill, gave Jacob one of the puppies his dam delivered earlier in the summer. Jacob named the male American Foxhound, Lance.

"I want to thank you all for the thoughtful gifts and for coming today," Jacob announced. "This is most definitely my best birthday yet, because in six short months, a wee babe will be joining our family."

As pledged, Christian and Marie moved into town. Marie brought her many cherished books and the precious cupboard her father lovingly crafted for the couple when they married back in Chawton.

Jacob and Sarah welcomed their first child into the family when they celebrated the birth of John Christian on 2 April 1794. An easy delivery for Sarah; she suffered no complications, and they baptized their strong and healthy son at All Saints' Episcopal on 3 May 1794.

Over the years, the mill earned Jacob a sizable profit. The family became respected members of the community. The men participated actively in the church, and Philip became known as an esteemed educator.

When John turned three, Sarah was expecting her second child in late October, after the fall harvest. Sarah began feeling quite fatigued, so it became necessary for Mrs. Swadener to take on more of the responsibility for John's care.

John loved Mrs. Swadener. He followed her everywhere, particularly now, with Sarah resting most of the day.

"Young John," Marta Swadener said. "Come to me so I can wash your face and hands."

John had been playing outside with the dog; both were caked with mud. "Lance and I are making pies."

"*Ihre Mutter* will be furious, *dein Vater* too when he sees his *Hund* covered in mud."

Eight months into Sarah's confinement, Marie arrived to stay until the baby's birth and to help Marta care for young John.

"Oh, Marie," Sarah cried. "I'm so worried for this baby and for my health as well."

"I am here for you, and Marta is an experienced midwife; you will be fine," Marie told her.

Jacob and Sarah welcomed Lydia Marie on 20 September 1797. While John's features were dark like his father's, Lydia's were fair like her mother's. Sarah was constantly worried. A quiet baby, never fussing and rarely crying, Sarah wondered if something might be wrong.

The Christmas season arrived cold and snowy, but the family was excited to celebrate the end of 1799.

On New Year's Eve, Jacob, Sarah, John, and Lydia went into town to celebrate with Christian, Marie, Margaret, and Philip.

Marie mixed cider and brown sugar in a large pan. She then placed cloves, cinnamon sticks, and allspice berries in a piece of cheesecloth, tied it, and added it to the cider and sugar mixture, simmering it for a quarter-hour. The mulled cider was then poured into the wassail bowl, to go "wassailing"—sharing the warm drink with neighbors. In England, they celebrated this tradition on Twelfth Night. But the family quickly found that folks held different traditions in America.

"Here we come a-wassailing among the leaves so green," Jacob, Sarah, Philip, and Margaret sang as they approached each of their neighbors' homes.

It was New Year's Day, 1800, and Marta prepared her pork and sauerkraut dinner with spaetzle dumplings, as the entire family gathered together at the mill. Marta grew cabbage in her large vegetable garden, which Alfonso made into sauerkraut. He shredded the cabbage and packed it with salt into a stone crock to ferment for several weeks. Marta put the sauerkraut into jars and stored the jars in the root cellar.

"It brings good luck to eat this meal on New Year's Day," Marta explained. "I plan to prepare it for many years to come."

"It must bring good luck, as I have wonderful news," Philip announced. "I've been appointed one of the founders of Frederick College, becoming its first professor of English literature."

The family had lived in America for almost a decade. No one believed they could be happier until Sarah once again found herself with child almost six years after Lydia's birth.

On 18 October 1804, the family celebrated the birth of Christina Elizabeth, a plump baby with big blue eyes.

CHRISTINA ELIZABETH WADE
1809 – 1810

"I am five years old today," Christina told her brother. "Grandmother Wade and Aunt Margaret are giving me a party."

"Yes, silly, I know," John said. "That's all I've been hearing for the past week. You better run upstairs and change into the new frock mother sewed, or we'll leave without you."

Christina loved her big brother, even though he teased her incessantly. A happy girl, Christina lived with her parents and siblings in the big millhouse by Carroll Creek.

"Tina, come and get dressed, or you'll be late for your party," Etta called from upstairs.

The Wades had hired Alfonso, Marta, and their son Harry eighteen years earlier. Alfonso worked as their farm manager for sixteen years until his death two years earlier. After Alfonso died, Harry accepted the position as farm manager.

At thirty-two, Harry married a young woman named Etta, who now lived in the small white cottage with him and Marta. Unfortunately, over the years Marta developed severe rheumatism in her knees and hips. Since she couldn't move around as she used to, Etta had taken over Marta's housekeeping duties at the millhouse.

When everyone was ready, John hitched the horses to the coach. At fifteen, John stood tall and handsome. He assisted his father at the mill but mostly enjoyed helping Harry in the fields. Jacob expected his son to read law with Judge Chase after college, but John secretly dreamt of being a farmer. Jacob drove to the front of the house. John helped his mother and two sisters into the coach and climbed onto the seat beside his father.

"Now that the crops are harvested and taken to market in Baltimore, you will no longer be needed at the mill, so you can start back to school next week," Jacob told his son.

"Only one more year studying under Professor Decker. I can't wait to go to college so I can study with Uncle Philip."

Understandably, Lydia was not allowed to attend Schley Grammar School for Boys, so Grandmother Wade tutored her in reading, French, and embroidery three days a week. Christina's grandmother planned to do the same for Christina if the child could ever learn to sit still. Sarah had never attended school. She was therefore thankful Marie offered to teach her daughters the things she couldn't. Sarah wanted both her daughters to become accomplished ladies like their grandmother.

Lydia had turned twelve the previous month. For her birthday, Christian had gifted his granddaughter a small fortepiano. When Lydia met with her grandmother, she also studied music with Mr. Barton—the organist from All Saints' Episcopal Church.

A shy and quiet girl, Lydia preferred to stay indoors with her mother rather than play outside. The opposite of her big sister, Christina was active from the moment she awoke in the morning until she went to bed at night. That day, she could not stop bouncing on the seat beside her mother.

"Christina, please stop, or you'll break the eggs Aunt Margaret asked us to bring."

Christina's grandparents lived in a large house at the corner of Second and Market Streets. When Jacob turned onto Second Street and pulled up in front of the house, they found Christian standing at the corner awaiting their arrival.

"Grandfather!" Christina shouted from the carriage window.

"Happy Birthday, little one," Christian said. "Let's go in and see your grandmother. Aunt Margaret is in the kitchen, and I think your Uncle Philip has a gift for you."

Christian opened the coach and picked up his littlest granddaughter, carrying her into the house.

"Christian, the child can walk," Marie scolded. "Happy birthday, Christina."

"How do you feel today, Lydia?" Philip asked, "How is your cough?"

Lydia had been complaining of a sore throat for several days. She would cough all night until her father gave her a spoonful of whiskey with honey to help her sleep.

"I feel well today," Lydia said. "It is such a warm and sunny autumn day; how could I not?"

Marie always kept games for the children at the bottom of the elm cupboard that held a place of prominence in the large dining room. Lydia and John set up the draughts board on the floor by the fireplace as Christina ran off to find her Aunt Margaret.

"Happy Birthday! Do you want to help me with your birthday cake?" Margaret asked.

"Yes, and here are the eggs you wanted Mama to bring you." Christina answered. "What sort of cake are you baking me?"

"Go into the dining room and ask your grandmother to fetch me two cinnamon sticks, three whole cloves, and the nutmeg from her cupboard," Margaret said. "I am making Marta Swadener's spice cake. You can help me mix the batter."

Margaret mixed a cube of lard with a cut of sugar and added one of the eggs Christina had carefully carried in her basket.

"I have already measured out two tumblers of flour, to which I'll add a pinch of pearlash. Then I'll grind the spices and mix them into the flour along with a handful of the walnuts Uncle Philip chopped for me, a heaping cup of currents and two gills of water, a jigger of molasses, and finally, the sugar and lard mixture. You can mix the batter while I grease the cake hoop. Once you are done, you can play with your sister while I put the cake in the oven and make the brown sugar drizzle."

After dinner, the family gathered in the parlor to present Christina with her birthday gifts.

From her mother and father, she received a dollhouse. Her father made the dollhouse, a replica of their house with a working mill and miniature furniture. He whittled tiny dolls out of wood to look just like her family, including Marta and Alfonso, although he was no longer with them. He even carved a replica of Harry behind a plow and horse. One of the miniature furniture pieces represented a cupboard precisely like the one Grandmother Wade brought from England. Her mother, Sarah, sewed curtains and tiny bedclothes and even wove a small rug.

Aunt Margaret made her a pretty straw bonnet with pink silk ribbons. Margaret worked as a milliner in England and now had her own shop in Frederick Town. Lydia gave her a small rag doll Marta helped her sew, and John made her a wooden box with a maple leaf carved into the lid, where she could keep her hair ribbons.

Philip loved presenting the three Wade children with books on their birthdays. He found a book in a local bookstore that he thought Christina might love. Because it had the longest title Philip had ever seen, he knew it would make Christina laugh. The 1762 publication of *A Little Pretty Pocket-Book, Intended for the Instruction and Amusement of Little Master Tommy, and Pretty Miss Polly with Two Letters from Jack the Giant Killer* came with a little pincushion. On the dedication page, he wrote: *To my niece on her fifth birthday from Uncle Philip, 18 October 1809.*

"Perhaps your sister might read you the book tonight before you go to bed," Philip said. "Once you learn to read it, you can read it to me."

"Before we eat our cake, everyone, please follow me to the Carriage House," Christian said. "It's where we'll find Christina's gift from her grandmother and me."

As they reached the Carriage House and Christian opened the door, Christina immediately saw her gift: a small grey mare about half the size of her father's grey stallion, with a big blue bow around her neck. Christina jumped up and down, pulling her grandfather's arm.

"Can I ride her?" Christina asked. "I love her so much."

"She's five years old," Christian said. "The same age as you."

A sudden lightning bolt lit up the sky, followed by a loud thunderclap.

"Oh, Grandfather!" Christina exclaimed. "I'm going to name her Lightning."

"Everyone, run back to the house before it starts to rain," Jacob said. "It looks like this storm may last a while. We'll need to wait it out before we can start for home."

Once inside, Margaret sliced Christina's birthday cake and served each person a large piece before they all retired to sit by the fireplace and wait out the storm.

Christina sat down to play with her new dollhouse, as Lydia entertained the family by playing the overture from the new opera, *Le caliph de Bagdad,* on her fortepiano. When Lydia reached the more difficult part, her grandmother finished the piece.

Suddenly, there came a loud banging on the front door. Philip opened the door to see Harry Swadener, drenched and breathing hard. They could tell he had ridden his horse fast. There was a look of alarm on his face.

"The mill is on fire!" Harry shouted. "Lightning struck the roof, and the mill is engulfed in flames. I don't think anything, or anyone, can save it."

"My coach is out front," Jacob said. "Philip and John, you and Father can ride with me; we must see what we can save."

When the men reached the mill, it no longer existed in its former form. In the early evening twilight, they could barely make it out.

Still, they could see the interior was completely gutted, the roof had fallen into the basement, the water wheel lay in the river, and the stone walls had started to collapse from the heat. Nothing survived the fire. The sight overwhelmed them.

"Whatever can we do, Father?" John asked. "Can we rebuild?"

"No, John," Jacob said, "I don't think it is possible. It will take more money than we possess to try and rebuild the mill to anything like how it was before the fire."

"We could build a smaller house and just farm the one hundred acres," John suggested.

"We could never make enough to keep our family fed without the mill's income," Jacob replied. "We'll need to think of something else."

"There is nothing we can do tonight," Christian said. "Come back in the morning to see what you can salvage."

At Sunday's church service, the congregation expressed their sorrow over the Wade's misfortune; each offered assistance to help them rebuild.

"If I were a younger man, I'd head west," Henry Nelson said. "Ohio became a state six years ago, and I've heard you can buy land for very little money. I talked to Mr. Marshall's son, Reggie, yesterday. He is interested in buying back the land his father sold you. You should talk to him. I can help you with the transaction if you decide to sell."

"Thank you for your advice," Jacob responded.

After much discussion, the family made the difficult decision to leave Maryland. Jacob sold one hundred acres of farmland back to Reggie Marshall for nearly double the price his father originally paid in 1791. He did not receive as much as he wanted, but he was happy to be one step closer to moving to Ohio.

Because Jacob considered the Swadeners family, he signed over the other one hundred and fifty acres to Harry in a Land Patent.

Jacob published the transaction in the *Frederick-Town Herald*, so the citizens of Frederick Town would know that Harry now owned the land outright.

"I will be leaving next week for Ohio with John and Father," Jacob told his wife. "We want to leave before the weather turns cold. The Foley twins will be coming with us. We'll load one of their Conestoga wagons with the tools necessary to clear the land and build cabins. They own a pair of oxen to drive the wagon whilst Father, John, and I will be traveling by horseback."

"Oh, Jacob," Sarah lamented. "With Lydia so sick, I don't know if I can do it alone."

"You aren't alone; you'll live here in the house with Mother. I'll be back by spring. Lydia should be in good health by then."

Christian, Jacob and John had been gone over a month. Marie worried for the men's safety but hid her fears from the others. Just after they left, Philip and Margaret moved out of their cottage and into the Wade's home.

Christina now slept in her grandmother's bedroom. This particular morning, she leaped from the bed and appeared especially high-spirited.

"Please wake up, Grandmother; it's Saint Nicholas Day."

That morning, the family gathered in the parlor to watch Christina search the stocking she had hung above the fireplace for the hidden orange and chocolate coins. While Lydia, still quite sick, lay on a cot near the fire.

"May I ride Lightning today?" Christina asked her uncle.

"Of course, we'll take her to the park later today. But we must start planning to sell this house and pack for our trip to Ohio. I'll bring the trunks down from the attic after dinner. Maybe you can help gather the things you want to take with us."

"Uncle Philip, I must be able to take my dollhouse father made for my birthday. Will it fit into a trunk?"

"It may not fit into a trunk, but we shall be sure not to forget your dollhouse or your little pony, Lightning. We'll even take Lydia's fortepiano."

Margaret and Marie moved to the kitchen to prepare breakfast while Sarah sat with Lydia in the parlor.

Christmas Day arrived cold and snowy, so Sarah bundled Christina into her heavy coat and hat. The previous night, the family decorated the house with evergreen boughs, and Philip burned the Yule Log.

"Mother must stay behind with Lydia," Sarah said. "Be a good girl for your grandmother at church today."

"When will Lydia get better?" Christina asked her mother. "I wanted her to read to me last night, but she could barely stay awake."

Arriving home from church, the family found a frantic Sarah. "Philip, go for the doctor!" she screamed. "Lydia started coughing up blood, and she is so lethargic; I can't wake her."

When Philip returned to the house with the doctor, Lydia had already passed. The doctor left for the undertaker's office to ask him to prepare a tiny coffin. Although quite shaken, Philip brought Christina to the park with her pony to distract her while the women washed and wrapped Lydia's body in a winding sheet.

"Christina, your sister departed this earth and ascended to heaven this morning," Philip said as he fought back tears. "She became an angel today."

"She won't be going to Ohio with us?" Christina asked. "If she is already in heaven, how can I tell her goodbye?"

"You can always talk to Lydia in your prayers."

On an unusually sunny day in early April 1810, Marie sat in the parlor embroidering a gift for Sarah and Jacob. Using silk floss and chenille on ivory silk ground, she portrayed Lydia as a grieving angel leaning against a willow tree. Marie used watercolors to paint the background, revealing Carroll Creek and the millhouse. Once Marie finished the mourning picture, Philip promised to make a wooden frame.

Sitting with her grandmother and playing with her dollhouse, Christina heard a horse and tiptoed tentatively to peer out the window. Whenever the child heard a horse coming up the street, she thought it might be her father. Some days, she dissolved into tears and needed to be consoled when she saw it was not him; this day turned out differently.

"Grandmother!" Christina shouted. "Father is home!" She immediately ran outside to greet him.

"Father, did you remember John's birthday? Uncle Philip told me Lydia went up to heaven."

Jacob rushed past his youngest daughter, nearly knocking her down.

"Where is Lydia?" Jacob called to his mother.

"She is gone, Jacob," Marie answered. "She passed on Christmas Day."

Jacob collapsed on the settee, buried his head in his hands, and wept.

That evening, as Christina sat on her father's lap, Jacob soberly recounted his trip to Ohio.

"We traveled to Cumberland, where we picked up Braddock Road to Pennsylvania. We were ferried across the Monongahela River at McKee's Port. From there, we rode down to Jefferson, Ohio, and were once again ferried across a river, the Ohio River, this time. We passed through the capital of Ohio at Zanesville and on into the small hamlet of Dayton. It was forty-five days from when we left until we reached Dayton on December 8. Fortunately, we enjoyed mild weather during the trip."

"The ferry must have been quite large to carry the wagon and the oxen," Philip said.

"Yes, large and frightening as the rivers were quite deep and very wide," Jacob said and then continued: "Before traveling to Cincinnati, we stopped at Newcom Tavern in Dayton for supplies. Colonel Newcom was quite the talker and kept us several hours recounting stories about Dayton. He said that Dayton is named after Jonathan Dayton, one of the signers of the Constitution who owns a significant amount of land but doesn't live in the area. He finally gave us directions to Mad River Road, telling us that it was laid out by a man named Daniel Cooper, a surveyor and miller who also laid out the town site of Dayton in 1795 and lives in town. We told Colonel Newcom of our mill fire and asked that someday he introduce us to Mr. Cooper."

It was getting late and Christina had fallen asleep, but Jacob had more to tell. So Sarah put the child to bed, Marie lit a few candles, and Jacob continued.

"Once in Cincinnati, we found the Federal Land Office, where we purchased four connecting square townships, six hundred and forty acres each. I bought one township and Richard and Robert secured one they were allowed to split. Father bought two townships. Father plans to sell Mr. Creager and Mr. Reich one hundred and sixty-acre parcels each. The land is an unspoiled forest with many types of trees. The survey map listed oak, maple, poplar, hickory, walnut, locust, and cedar. We will need to clear the trees before we can start farming. A tributary of the Ohio River runs through the back of our property. The river is named the Little Miami, after the Miami tribe, and is said to have many different fish species."

"Miami tribe?" Marie asked.

"The Miami Indian tribe has moved westward," Jacob replied. "The entire area is called the Miami Valley. The large river that runs through Dayton is named the Great Miami."

"What did you pay per acre?" Philip inquired.

"At auction, we paid two dollars per acre," Jacob said. "They allow you to pay on credit over time, but we paid in cash. Father plans on constructing a church and a school."

"Where exactly is this property located?" Marie asked.

"Here, let me show you on the map." Jacob opened the map and spread it across the dining table. "The property is in southwestern Ohio, north of the Ohio River and east of the Great Miami River, in Greene County."

"Thank you," Marie said. "How are Father and John?"

"They are good and working hard. They stayed back to finish building the two cabins we started before I left to return to Maryland. They should be completed by the time we arrive. Robert Foley stayed with them, and Richard came back with me. Be prepared, Mother, these log cabins will be like no house we have ever owned."

Jacob looked up to see Christina out of bed and sitting on the top step.

"Am I going to Dayton?" Christina asked her father.

"Yes, darling, you will not be left behind on this trip," Jacob said as he held back his tears, realizing Lydia would not be joining them.

Mr. Nelson found a buyer for the house in the city and Margaret closed her millinery shop. Philip tendered his resignation from Frederick College, effective at the end of the term.

Plans were made to meet at the Foley farm on May 15. A few days before, Jacob purchased six draft horses from Jonathan Hager in Elizabethtown and a Conestoga wagon from Henri Reich, which he and Richard Foley would drive. Philip planned to drive the coach with Marie, Margaret, Sarah, and Christina inside. Jacob's horse and Christina's pony were to be tied to the back of the coach.

Along with the Wades were eight members of Henri Reich's family and eight members of the Creager family, all heading to Ohio together. The wagon train would include five Conestoga wagons, three coaches, twelve draft horses, six carriage horses, six oxen, six saddle horses, one pony, and twenty-three travelers. The men unanimously elected Jacob captain of the wagon train. (Years later, folks still called him Captain Wade.)

"Look, Mother," Christina said. "Father's wagon is blue with red wheels, and a star, a bird, and a clover are painted on the back. Isn't it pretty? It's nicer than that old hay wagon we gave Harry."

On the first day, they traveled as far as Boonesborough, Maryland. William Boone allowed the wagons to camp on his farm. The men circled the wagons to keep the horses and oxen from wandering off in the middle of the night. They then pitched several tents before everyone shared in a communal supper.

"Say your prayers, Christina," Sarah said. "And don't forget to say goodnight to your sister, Lydia; she will always be your guardian angel."

"Mr. Boone gave me some apples. He said after I eat the apple, I should save the seeds and plant them when we get to Ohio. That way, we can take a part of Maryland with us. I told him about Lydia; he said we should plant the apple trees in her memory. I miss Lydia so much; I don't understand why she is in heaven. Mother, please don't be sad and cry anymore."

Anyone who looked at Sarah could tell she still grieved the loss of her precious Lydia. She rarely spoke to anyone and appeared frail and small. She reminded Jacob of the terrified sixteen-year-old girl who left Farnham in Surrey nineteen years earlier.

When they arrived in Cumberland, they picked up one more wagon owned by James O'Sullivan. He was traveling to Ohio with his wife Kiera, and their one-year-old son, Jamie.

"Captain Wade?" James O'Sullivan asked. "I heard from old Mr. Creager that you own some land you might sell to me."

"How much can you afford?" Jacob asked. "I can sell it for what we charged Mr. Creager, two dollars and ten cents an acre."

"I can afford forty acres."

"I can sell you a very nice parcel with a creek. It sits right next to where we plan to build the main road," Jacob said. "Let me show you on the map, and if you agree, I can write a transaction contract for you to sign."

Mr. Creager's son, David, volunteered to help Mr. O'Sullivan drive his wagon. Mrs. Creager invited Kiera and her baby to ride in her coach.

"Mother, there is a tiny baby in Mrs. Creager's coach," Christina said. "Come see him; he is so precious. He has bright curly red hair and fat little rosy cheeks. Mrs. Creager asked if I would like to ride with her and her daughter in their coach. Little Jamie is riding in their coach, and Nancy is five years old, just like me. May I?"

Mrs. Creager and her daughter, Nancy, were riding alone in their coach, so Kiera O'Sullivan, little Jamie, and Christina were welcome company.

The coaches could start to feel cramped. And sitting on a horse all day could become quite uncomfortable, so the women and men often walked for short distances. Christina loved holding baby Jamie whenever Kiera felt the need to walk.

"What part of Ireland do you hail from?" Mrs. Creager asked Kiera.

"I am from Killarney in County Kerry. Killarney has mountains and hills as you have here, but I'm not sure I like the wildness of this country. Perhaps I'll become used to it, but it's so different from Killarney. My husband, James, was born in County Kildare, near Dublin."

"When did you come to America?"

"James came over in 1798 when he was nearly sixteen years old. My parents and I arrived six years ago, when I was nineteen. We have been living here in Cumberland with my husband's uncle, George; James is his ward."

"I love your baby," Christina told Kiera. "Someday, I hope to have a baby just like him."

The wagon train headed north. Although it added a few extra miles to the trip, the wagons could not have been able to traverse the hilly terrain of the Appalachian Range. When they reached McKee's Port, the travelers had been on the road for nearly four weeks.

They arranged payment with the ferryman, John McKee, to ferry all the wagons and coaches across the Monongahela River. After making multiple trips across, they found a small clearing to set up camp for the night.

"Where are we?" Christina asked her father.

"Still in Pennsylvania," Jacob said. "But more than halfway home. It should only be another three or four weeks."

Though the men had followed this same route the previous year, this was a much longer journey. They changed two broken wheels while on the road and stayed in Cumberland an extra day to reshoe four horses. It would be almost another week before they would reach the ferry in Jefferson. Then another two hundred miles before they arrived in Dayton.

"Why is it taking so long? I'm so tired of riding in the coach."

"Why don't you ride with Uncle Philip tomorrow?"

So the next day, Christina decided to ride on the coach seat next to her uncle.

"Uncle Philip, my friend Nancy told me bears live in these woods. I'm afraid of bears; some nights, I hear animals howling."

"This is where the animals live," Philip said. "They merely want to warn us to be careful and not to disturb them. If we respect their space, they should not harm us. They are probably more afraid of you than you should be of them. We just need to be vigilant."

"Grandmother Marie has been helping me with my reading and numbers," Christina told him.

"As soon as we reach our new home, we plan to build a school where I will be the schoolmaster," Philip replied.

"I want to go to school just like John," Christina said. "Can Nancy and Jamie go to school with me? When Jamie is older, of course."

"Of course," Philip assured her. "I will teach you the same subjects I teach the boys. You will learn reading, arithmetic, and writing. When you are older, we could even add Ancient History, Latin, French, and perhaps even English literature."

By the time they reached Jefferson, most everyone was exhausted. Arguments broke out amongst some of the Reich men, which forced Jacob to intervene.

"I think we need to stop here for a few days before attempting to ferry across the river," Jacob told the group. "Let's eat our supper, and maybe James O'Sullivan would agree to play his fiddle."

Two days later, after replenishing their supplies and their spirits, the ferryman in Jefferson, Absalom Martin, made expeditious time getting all the wagons across the vast and rain-swollen Ohio River.

"You people are lucky this old river is down some," Mr. Martin said. "Just last week, Colonel Zane had two wagons slip off his ferry into the river over in Wheeling and sink. No one was hurt, but the journeyers lost everything, including their horses. I told old Ebenezer there was too much weight on his ferry, but he never listens to me. Did you know the name Ohio comes from the Iroquois word for *good river*? Well, it wasn't so good that day."

Once they crossed at Jefferson, they picked up Zane's Trace for the seventy miles to Zanesville, the capital of Ohio. The road followed ancient footpaths but was now wide enough for wagons. Unfortunately, the deep ruts and the steep grade made travel difficult. They also needed to be ferried across the Muskingum, Licking, and Scioto Rivers.

Before they reached Zanesville, they celebrated the Fourth of July by dancing and singing while camped near Pleasant Hill. James O'Sullivan played his fiddle, while his wife, Kiera, sang several Irish folk songs. Mrs. Creager brought out her zither and played some melancholy tunes before James and Kiera finished the night's festivities with *Shule Aroon*.

Zanesville appeared to be a booming city with many small shops and businesses. It boasted a sawmill, a blacksmith, and a grain mill.

"Purchase as much grain and food as you can; you won't find many stores when we arrive in Dayton," Jacob warned. "There is an old cabin in Dayton, best known as a crossroads tavern, with limited supplies."

The travelers picked up soap, candles, beans, flour, and other foodstuffs. They bought grain for the livestock. They even repaired the two broken wheels before their final push to Dayton. Now in high spirits, the group realized they only needed to endure one more week's travel before reaching their destination.

They passed through the small town of Franklinton and continued, heading west. They finally reached Dayton on July 14, 1810.

"Captain Wade got us safely to Dayton," David Creager bellowed. "Let us all give three cheers for Captain Wade."

As they entered a small clearing, Christina saw her grandfather and brother waiting for them, standing in the doorway of a house made from logs, the tiniest house Christina had ever seen. Philip helped Christina down from the coach seat, and she ran into the two men's waiting arms.

MARIE ELIZABETH BAILEY WADE
1810 – 1813

"Nobody, who has not been in the interior of a family, can say what the difficulties of any individual of that family may be."

Jane Austen, *Emma*

18 October 1810
Ronald Lewis Bailey
Hawthorne Hall
Chawton, Hampshire
England

My Dearest Brother,

I was pleased and comforted when I received your letter today. It assured me you received mine, in which I informed you that we reached Ohio safely.

I hope this latest letter finds you and Susan well and that my nieces and nephew remain healthy. At the same time as my letter to you, I am writing to our brothers, and I yearn for their prompt reply.

These past twelve months have been extremely taxing, what with the mill fire and Lydia's death. And now, your report of the death of our parents. The news of Mother dying from a fall and then Father in his sleep two days later saddens me deeply. I am comforted only to know they are together. I will always cherish the cupboard Father made for my marriage to Christian. It always brings good memories to mind.

Christina is our shiny little bauble who keeps us smiling and provides much entertainment. Today is her sixth birthday, and we are planning a joyful celebration. We invited the families of those who came with us on the wagon train. Margaret and I will prepare enough supper for all to enjoy. We expect twenty-eight, counting our family. It will be nothing like the Wade's fall harvest fête back in Alton, but festive nonetheless. Jacob and John built a large trestle table with two long benches so that we could hold our celebration outside. There is definitely no room in our small log cabins for any entertaining.

I did not explain in my last letter, so let me tell you about our living arrangements. Before the rest of us arrived, Christian and John erected two small round-log cabins from the abundant oak and poplar trees on our land. They carried mud from the river to fill the gaps between the logs to keep out the cold and wind. Each two-room cabin has one main room with a large fireplace for heating and cooking.

One cabin is for Margaret, Philip, Christian and me. Margaret and Philip have graciously surrendered the small back room to Christian and me as our sleeping area. The other cabin is for Jacob, Sarah, Christina, and John. John sleeps in a loft built over the main room in Jacob's cabin and Christina sleeps with her parents. These humble structures will have to do until we can build a more permanent home. Our two cabins appear nothing like what you enjoy at your fine estate in Chawton or the townhouse in London, but please do not think I am ungrateful or complaining about my current situation.

A creek runs near the house, supplying water for drinking and cooking, which we named Buckeye Creek. Let me explain. We have many horse chestnut trees. The Indians call the nuts from these trees Hetuck, which means "buck eye," because the nuts resemble the eye of a deer. Although inedible, the nuts are said to bring good luck if you carry one in your pocket.

Sometimes, we see an Indian when we shop in Dayton. They come to barter and trade, but most moved farther west into Indiana Territory before we arrived. The Little Miami River runs through the back of our property, but Christian and Jacob have no plans to build a mill.

Ohio is truly a wilderness like none I've ever seen. I feel like I am living in a cabin in New Forest. The men work so hard; I have even seen some women helping to clear the land. Once they felled the hundreds of trees needed to build the cabins, oxen were used to pull the logs to the building site. They used picks and shovels to clear a large portion of the land, preparing it for spring planting. We were able to sow some vegetables this past summer. What with the abundance of rabbits and squirrels we should not starve this winter.

Once the men cleared the land and built the homes, they excavated the land around our property to create travelable roads. It makes it much easier when we must travel to Dayton or Cincinnati for supplies. In the next few years, the men plan to build a church and a school.

Everyone helps the others with the building of the cabins and barns. Just today, they finished James O'Sullivan's cabin. The O'Sullivans are one of the families I mentioned in my last letter who came with us on our trip west. Their cabin is near enough that we see them almost daily. James and his wife, Kiera, have a young son named Jamie, whom Christina adores. They should grow up fast friends.

In addition to Christina and John, Philip is tutoring three young students. They come to our house whenever their parents do not need them for farm chores. David Creager just turned thirteen, his sister Nancy is six, and Peter Reich is eight. Our

John is sixteen but still enjoys studying with Philip when he's not helping his father.

I wrote to Mr. & Mrs. Langley to inform them of their granddaughter Lydia's death before we left Maryland but did not hear back. I am enclosing another letter in hopes you might deliver it. Sarah has no brothers or sisters, so I fear her parents may have passed on. If not, I pray they write to Sarah. Perhaps a letter from her parents might boost her spirits, as Sarah still grieves her daughter's death. Please let me know in your next letter if you find any information regarding Sarah's parents' situation.

I still write in my diary every night, and Philip tells me he also keeps a journal. We both want to document the events, good or bad, so my grandchildren and great-grandchildren learn how we lived and worked.

After conferring with the other families, they agreed to name our settlement Christiansburg. Christian felt extremely humbled. But with him being the largest landowner and the senior member of our small community, it only seemed fitting to be named after my husband.

Until we can establish postal service directly to our community, continue to send your correspondence to: Christian Wade, c/o Colonel George Newcom, Newcom Tavern, Village of Dayton, Ohio, United States of America.

Your loving sister,
Marie

Unlike the mild winter of 1809, 1810 was extremely frigid, with heavy snowfall.

"We are so blessed to have enough firewood, grain for the animals, and food preserved for our needs," Marie said to her husband. "Water is the only commodity in short supply, what with the creek frozen again."

"Philip broke through the creek this morning to bring us fresh drinking water," Christian replied. "Jacob and John left to tend to our livestock, and I'm sure they can easily break the ice on the pond. I'll bundle up and walk to Jacob's cabin to see how Sarah and Christina are faring this morning."

He found Sarah cooking porridge in a kettle over the fire.

"Welcome, Father Wade," Sarah said. "I cooked more than enough if you need sustenance this morning."

"Sarah, it is good to see you looking so well. Marie prepared me a large plate of fried pon haus before I came over," Christian said. "Just like Marta Swadener used to make for us back in Maryland. And how is my little lassie this morning?"

"I'm fine," Christina replied. "I want to go outside and play in the snow, but I have a case of the sniffles, and Mother says I must stay indoors."

"Only a few more weeks, and we can all go outside and play," Christian said. "Hopefully, a good January thaw brings us better weather, as Philip and I plan to travel to Cincinnati for much-needed supplies."

Several settlers traveled with Christian and Philip to Cincinnati that spring and returned with new farm implements and seeds, ready to plant their crops.

The Wades intended to plant corn, whereas the Foleys and the O'Sullivans would plant wheat. Other settlers offered to plant oats, barley, rye, or buckwheat. They all agreed to trade and share their crops.

While in Cincinnati, Philip found several glass windows. Because the glass was cracked (deeming the windows unsuitable for construction projects), he paid practically nothing. Philip used the windows to construct a large cold frame where Marie planted lettuce, leeks, carrots, and beets.

As soon as the ground could be worked and any threat of frost passed, Marie, Margaret, and Sarah worked together to start a large kitchen garden with the vegetable seeds, onion sets, and seed potatoes the men brought back from their trip.

In their freshly tilled garden beside the barn the ladies planted several rows each of onions, pole beans, early peas, turnips, pumpkins, parsnips, potatoes, squash, and cabbage. In a small herb garden they planted chives, marrow, sorrel, tarragon, mint, and sage. The ladies would spend most of the summer and fall preserving their vegetables and herbs in the root cellar Jacob dug into the side of the hill near the house.

On a warm morning in early summer, Sarah, Marie, and Margaret rested on a bench in the garden. They had been pulling weeds for over an hour and needed a short break before continuing.

"I received a long letter from my parents yesterday, and they seem to be doing quite well," Sarah said. "Mother advised me my father is still working the farm, and last spring my cousin and his wife came to live with them. My parents are getting older and could use their help."

"I'm so glad," Marie said. "I hope you continue to correspond with your parents."

Christina was sitting on her grandmother's lap. "Grandmother?" Christina asked. "Where can I plant my apple seeds Mr. Boone gave to me when we stayed at his farm in Maryland?"

"I can give you a small plot here in my vegetable garden. Then, when the young saplings emerge, we will plant the trees behind the barn. Maybe we can plant an entire orchard of apple trees, like my orchard back in England."

"The corn has been cut and shocked and is now ready to be husked," Jacob told his mother one evening in early October. "Let's plan a real fête for Christina's seventh birthday and invite all our neighbors. Just like the festivals we had in England."

A week later, thirty-five people descended onto the Wade's property for a harvest festival and corn husking bee.

"I've brought the corn into the barn and divided it into two piles, Jacob said. "I chose Henri Reick and James O'Sullivan to be the captains, and they, in turn, choose their teams. Let's start the contest to see which team fills their baskets first. The winning team has bragging rights for a whole year. Plus, the man who finds a red ear may kiss the lady they choose."

As the husking began, so did the taunting, shouting, and laughing. Each side tried to outstrip the other until all the corn was finally husked, and Marie rang the supper bell.

Tables laden with venison, stewed squirrel, chicken pie, cornmeal flatbread, jars of wild honey, and stewed pumpkin had been brought into the yard. Margaret made her incredible spice cakes, and Mr. Reich brought several jugs of cider, which were passed around from neighbor to neighbor.

After supper, they removed the tables, lit several fires, and the dancing began. James O'Sullivan played his fiddle, and everyone danced; no one stood still. When they were too tired to dance, some folks sat around the fire and told ghost stories or recited poems. The older ladies and gents went home after supper. But the young people didn't trudge home until daylight. Everyone agreed there should be a harvest festival at the Wade homestead every year on 18 October, Christina's birthday.

"Jacob tells me he and John met a strange mountain man in Dayton yesterday," Marie told Margaret one night while sitting by the fire. "His name is Martin Owen, and he has been trapping furs up north in Michigan Territory. He sold his furs to trading companies near the outpost at Detroit and bragged about how much money he'd earned. Now, John wants to go back with him. Sarah is beside herself with fear and anxiety over his possibly being hurt."

"What does Jacob know about this man?" Margaret asked.

"He fought with Colonel Newcom during General Anthony Wayne's campaign against the Indians. From what Colonel Newcom said, he is a good man. I know it must be hard for Sarah, but she may need to learn to let go, or John could come to resent her. John will be eighteen by next spring, and there's not much Sarah or Jacob can do then."

John and Martin Owen left in late October, promising to return for spring planting season. Mr. Owen had all the needed equipment, including a horse and two pack mules. Jacob allowed John to take one of the saddle horses and Jacob's old flintlock rifle.

"Mother, please don't worry," John implored. "We plan to take plenty of food, and Mr. Owen knows how to make shelter. I want to learn how to trap, and I'll be back early next year."

"I promise I'll keep him safe," Mr. Owen said. "We'll be living and working out of Fort Detroit. I retain a good relationship with the British and the fur trading companies, and the Indians always leave us alone to trap all we can. Your boy should come home a rich man."

The winter of 1811 began relatively mild. The men caught up on the repairs of their outbuildings and fences. The good weather was a welcome change from the previous year.

Soon after they arrived in Ohio, Christian secured two cows for milk and two dozen chickens for their eggs and meat. This particular morning, Margaret milked the cows as Marie collected the eggs.

"Do you remember how Sadie collected eggs for us every morning?" Marie asked Margaret. "I never thought I would be collecting eggs, milking cows, or churning butter someday. How our lives have changed."

Marie used her apron to wipe a smudge from Margaret's face. As she did, the two women laughed until they cried.

One day in early February, Jacob entered his mother's cabin with news to share.

"I met a man who agreed to come out next week and help me tap our sugar and black maple trees to make sugar syrup," Jacob said. "He teaches me, and we agreed to split anything we make."

They tapped the trees the next week, and Jacob built a sugarhouse for boiling and evaporating the sap.

It was mid-March, and as Jacob was working on his second batch of syrup, John came riding up to the house.

"What's that amazing smell?" John asked.

"Son, you are truly a sight for sore eyes. Your mother pined for you the entire time you were gone. Come in and tell us all about your trip. Everyone is in your grandmother's cabin; wait until you taste this syrup on your porridge."

Marie fixed a hearty breakfast, and John tasted maple syrup for the first time.

"Grandmother, this is the best thing I've tasted since my last big slice of Aunt Margaret's spice cake with brown sugar drizzle that she made for Christina's birthday last year."

"Well, go on, son, tell us about your trip," Jacob implored.

"Mr. Owen and I trapped over two hundred beaver pelts. They sold for six dollars a pound and he paid me five hundred dollars! We plan to return next year, and he said I could keep half of the furs we trap. Martin doesn't work for one of the big fur trading companies. He's an independent trapper who can keep all the money he earns. Tensions are increasing between the folks living up in Michigan Territory and the British, so we may need to try a different territory, maybe farther west. Mr. Owen thinks the British might incite the Indians to take up arms against us. He reckons there may be another war with England."

The next morning, as Marie stepped outside to collect eggs and feed the chickens, she saw that several inches of snow had fallen overnight. It was one of those heavy, wet spring snows that cling to the tree branches, making it look and feel like something out of a fairytale.

After breakfast, John retrieved the sleds from the barn he and Jacob had made the year before, and the family headed out. Everyone got a turn sledding down the big hill, which sloped to the river. Even Marie and Christian took a go. Now that John had returned home, Sarah seemed healthier and happier.

"I have an idea," Marie said. "John, go into the house, bring out all our tin bowls and some spoons, and fill each bowl with snow. Then, I'll pour some of Jacob's fine maple syrup over it. Margaret, I wonder if we could make maple candy? Jacob, you should take some of your jars of syrup into Dayton to see if Colonel Newcom might buy them."

Jacob and John agreed. Later that afternoon, they chose one hundred jars of maple syrup to sell at Newcom Tavern. George Newcom gave Jacob twenty dollars for the lot. With the money, Jacob found a bolt of gingham fabric and some ribbon for Sarah to make her and

Christina new dresses. He bought Margaret yarn for knitting socks and mittens for next winter, Philip a new journal, his mother a tin of fine English tea, and for his father a new belt knife with leather sheath.

"What would you like for your birthday, John?" Jacob asked. "How about a new flintlock rifle? Let's head down to Mr. Ludlow's gun shop and see what he has in stock."

Before they left Newcom Tavern, John noticed a young girl with her father and mother. She couldn't have been more than sixteen, with lovely blond curls and blue eyes. John seemed smitten. He overheard her mother call her Cynthia, and he knew he must meet her.

"Colonel Newcom?" John asked. "Do you know the family who just left?"

"Might you be referring to Brother Daniel? He is a Jesuit missionary from Cincinnati. He's looking for a plot where he might establish a Catholic church here in Dayton."

A few weeks later, Brother Daniel and his family stopped at the Wade's homestead to speak to Christian.

"Colonel Newcom told me that you plan to establish an Episcopal Church," Brother Daniel said. "If you need a minister, I know a man in Cincinnati, The Reverend David Thomas, who moved there from Philadelphia last year. I shall give him your information, and he can send you a letter of introduction."

"We plan on building our church this spring," Christian said. "I'll be anxious to hear from Reverend Thomas."

"Please stay for supper," Marie said. "I made a large pot of stewed rabbit."

John couldn't believe his eyes when he saw who had come to visit his grandfather. He immediately invited himself to dinner.

John, Jacob, Christian, and Philip made quick work of two log buildings before the arrival of Reverend Thomas and before planting season started.

They completed the church, along with several benches, and even built a fine pulpit. Next, they constructed a one-room cabin for the Reverend's home. As a tithe, Christian agreed to pay him three dollars a month, some of the money coming from the lumber Christian sold.

Once the church and cabin were completed, the men crafted a kitchen table with a bench, a bedstead, and a small side table.

The ladies sewed a mattress and pillow from ticking, stuffed each with duck down, contributed cooking utensils from their kitchen cupboards, and planted a small vegetable patch.

"I want to donate Lydia's fortepiano to the church," Marie told Christian.

"That is a fine gesture," Christian replied.

Although the O'Sullivans were Catholics, and the Reichs and Creagers were Lutheran, out of respect for the Wades and all they had done for their small settlement, they all attended the first service at the new Christ Episcopal Church of Christiansburg.

And so, on Marie's sixty-third birthday, 14 June 1812, twenty-seven worshippers joined the dedication service of the new church. Much to John's delight, Bother Daniel brought his family and stayed for the supper Marie prepared. John made certain that he sat next to Cynthia Daniel.

Four days later, the announcement came that President James Madison had signed a declaration of war against Great Britain, marking the beginning of the Second War of Independence.

After the announcement, Governor Meigs appointed Dayton as the assembly point for Ohio troops. Before long, 15,000 men assembled. Three regiments encamped nearby, one just two miles from the Wade homestead.

By August, they received word that 2,500 men stationed at Fort Detroit surrendered to the British, including the 1,600 men who traveled north from Dayton in May. John had watched them go. He longed to accompany them. The men, dressed in homespun and carrying crude guns, appeared to John to possess stout hearts. They marched out of Dayton, singing. John could faintly make out the lines from the song "In freedom, we're born, and in freedom, we'll live."

"General Hull should be court-martialed," John told his grand-mother as they sat down to breakfast. "I have half a mind to join. I want to fight for my country."

"John, don't be hasty. Besides, I don't think your mother could take you leaving; she has begun to look very fragile lately. Plus, your father needs you here for harvest."

Fall came, and John realized Mr. Owen had taken off to trap without him. Disappointed, John threw himself into the harvest, even helping the Foley brothers harvest their tobacco. It was backbreaking work cutting the tobacco by hand and then hanging it in the barn to dry. But it kept his mind off the war, the money he could have earned fur trapping, and Cynthia Daniel.

"John, you must be working too hard," Marie told her grandson at breakfast. "You look to be all skin and bones."

"I'm so darn mad at that old codger for going off and leaving me behind," John said. "Can you believe he went out west to trap along the Oregon River? He told me British and French-Canadian fur traders occupy it, and it is almost as many miles away from Ohio as we live from England. It would have been grand to go out West. I doubt he will be back."

"Well, I can't say I'm disappointed you are staying here; we would miss you more than you know. I love you, boy, and I hope you never leave the homestead here in Ohio."

"Awe, Grandmother, I love you too."

Another year was coming to an end as the Christmas season arrived. The family walked to church Christmas morning, joined by the O'Sullivan family. Marie invited them to Christmas dinner, and they graciously accepted.

"I can't believe how much our children have grown," Marie told Kiera. "Our little Christina turned eight in October, and your little Jamie turns four next May. It seems like barely yesterday when we traveled here from Maryland."

"I am bursting to tell someone," Kiera said. "I'm going to have a baby in the spring, probably in late June."

"Oh, Kiera that is magnificent news! Shall we announce it to the rest of the group?"

"Yes, of course."

"Everyone," Marie announced. "Mrs. O'Sullivan is with child; let's raise our glasses high and give her a salute."

"I'll make more eggnog," Margaret said. "This is a celebration!"

Spring arrived early in 1813, and the men started planting a new year of crops. The Wade men worked all winter to clear twenty-five more acres and planned to rotate their crops, planting corn on the new field and spring rye in the old field.

Kiera named her baby June for the month in which she was born. They gave the child the middle name Brigid, after the Irish saint, Saint Brigid of Kildare.

"John, may I ask you to go into Dayton and purchase a pound of flour?" Marie called from her doorway. "I want to make a cake for our Fourth of July celebration."

As Marie awaited John's return, she searched her large cupboard for the cookbook her mother had gifted her on her wedding day: *The Art of Cookery Made Plain and Easy*. In it, she found the recipe for pound cake.

To make a Pound Cake

T A K E a Pound of Butter, beat it in an earthen Pan, with your Hand one Way, till it is like a fine thick Cream; then have ready twelve Eggs, but half the Whites, beat them well, and beat them up with the Butter, a Pound of Flour beat in it, and a Pound of Sugar, and a few Carraways; beat it all well together for an Hour with your Hand, or a great wooden Spoon. Butter a Pan, and put it in and bake it an Hour in a quick Oven.

For Change, you may put in a Pound of Currants clean wafh'd and pick'd.

Upon John's return, he exploded through his cabin door, his face flushed red. He was angry as he yelled at his parents. "Richard Foley said he heard the British burned Georgetown in Kent County and Frederick Town!" John shouted. "I am meant to go back and fight for my home."

"Hold on, John," Jacob said. "Ohio is your home now."

"Richard Foley and I leave tonight, and you can't stop me."

"No, John," Sarah said. "I won't let you go gallivanting all over the country on such a foolish expedition."

"It's not foolish, Mother."

"Take your grandmother's provisions to her, and when you come back, we can discuss it," Jacob said.

Unfortunately, John could not be talked out of going.

"Sarah," Jacob said, "if John has decided to go, there is nothing we can say or do to stop him. But I cannot let him go alone; I must go too."

To properly prepare for the trip back to Maryland, Jacob talked John and Richard into waiting to leave until the end of the week.

"Robert Foley and James O'Sullivan agreed to help you and Philip with the harvest," Jacob told his father. "We should be home before Christmas."

It had been almost three months since the men left Ohio to fight the British. Inconsolable, Sarah would not eat and cried almost daily. Marie moved into the cabin with her and Christina, primarily for Christina's health and safety.

"Sarah just rocks in her old rocker day and night," Marie told her husband. "I can't convince her to eat or sleep; she does not even talk to me, just stares at nothing. It's unhealthy for Christina, and I'm at a loss as to how to help Sarah. I'm going for Reverend Thomas to see if he might offer her some guidance on how to cope with her grief."

Reverend Thomas came and prayed with Sarah, but nothing helped, and Sarah continued to do poorly.

"It is less than a month before your ninth birthday," Marie told Christina that morning at breakfast. "With your father and brother away, we won't be hosting a harvest festival this year. But do not worry, the family will still celebrate your birthday. Let's you, me, and Aunt Margaret take

Grandfather and Uncle Philip a cool drink. They've been working in the field all morning and should be thirsty by now. Since your mother is feeling unwell today, we might prepare some warm bone broth when we return. It should make her feel much better."

Marie, Margaret, and Christina walked out into the field to find the two men. When they returned to the cabin, they found Sarah unconscious on the floor.

25 September 1813

Mr. & Mrs. John Langley
Guildford Road
Farnham, Surrey
England

Dear John & Martha,

It is with deep regret that I must inform you of your daughter Sarah's death. She died yesterday at her home in Christiansburg.

Sarah never stopped grieving after her own daughter's death. We all believe she died of a most severe case of melancholy. Margaret and I found her fainted and carried her to her bed, where she died soon after. We, along with her young daughter Christina, were with her at her time of passing.

Unfortunately, Jacob and John are away fighting the British in Maryland and are unaware of Sarah's death. We expect the men home within the next few months. It may be difficult to explain why their beloved wife and mother is no longer with us.

Sarah was buried today in the graveyard of Christ Episcopal. She is the very first to be buried next to our new church. We dressed her in the dress she was married in, her favorite yellow frock, which she had kept all these years. We obtained a second cutting of our beautiful lavender and laid a bouquet in her arms. I've enclosed in this letter a sprig of lavender from Sarah's funeral bouquet.

The Reverend David Thomas officiated the funeral and graveside service. He read from The Book of Common Prayer and gave a joyful sermon based on the hope of resurrection. We sang hymns, and Christian gave a heartfelt eulogy. After the service, we held a supper at our cabin for Sarah's many neighbors and friends.

Christina is living with us until her father returns. She sends her love and even drew you a picture of herself, which I enclose. Christina is like a breath of fresh air. She will be nine years old next month and is a sweet, loving girl who looks very much like her mother.

Very sincerely and with my deepest sympathy,
Marie Wade

JOHN CHRISTIAN WADE
1813 – 1815

"Where the mind is perhaps rather unwilling to be convinced, it will always find something to support its doubts."

Jane Austen, *Sense and Sensibility*

Sunday, 4 July 1813

Dearest Cynthia,

If I see you now, I might decide to stay. So I asked my grandfather to deliver this letter since I will be gone when you receive it. My father and I and Richard Foley plan to leave today for Maryland to fight the British. We are joining the 16th Regiment of the Maryland Militia.

As you know, our troops captured and burned the city of York in April. Then, in May, our Ohio soldiers at Fort Meigs held off two assaults, the first by the British and the second by the Shawnee leader, Chief Tecumseh. Though I currently live in Ohio, in my heart, I am still a Marylander. Right now, Maryland is being burned and looted, so I must go.

The enclosed lace handkerchief is the birthday gift I had planned to present to you next week. I hope you think of me and carry it whilst I'm gone. I promise you that I shall return, and when I do, I hope you agree to be my wife. We both know your father disapproves of our relationship because we are so young. It does not help me being Episcopalian and you Catholic. I feel confident we can change his mind. So, I leave my proposal of marriage entirely in your hands.

Dayton is having its Independence Day celebration tonight, with cannon firings, toasts, music, and dancing. I had hoped to celebrate with you, but we must make haste in our expedition to help save Maryland and America. I remain faithful to only you and will abide by whatever your decision may be.

I will always be forever your ardent admirer,
John Wade

It was four weeks before the three men reached Frederick Town. Although it had been nearly three years since they left to settle in Ohio, they found the town surprisingly unchanged.

"There doesn't appear to be any damage here," John said. "We should stop at Mr. Nelson's office; perhaps he can enlighten us about what may be happening here."

"After talking to Mr. Nelson, John and I intend to go to Mount Olivet Cemetery to visit Lydia's grave," Jacob told Richard Foley. "We also want to stop at the site of our old mill to see the Swadeners."

"I'm going to ride on to my brother's farm to see what he knows," Richard told the pair.

"We'll met you at Will's sometime after sundown," John said.

Richard rode off while John and Jacob turned onto Court Street, stopping in front of Mr. Nelson's law office. Though young Mr. Francis Key had moved his family and settled in Georgetown years before, the shingle over the door still read *Law Office of Nelson and Key.*

"Jacob and John Wade, as I live and breathe," Mr. Nelson cried. "Come in, come in. General Key is here today; he shall be most pleased to see his old friends."

"General Key," Jacob said. "It is so good to see you. How, may I ask, is your family?"

"You missed Francis," General Key said. "He came down last week to Terra Rubra for his thirty-fourth birthday celebration. His wife, Mary, stayed in Georgetown as they are joyfully expecting their sixth child next month. How are your parents, Jacob, and your wife, Sarah? I trust they are doing well and remain happy in Ohio."

"Yes, the family is doing very well, thank you."

"So, what brings you and young John to Frederick?" Henry Nelson asked.

"We heard the British raided Frederick Town, and we came to join the fight against the bloody bastards," John announced.

"My heavens!" Henry exclaimed. "Fortunately, you've been given some false information. The British have been terrorizing towns all along the Chesapeake Bay. However, the raid you speak of happened in May on two villages along the Sassafras River—Georgetown, and Fredericktown—not here. A landing party from the HMS *Mohawk* marched into those two settlements. It destroyed thirteen dwellings, four schooners, a cobbler's shop, a tavern, a granary, and storehouses of sugar, lumber, and leather. The nearly four hundred men of the Kent County militia were forced to retreat and the townspeople to flee. Some of the residents of those towns came to Frederick. I don't believe those two villages will ever recover."

"We still plan on joining the militia here in Frederick," John said. "We came to fight wherever, and for however long you need us."

"Then you need to talk to Reverend Slater," Henry advised. "He is calling for volunteers. We need men the most along the Maryland border and the ports up and down the coast. He most likely will send you to Camp Hampstead in Baltimore."

John and Jacob left their horses tied in front of Mr. Nelson's office and set off on foot to Mount Olivet Cemetery. They passed the Wades' former house on Second Street, Margaret's old hat shop on Market, and the park on Hill Street where Christina often rode her pony, Lightning. Once they entered the cemetery, Jacob guided John to Lydia's gravesite.

"I remained in Ohio, not knowing Lydia died," John lamented. "My tender and precious sister gone so young. Let me read aloud the epitaph engraved on her gravestone: *Lydia Marie Wade, born 20 September 1797, died 25 December 1809, 12 years, three months, and five days. Step softly; one of God's angels lies buried here.*"

"I'm so pleased with the marble angel Father commissioned from Italy," Jacob said. "It reminds me of Lydia, graceful and delicate, with its outstretched wings, standing watch as Lydia rests, transporting her soul and giving hope for eternity. I was also in Ohio when she died; the guilt is with me daily. I hope never again to be away when someone I love needs me."

"If you are worried about grandfather and grandmother, they are strong and healthy," John told his father. "And Lydia wouldn't want you to feel guilty. She never complained. Even the doctor did not know she suffered from consumption. Besides, she seemed excited about going to Ohio; she told me so the night before we left, and that is how I plan to remember her."

"You are undoubtedly right, Son."

"Father?" John asked. "Who do you presume left the flowers on Lydia's gravestone?"

"It must be Marta Swadener," Jacob supposed. "She said she loved Lydia as if she were her own daughter. Let's visit Marta, Harry, and Etta; they should raise our spirits, especially if they share some of that fine ale Harry brews."

Marta stood at the kitchen window of their new house preparing a chicken with dumpling stew when she saw two men riding up the path.

"Etta, come quickly!" Marta exclaimed. "I believe, even with my dim sight, I see Jacob Wade and his young son, John, riding toward the house."

"Yes, Mother Swadener," Etta said. "Your old eyes do not deceive you today. I also see Harry walking with them. He must have met the pair while coming home from the back meadow."

Before Jacob and John reached the house and could dismount, they spotted Marta opening the gate, ready to embrace the two men with a warm, motherly hug.

"What is this you wear?" Marta asked. "You look as if you plan to hunt bears."

"We plan to hunt Redcoats," John announced. "These buckskins become necessary if you do not wish to end up with saddle sores in delicate places."

"You must be hot, tired, and hungry," Harry said. "Come inside where it is nice and cool."

After the mill burned down, Harry salvaged the stones to construct a fine two-story home near the site of the old cottage.

"You have accomplished so much in the three short years since we left," Jacob said. "The fields look ready to harvest. And who is this fine young man clutching to this mother's leg?"

"This is our son, Alfonso," Etta replied.

After supper and several pints of Harry's home-brewed ale, John realized his father appeared in no shape to ride to Will Foley's farm. So John said his goodbyes to the Swadeners, promising to come by the next morning, Sunday. They wanted to talk to Reverend Slater before he started his early morning service.

When John reached Will's farm, the clock on the mantel in the Foley's kitchen chimed nine. Before bed, he asked for a candle, paper, a quill, and ink. He sat at the table and wrote a letter to his grandfather.

7 August 1813

Mr. Christian Wade
The Wade Homestead
Christiansburg Highway
Christiansburg, Ohio

Dear Grandfather,

We arrived in Frederick Town at noon today. We stopped first at the law office of Henry Nelson. Henry informed us the British did not raid our Frederick, but Fredericktown in Cecil County, as well as Georgetown in Kent County. Grandfather, in those two towns the British burned dozens of houses and businesses. The townspeople fled, along with the Kent Militia. In April, the British went up the Rappahannock River and captured or destroyed fourteen American ships.

A British officer named George Cockburn is responsible for much of the looting and burning of the private property of civilians in the villages and towns who oppose him landing his ships and barges. They are interrupting commercial traffic and capturing American vessels and supplies. You surely already heard that the British were even taking sailors off American merchant vessels and impressing them into service with the Royal Navy; these sailors became nothing more than prisoners. The British are causing destruction all up and down the coast, and Father and I plan to assist by offering protection to the many ports within the Chesapeake Bay area.

We plan to meet with Reverend Slater before the early service tomorrow morning at St. John the Evangelist. He is instrumental in recruiting volunteers for the militia. Mr. Nelson surmised we would be sent to Camp Hampstead in Baltimore.

Father and I stopped at Mount Olivet Cemetery after we met with Mr. Nelson. Lydia's monument is breathtaking, and we were moved by the epitaph engraved on her gravestone.

We shared supper with the Swadeners this evening. Harry and his wife, Etta, have a two-year-old son they named Alfonso, after his grandfather. They are all well, except for Marta, who is nearly blind. I left Father there for the night as he drank more than his share of Harry's ale.

I hope all is well at home. Give our love to everyone.

Respectfully, your Grandson,
John

When they reached St. John the following morning, several other men were waiting to speak with Reverend Slater.

"Jacob and John Wade," Reverend Slater called. "Mr. Nelson advised me you have traveled here from Ohio to volunteer. It pleases me to see you brought your muskets and horses. I can provide you with a coat, vest, and two pairs of cotton pantaloons. We can also provide you with two pairs of shoes, two shirts, one stock tie, and one cap."

"If you don't mind, sir, I prefer to wear my shirt and britches," John said. "My boots serve me well, as does my buckskin jacket. I also like my wide-brimmed beaver hat; it works fine to keep my eyes shaded from this bright Maryland sunshine."

"That is perfectly fine with me, John," Reverend Slater replied. "However, Jacob, I want to appoint you captain of this company of eighty volunteers from Frederick, and so I need to ask you to wear the blue jacket and white pantaloons, as well as the cap recognizing the 16th."

"I am honored, Reverend Slater. I shall proudly wear the color and insignias of the 16th Regiment of the Maryland Militia."

"Richard Foley, I appoint you lieutenant under Mr. Wade. You too must wear the militia's uniform. You both need to visit Mrs. Wren's shop on Market Street; she can issue you everything you need. It would be best to leave for Camp Hampstead in the morning. However, I have one last thing to say before you go. You men shall be instrumental in protecting Maryland's borders, Baltimore, and our nation's capital. It is a monumental task, but whether a farmer or a fisherman, we Marylanders will always fight for the good of this great nation. Thank you, men, and may God bless you."

The first night, the company of eighty men camped on the outskirts of New Market at the farm of William Plummer. Mr. Plummer called a meeting of several local men, and Jacob enlisted thirty more volunteers.

From New Market, they made their way to New Lisbon and then Ellicott City. At each stop they recruited more volunteers. Each brought a musket, and every man wore their everyday farming clothes. By the time they reached Camp Hampstead, the 16th Regiment had swelled to nearly two hundred men, mostly farmers.

Upon their arrival at Camp Hampstead, a young soldier ushered Jacob to the tent of Major General Samuel Smith, commander of Baltimore's militia.

"Captain Jacob Wade reporting, Sir. I've brought one hundred ninety-five men from the 16th Regiment of the Maryland Militia. This is Lieutenant Richard Foley, who will assist me in training our men and aiding with our regiment's everyday duties."

The major general stated, "General Key sent me a dispatch, telling me you are originally from the area. He said you are familiar with organizing personnel, what with your experience captaining a wagon train from Maryland to Ohio. Therefore, I'm also putting you in charge of training the new men in the Baltimore militia. You will report directly to me. My aide can direct you to an area where your men may set up their tents. It may only be temporary, as most will be heading into battle."

"I stand ready to fulfill my duties to the highest level and will begin training the troops immediately."

"One other important request," Major General Smith announced. "Is there a man in your company who could act as a scout, a young man who is strong and willing to take on such a dangerous task?"

"My son, John, who was born in Frederick, knows this area well. He spent several months trapping furs near Fort Detroit a few years back. He is a strong young man and a perfect candidate. I'll bring him by your tent tomorrow."

"Be here at noon."

After his meeting, Jacob spent the rest of the day organizing his troops, setting up camp, and assigning duties. He discussed with John what was expected of him as a scout. He then suggested that each man find paper to write a letter home.

13 August 1813

Mr. Christian Wade
The Wade Homestead
Christiansburg Highway
Christiansburg, Ohio

Dear Grandfather,

Father and I arrived in Baltimore early this morning, ready to protect Baltimore and Washington if the British attack. Major General Samuel Smith placed Father in charge of training the new volunteers for the Baltimore Militia and our 16th Regiment. We have cooks, tailors, cobblers, and gunsmiths. They keep us fed and the uniforms and guns in top condition. Some men were assigned tasks based on their previous occupations.

Tomorrow morning, we will be awakened at five by a long drum roll outside our tents. Once up, we must straighten our bunk, wash, and shave. Some men have the task of emptying the toilet bucket while others fetch fresh water. There is no time for a smoke, so men plan to chew their tobacco. Parade and inspection start at six. Father will begin training the fighting troops while the other men complete their assigned duties. We won't have breakfast until well after nine.

Father is taking me tomorrow to meet Major General Smith, as he recommended me as the major general's scout. I shall be exploring all up and down the Chesapeake Bay area, so it will be impossible to receive any mail. Father advised that none of us would be able to receive correspondence even while here in camp. Therefore, it would be futile for you to try to send us any letters at this time. I will attempt to write as often as they allow ink and paper.

Father feels certain we are capable of defeating the British by Christmas. Look for us coming home sometime early next year. Please wish Aunt Margaret a very happy birthday from Father and me. I suspect Mother found enough fresh spices hidden in Grandmother's old cupboard to make Aunt Margaret a fine spice cake covered with Father's thick maple syrup. My mouth is watering, merely thinking about it.

Your faithful Grandson,
John

For six months, John scouted up and down the coast of Maryland, returning to Baltimore after each expedition to report to Major General Smith. He counted British troops and verified their location. Because he wasn't allowed to engage with the enemy, he was forced to watch in horror from a distance as they looted and burned towns and villages. Christmas came and went, with no end to this new war with Britain.

John found the time to write to his family, unaware that his mother had passed away over four months before.

4 February 1814

Mr. Christian Wade
The Wade Homestead
Christiansburg Highway
Christiansburg, Ohio

Dear Grandfather,

I have not seen Father in months. Soon after my second scouting mission, the army transferred him and Richard Foley to Fort McHenry. I pray he wrote to you and my mother and all is well at home.

Well, Grandfather, our plan to come home after Christmas has been delayed. Our work is vital for the safety of our citizens. I am hopeful that you and the rest of the family understand its importance. I've been on dozens of scouting missions and will likely be sent out again soon. But for now, Major General Smith gave me some time off to rest before my next assignment. He is allowing me to visit Father at Fort McHenry.

Please give everyone my best and a happy early birthday to you. Please tell Mother how much I hated not being with her on her birthday. How many birthdays have I missed, and how many slices of cake? I do hope you continued with the harvest festival on Christina's birthday.

I spent Christmas in a tavern outside of Havre de Grace. You may remember it as one of the villages the ruffian Cockburn plundered last May when they burned nearly forty of its sixty houses. They even looted the Episcopal Church, although it still stands. Pray for Father and me at next Sunday's service at our charming little church, Christ Episcopal. I shall write to you again as soon as I am able.

Love to you, Grandmother, Uncle Philip, Aunt Margaret, Mother, and little Christina.

John

Before heading down the Patapsco River to Fort McHenry to visit his father, John wrote a letter to his sweetheart.

4 February 1814

Miss Cynthia Daniel
c/o Brother Ebenezer Daniel
100 Water Street
Dayton, Ohio

My Dearest Cynthia,

I spoke in my last letter that father and I planned to be home by Christmas, but as you can see, those plans have changed. I selfishly asked you to wait for me. I truly understand if you feel at all unable or unwilling. My mission here is to "boot" the British back to England, and I hope you agree with what I believe is a noble cause.

As I scout up and down the coast of Maryland, I have seen, first-hand, many atrocities committed by the British on our charming waterfront villages and many flourishing plantations, now burned and lying in ruins.

My beloved, I miss you more than you will ever know. Pray this war ends soon, and once my father and I come home, you and I shall celebrate our love with the most splendid wedding.

All my devotion,
John

By summer, John saw more and more activity along the Anacostia River. On a hot and humid day in August, he encountered a regiment of about fifteen hundred British troops near Bladensburg, some eight miles from Washington.

As he entered Bladensburg, he came across many of the men from the 16th Regiment. Among them was their family friend, Francis Key, who was serving as a lieutenant and quartermaster in the Georgetown Artillery.

"Lieutenant Key," John called. "It appears you hold the advantage of the high ground, defending the bridge the British would need to cross."

"John Wade," Francis Key replied. "I heard that you and your father traveled here to assist us fellow Marylanders once again defeat the British."

"As Major General Smith's scout, I am headed back to Baltimore," John explained. "I shall report that all is well here."

As John rode off, he chose to stay and watch the battle from a safe distance. Sitting on a hill among a line of beech trees, he observed the British bypassing the bridge and fording the river. Unfortunately, it was too late to alert Francis.

After nearly three hours under a barrage of British rockets, the American line crumbled, and the men fled. John couldn't believe he had witnessed such a devastating defeat. Stunned, John knew he needed to buck up. He had a duty to return to Baltimore and warn Major General Smith. He rode as fast as he could, but he didn't reach Baltimore until the following day.

Arriving in Baltimore, John found they had already received word that the British had captured and were burning Washington.

"John," Major General Smith said, "I'll need your assistance in getting the word out to the people of Baltimore to bring all the pickaxes, spades, wheelbarrows, and shovels they can procure to begin digging entrenchments along Hampstead Hill. The British will be coming up Philadelphia Road, and we must be ready. As a veteran of the Revolution and a Marylander, I tell you the British will not capture Baltimore on my watch."

In addition to the residents of Baltimore, thousands of men from the militias of Delaware, Pennsylvania, Virginia, and, of course, Maryland, helped build a mile of earthen fortifications from the waterfront northward. John felt relatively sure Baltimore was now safe, but he worried about his father stationed at Fort McHenry.

Several days later, John learned that President Madison had fled to Brookeville after the defeat at Bladensburg, and most of the citizens of Washington had also run away. Georgetown and Alexandria surrendered to Cockburn in exchange for their cities being spared.

"It was so hot, and the heat only exacerbated the fires," Caleb, a man John knew from Frederick, said. "They burned the Presidential Mansion and the Capitol Building in revenge for us burning the town of York. Then, just as we moved for a counterattack the following day, the skies darkened, and it began to rain. Next, a thunderstorm formed like no other I'd ever seen. It looked like night had come in the middle of the day, and the winds caused as much damage as the fires. By nightfall, rain extinguished most of the fires. We soon found the British had taken this opportunity to leave their campfires burning and sneak away."

"I saw a tornado pass directly through the city!" another man exclaimed.

Major General Smith sent John out to scout along the Patapsco River. John reported back that dozens of British vessels were headed toward Baltimore to unload several thousand troops.

"For now, we can stall a land attack on Baltimore. However, it appears that the British Navy is planning a bombardment of Fort McHenry. If successful, it could allow the ground soldiers another attempt to take Baltimore," said the major general. "Thank you for this valuable information, but I need you for an even more important mission. President Madison enlisted the help of Francis Scott Key to assist in procuring the release of an elderly civilian physician, Dr. Beanes, taken prisoner by the British as they left Washington. Attorney Key asked that you accompany him and the U.S. Agent for Prisoners of War, Attorney John Skinner, as their protection officer on this mercy mission. Plan to leave early tomorrow."

On 5 September 1814, John boarded a ship with Mr. Key and Mr. Skinner and headed down the Patapsco River, hoping to meet the British fleet in the Chesapeake Bay. Two days later, the three men boarded the British vessel holding Dr. Beanes. After nearly six days of negotiations with Admiral Cochrane, they gained the doctor's release but were not yet allowed to return to Baltimore.

The men were finally transferred back to their truce ship but were tethered to a British vessel. Admiral Cochrane worried the Americans would relay any battle secrets they may have overheard back to Major General Smith.

On the morning of September 13, from at least four miles away, John witnessed the beginning of the bombardment of Fort McHenry by the British. The helpless feeling of knowing his father was at the fort was unbearable. Most of the men aboard the American truce ship stood on deck for twenty-four hours as they watched the assault on Fort McHenry. Once the smoke cleared the following morning, John could see through the lens of a borrowed spyglass that the American flag with its fifteen stars and fifteen stripes was still waving.

"After last night, I am truly inspired by what I have witnessed this morning," Mr. Key told John. "Thank you for accompanying us. Your presence made me feel much less threatened. Baltimore is saved, and this war should be over soon."

On John's return to Baltimore, Major General Smith said he'd received a message that John's father had been injured during the bombing of Fort McHenry.

"I release you from your duty to me as my scout. Go to Fort McHenry and find your father," Smith said. "Your assistance in our ongoing protection of the entrance to Baltimore's harbor is needed much more, so I am sending you and several others from the 16th to Fort McHenry."

Arriving at Fort McHenry, John found his father sitting outside the fort's hospital with bandages wrapped around his head. Jacob had sustained a mild head injury and concussion from one of the many bomb blasts that hit the fort, but he appeared well on his way to recovery.

Jacob and John spent the balance of their time at Fort McHenry, even though the British were no longer a threat to Baltimore. After the battle of Bladensburg, Richard Foley left Baltimore. He escorted several hundred British prisoners of war back to Frederick for incarceration at Hessian Barracks. By late January 1815, they heard tales about the defeat of the British by Andrew Jackson at the Battle of New Orleans. News came a few weeks later that President Madison ratified a peace treaty, declaring the war officially over.

In early February, John and Jacob mustered out, heading to Frederick to meet up with Richard Foley for the journey back to Ohio. Arriving at the Foley farm, they were greeted by Will, who handed Jacob and John two letters: one from Christian and one from Marie. The letters had been written seventeen months earlier, and the men were anxious to read them. Jacob instructed John to bring the two letters into the Foley's orchard and asked him to read each letter aloud.

"It appears that the letter from your grandfather came first, so you should read it first," Jacob said.

10 September 1813

Misters Jacob and John Wade
c/o Mr. William Foley
Frederick Town
Frederick County, Maryland

Dear Jacob and John,

We received your letter and are glad you arrived safely at the Foley's farm. We rejoiced when you told us that the British had not burned our beloved Frederick. But then we offered prayers at church on Sunday to the many victims of Georgetown and Fredericktown.

It is difficult for me to comprehend how people from our motherland could commit these horrendous atrocities against innocent civilians. We always thought of the English people as righteous and honorable. Many of our neighbors blame much of this on Napoleon. However, I stand with President Madison. I also stand on the side of the French people and their desire for independence. Unfortunately, I am not confident Napoleon is doing what his people want as he attempts to take more power. If Great Britain defeats Napoleon, I fear the British would turn their entire focus on America.

We here in Southern Ohio do not feel the trade restrictions as much as the people of Maryland, so we commend your efforts in fighting to protect their rights. Even after our army invaded British North America last year, the war is still mostly north of us. Your mother and grandmother are worried about it moving southward. We are worried not as much about the British but about the American Indian tribes, who oppose our expansion into their territories. I hope they come to accept us as equals and that America is a large enough country in which all of us may learn to live together in harmony.

Jacob, Sarah received your letter, which appeared to brighten her day. She misses you both and wished me to ask you to come home as soon as possible.

Most important to you, John, I gave your letter to Cynthia. Her father asked that you speak to him when you return, which is a good sign that he might be agreeable to your marriage.

Many of our neighbors are building more permanent homes. So, Philip and I started plans to build a large two-story house.

John, you and Cynthia are welcome to live in one of the smaller cabins once you are married. We will make sure it is suitable for a young couple by first replacing the packed dirt floors with oak boards and the greased paper windows with glass. We've already begun putting white plaster on the interior walls.

The logs for the new house will be hewn by hand. Therefore, both the outside and the inside walls will be flat instead of round like our older cabins. We may decide to line the interior walls with pine planks.

Philip has been instrumental in designing the new house, with help from an architect in Cincinnati. The new house will boast three bedrooms, and we hope to start building as soon as you return. Be quick, and come home to us safely. Think of yourselves and us.

Love and farewell,
Father

"An excellent letter," Jacob said. "I hope they forgive us for having been gone so long. The new house is welcome news. Now, please read the letter from your grandmother."

30 September 1813

Misters Jacob and John Wade
c/o Mr. William Foley
Frederick Town
Frederick County, Maryland

My Dearest Son and Grandson,

I hesitated for several days, contemplating whether I should send this letter. Father worried you might hear this news from someone else before you could hear it from your family. We hope you are still in Frederick Town to receive this letter, and once you read my message, you will come home immediately.

Jacob, your precious wife, and John, your dear mother, died last week. Margaret, Christina, and I stayed with her until her last breath. Do not be disheartened. She passed peacefully. She lies in the graveyard next to our new church, and Father commissioned an exquisite headstone.

The Reverend David Thomas read from The Book of Common Prayer and gave a joyful sermon based on the hope of resurrection. We sang hymns, and your father gave a heartfelt eulogy. A tender, sweet woman, she will be sorely missed.

We welcomed Christina into our home, and she is doing well. And so, I write no more; my heart can no longer bear to put ink to paper.

It is with love and affection that I sign this letter,
Mother

John no longer held back his emotions. After reading his grand-mother's letter, he wept.

"Your mother, my sweet Sarah!" Jacob cried. "We should never have left her."

John sat down beside his father. The two men wept like small children as they held each other.

"Let's go home, Father. Christina needs us."

PHILIP ALISTAIR CRANE
1815 – 1822

"I should definitely prefer a book…"

Jane Austen, *Pride and Prejudice*

*J*acob and John arrived back in Christiansburg on Easter Sunday, 26 April 1815. Realizing the family was most likely at worship, the two men rode to the small church, first stopping to pray over Sarah's grave.

When Christina realized the men were home, she ran from the church into her father's open arms. Father and daughter cried tears of joy as well as tears of sorrow. They were joyful, because they were together again but also felt a deep sadness because Sarah was not there to share in their reunion.

"Philip," Jacob declared once they were all back at the homestead, "I'm anxious to see the plans for the new house."

Philip spread the drawings across the table for all to see. "With the front door facing south, the house will catch the sun all day. The front door will open to a large sitting room, with a bedroom at the back for Christian and Marie. The stone Inglenook fireplace will be here, with seat alcoves and a bread oven, just as Marie requested. Here is where we will place Marie's cupboard. The staircase will be located opposite the fireplace, with a pantry and additional storage underneath. Large beams will support the second floor where two bedrooms will be created on either side of a small landing. A Rumford fireplace will be placed along the back wall of each upstairs room."

During the two years Jacob and John were in Maryland, Philip and Christian had laid the stone foundation for the new house. All the logs were cut and hand-hewn, with help from David Creager and James O'Sullivan.

Jacob and John planned to put all their energies into helping with the construction of the new two-story hewed-log home. But Jacob had no desire to move into the new house; he sought the privacy of his old cabin. And once John and Cynthia were married, they agreed to take the other small cabin as their new home.

Carts pulled by oxen brought bricks from a brickyard in Dayton that Philip and Christian used to construct a new brick summer kitchen where the ladies would cook much of the year. The daily cooking would resume inside the main house once winter arrived and the canning season was over. Philip proudly showed Jacob and John the finished building.

"Once the back porch of the new house is built, a brick path will lead from the back door to the summer kitchen Christian and I completed whilst you both were gone. Now that you are home, we can work on building a larger smokehouse, an icehouse down by the river, and enlarge the cramped root cellar. We could also expand the old lean-to or perhaps build a barn with a hay loft and enough stalls to provide the cows and horses shelter during the long, harsh Ohio winters."

There were many times when Jacob and John felt extreme sadness and guilt. If they had stayed back in Ohio, instead of going off to war, all the building projects would be finished and Sarah would still be alive. But they never displayed their emotions; not even to each other.

"I must say, Philip, I am quite impressed with your plans and also for your diligence and fortitude," Jacob said. "You and Father worked extremely hard, and your merit has not gone unnoticed.

What a stately home this will be, what with the wide oak floors, many windows, and pine interior."

John complimented his uncle further: "In addition to being an esteemed educator, you are now a skilled carpenter, furniture maker and experienced farmer."

Philip, the second son of Martin and Lucy Crane, was born at Crane Hall in the village of Deane in Hampshire, England, on 4 May 1767. Philip's father, a wealthy landowner, also owned a successful brewery in Basingstoke, Crane Brewery.

When Philip turned seven, he and his older brother, Martin, were sent to Steventon to study with Reverend George Austen, the rector at Steventon and Deane. Upon the death of their father in 1782 Philip's older brother left the Austens.

As the eldest, Martin inherited the large manor house, the land, and the brewery. As the youngest son, Philip knew he would not inherit his father's estate. Fortunately, Reverend Austen made such a great impression on him that Philip decided at an early age to become an educator.

In addition to studying Latin, French, and English literature, Reverend Austen encouraged his students to read from his extensive library. Also, while living at the parsonage, Mrs. Austen taught Philip how to care for her prized beehives. He assisted her in harvesting the honey as well as making her excellent honey wine. Philip learned as much from Mrs. Austen as he did from Reverend Austen. He helped in the dairy, the poultry, the piggery, and the large vegetable garden, but Philip was most interested in learning the art of beekeeping.

While boarding with the Austens, his best mate was Reverend Austen's son Edward, or Neddy, as everyone called him. Being the same age, Neddy and Philip roomed together in the large bedroom at the top of the house.

About the time Philip's brother departed Steventon, relatives of Reverend Austen adopted Neddy, and he left to live with Thomas and Catherine Knight at Godmersham Park.

Philip continued to board at the parsonage with the Austens for two more years. On Philip's seventeenth birthday, his brother Martin sent him to Winchester College to begin his studies of the classics.

Philip saw little of his childhood friend after Neddy moved from Steventon, but over the years, the two men corresponded regularly. (Years later, Philip learned that in addition to owning three estates, Neddy became the High Sheriff of Kent.)

Even with all the prestige of a wealthy man, Neddy remained a good and faithful friend. Edward, as he now desired to be called, had been obliged to change his surname from Austen to Knight.

While Jacob and John were away in Maryland, Philip, with help from James O'Sullivan, built a piggery. Together, the two families purchased several gilts and one giant boar. Once the piglets reached six months they were slaughtered. The men packed the fresh meat in salt for six weeks, then hung the hams and slabs of bacon in the smokehouse for another two weeks. Finally, the smoked meats were stored in the Wade's root cellar to be shared with the O'Sullivan family.

Philip knew the large trestle table John and Jacob built their first year in Christiansburg would fit perfectly in the new house. However, instead of using the long benches built originally, Philip crafted eight straight-back chairs from poplar wood. The long benches could now be used in the new school. The women harvested and dried leaves from the cattails that grew near the pond, weaving seats for the new chairs.

The construction of the new house was progressing.

James O'Sullivan instructed Philip on how to build a bread oven inside the Inglenook fireplace. Once the bread oven was completed, Philip installed an iron door he purchased from Colonel Newcom to fit over the front.

New six-over-six sash and leaded glass windows were ordered from a large building supply company in Cincinnati. The plans called for five windows on the front of the house, one on either side of the door, and three across the second floor. Two more windows on both sides of the house and two in the back. Smaller windows were ordered to replace the greased paper windows in the two original log cabins.

Margaret and Marie used scraps of wool, cotton, and burlap left-over from their sewing projects to create braided rugs. They intended to place the rugs in the sitting room and each of the three bedrooms in the new house. They also sewed bright curtains for the many windows. Additionally, the ladies made curtains and braided rugs for the smaller cabins' new windows and floors.

For the last task in the building of the new house, Christian commissioned a sign maker in Dayton to create a sign to be placed at the end of the lane. It arrived just days before they completed the house. The four men erected the large signboard that read: *The Wade Homestead Est. 1810.*

With the building projects on the homestead nearly completed, Philip focused on building a one-room schoolhouse with help from his neighbors.

The plans for the schoolhouse included a small fireplace to be built in the front corner. The boys would be required to carry wood from the woodshed to keep the schoolhouse warm during cold weather. Two privies were built behind the schoolhouse—one for the boys and one for the girls.

Mr. Creager finished an addition to his home. When he replaced six windows, he gave the old windows to Philip. The donated windows were hung high to better catch the light and prevent the students from peering out the window during class time.

Philip spent several weeks building his desk from an old walnut tree that had fallen near the new house. Fitted with brass hinges, the top tier lifted to reveal a spacious cubby for his papers and books. He placed the desk on a raised platform at the front of the room. He also built a matching stool but planned on standing most of the day.

Two long slabs of wood were attached to either side of the room, creating two long desks with a long bench underneath. The boys would sit on one side of the room, the girls on the other side. The younger children would sit on benches in the center of the room, facing Philip.

One sunny day, Philip was surprised when he saw Colonel Newcom's wagon approach the half-finished school building. Having been recently elected to the Ohio Senate, Colonel Newcom had sold his tavern and moved from the area.

"Let me be the first to congratulate the citizens of Christiansburg on the fine school they have built for the young folks of their community," Colonel Newcom announced. "I am honored to bestow this school bell to my good friends of Christiansburg and ask you to ring it proudly every school day for years to come."

The men unloaded the large iron bell, including a bell yoke and rope, from the Colonel's wagon. They dug a deep hole and firmly mounted the bell to a thick wooden post near the school's front door.

In just three weeks, the small one-room log schoolhouse was finished.

In addition to building the new schoolhouse, Philip and Margaret envisioned someday owning a mercantile. They intended to sell fruits, vegetables, canned goods, bread, maple syrup, and food staples like sugar and flour. They could also sell dry goods, farming, and building supplies. An excellent seamstress and milliner, Margaret dreamed of someday selling her designs to the women of Christiansburg, perhaps even those of Dayton.

Philip also planned to build several beehive boxes to start keeping honeybees, much as he had in England with the Austen family. He desired to become a master beekeeper and sell honey and honey wine at his and Margaret's future general store.

Several months earlier, Philip had written to Dr. Hahn in Frederick, advising him that Christiansburg needed a physician. Did he know someone he could recommend? Within a month, a doctor from Columbus answered Philip's inquiry. With the promise of a house, Dr. Jedediah Smith agreed to move his practice to Christiansburg.

Before the doctor and his family arrived, James O'Sullivan enlisted several men to help him build the doctor's new house. James had learned the building trade while working at his uncle's company in Maryland. He acquired lumber from the sawmill in Dayton and built a large two-story clapboard house to accommodate the doctor and his young family as well as to become the doctor's office where the sick could come for treatment.

Philip was particularly pleased that Dr. Smith and his wife, Anne, had three young children who would be attending Philip's new school. The little town of Christiansburg was growing and thriving, and Philip was genuinely enjoying his new life in Ohio.

At dinner one evening, John observed, "We should have a good harvest this year. My attention is now focused on my wedding and bringing Cynthia to the homestead. But don't fret, little Christina, we will plan a splendid harvest festival for your birthday."

John remained a farmer at heart. He'd loved working in the fields with the Swadener men in Maryland and now at his new home in Ohio. John helped with the building projects but focused most of his time and attention on farming. He decided to sow hay and alfalfa, with a few acres of tobacco as an experiment. Philip and Christian had planted corn while John and his father were fighting in Maryland, so John felt hay and alfalfa would be a good choice for rotating the crops. He planned to barter with the other homesteaders for corn and oats.

"With no corn to harvest, it appears we won't be having a corn husking competition this year," Jacob teased John. "We must think of a new game for this year's gathering. Maybe we should organize a competition to see who dances the best jig: the Irish or the English."

Much to the dismay of his grandfather, John had converted to Catholicism a few months after returning to Ohio. The war had a profound effect on John; he spent much of his free time discussing his faith with his soon-to-be father-in-law, Brother Daniel. John also spent many evenings in his cabin with his father and Uncle Philip, discussing his decision and how his grandfather might react. He greatly respected his grandfather and didn't want to disappoint him.

In 1814, while John was in Maryland fighting the British, Cynthia's mother died. Since both John and Cynthia's mothers had passed on, it was left up to the surviving family and friends to help create a happy celebration for the new couple. So on 9 September 1815, John Christian Wade and Cynthia Jane Daniel were married at St Joseph's Catholic Church in Dayton.

Margaret designed and stitched an ivory linen gown for Cynthia, to which she added a blue-ribbon sash. A large hoop underneath made the already full skirt even fuller. Margaret asked Marie to embroider delicate blue flowers across the bodice. Marie loaned her blue sapphire earrings to Cynthia, knowing how they would nearly match Cynthia's vivid blue eyes. Christina gathered the last of the blue cornflowers from the meadow for Cynthia's bouquet and fashioned a wreath for Cynthia to wear over her golden curls.

John owned no formal outfit, so he borrowed one from his Uncle Philip. He looked quite genteel in one of Philip's three-piece ensembles, consisting of a black wool tailcoat, ivory cotton twill pants, and a vest of black satin with a cut-velvet woven floral pattern. Under the vest, John wore a white ruffled shirt with a white silk scarf. After the ceremony, Brother Daniel held a wedding breakfast for thirty guests at his Dayton home.

Once John and Cynthia were settled in their cabin and the rest of the family in the new house, plans turned to the combined housewarming, harvest festival, and Christina's eleventh birthday.

Philip set about lighting a fire in Christina's fireplace before saying goodnight and closing her door.

"It is cold and rainy tonight for late September," Margaret observed as Philip lit a fire in their bedroom. "I see you received a letter and quite a large package from your friend back in England. What did he send you?"

"Please read his letter aloud while I open the package," Philip asked his wife.

31 August 1815

Mr. Philip Crane
The Wade Homestead
Christiansburg Highway
Christiansburg, Ohio
United States of America

Dear Philip,

I enjoyed reading your last letter about your new house and the school you are building. I am also quite thankful to hear that Jacob and John returned safely from the second time you Americans were fighting us English. I bear no animosity against the American people because I was busy battling Napoleon during your second war with Britain. Life in America seems to suit you.

My children are doing well, considering it has been seven years this December since their dear mother's death. I wish you had met my precious Elizabeth, but when we were starting our married life, you were already married to Margaret and establishing yourself in Maryland.

My darling Fanny Catherine is now twenty-two and has an abundance of suitors calling on her. As yet, she has little interest in anyone. Elizabeth, Marianne, Louisa, and Cassandra are tutored in drawing, dancing and piano.

Louisa and Cassandra were so young when their mother died. Even with the many servants to help with the care of the children, I am thankful their aunts, Cassandra and Jane, visit Godmersham Park often to see their nieces and nephews. My sister Cassandra now calls on me much more often than Jane, as Jane has experienced numerous health issues over the past few years. I wonder if all her writing contributes to her eyes' redness and pain. As I told you in a previous letter, Jane, our sister Cassandra, and our mother took up residence in a cottage I own in Chawton. It has been six years, and Jane seems more rested these days.

The boys—Edward, George Thomas, and Henry—have become first-class amateur cricketers. William and Charles are not as interested in playing cricket, but they are excellent students. Even young Brook John, who is six, also loves the sport. As you know, Brook John was only one month old when Elizabeth left us. Little Brook John turns seven next month, and his aunt Cassandra and I are planning an exceptional birthday party. The boys' current tutor is Mr. Adams. He is notable, but I would have greatly fancied for you to have been their professor.

Indeed, you may be wondering what is contained in the rather large package if you haven't already opened it out of curiosity. I have sent you copies of the three published novels my sister Jane has most eloquently written. She comes to Godmersham Park to use my extensive library, and I believe one of the novels I've enclosed is based on my home here in Kent, most likely the one titled Mansfield Park. A fourth novel is set to be published later this year. I shall send it and any future books as soon as they are published.

Each of the three novels in this package were published in three volumes, so as you see, there are nine books in total. As I mentioned in my previous letters, Jane did not receive credit as the author of these books. My brother Henry and I hope to remedy this situation some time very soon.

You could include these in your teachings as a nod to Jane. I realize she is much younger than you and I, but she looks up to you as much as she does me. We consider you family, so you should own copies of these precious books.

Cassandra and Jane send their love. Take care, my friend, and I hope to hear from you again soon.

Your mate,
Edward "Neddy" Austin Knight

"What are your plans for these books?" Margaret asked. "They seem too special to add them into the new school's library."

"I feel these books should stay within our family," Philip said. "My idea is that, each year for the next three years, to present one of these three novels to Christina on her birthday. I have never discussed my Hampshire family with Christina. I am anxious to tell her about my childhood living with the Austens. I want her to know about my childhood friends, Edward and his young sister Jane. Do you think she might be interested?"

"I am certain Christina will love to hear the stories about your childhood," Margaret said.

Philip never mentioned his parents or his brother, Martin, and Margaret knew it best not to ask questions. She perceived that he and Martin had suffered a serious falling out at some point in Philip's latter teen years.

The following day, Philip and John traveled to Cincinnati to stock up on much-needed provisions. The rain finally stopped, and the morning sun brought much warmer weather. Philip required supplies for the school: small framed slates for each child, white slate pencils, and books to fill the library. John needed to purchase some clevis fasteners to repair the old plow head.

Several weeks before, Philip had found a shop in Dayton that carried black paint. He'd painted several coats onto a large wooden board he hung on the wall behind his desk. He'd used a slate blackboard in Maryland but was unable to find one in Ohio; the makeshift board would have to do for now. While in Dayton, Philip felt extremely lucky to find white limestone chalk for writing on the wooden board.

Marie gave John a list of supplies for the festival. The young apple trees were not yet producing enough apples to make cider, so Marie instructed the men to purchase several large casks of cider. She also asked them to buy a sack of sugar and one of flour to make Christina's cake and the crust for the dozen or more fresh raspberry and blackberry pies she planned to serve at the festival.

The two men spent the night at a small hotel in Cincinnati, arriving back in Christiansburg after the midday meal the next day. It turned out to be a very successful trip.

Christina's birthday dawned warm and sunny, with the trees in their full fall glory of red, yellow, and soft hues of brown. Christina's birthdays always happened on perfect autumn days. The one exception was the storm on her fifth birthday when a lightning strike burned down their Maryland home.

The morning of the festival, Uncle Philip and Aunt Margaret gave Christina a brightly wrapped package. Inside, she found a three-volume set of wonderfully bound books titled *Sense and Sensibility*. Philip wrote on a card tucked under the ribbon: *To my niece on her eleventh birthday from Uncle Philip 18 October 1815.*

"This book was written by a dear friend of mine back in England, Miss Jane Austen," Philip said. "She is now a grown woman, but was a little girl when I lived with her family. I hope you love these books as much as I love you."

When Christina opened the first book to the title page, the author had scratched out "By A Lady" and written, "By Jane Austen."

"I will place these books into Grandmother Marie's big cupboard and read a chapter to everyone each night after supper," Christina told her aunt and uncle. "Thank you so much."

The annual Wade Harvest Festival continued to be a huge success. That year, there was almost double the amount of attendees as the first festival five years earlier.

"So much has happened in the last five years," Philip said to Margaret when most festivalgoers had left and the couple was settled into bed. "We live in a handsome new home, and our little town's population has almost doubled. I am so sorry Sarah and Lydia are not here to see all we have accomplished."

"Yes, but I know they are looking down on us with approval," Margaret said. "Plus, your new school starts in just over a month, and you now have seven new students."

On 20 November 1815, Christiansburg's first school opened to ten eager students. The first to arrive was Peter Reich.

Philip split the school year into two semesters to coincide with the planting and harvesting seasons. The spring semester started in late May and would run for ten weeks, ending in early August. The winter semester would begin in late November and run for ten weeks, culminating in early February, with a week off for Christmas.

Of the five children studying with Philip in his home for the past five years, only Nancy Creager, Peter Reich, and Christina would be joining Philip at the new school. David Creager and Philip's nephew, John, were both married men. David even had a baby on the way.

At thirteen, Peter Reich prepared to spend the next ten weeks studying for his eighth-grade exam without intending to continue his education beyond the eighth grade. Philip would schedule a graduation ceremony for Peter at the end of the term, as the young man would be the school's first graduate.

"There is a slight chill in the air this morning," Philip said to Peter. "Can you please bring in a load of firewood and start a nice warm fire?"

When Philip stepped out to ring the bell, he found all the children anxiously waiting to start their first day.

As the children entered, they found hooks for their coats and jackets by the door. Individual slates sat on the desks. Philip had painstakingly painted their names on each slate so they could quickly find their place.

"I see you found the coat hooks and your seats," Philip announced. "Tin cups are hanging near the water bucket by my desk. The other bucket sitting by the fireplace is to wash your hands. Each morning, I need a volunteer to fetch water from the creek."

The children were seated from youngest to oldest, so each child had a good view of Philip. On the boys' side, starting in the front, were Matthew Smith, fourth grade; Harry Vance, sixth grade; and finally, in the back, Peter Reich and Russell Smith, eighth grade. The girls who sat along the opposite side were Nancy Creager and Christina Wade, fifth grade; Sarah Vance, sixth grade; and Molly Smith, seventh grade. On two separate benches, the youngest children sat directly in front of Philip: Jamie O'Sullivan, first grade, and Claude Vance, second grade.

"Before we begin our studies, I must first explain my rules," Philip said. "The bell will ring at a quarter to nine each morning. You must be in your seat promptly at nine o'clock. You shall be given one hour off for lunch, from noon to one o'clock. During this time, you will eat the lunch you brought from home. Afterward, you may play outside. You may go home for lunch if you live nearby, but you must advise me before leaving the school grounds. You may bring toys from home to play with during the lunch hour. Do not go so far that you cannot hear the bell. If you want to bring a potato, we can place it on the fire in the iron bucket, so you can enjoy a hot jacket potato for lunch. Always raise your hand if you need my attention, want to answer a question, get a drink, or need to use the privy. You will address me as Sir or Mr. Crane, and there will be no whispering during class. You could be assigned additional homework if any of these rules are broken."

Philip owned dozens of books from when he taught in Alton and Frederick, which the older students could use. While in Cincinnati the previous month, he'd used his own money to buy twenty books for the younger children.

"There is an extensive library in the bookcase at the back of the room, but if you want to bring books from home, feel free to do so," Philip continued. "You can also bring your Bible to read in your spare time or during nooning. We begin every Monday morning with a recitation from your readers in front of the class. We will have a spelling bee every Friday morning. At the end of each day, each student must straighten their desk. I will ask for volunteers to clean the large blackboard, sweep the floors, and empty the water buckets. And always remember to sit up straight, no slouching."

Philip prearranged with each parent that he would not charge tuition but would accept payment in kind. Some of the parents had given Philip either a tin of coffee, a bag of sugar, a chicken, or a jar of pickles. One parent even gave Philip a looking glass. Most of these were farmer's children, and Philip was merely happy to be teaching again.

The previous spring, Robert Foley married widow Mary Vance. The Vance children attended school in Dayton before the family moved to Christiansburg. Dr. Smith's children had attended school in Columbus before settling in Christiansburg. Even little Jamie knew his ABCs. On the first day, Philip assessed each child's progress by asking, one by one, to stand up in front of the room and recite from their readers. After they finished, Philip stood satisfied that he had placed each student into the appropriate grade according to their abilities.

Next, Philip assisted each student in making a copybook out of five pieces of scrap paper. After stitching the pages together, the books were folded down the middle.

"These copybooks will be used to practice your penmanship using ink and quills," Philip said.

During the nooning hour, Nancy and Christina sat quietly at their desk, eating lunch. Christina opened the berry pail her Aunt Margaret packed to find a hard-boiled egg, an apple, and a slice of freshly baked bread folded in half with plenty of butter. Grandmother Marie must have slipped in the piece of maple candy.

After eating, the children ran outside to find it had been snowing all morning. Not enough snow fell to build a snowman, but the children were able to gather enough to throw snowballs at each other.

That first day, Philip taught arithmetic, history, grammar, and geography. Of course, each student heard the lesson regardless of age. A skilled teacher, Philip kept the day organized and each child fully engaged. At about three o'clock, Philip noticed Jamie had fallen asleep on his bench.

"Christina, please fetch Jamie's jacket off the hook, roll it up, and place it under his head," Philip instructed her.

Christina did as Philip bade, then removed her jacket and laid it across his tiny body. At six years old, Jamie found staying awake until the four o'clock dismissal challenging.

The winter semester ended in early February 1816. Peter Reich passed his eighth-grade exam, so Philip arranged a graduation ceremony. Though the day started a bit chilly, most Christiansburg residents attended. Henri Reich invited everyone back to their home for cake and his wife's hibiscus punch.

In early March, Philip heard of a beekeeper who sold ready-built hives and beekeeping equipment. After several letters back and forth, Philip and Jacob drove to Waynesville to meet Simon McDonald and to pick up four new hives. Philip had already discovered several wild swarms in the woods and plotted with Jacob to capture and relocate the bees.

"Well, I must say, I never thought I would be helping someone capture honeybees," Jacob mused as they returned with the new hives. "I find them somewhat a menace, but I do like honey."

Philip and Jacob spent two days collecting the wild bees in boxes and reorienting them to their new location in Phillip's apiary near the apple orchard and a large meadow of clover. Once again, Philip was ready to preserve honey and make some flavorsome honey wine.

Spring semester would not start until the last week in May. So over the next two months, Philip set about planning the opening of his mercantile.

Philip and Margaret used much of their savings to purchase a small lot next to Dr. Smith's. They hired James O'Sullivan to build a large two-story wood-plank building. A blacksmith and a livery were located a few steps from where their new mercantile would be built. Plenty of empty lots were already planned for other businesses to become established on what the citizens named Front Street.

By the end of the school's spring semester in August 1816, Philip and Margaret were ready to open Crane Mercantile. Their store stocked plenty of home-canned vegetables, Jacob's maple syrup, Philip's honey, and the honey wine he brewed and bottled in the summer kitchen back at the homestead. Margaret stocked bolts of cotton fabric in solid and gingham, along with many colored ribbons and sewing threads. She made herself available to sew for ladies who had neither the time nor the skills; she even started making hats and bonnets again.

John and Jacob helped Philip procure farming and building supplies at wholesale. Soon, their general store stood ready to serve its first customer. Christina even asked to help at the store during her school breaks to earn a little spending money.

On 18 October 1816, Philip presented Christina with the second of Jane Austen's novels, *Pride and Prejudice*. He intended to give Christina the third novel, *Mansfield Park,* on her thirteenth birthday.

True to his word, Edward Austen sent Philip a copy of Jane's fourth novel, *Emma.* Philip saved it, planning to give it to Christina on her fourteenth birthday.

As Christina received each new book, she placed them in her grandmother's big cupboard in what she considered a place of honor.

Several months before Christina's thirteenth birthday, Philip received a letter from Edward stating his dear sister Jane died on 18 July 1817. In his letter, Edward advised Philip that as soon as they were published, he promised to send two more of Jane's novels: *Northanger Abbey,* and *Persuasion.* Edward's letter included a clipping from the *Courier* of Jane's obituary. That evening at dinner, Philip read it aloud.

> *On the 18th of this month at Winchester, Miss Jane Austen, youngest daughter of the late Reverend George Austen, Rector of Steventon, in Hampshire, and the Authoress of Emma, Mansfield Park, Pride and Prejudice, and Sense and Sensibility. Her manners were most gentle; her affections ardent; her candor was not to be surpassed, and she lived and died as became a humble Christian.*

Philip sent a letter of condolence to Edward and felt quite melancholy for several days.

The years passed quickly, and the family found they were about to grow in number as Cynthia and John were expecting their first child.

On 2 February 1820, Emmett Ryker Wade came into the world, crying and hungry. Sadly, his twin sister entered the world stillborn. They buried little Emma Marie next to her Grandmother Sarah. She was only the second Wade to be laid to rest in the small graveyard at Christ Episcopal. That evening, Margaret entered the birth of the two children and the death of Emma into the Wade Bible.

Life returned to as near normal as possible after the tragedy suffered by John and Cynthia, with the loss of their precious Emma.

Ten years had passed since the Wades first came to Ohio. Remarkably, the town of Christiansburg had more than doubled in size from that first year. Because of the abundance of good, tillable farmland and fresh water, farmers and shopkeepers found it a great place to bring their families and start their businesses.

More shops opened along Front Street, including a small tavern and inn operated by John Archer named the "Sign of the Crossed Keys." The tavern became a favorite sojourn for Jacob. In fact, according to his sister Margaret, it happened to be too much of a good thing. Although, in his defense, Jacob still grieved for his young wife, Sarah. After a hard day working on the farm, he found comfort in the lively music and good food and drink he encountered at the tavern.

(Years later, the Christiansburg residents voted John Archer for the position of postmaster, and he then managed the post office out of his tavern.)

Over the years, Philip instructed and graduated countless students; first in Alton, then in Frederick, and now in Christiansburg.

Of the original ten students from 1815, four were still enrolled by the end of the semester of 1822. Claude Vance was fourteen, and Jamie would turn thirteen in May. The two boys would be entering the ninth and eighth grades in November. Nancy and Christina stayed with Philip for one more semester to assist him with the younger children and to study Latin, Greek, and English literature. At the end of the semester, with great pride, Philip organized a graduation ceremony for his niece Christina and her lifelong friend, Nancy Creager. Aunt Margaret stitched two matching white dresses, which she embellished with pink and blue ribbons.

On a sunny morning, 9 February 1822, the school held a graduation ceremony at Christ Episcopal. Reverend Thomas played Lydia's fortepiano as the girls marched into the church. Each of the girls gave a prepared speech. Finally, Philip presented each young lady with a diploma, which he had hand-lettered, rolled, and tied with a gold ribbon.

Both Nancy and Christina were turning eighteen on their respective birthdays. Nancy wanted to stay and assist Philip, as fifteen students were enrolled for the upcoming spring semester. Christina, however, wanted to see what lay beyond Christiansburg. She asked her Uncle Philip to help her find a position teaching at a large city school, perhaps in Dayton.

Philip did assist Christina in acquiring a teaching position, but not in Dayton. It was at a new school in Madison, Indiana. The town of Madison sat on the north side of the Ohio River, about seventy-five miles from Cincinnati. Christina would leave for Indiana in September, much to Christina's delight and Philip's satisfaction. Aunt Margaret, Grandmother Marie, and Jamie O'Sullivan were not as enthusiastic.

After Philip returned from escorting Christina to Indiana, he wrote in his journal:

9 September 1822

Yesterday, I returned from delivering my niece, Christina Elizabeth Wade, to her first teaching assignment in Madison, Indiana. I will think of her all day today, as it is her first day as the new teacher at St. Paul's Episcopal School.

On an early fall morning, 6 September 1822, Christina, her father Jacob, and I rode to Cincinnati in the family's small carriage. Once there, we proceeded to where they docked the Bella Queen. Christina and I boarded the large steamboat. A young porter delivered our bags to our cabins. We walked to the rail to wave a jubilant farewell to Jacob. There were tears in Christina's eyes, along with a courageous smile on her face.

That night, we ate dinner in a red and gold extravagantly decorated dining room with velvet chairs and waiters wearing black suits and white gloves. An orchestra played Schubert while we dined on steak with scalloped potatoes, creamed spinach, and a luscious chocolate cake for dessert. It has been many years since I dined in such a stylish dining room.

After a restful night, we arrived in Madison the following day and were greeted by Reverend Isaiah Morris and his wife, Maryann. As he drove to the newly built red brick schoolhouse with its large white cupola, we passed the parsonage, where Christina will live with the Morris family.

Christina and I toured the school with Reverend Morris and were highly impressed with the facilities. Each student benefits from having their own desk, complete with an inkwell and book storage. The extensive library is equally impressive. Behind the large oak desk hung a slate blackboard and maps of the world and the United States. In the corner stood a small piano, which Christina can play brilliantly, having learned on her sister's fortepiano. Christina seemed nervous, but I am confident she will excel at her assignment; she was meant to be a teacher.

Christina rode with Reverend Morris in his carriage as they drove me back to Madison's Port Authority. I waved farewell to my young charge and wiped away a few tears. I remember her as the little girl in Frederick Town on that cold Christmas morning in 1809 when I escorted her to the park to ride her pony. I had the difficult task of explaining to a wee five-year-old girl that her sister had gone to heaven and was now her guardian angel.

I know in my heart that her mother, Sarah, and her sister, Lydia, are looking down on Christina today, and always.

PAC

CHRISTINA ELIZABETH WADE O'SULLIVAN
AND
JAMES "JAMIE" KEAN O'SULLIVAN III
1822 – 1839

"One half of the world cannot understand the pleasures of the other."

Jane Austen, *Emma*

*C*hristina rode with Reverend Morris to drop Philip back at Madison's Port Authority in time for him to catch the last steamboat to Cincinnati. Upon their return, Reverend Morris stopped and parked the carriage in front of the parsonage. A man emerged from behind the house and drove the carriage away.

"Thank you, Reginald," Reverend Morris told him.

Located on West Second Street, the Morris's house sat alongside other large homes. Paved with bricks, Second Street looked nothing like Front Street back home; it was still paved with packed dirt. Madison looked and felt entirely different from Christiansburg.

Seeing the house, Christina developed an odd feeling. Where had she seen this house before? Once inside, she realized how similar it was to Grandpa Wade's home in Frederick. Although she'd been five when she left Maryland, Christina remembered the house as a three-story redbrick, with a white front door to the left. It sported two dormers at the top, the same as the Reverend's house.

"Your home is lovely," Christina told Reverend and Mrs. Morris. "It reminds me of my grandfather's former home in Maryland."

"Thank you, Christina," Mrs. Morris said. "Dinner will be ready in one hour. Perhaps you might like to freshen up and change out of your travel clothes."

"Reginald," Reverend Morris called out. "Please take Christina's trunk upstairs to her bedroom."

Christina followed Reginald up a grand curved staircase to a small bedroom on the third floor. She gasped when Reginald opened the door. She had never seen an airier, more light-filled bedroom. There was a four-poster bed with a white goose-down comforter. Crisp white curtains hung at the two dormer windows. A small washstand beside the bed held a blue and white washbasin and pitcher. Christina was pleased that the room also contained a small writing desk with a sturdy chair and a comfortable-looking rocker.

Christina learned later that Reginald and his wife Martha lived in a bedroom at the back of the house. Martha tended the garden and cooked the meals. Reginald ensured the house stayed warm in winter and did anything else asked of him, including attending to the horses and keeping the house in good repair. Penny, a fourteen-year-old girl who lived across town, came daily to do the washing and house cleaning.

Grandma Marie often told Christina stories of when, as a young girl growing up in England, Christina's great-grandfather employed a dozen or more servants. Christina treasured one story most: how her grandmother's personal lady's maid combed her grandmother's hair and helped her dress.

Before she left for Madison, Aunt Margaret helped Christina sew three new day dresses, using one of her aunt's Lowell Mill patterns.

In addition to the dresses, Christina stitched herself a new corded petticoat, Grandma Marie knit Christina a dark brown shawl for cool weather, and Margaret made Christina a lovely black velvet bonnet to match her black wool cape. Christina owned a small straw hat but planned to wear her new bonnet when winter came. Luckily, Christina did not need to travel far, as the parsonage stood a short walk from St. Paul's Episcopal Church, and the school sat right next to the church.

After unpacking her trunk and placing her clothes into a large clothes press that stood between the two windows, Christina washed her face. She drew her hair into a tight bun and changed into one of her more stylish dresses.

Christina checked the pendant watch her family gave her as a graduation gift, then hurried downstairs to be on time for dinner.

Jamie's father spent most of his time with a crew of men building new homes for the wealthier residents of Dayton. At thirteen, Jamie did not need his father's help. He was quite capable of tilling and seeding their nearly forty-acre corn crop on their farm in Christiansburg. Jamie's mother, Kiera, tended their extensive kitchen garden with help from Jamie's three young siblings: June, nine; Finn, seven; and Liam, six.

But when Jamie could get away from his chores at home, he helped the Wades plant and harvest their crops. In return, they helped Jamie. That day, Jamie assisted Jacob and John with their tobacco crop's fourth and final cutting.

"Once we hang this last load into the Foley's tobacco barn, we can call it a day," Jacob announced. "Jamie, you are welcome to share our supper."

"Thank you," Jamie responded. "My mother is expecting me, so I must go home."

Jamie thought of Christina all day while working with Jacob and John in the fields. As her birthday approached, he sadly realized she would not be home to join everyone at that year's annual harvest festival. He had known Christina since before he could remember. She helped him in school when he had trouble with his numbers. On a warm summer day, she might take him fishing in the large pond by her house. Some days, they sat high in an apple tree while she read to him from one of her Jane Austen books. He looked up to her as a big brother might look up to his older sister, and he missed her terribly.

Back at the house, Jamie realized his father had come home early. He quickly washed and changed his clothes.

"Jamie," his father announced at supper, "I will allow you to attend school for one more year here in Christiansburg. Then I want you to come and work with me. I plan to start my own business. I will be naming it O'Sullivan and Sons Building Company. This year, I saved much of my pay to buy our equipment and supplies. Someday I may want to sell the farm and move to Dayton permanently. This new venture should make us wealthy business owners, much like my uncle back in Maryland."

Jamie felt like his world had fallen apart. He pined for his friend Christina and feared that soon, he'd never see Christiansburg again. Jamie cared nothing about becoming wealthy. He cared about the farm, his incredible friends, and his many neighbors.

Christina comfortably settled into a daily routine. Before school began, she ate breakfast in the nursery with the Morris boys, Alfred and Nicholas. Alfred, or Freddy, was ten, and Nicholas, or Nicky, was eight. Both boys attended school, but Reverend Morris hired Christina as the boy's nanny when school was not in session.

"Today is your eighteenth birthday, Miss Wade," Nicky announced. "Martha is baking you a nice cake for dinner."

"Well, before we can think about cake, have you studied your spelling words for today's spelling bee?" Christina asked the boys. "Today is Friday."

"Oh, yes!" they exclaimed in unison.

Christina received a large packet in the mail that day. Once she retired to her bedroom after dinner she lit a candle, settled into bed, and opened the packet to find dozens of letters from home. She received letters from each of the children she'd helped the previous year with Uncle Philip and a letter from every one of her family members. Her two-year-old nephew, Rye, drew her a picture. Even Nancy Creager included a letter, but there was no letter from Jamie.

She decided she must stay up a few minutes longer and write home to thank them for the letters and include the recipe for Martha's luscious cake.

October 18, 1822

Mr. Jacob Wade
The Wade Homestead
Christiansburg Highway
Christiansburg, Ohio

Dearest Family,

I miss each and every one of you so very much, but I must say that the letters you sent helped lift my spirits. The Morris family gave me the most beautiful silk and ivory hand fan, and their cook, Martha, prepared a delicious meal. The cake she baked was like none I have ever tasted, so I asked her for the recipe, which I have written below. Please ask Grandmother Marie to put this recipe into the small wooden box she keeps in her big cupboard. Aunt Margaret, you must make this for the family; you can use the blackberry jam we preserved last year.

Martha's Kentucky Blackberry Jam Cake with Caramel Glaze

In a large bowl, combine three coffee cupful's of flour with a coffee spoonful of ground cinnamon, a dash of ground cloves, a dash of cracked nutmeg, a pinch of salt, and a smidgen of pearlash.

In a separate bowl, cream a packed fistful of brown sugar with a heaping coffee cup of white sugar and a chunk of lard. Add one coffee cup of seedless blackberry jam and three large eggs and mix well. Add half the flour mixture and a teacup of buttermilk and mix well again. Repeat with the second half of flour and another teacup of buttermilk. Using a wooden spoon, mix until the batter is smooth, and then fold in one coffee cup of chopped walnuts.

Divide batter into two small round cake pans greased with lard and floured. Bake in a rather hot oven for one-half hour. Once cool, spread a smear of blackberry jam between the two layers and stack one on the other. Cover with caramel glaze.

Caramel Glaze

Add one packed fistful of brown sugar to two cubes of melted butter. Once that comes to a boil, add a teacup of milk and a dash of rum. Continue to cook until it becomes thick. Once cooled, you may pour over the cake.

If I were there, I would give each of you a big hug. Please also tell Jamie hello from me.

Love,
Christina

The year went by quickly. Before Christina realized it, the end of December arrived, and the school year was nearly half over.

Christina attended church with the Morris family on Christmas Eve. On Christmas Day, Martha prepared a Christmas goose with all the trimmings. The Morris family gave Christina a small black velvet purse. She, in turn, gave Reverend and Mrs. Morris a box of assorted nuts. She gave the boys a book by Mary Martha Sherwood titled *The History of the Fairchild Family*. But Christina's most cherished gift was the letter from Jamie.

18 December 1822

Miss Christina Wade
c/o Reverend Isaiah Morris
314 West Second Street
Madison, Indiana

Dear Christina,

I have been studying feverishly for my eighth-grade exam and should graduate next February. I asked Mr. Crane to hold my graduation ceremony until you return home in May.

I must apologize for my behavior the day you left Christiansburg. I was so upset to see you go. I consider you my best friend, and if my family decides to move back to Maryland or even Dayton, I shall miss you terribly.

I hope you enjoy a fine Christmas. I anxiously await your return.

Your friend,
Jamie O'Sullivan

Jamie completed the spring planting and hoped his father might allow him a few weeks of lazing around with his friends before starting work in Dayton. He dreamed of swimming in the Wade's pond, fishing in the river, and spending time at the "Merc" with Christina and his many friends.

Christina had been home for several weeks when, on 21 May 1823, Jamie turned fourteen. The following Sunday, Philip arranged a graduation ceremony for Jamie at the church. Afterward, Kiera served bowls of freshly picked strawberries with cream.

"I know this is your day off from the store, but if you walk with me to the Merc, I will buy you a peppermint puff. Or perhaps you prefer a pickle from the big barrel?" Jamie asked Christina.

Christina laughed. "No thank you on the pickle, not after strawberries. But it is a beautiful day. I would love to walk with you more than ever if you buy me a peppermint puff."

"I overheard my mother and father discussing the possibility of moving back to Maryland," Jamie lamented. "I asked Jacob if I may live with him if they do."

"The opportunities for building new homes here in Christiansburg and Dayton are too good to pass up," Christina said. "I doubt they'll move back to Maryland. Besides, even if your family does move to Dayton, it is only a short ride away."

Luckily for Jamie, most of the building projects he worked on for his father that summer were in Christiansburg. And since Christina was helping Philip and Margaret at their store, Jamie frequented it often to visit Christina whenever he wasn't working.

As a gathering place, the Crane's store had become almost as popular as John Archer's tavern. That summer, with planting mainly completed, Philip built a counter where the farmers could sit and relish a glass of his much-celebrated honey wine. Or the customers could play checkers while they nattered away for hours.

Unlike when she taught school, Christina no longer wore her long hair in a tight bun but merely tied it back with a bright ribbon, letting it cascade onto her shoulders. Jamie's stomach was full of butterflies whenever he looked at her; he was confused by his feelings for his old friend. And he was miserable when he realized she would be returning to Madison at the end of the summer for another long school year.

Finally, Christina's two-year agreement to teach at St. Paul's Episcopal School ended. Although this felt bittersweet, Christina was happy to be returning to Christiansburg. Just as she finished packing her trunk, Martha brought her a letter delivered by the post that morning.

20 May 1824

Miss Christina Wade
c/o Reverend Isaiah Morris
314 West Second Street
Madison, Indiana

Dear Christina,

Russell graduated from Ohio University in May with his AB in History. He has been appointed assistant librarian at the State Library of Ohio in Columbus. Russell asked my father for my hand in marriage last Christmas, and we are being married next month.

You and I were mere children when you came to ride in our carriage as we left Maryland. I possess no other friend for as long as I have known you. Therefore, will you stand with me at my wedding? Your Aunt Margaret is making my wedding dress and has offered to make you a fashionable dress as well.

I cannot wait to see you so we can discuss all the details of my wedding.

Your best friend,
Nancy

Russell Smith was Dr. Smith's eldest son. He and his younger brother, Matthew, stayed beyond the eighth grade to study with Professor Crane. After serving a six-month apprenticeship with his father, Matthew planned to attend the University of Pennsylvania Medical School.

Philip told Christina of Nancy's resignation, and Christina appreciatively accepted the full-time teaching position at Christiansburg's school. Philip now taught only part-time so he could assist Margaret at their store.

Nancy Creager and Russell Smith were married on 12 June 1824. The couple stood beneath Mrs. Creager's rose arbor, where hundreds of fragrant red roses were in full bloom. Pastor Secrist, from St. John's Lutheran Church in Dayton, performed the wedding service. The happy couple left for Columbus immediately after the ceremony.

Jamie and Christina left and strolled back to the homestead while some guests stayed for wedding cake and tea in Mrs. Creager's garden.

"Do you think you will ever marry?" Jamie asked Christina. "I wonder when you realize you love someone enough to ask that person to marry you."

"I cannot say I have given it much consideration," Christina replied. "Only if I truly love a person will I agree to marry. You will find the right person when you are older."

A few days after the Wade's Harvest Festival of 1824, Jamie's father received word that George O'Sullivan had died unexpectedly. Obligated to be present for the settlement of his uncle's estate, James left immediately for Cumberland. It would be several weeks before he returned, so he asked the Wades to watch over his family while he was gone.

"Tell me about your father's uncle," Christina asked Jamie as they huddled on a blanket under the apple trees in the orchard one evening.

"My father's uncle brought him to the United States when my father was sixteen," Jamie said. "During the Irish Rebellion against the English, my grandfather, a member of the Society of United Irishmen, was arrested when the taking of Dublin failed. My grandmother asked her brother-in-law, George O'Sullivan, to leave Ireland and bring my father, her son, here to the United States. My great-uncle sent many letters to Ireland but never heard back from my grandparents. It's like a hole in my existence, so I can only imagine how much it must hurt my father not to know what happened to his parents. You are fortunate that your grandparents are still alive. They are such a huge part of your life, Christina."

"How awful for you and your father, but such a fascinating story," Christina said. "We should all know our family's history to better appreciate everything we hold dear. Maybe someday you might learn whatever may have happened to your grandparents."

Jamie's father returned to Christiansburg a few days before Christmas. He immediately negotiated the sale of his farm to David Creager Jr. and moved his family into a lovely home on East First Street in Dayton. It was a house that James had worked on years earlier when he was just a carpenter. James had always admired the splendor of the three-story stone-faced brick residence resting on a limestone foundation, built in the Italianate style of architecture. To finish it, James and Kiera commissioned a house full of furniture from a prominent Philadelphia furniture and cabinetmaker. They covered all the walls with decorative wallpaper in floral chintzes and toiles to make their home even more lavish and opulent.

It was evident to all who knew him that James O'Sullivan had inherited a large sum of money from his uncle.

That summer, Philip called a meeting of the townspeople to discuss the need for a new and much larger school.

"As you are all aware, the Ohio legislature established common schools by implementing a half-mil property tax," Philip announced. "We now control the funds to build a new school and pay our teachers a livable wage."

Christian added, "As the largest property owner here in Christiansburg, I am more than willing to pay my fair share to ensure our children become well-educated. Now all children can attend our school without having to pay tuition. I motion we use James O'Sullivan and his crew of competent builders to build our new schoolhouse."

Everyone in attendance agreed. With the new school building approved, construction started immediately. The citizens also established a newly organized school board and appointed Philip its first president.

To further comply with the state's suggestion, the school board changed the two ten-week semesters to a nine-month consecutive year. The school year would run from the first week in September to the last week in May. A summer session would be available from May to August so those who still helped their parents on the farm could make up any school they missed.

Known as the Red Brick Schoolhouse, Christiansburg's newly built school opened in September 1825. Four long desks on either side of a large wood stove faced a long overdue new chalkboard. The stove stood in the center of the schoolhouse. With its capacity to seat five students at each long desk, the school could easily accommodate forty students.

Twenty-eight students enrolled that year. Christina felt fortunate to retain Claude Vance as her classroom helper. Claude was one of the few students to complete the twelfth grade. Christina believed he was meant to become an excellent educator in his own right.

The first year in the new school passed quickly, and as the school year ended, Philip declared his plans to retire. Only six students had signed up for summer school, so he agreed to teach the summer session. With her uncle taking over the summer session, Christina gained the entire summer to do as she pleased.

"Aunt Margaret?" Christina asked. "May I help you at your store again this summer?"

"Why, yes," her aunt replied. "We can always use your assistance."

Christina loved working at Crane Mercantile. Waiting on people as they shopped for supplies was a welcome change from teaching.

It was a hot day in early August when Molly Smith entered the store.

"Christina!" Molly exclaimed. "My mother and father want you to join us next week. They are planning a trip to Columbus to visit Nancy and Russell. We shall be gone for about a month. Can you come?"

Christina only imagined how Columbus must have changed since fifteen years earlier, when she'd traveled on a wagon train through the small town known at that time as Franklinton. It was now the capital of Ohio, named after the explorer, Christopher Columbus.

"We will stay with my aunt and uncle while Mother and Father take Matthew to Philadelphia."

"Aunt Margaret?" Christina asked. "Can you possibly manage without me for a whole month?"

"Absolutely! You deserve a holiday."

"I would love to go, Molly, as long as I return in time for the start of my school's fall term."

Jacob drove the five passengers to Dayton, where they caught the weekly mail stagecoach to Columbus. The trip required two days to reach Columbus, with an overnight stop in Springfield.

Christina loved her time in Columbus with her old friends Molly, Nancy, Russell, and Matthew. One evening, after the family finished supper, Matthew asked Christina to walk with him to the Public Square near the Statehouse.

"It is such a fine evening. Walk with me?"

"Of course, Matthew."

"Will you write to me while I am at school?" Matthew asked. "I have always admired you, and I am hopeful we might become more than friends."

The next day, Mr. and Mrs. Smith would accompany Matthew to Philadelphia to start medical school. Christina was flattered by his request. However, knowing he would not return to Christiansburg for at least three years, it was with some reluctance that she agreed.

Once Christina was alone in her bedroom, she was startled when Molly burst through the door.

"Oh, Christina!" Molly exclaimed. "Matthew told me he has asked you to write to him while he is away at school. You, Nancy, and I may someday be sisters."

When Jamie turned seventeen, his father allowed him to oversee the smaller building projects in Christiansburg and manage two young men who lived in town. Jacob offered to let Jamie stay in the loft of his cabin and take his meals with the rest of the family in the main house.

Grandma Marie was most content with lots of company to cook for, as nine now sat around the table each night. Marie never complained, but Jacob noticed his mother's feet and legs were always swollen. Dr. Smith advised Jacob that his mother's heart was failing.

"Allow her to rest as much as possible and keep her legs elevated while she's resting," Dr. Smith told Jacob.

Despite all the attention everyone spent caring for Marie, she became more frail as the weeks passed. She often ate her meals in her bedroom, but she always came out to sit in her rocker and listen to Christina read to the family after supper.

One warm evening after Christina finished reading William Cullen Bryant's poem "To a Waterfowl," Jamie found Christina alone on the back porch. He confronted her with some gossip he had heard from Molly Smith.

"I enjoyed your reading tonight; you spoke most eloquently. However, I must ask you something I heard from Molly. Is it true? You are writing to Matthew?" Jamie asked, looking upset.

"Matthew and I are purely friends."

"Molly thinks you and her brother are now betrothed."

"Not at all, Jamie. But why do you care?"

"Because I think I love you," Jamie announced.

After his confession, he turned around and marched to Jacob's cabin, slamming the door and leaving Christina in shock.

It was days before either one spoke to the other, and then merely a brief acknowledgment that the other person was in the room.

On the night of the annual festival and Christina's twenty-second birthday, Jamie reluctantly approached her.

"I am leaving Christiansburg tomorrow and moving to Dayton permanently, as I have plans to start building my own house," he said. "I will not be back until Christmas. If you can muster enough strength after writing all those letters to Matthew Smith, will you write to me?"

"Oh, Jamie," Christina laughed. "I will most definitely write to you."

She placed a soft kiss on his cheek before they said goodnight.

Jamie and Christina wrote dozens of letters over the next two months, and by the time Christmas approached, Christina looked forward to Jamie's arrival with great anticipation. Jamie spent Christmas Eve with his family in Dayton but rode to Christiansburg early Christmas morning. He first stopped at Jacob's cabin.

"Sir," Jamie said. "I have come to ask you for your daughter's hand in marriage."

"You have my blessing," Jacob replied.

The two men walked the short distance to the main house, where the entire family gathered for Christmas dinner. Once inside, Jamie reached for Christina's hand, lowered his voice, and whispered in her ear.

"Will you marry me, Christina?"

"Yes, Jamie, I will marry you."

Not only was it Christina's twenty-third birthday, but 18 October 1827 was the day she would marry her longtime friend and now the love of her life, Jamie O'Sullivan.

At eighteen, James Kean O'Sullivan III had grown into a tall, muscular, and quite handsome young man. He had curly red hair and now possessed a red mustache and full beard.

While Christina and the family remained at the house, Jamie stood at the altar of Christ Episcopal with Reverend Thomas. A choir of twelve young schoolgirls led the congregation in the singing of hymns.

Nearly all of Christiansburg's citizens awaited the bride's arrival. Many of the townspeople stood outside the church because there weren't enough seats inside for everyone who wanted to witness the marriage of two of Christiansburg's original pioneers.

Margaret created Christina's gown from light blue satin. The sleeves were puffed into an enormous billow from shoulder to elbow and the tapered lower part of each sleeve came to a point over her hands. Elaborate dark blue silk velvet trim adorned the hem, sleeves, and bodice.

Cynthia styled Christina's hair high on her head with curls on either side. Her head was covered by a light blue satin turban that matched her dress. Margaret used blueberries to dye marabou feathers a light blue, attaching them to the turban. Marie helped Margaret design the hat after one Marie had worn as a young girl in England. And of course, Christina wore the blue sapphire earrings passed down from Grandmother Marie.

Before the family left for the church, Marie called everyone into her bedroom.

"Christina, my love, you look breathtaking," Marie gushed. "I so wish I could be at the church this evening to witness your nuptials.

Unfortunately, I feel a little under the weather today. Your grandfather and I discussed your wedding gift with the family, and we all agreed. We want you and Jamie to take the cupboard my father made and gave to your grandfather and me on our wedding day to your new home in Dayton. It is no longer my cupboard; it is now yours."

"It is now Christina's cupboard," her grandfather added.

Christina hugged her grandfather then leaned down and kissed her grandmother's cheek. "I am thrilled to receive your kind gift; I will forever treasure and cherish 'our' cupboard."

After the ceremony, the townspeople gathered at the Wade homestead to participate in the combination birthday celebration, wedding reception, and harvest festival.

The wedding couple toasted with some of Philip's excellent honey wine. Margaret and Cynthia made dozens of iced fruit cakes to divide among the wedding guests. Jacob and John roasted one of their prized pigs, and Christian brought out jugs of his now-famous apple cider. The townsfolk also brought food and drink to share. Christiansburg's harvest festival was finished for another year, and Christina and Jamie were ready to start their new life together.

The Harvest Festival of 1827 was one of the most memorable.

Jamie's latest construction job was enlarging Christ Episcopal. The town had outgrown the old one-room log church. Also, because the newly married couple's house in Dayton was still under construction, they settled into Christina's old bedroom at the homestead until the church's addition and their new home in Dayton were completed.

The day, 15 January 1828, dawned frigid cold. Cynthia and Christina cleared the breakfast plates. John left to take Rye to school, and Jacob walked to the barn to feed the livestock. Philip and Margaret went to open their store while Jamie started his day putting up braces to stabilize the outside wall of the church's new Sunday school room. Christian walked back into his bedroom to clear Marie's dishes. When he emerged from the bedroom, he calmly announced, "My lovely Marie has died."

Cynthia frantically ran outside to call Jacob. John returned home, then walked back out into the frosty morning air to fetch Rye from school. Then Jacob sat with his father while John rode into town to bring Philip, Margaret, Jamie, and Reverend Thomas to the house.

Marie's funeral and burial were planned for the following day. They would bury Marie Elizabeth Wade beside Sarah Jane and Emma Marie in their church's graveyard.

Christian wrote to Marie's brother, apologizing for bringing Marie to live and die in what Christian felt was a cold and cheerless cabin compared to the elaborate homes she'd grown up in back in England. Several weeks later, Christian received a large packet from Marie's brother.

12 February 1828

Mr. Christian Wade
The Wade Homestead
Christiansburg Highway
Christiansburg, Ohio
United States of America

Dear Christian,

I am sending you a packet of Marie's letters, which she sent me over the past 37 years. There are over seventy-five letters in this packet, some dated as early as 1791, the year you arrived in Maryland. They should prove to you how much she adored you, her family, and her life in America.

Never once did I know Marie to ever complain about her situation. She always made it sound as if her life with you was one remarkable adventure after another. She spoke of how much she enjoyed working in her garden and cooking for her family. She was more than satisfied listening to her granddaughter read in the evening after supper with a few bright candles to light the faces of her loved ones. Please never doubt either her love or her happiness.

Your old friend and devoted brother-in-law,
Ronnie Bailey

The house in Dayton was completed on 1 March 1828. Jamie built a magnificent two-story stone house with a brick foundation. Jamie and Christina's new house was on Elm Street, west of Main Street, and just three blocks from his parents' house.

Jamie added a two-story veranda to the back, while pilasters with Ionic capitals separated the three second-story windows in the front. A hip roof covered the house, pierced by chimneys on either side.

A week after Christina and Jamie moved to their new house, the entire Wade clan came to Dayton for a special housewarming and to bring Christina her cupboard. It was apparent to Christina that Grandpa Wade was still grieving Grandma Marie's death, so she invited him to stay with them for a few weeks. But what started as a few weeks turned into more than a year.

"Christina?" her grandfather asked. "Have you met your new neighbors across the alleyway? They don't look to be more than eighteen years old."

"Yes," Christina replied. "They are a recently married young couple named Simon and Ann O'Malley. He is a salesman for one of the large dry goods stores in town. Ann says she will be pleased to help me when the baby is born."

It was an unseasonably warm, sunny day in mid-February. Christina and Grandpa Christian sat on the veranda awaiting Jamie's return from work. Christina was knitting a baby blanket for Christian's second great-grandchild—her first child was due in late August.

"You will be a wonderful mother," Christian told her. "It is sad, indeed, that your mother and grandmother are not here to witness the birth of this dear baby."

Sarah Jane O'Sullivan was born on 16 August 1829, a baby girl with wisps of blond hair and large blue eyes.

"She looks so much like you when you were just a wee babe," Christian told Christina. "With a new baby in the house, it's time for me to return to the homestead."

Not two years later, James Kean O'Sullivan IV was born to Christina and Jamie on 27 February 1831. Little Jamie was a loud and boisterous little one, with nearly a full head of red curls.

When baby Jamie wasn't even a week old, Christina looked through the front window, and much to her surprise, she saw her Uncle Philip's carriage pull up.

"Why, Uncle Philip, are you here to see the new baby?" Christina asked.

"I would love to see Little Jamie, but I have come on another, more serious, matter," Philip replied. "I bring very sad news. Your Grandfather Christian died last night."

At only the beginning of her lying-in period, Christina was confined to her bed for at least the next month. Being unable to attend Christian's funeral caused Christina great sadness. Christina's neighbor Ann came to stay with Christina while Jamie, his parents, and Jamie's three younger siblings traveled to Christiansburg with plans to return in two days.

Jamie's brothers, Finn and Liam, would turn seventeen and sixteen on their next birthday, while Jamie's sister, June, would soon be eighteen. The younger O'Sullivan children had many friends and enjoyed living in Dayton while studying at St. Joseph's School with Father Leo. They had all known Christian their entire life and loved him as if he were their grandfather. However, Jamie would never understand how his sister and brothers choose busy, noisy Dayton over growing up in the clean, open country of Christiansburg.

Easter fell on the seventh of April in 1833. With only June living at home (Liam and Finn were studying at Harvard), James and Kiera invited the entire family to share Easter dinner. Thirteen people gathered around the table in the O'Sullivan's large home.

Jamie's parents invited Philip and Margaret to stay over at their home. Jacob, John, Cynthia, and Rye stayed the night with Christina and Jamie. The two houses were full of love and laughter now that three-year-old Sarah and two-year-old Little Jamie were there to make the celebration even merrier.

Four short months after the family's joyous Easter gathering, tragedy struck Dayton. It rained almost nonstop the entire month of August. The streets and yards were full of water. This caused the privies to back up and fill the yards with sewage.

"I was talking with Simon O'Malley. Their little son, John, is very sick," Jamie told Christina. "Keep the children in the house. I do not want our babies to contract this sickness."

"What do they suppose is the illness?" she asked.

"Cholera."

Late that evening, Christina and Jamie observed the local undertaker, Mr. Meyers, drive up to the O'Malley home.

"I am going over to see if I can help," Jamie said.

"Oh, I pray our children do not grow sick," Christina lamented.

On 14 August 1833, at two years and six months old, James Kean "Little Jamie" O'Sullivan IV died of cholera. The next day, 15 August 1833, his sister, Sarah Jane O'Sullivan, died of cholera, one day before her fourth birthday.

After the funerals, a distraught Christina spent the next three months in Christiansburg. She could not bear to live in the house where her children suffered and died. Perhaps she would return to Dayton sometime after Christmas.

By March 1834, Easter with Jamie's parents was becoming a family tradition. Everyone was gathered in the large dining room when Christina announced that she and Jamie were expecting a baby in November. Mary Jane O'Sullivan entered the world on 10 November 1834.

Jamie sat in his parents' parlor a few weeks after his daughter's birth. "There could be no more cherished child on God's earth than our Mary Jane," he told his parents. He paused before asking, "How are June's wedding plans progressing?"

Jamie's sister, June, was marrying a school friend, Roger Taylor, and having a Christmas wedding.

"The plans are progressing quite well. Did I tell you that June's cream silk dress came from a designer in New York?" Kiera asked. She continued before Jamie could answer. "Lace covers the bodice and sleeves, and she will wear a lace veil. As an early Christmas gift, we gave June emerald and diamond earrings, which will flatter her striking red curls. Did I also tell you that Roger's mother is baking the wedding cake from a recipe she found in a book she owns: *The American Frugal Housewife* by Lydia Maria Child? I'll write out the recipe for Christina. I know she'll want to keep it for when she makes one for Mary Jane's wedding."

Jamie smiled. "I think we have some time before Mary Jane gets married, but I'll be sure to pass the recipe on to Christina," he said.

"Liam and Finn are coming home for Christmas this year to witness their sister's wedding," James told Jamie. "This will be such a wonderful Christmas, what with the new baby, the wedding, and all my children home."

The moment Jamie arrived home, he gave Christina the recipe from his mother, much to Christina's amusement.

Wedding Cake

Good common wedding cake may be made thus: Four pounds of flour, three pounds of butter, three pounds of sugar, four pounds of currants, two pounds of raisins, twenty-four eggs, half a pint of brandy or lemon-brandy, one ounce of mace, and three nutmegs. A little molasses makes it dark colored, which is desirable. Half a pound of citron improves it; but it is not necessary. To be baked two hours and a half, or three hours. After the oven is cleared, it is well to shut the door for eight or ten minutes, to let the violence of the heat subside, before cake or bread is put in.

The tragedies of the past few years were forgotten, and the Wade and O'Sullivan families enjoyed more joyful days. The homestead was prospering, as were most families now living in Christiansburg—both new residents and the small number of original settlers.

When not planting in the spring or harvesting in the fall, John and his son, Rye, were trapping. Cynthia was helping Philip and Margaret at the store, and she was becoming a fine seamstress. Jacob tried to stay busy but found himself more often at John Archer's tavern than at home.

Not a year later, June's first baby, a boy, was born. They named him Roger, after his father. Liam and Finn graduated from Harvard Law School with honors and were hired at a large Boston law firm.

Jamie and his father stayed busy with their construction projects. Christina was happy being a mother to Mary Jane. She also fancied herself as a hostess to her many neighbors for an afternoon tea or a late dinner.

Jamie and Christina felt their life together could not be any more blissful than it was at that moment.

A few weeks after the start of the new school year, Philip stopped to see Claude Vance and give a short speech to the young students. Philip learned that Claude had hired a new teacher, a young lady who, with her parents, had recently moved to Christiansburg from Frederick, Maryland.

After supper, Philip excitedly told the family about the new schoolmistress.

"I enjoyed meeting all the new students at school today. I was thrilled to meet the new assistant schoolmistress. Ironically, she is from Frederick. Her name is Susan Meijer. I shall write a letter to Will Foley to ask if he may know the Meijer family."

"Next week is your sixty-sixth birthday, Jacob," Margaret said. "Philip and I are planning to host your birthday dinner, and Cynthia is baking your favorite cake. All your Dayton family are coming, so you cannot spend your entire evening at John Archer's tavern."

"Well, I guess I better mark 23 September 1838 on my calendar," Jacob teased.

"Philip sent me home from the store early, advising me to drink some hot tea with his wonderful honey," Margaret told Jacob on his birthday. "I have a stiff neck and a sore throat, so you should all probably stay away until I feel better. I apologize for not being able to host your birthday dinner tonight; we will celebrate next week. Please send Christina and her family home when they arrive."

After Philip closed the store for the day, he stopped at Dr. Smith's office to ask if he could visit Margaret at the farm.

"I sent Margaret home with a sore throat," Philip said. "Can you come to our home today and examine her?"

"I sent two young children home from school yesterday," Dr. Smith said. "I diagnosed both with diphtheria."

Dr. Smith examined Philip's throat. A thick gray membrane covered his tonsils, consistent with diphtheria.

"Go home, rest, and tend to Margaret. There is nothing I can do."

Four days after his birthday, Jacob noticed a note nailed to the main house's front door.

Jacob,

Do not come into the house. My precious Margaret died right before midnight. I am having extreme difficulty breathing and am dying also. Please ask John to assist you in building two plain coffins.

Philip

Several weeks after Philip and Margaret's funeral and burial in the old graveyard next to Christ Episcopal, Jacob rode to Dayton to discuss a business proposition with Christina and Jamie.

"Philip and Margaret left me a fair amount of money," he told them. "They also gave me full ownership of the store, which I have arranged to sell to John Archer. He plans to change the name to Archer's Mercantile."

"He can call it whatever he wants, but I'll always call it Crane Mercantile," Christina declared.

"There is nothing in the big house in Christiansburg I wish to save," Jacob said. "It holds only bad memories. I want to tear it down and build a fine new house in its place so you and little Mary Jane will come back to live at the homestead in a house that Father, Mother, Sarah, Lydia, Philip, and Margaret would be proud of if they were alive."

"I know a great architect we can use to draw up plans for a Greek Revival design," Jamie said. "This style is becoming quite fashionable. The house would boast a large front porch with four massive columns. But I will only help build it if you leave the small cabin and live with us in this grand house."

"Fine," Jacob replied. "But I don't want to tear down my cabin, and I want to help John expand and make repairs on his."

"If we decide to move back to Christiansburg, I must first discuss with my father how we can divide our projects," Jamie said. "I am sure we can work something out."

By February 1839, the old house had been demolished, and most of the lumber and other building products were sold or given away. Jamie added four men to his crew to ensure the completion of the new house before winter. During the construction, Christina stayed in Dayton because she was expecting another baby in May.

"I shall miss our daily afternoon meetup," Christina told Ann O'Malley. "You are invited to visit us in Christiansburg anytime, especially on my birthday when we host our annual harvest festival."

Thursday, 23 May 1839 saw the birth of Elizabeth Marie O'Sullivan, who was born in Dayton, a city that had grown to over six thousand citizens. But knowing Mary Jane and the new baby would enjoy plenty of sunshine and fresh air growing up in Christiansburg gave Christina hope that no other death would harm her family for many years.

Finished to a high standard, the new house was completed in late September, and Christina moved back to Christiansburg with her two little girls.

By Christina's thirty-fifth birthday, Christiansburg would celebrate its twenty-seventh harvest festival. It should have been the twenty-ninth, but they'd held no festival when Jacob and John were fighting the British in 1813 and 1814. At their first festival in 1810, up to thirty homesteaders were in attendance. Christina estimated that nearly two hundred homesteaders, farmers, and merchants would be coming to the farm today.

It was quite the celebration. Christina invited her good friends Simon and Ann O'Malley and their new baby, Virginia, to spend the week. Plenty of laughter and love blessed their new house and helped erase the darkness from the days gone by.

MARY JANE O'SULLIVAN
1839 – 1842

*"I always deserve the best treatment because
I never put up with any other."*

Jane Austen, *Emma*

"I am five years old today," Mary Jane told her uncle. "You, Mama, Papa, Grandfather Wade, and Aunt Cynthia are giving me a party."

"Yes, silly, I know," John said. He recognized Mary Jane as the image of his sister on her fifth birthday. "I believe the last time someone said those same words to me was thirty years ago when your mother turned five."

"My mother was never five."

"Yes, your mother was once five, and she and I had this same conversation. Now, run inside and prepare for church before you freeze your little biscuits."

"Oh, Uncle John, you are so funny," Mary Jane said. "I already ate my biscuits at breakfast this morning. I will go in as soon as I find Cousin Rye. I need to tell him about my birthday party."

A happy girl, Mary Jane loved everyone; mostly, she loved her cousin Rye. She followed him around all day when he was trying to work. Rye would turn twenty in February, and he was unaccustomed to having a small child following him everywhere.

Mary Jane gently knocked on the door of the small cabin.

"Come in, little one," Cynthia called. "You are going to freeze; it is cold today."

After a sunny and warm October, November had arrived cold and rainy.

"Today is my birthday," Mary Jane announced. "Davey Creager and Ginny O'Malley are coming to my party. Ginny's a baby—like my little sister. Of course, my little sister Lizzy will be there too, but she and Ginny are not allowed to eat cake. I hope Papa gets me the lamb I asked for, like the one in the book Mama reads to me at bedtime. As soon as I am old enough to go to school, I will take my lamb, even if it is against the rule. I hope Cousin Rye can come to my party. Where is he?"

"Ryker is out checking his traps," Cynthia said. "He will be back in time for your party. You better run home and prepare for church; your mother will be worried."

"Yes, before I freeze my biscuits." Mary Jane laughed as she realized John had been teasing her.

In addition to Davey Creager's and Ginny O'Malley's parents, Christina invited the newest family in Christiansburg, the Meijers: Hans, Maria, and their daughter, Susan.

They held Mary Jane's party in the large dining room off the home's front hall. Christina served a fine dinner with pepper pot soup as the first course. The main course consisted of roast venison with boiled potatoes and onions in a rich cream sauce. Jacob served the adult guests a glass of Uncle Philip's rare honey wine.

The thirteen adults sat at the large dining table. The children found themselves seated around a smaller table off to the side. After dinner, Christina brought out two iced gingerbread cakes, Mary Jane's favorite.

"Christina, you must give me your recipe for this luscious cake!" Maria Meijers exclaimed.

After dinner, everyone retired to the parlor, a large comfortable room opposite the dining room.

Grandpa Wade and Uncle John had made a large white dollhouse for Mary Jane. It looked exactly like their new house here in

Christiansburg, with its large front porch and four white pillars. Rye whittled miniature furniture pieces and a family of four to fit inside the dollhouse. Aunt Cynthia stitched curtains for the windows and rugs for the floor. Now Mary Jane owned a dollhouse she could play with. She had always admired her mother's dollhouse, which now sat under a glass case on a small table in the library. Mary Jane was only allowed in the library with a grownup present to admire the dollhouse, with her hands clasped securely behind her back.

Next to the old dollhouse stood her mother's prized cupboard, full of books and games. Some books were very old, brought over from England by Mary Jane's great-grandmother, Marie. On the wall hung an expertly embroidered piece depicting an angel leaning against a willow tree, with a mill in the background. The mill in the embroidered piece looked exactly like her mother's dollhouse. Mary Jane's mother told her the angel in the picture was her mother's older sister, Lydia, who died in Maryland years ago.

Even at a young age, Mary Jane understood that she and her mother both had an older sister who died young. Regrettably, Mary Jane also had an older brother who died before she was born.

When Mary Jane finished opening her gifts, Grandpa Jacob made an announcement: "Let us all go outside," he said. "It is time to show my little granddaughter her birthday present from her papa and mama."

Jacob led everyone into the horse barn and Mary Jane caught the first glimpse of her gift: a small gray Welsh pony. It was love at first sight; Mary Jane ran to give the little horse a big hug. Jamie had acquired the pony from the Meijer family. Susan Meijer brought the pony from Frederick, but at nearly nineteen, she no longer rode him.

"I named my first horse Lightning," Christina told her daughter.

"It is a very nice name, Mama, but I plan to name my little horse Lamb."

Lamb was gentle with Mary Jane, but to her dismay, her parents forbade her from riding her new pony pending better weather and a warmer day.

Later that evening, while the men retired to the library, the ladies relaxed in the parlor to listen to Susan sing and play the O'Sullivan's newly purchased fortepiano. Jamie bought it in hopes that Mary Jane might someday learn to play and become as accomplished on the instrument as her mother.

Hearing Susan sing, Rye left the library and stood in the hallway to better listen; he was captivated by her voice.

As the Meijer family was leaving, Rye asked Susan if he could call on her the next Sunday.

"Rye, if you are going to see Susan this afternoon after church, could you please take this recipe to her mother, along with a jug of our maple syrup?" Christina asked her nephew.

Iced Gingerbread Cake

In a large mixing bowl, sift together two coffee cups of flour, two teaspoons of cinnamon, one teaspoon of ground ginger, one teaspoon of baking soda, and a pinch of salt.

In another bowl, cream together one cube of butter and one teacup of firmly packed brown sugar. Add two hen eggs, one at a time, and beat well. Finally, add one-half coffee cup of maple syrup and beat well to combine all ingredients.

Next, alternate between adding the flour mixture and a tumbler of milk to the butter, sugar, and eggs until all has been added. Pour the batter into a square pan that has been greased with lard and dusted all over with flour.

Bake in a moderate oven for three-quarters of an hour. Drizzle over the cooled cake a mixture of powdered sugar and water you have mixed until smooth. This recipe will make one cake cut into nine pieces.

Mary Jane's other grandparents had spent the previous three weeks visiting their sons, Liam and Finn, in Boston and were unable to attend Mary Jane's party held on her birthday.

Now home, they traveled to Christiansburg with Mary Jane's Aunt June, Uncle Roger, and Roger Jr., Mary Jane's three-year-old cousin, whom everyone called Chip. It would be a full house, so Jacob volunteered to return to his old cabin for the next few nights. With four bedrooms in the new house, there were enough beds for all the guests.

"You missed my party, Grandfather O'Sullivan," Mary Jane said.

Her grandfather placed five brightly wrapped gifts on the reception table in the foyer. "Yes, I know, but we are having another birthday party for you today," he told her. "Look at all the fine presents we brought you from Boston."

He turned to look at Jamie and Jacob. "I must say, you both did a fine job on this house."

"A difficult task at times, but we could not have accomplished it without your assistance," Jacob said.

"Yes, Father, we have so much to thank you for," Jamie added.

Cynthia and Christina were fixing a light supper when Mary Jane ran into the kitchen.

"Grandma and Grandpa O'Sullivan brought me five presents," she squealed. "I want to open my gifts."

"I think one of those five gifts is from your aunt and uncle," Christina told her daughter. "You must be patient; we have hungry guests to feed first. I made your favorite: pork pie."

"Well then, I will take Grandpa O'Sullivan to see Lamb."

"Put on your coat," Christina called out.

"Put on your coat, Grandpa!" Mary Jane shouted. "I want to take you outside to meet my Lambie Pie."

Once inside the horse barn, Mary Jane showed her grandfather her pony.

"I have ridden him a hundred times," Mary Jane fibbed. "Please put his saddle on and open the barn door. I will show you how well I can ride."

James did as his granddaughter requested. Riding Lamb out of the barn, Mary Jane trotted off toward the woods. Walking back from setting traps, Rye saw Mary Jane riding toward him. He quickly caught up to her and grabbed the reins.

"Didn't your father declare you couldn't ride this horse until warmer weather?" Rye asked. "I am sorry, sir, I did not know you were here with her," Rye said to James once he noticed him standing by the barn.

"Let's not tell her mother and father," James said guiltily.

Once everyone sat down to dinner, Mary Jane announced, "Grandpa O'Sullivan put the saddle on Lambie Pie, and I rode her to the edge of the woods all by myself, didn't I, Cousin Rye?"

"Mary Jane O'Sullivan," Christina said sternly, "you are in such big trouble."

"Don't blame our sweet little Mary Jane," James said sheepishly. "It was my fault."

Everyone enjoyed the luscious pork pie. Accompanying the pie was a hot apple crumble with diced apples, flour, sugar, and cinnamon. Christina combined flour, baking soda, salt, brown sugar, cinnamon, and butter for the topping. When she brought it to the table, it was bubbling hot, with the top a golden brown.

For dessert, Cynthia brought out a rich fruit cake and then passed a pot of warm buttered rum sauce to the adults so that they could drizzle it over their slice.

"I know you have asked for this recipe in the past," Cynthia said to June. "So I wrote it down for you."

Mild Fruit Cake

Bring to a boil a heaping coffee cup of sugar, the same of water, one tumbler of raisins, butter about the size of a walnut, two large finely grated carrots, one kitchen spoon of both ground cinnamon, ground nutmeg, and half that of ground cloves. Simmer for five minutes and then let stand overnight.

After the liquid has stood for at least twelve hours, add one tumbler of chopped walnuts, two and a half coffee cups of flour, a coffee spoon of salt, a coffee spoon of baking soda, and one of cream of tartar.

There is enough batter to make two loaves. Bake in a very slow oven for one hour. Serve with warm rum sauce.

Rum Sauce

Heat a cooking spoon of rum with the same amount of water along with a dollop of butter until nice and warm. Add one teacup of powdered sugar and mix. Pour into your prettiest coffee creamer so your guests can pour what they want.

After everyone settled in the parlor, Mary Jane began opening her gifts.

"This first gift is from your Aunt June, Uncle Roger, and Cousin Chip," Kiera said.

Inside the box was an expensive-looking doll. Her porcelain face was painted with rosy cheeks and big brown eyes. The doll's black hair curled up under a yellow bonnet trimmed in white lace that matched her yellow dress.

"I think I shall name this doll Sarah Jane, after my big sister," Mary Jane announced. "She will be my angel."

Next, Mary Jane started opening the four gifts from her grandparents. Peeking inside a small hat box, she pulled out a red velvet widebrimmed bonnet with a red ribbon. It was extravagantly trimmed with brown beaver fur. Tears came to Christina's eyes as memories of the bonnets her Aunt Margaret made came rushing back.

Mary Jane promptly put the bonnet on her head and skipped into the foyer to peer at herself in the large mirror. "Don't I look fancy!" she shouted from the hallway.

Next, she opened a box that contained a red velvet coat with an attached cape trimmed in brown beaver fur, which exactly matched her bonnet. A brown beaver fur muff was hidden in the bottom of the box under a mound of white tissue paper.

In the third box, Mary Jane found more tissue paper, a brown silk dress, white stockings, and white pantalettes with lace around the ankles. When Mary Jane opened the smallest package, she found a pair of brown kid leather shoes with ankle straps and the teeny-tiniest red bow on top.

"Now, with your new pair of shoes, you are all set to go on an adventure," Grandpa O'Sullivan told her.

"You had a wonderful birthday this year," Jamie said as he tucked his daughter into bed. "You received more gifts than any little girl I know."

"Yes, Papa," Mary Jane said sleepily. She whispered, "I love my pony and all my gifts, but my favorite gift is my dollhouse."

Once the children were settled in bed, the men retired to the library to sample the fine port James brought from Boston and discuss next year's crops and politics. They ended the night listening intently as Jacob and John told stories of the second war of America's independence from Britain.

The four ladies stayed in the parlor to play charades. Much laughing and commotion emerged from the parlor before Kiera and Cynthia were finally declared the winners.

"I don't know about you ladies," Kiera said. "It is well after midnight, and I am ready for bed."

"Where is Mary Jane going to wear those silly clothes?" Christina whispered once Jamie closed their bedroom door. "The dress will be ripped and torn not two minutes after she puts it on. And those shoes!"

"She could always wear them to church," Jamie suggested.

"And have our friends think we are somehow better? They think that now. Did you see the disappointment on my father's face? How will Mary Jane liken the gifts from your family to a homemade dollhouse?"

"Don't worry, Christina," Jamie said. "Just like you, Mary Jane can keep her dollhouse forever, while those clothes will be forgotten before she outgrows them."

"I wish your father didn't feel the need to flaunt his wealth. He was humble and kind before he inherited the money from his uncle. What happened to him?"

"I guess wealth can do that to some people. Let's not worry; you are getting all worked up over nothing. He loves Mary Jane and merely wants to give her the best. Did you see poor Chip in that ridiculous sailor suit?"

The next morning, Mary Jane came downstairs wearing one of her favorite daytime smocks, her new red bonnet and new leather shoes.

"Mary Jane, you look lovely, but you must take off your bonnet and put on your small lace cap before you can sit at the table and eat breakfast," Christina said.

"Look, Grandpa O'Sullivan! I am wearing my new shoes," Mary Jane called out. "Where are we going on our adventure today?"

"I've already asked your parents," James told Mary Jane. "You are coming to Dayton to stay with Grandma and me at our house for a few weeks, and in addition to your new shoes, you must bring all your pretty new clothes."

"Is there enough room in your carriage?" Christina asked.

"There is adequate room for Mary Jane, or she can sit on my lap," James replied.

The following day, James's postilion returned with the coach. He arrived in full-dress livery: a scarlet jacket with gold buttons, a decorated cap, a white shirt, white leather breeches, and leather boots with an iron leg guard. Jamie had heard the O'Sullivan's private carriage ran remarkably fast. His father likely paid an exorbitant price for the carriage and the two massive bay Morgan horses pulling it.

As the carriage pulled away, James called out, "We will be back before Christmas!"

Jamie could see the worry on Christina's face.

"Do not fret, my dear," Jamie said. "My father will let nothing happen to our little darling, and she can wear all her fancy new clothes in Dayton."

James delivered Mary Jane back to her parents a week before Christmas and three days before a major snowstorm. Snow fell all day and all night. When the family woke on Christmas Day, three feet of snow covered the ground, with much higher swirling drifts.

"I am pleased we had the foresight to gather some pine boughs to decorate the mantles before this snowstorm," Christina said.

"I am grateful we had the foresight to bring in a good supply of firewood and fresh water," Jamie teased.

"Open the door, Papa," Mary Jane declared as she peered out the front window. "Here comes Uncle John, Aunt Cynthia, and Cousin Rye."

Draped over John's arm was a large basket filled with Cynthia's homemade preserves and several jars of tomatoes and beans. Rye was carrying a fresh rabbit and two small squirrels, likely ones he found in his traps not buried by the snow. It appeared as if Cynthia had fallen into a significant drift, and they were all laughing heartily when Jamie finally opened the front door.

"Well, at least we won't starve," Jacob announced. "Merry Christmas, everyone."

January turned bitterly cold. Not until later that month did the snow finally start to melt. On an unseasonably warm day, Jacob walked with Mary Jane to Archer's Mercantile to buy Rye a gift for his birthday.

"I want to buy Cousin Rye a new hat," Mary Jane said. "What are you buying him, Grandpa?"

"I think Ryker needs a new knife and sheath. Let's sit down, and I'll teach you how to play checkers. Oh, and before we leave, remind me to buy you a peppermint stick."

On Sunday, 2 February 1840, Rye turned twenty. He would not be home for Sunday dinner, because he planned to spend his afternoon at the Meijer's home.

"Who is my teacher this fall, Miss Meijer or Mr. Vance?" Mary Jane asked her mother at breakfast.

"Miss Meijer teaches first and second grade."

"I don't like her," Mary Jane announced as she sat at the small table in the kitchen, eating her mush.

"Mary Jane!" Christina scolded.

"Cousin Rye likes her better than he likes me," Mary Jane whined. "When can I give him my gift?"

"You know your cousin loves you," Christina said. "He will be home for our late supper, and you can give him your gift then. How about I let you wear your new red coat to church today? Now, go upstairs and get dressed."

When Rye arrived home that evening, they sat down to a light meal of cornbread, frizzled beef, and stewed apples. For dessert, Cynthia saved her milk, butter, and eggs to make a luscious sugar pie, Rye's favorite.

"It's time for presents," Mary Jane announced. "You must open mine first; it's a hat."

In addition to the hat from Mary Jane, Rye received a knife and sheath from his grandfather, a Springfield Model 1835 flintlock musket from his parents, and a new capote blanket coat from Uncle Jamie and Aunt Christina.

"Thank you all for the wonderful gifts. Now I have a request," Rye said. "How does the family feel about me moving into Grandpa's cabin? I am more than willing to fix the roof."

"Son, have you come to a decision concerning you and Susan?" John asked.

"No sir, not yet anyway. She is only nineteen. Perhaps when she turns twenty next summer, I might ask her to marry me."

"No…no…no!" Mary Jane exclaimed. "You cannot marry Miss Meijer; she is my teacher."

Jacob and John sat on their porch one Sunday after dinner, making small talk.

"At sixty-seven, I would be more than happy to pay someone to help with the planting and harvest," Jacob said.

"I have spoken with Harry Vance," John told his father. "He is happy with the arrangement I proposed. Unfortunately, Richard

Foley is in poor health. I don't know how long Harry can continue if we hire someone, as he will still need our help harvesting his tobacco."

After the death of Harry's mother and stepfather, his sister, Sarah, and her husband moved to Indiana. Harry inherited the farm from his stepfather, Robert Foley, but couldn't farm it by himself. So he sold the farm, and he and his brother, Claude, moved in with their elderly step-uncle, Richard Foley.

Harry and John agreed that no money would change hands. They decided to help each other until John and Jacob could come up with a better idea. Jamie, busy with his building projects, had stopped farming years earlier.

As the men talked, they were unaware of Mary Jane as she sat on the porch playing with her dolls.

"Why don't you build houses like my papa instead of growing corn?" Mary Jane asked.

Jacob chuckled. "We may do just that one day."

The spring planting was successful. The summer was hot. The crops were stored in the barns, and the women busied themselves with canning their garden's abundant vegetables to be put away in the root cellar. Before long, it was time for Mary Jane to start her education.

School started on 7 September 1840. Mary Jane was so excited that she could barely eat her breakfast. Small for her age, Mary Jane was just shy of her sixth birthday.

"Your cousin needs to pick up supplies at the Merc this morning, so he has volunteered to walk you to school," Christina said. "Mama must stay here with baby Lizzy. Your McGuffey Reader, spelling book, slate, and lunch are packed in your tote and ready for you to take to school. Now, please eat your porridge."

"My tummy feels funny," Mary Jane complained. "The cat can eat my porridge this morning."

"No, the cat cannot eat your porridge."

Mary Jane sat at the table with her head in her hands. She wore her purple dress with white pinafore and pantalettes. Her father had polished her black boots the night before. They were so shiny that Mary Jane could almost see her reflection when she looked down.

"Davey Creager will be walking with you this morning," Christina told Mary Jane.

The Wade and Creager homes were so close that Davey and Mary Jane could stand on their front porch and wave to each other.

Davey's great-grandfather and great-grandmother had come with the wagon train from Maryland in 1810 and still lived on their original farm. Davey's grandparents bought the O'Sullivan farm almost fifteen years earlier, when James moved his family to Dayton. When Davey's grandparents moved to Columbus to live with their daughter, Nancy, young Davey's parents moved into the old O'Sullivan homestead.

Once the children reached school, they were allowed to play outside until Mr. Vance rang the bell. Several older boys played Annie Over by tossing a ball over the privy until Mr. Vance stopped them. One of the boys brought a hoop while some of the older girls played hopscotch.

Rye wanted to talk to Susan before he left for the Merc but felt a slight nod more suitable.

Miss Meijer assembled the first and second graders in small chairs in a circle off to the left of Mr. Vance's desk. They recited their numbers and letters. After lunch, they sat at their benches to listen to Mr. Vance give a lecture on Ohio history.

After recess, Miss Meijer played the piano while everyone sang. Mary Jane's favorite song was "Twinkle, Twinkle, Little Star." The younger children returned to the reading circle. Miss Meijer read a story titled *A Little Field Mouse Named Ted*. Mr. Vance schooled the older children on their arithmetic. Before Mary Jane knew it, her first day of school was over.

"Rye?" Mary Jane asked her cousin. "It's summer, and school is out. When are you asking Miss Meijer to marry you? No more lollygagging."

"You better not let your mother hear your language. Did Davey teach you that word?"

"That nincompoop?"

"Mary Jane!" Rye exclaimed.

"Well, he is," Mary Jane insisted.

"Why don't you come with me to check my traps? Go ask your mother. Also ask her to pack us a big lunch. Maybe I'll let you wade in the creek with Scout."

Rye had received Scout, a brindle mastiff, as a puppy from his father the previous Christmas. At a mere six months old, he was already a large, powerful dog, but also a gentle giant. Rye kept Scout in his cabin, and Mary Jane visited almost daily. Rye trained Scout to be well-disciplined. Friendly to everyone, Scout loved playing with the children who came to play with Mary Jane and Lizzy, but he proved very protective of his family when strangers came around.

As Rye and Mary Jane crossed the creek and entered the deepest part of the woods, Scout gave a low growl. Rye spotted a small black bear with her cub just across their path.

"Mary Jane," Rye said in a hushed voice. "We need to turn around and walk slowly back up the path toward home."

Suddenly, the bear started to advance. Scout ran toward the bear; it looked like a fight might occur. However, once the bear saw the massive dog charge, she turned and ran with her cub on her heels.

"Scout!" Rye shouted. "Come here, boy."

Scout obeyed, and the three headed quickly back to the house.

"Silly old bear," Mary Jane said. "She ruined our adventure, and I dropped our lunch. Just wait until I tell Davey how brave my Scout Boy is."

On a warm summer's eve, Rye returned to the house after visiting Susan. "I asked Mr. Meijer if I could marry his daughter," Rye told the family over dinner. "He said she is too young and to wait a few years. I'm thinking of taking a hunting trip. I will be gone for a few weeks; I need to clear my head."

True to his word, Rye left for several weeks, returning a week before harvest. It was then that his father and mother told him their news.

"We are leaving in the spring for Oregon Country, near the Bitterroot River Valley," John told him. "Grandfather Daniel is part of a Jesuit missionary expedition to build a chapel for the Salish Indians and cabins for the missionaries. He has asked us to travel with him. An established mission is nearby, so we will live with other missionary folks. If you decide not to come, we understand. We should be back in a few years."

Later, John and Cynthia went to the main house to discuss their decision with Jacob, Jamie, and Christina.

"We will travel with Brother Daniel. Once the mission is established, we will return home," John said. "We'll be gone two years—three at the most. In the meantime, you may need someone to help with the farm; they could live in our cabin until we return."

"It sounds like your mind is made up," Jacob replied. "How are you traveling?"

"We will take a steamboat down the Ohio River and then up the Mississippi to St. Louis. Then we will pick up the trail west, traveling by wagon train with forty other wagons. We hear the trail is relatively flat until we enter the mountains out West. We will travel with a brigade from the American Fur Company, so we should be safe. The plan is to leave Christiansburg by mid-April."

"Is Rye going?" Jacob asked.

"Only if Susan will come with him."

Before bed, Jamie and Christina discussed John's announcement.

"It sounds like a boondoggle to me," Christina cried. "I know John and Rye too well, and they won't return. I pity poor Cynthia."

"They promised to come back," Jamie assured her. "They'll be back before you know it."

On 2 April 1842, John turned fifty-two. The family awaited Rye's return from Susan's house before celebrating John's birthday.

"I gave him mother's posey ring," Jacob said. "The one my father gave to my mother when he asked her to marry him back in 1766. I hope Susan says yes."

When Rye walked in the door, his downcast face told everyone the news was not good.

"She said no," Rye sighed. "Her father will not allow her to marry a man who is not Lutheran, especially if he is leaving to go out West. Here's the ring back, Grandfather."

Jacob and John hired Henry Ames to help with the planting and the harvest. Henry and his family had recently moved to Christiansburg from Philadelphia. He had been staying with his brother, who owned a nearby farm.

Henry, his wife Sharon, and their six-year-old daughter, Sissy, would live in John's cabin until John and Cynthia returned. Henry's fifteen-year-old son, Tom, would live in Rye's cabin. Henry assured Jacob he and Tom could easily farm their two-hundred-acre field. Sharon offered to help Christina in the main house with gardening, canning, cooking, and cleaning.

"Mama!" Mary Jane cried. "I will miss my family so much. I don't want them to go. Miss Meijer showed me on the map where they are going, and it is far."

"Just think about how much fun you can have with your new little friend, Sissy. And how lucky you are that Rye has given you Scout to look after."

Unable to take Scout, Rye asked young Tom to look after his dog.

"Scout is my cousin Mary Jane's dog, but he must stay with you in your cabin as he is not allowed in the main house, and he's used to living here," Rye explained to Tom.

On 9 April 1842, Jacob offered to drive Brother Daniel, John, Cynthia, and Rye to Cincinnati to meet the steamboat bound for St. Louis. Before leaving Christiansburg, dozens of townsfolk came out to wish them farewell. Susan was not among the well-wishers.

"Are you sure you don't want to come with us, Grandfather?" Rye teased.

"I survived one wagon train; I think I'm good for a lifetime," Jacob responded.

"Are you sure, Captain Wade?" John continued the teasing.

"I'm sure."

"John, wait! I almost forgot—I have something to give you!" Jacob called. Jacob ran back into the house and came out a few minutes later. "I want you to have your grandfather's pocket watch. It has a miniature of your grandmother inside. Perhaps someday you can pass it on to Ryker."

"I will treasure it forever."

Once the farewells had been said, the O'Sullivan family walked silently into the house and closed the door.

EMMETT RYKER "RYE" WADE
1842 – 1846

*"We certainly do not forget you as soon as you forget us.
It is, perhaps, our fate rather than our merit."*

Jane Austen, *Persuasion*

"I was a young man, just seventeen, or maybe eighteen, when I spent a season trapping beaver with a man named Owen," John said. "It was up north, near Detroit, before Michigan was a state."

John stood on the deck of the *Empress Mary*, the steamboat taking them to St. Louis, reminiscing with his son, Rye. Rye had heard these stories a dozen times before but always listened intently out of respect for his father.

"It's how I learned to trap and knew what was needed to teach you. Owen said he would take me out West the next year but reneged. Now here we are, traveling toward Oregon country, as I wanted to do thirty years ago."

"I'm surprised St. Joseph's Catholic Church in Dayton controls enough funds to send eighty missionaries out West," Rye said. "Forty wagons, each pulled by two oxen, must cost a small fortune. I am glad they have allowed us two wagons. It should make the next five months more comfortable, especially for Mother. I heard the plan is to move a great load of farm implements and supplies."

John laughed. "The last time I drove a team of oxen was way back in '09 when I first traveled to Ohio with father and grandfather. Occasionally, I held the reins of the Foley's Conestoga wagon. The wagons we are taking look very different from a Conestoga. I think the Conestoga is a work of art compared with these old farm wagons."

"Yes, but you can't ride in a Conestoga," Rye said. "The men I talked with this morning said you could stand upright along the center line in the wagon we'll take out West."

"I heard the dinner gong. We should go and meet your mother and grandfather; they are probably already in the dining room."

They spent eight nights on the *Empress Mary*, traveling first down the Ohio and then up the Mississippi. On the ninth day, they arrived in St. Louis.

"We'll be spending three nights here in St. Louis," Brother Daniel said. "How extremely lucky to secure these four tickets on the next weekly mail stagecoach. Prepare yourselves for two long days on the road before we pick up the wagon train in Independence."

By the time the travelers arrived in Independence, they had endured the most uncomfortable ride, traveling on the stagecoach day and night for almost forty hours. They'd stopped at way stations five times to change horses or drivers, quickly scoffing down a lousy meal and a cup of extremely strong coffee, with no time to rest.

The church arranged for the group to stay with local families until they were ready to start their journey. As soon as they were settled in with their host family, Rye procured paper and ink to write to his family in Ohio.

Sunday, 24 April 1842

Mr. Jacob Wade
The Wade Homestead
Christiansburg Highway
Christiansburg, Ohio

Dearest Family,

We arrived here in Independence, Missouri, a few days ago. We have been actively preparing our two wagons for the trip west. Today, Grandfather Daniel, Mother, and Father went to Mass, while I stayed back for some quiet time to write you this letter.

The trip on the steamboat was quite restful. Once we reached St. Louis, we boarded a stagecoach to Independence. The stagecoach traveled over very rough terrain, so it made for a hot and dusty trip. It was a long two-day journey. We only stopped to eat and to change horses or drivers.

The wagons are just farm wagons. Father and I built a false floor in each of our two wagons for storing reserve supplies, giving us more living space. Six bows of bent hickory go up the wagons' sides, covered by a heavy twill fabric we waterproofed by painting it with linseed oil. The covering is very efficient, with flaps on the front and a drawstring at the back. You can completely close it or open it for airflow. I'm sure it turns pretty hot when you reach the open prairie. One man told me you should take the top entirely down if you head into a robust, westerly wind. Our biggest concern is a snapped tongue or broken axletree. These wagons aren't as heavy as the Conestoga, and about half the size, so there is less stress on the oxen. Some call them prairie schooners because they look like sailing ships.

If all goes as planned, we, and the eighty missionaries, hope to depart on 2 May. Not only are we taking forty wagons, each pulled by two oxen, but also transporting over two hundred head of oxen and cattle. I heard a rumor of a much larger wagon train headed out after us from Elm Grove, primarily farmers and pioneers headed to Willamette Falls. We've met our five guides, fur traders employed by the American Fur Company. They leave us at Fort Hall, where a Salish man from the Flathead Tribe will guide us north to the Bitterroot Valley and St. Mary's Mission.

When we stop at a trading post or military fort that sends mail going east, I'll send another letter. We should hopefully arrive at St. Mary's Mission sometime in September or October before moving to the building site for the St. Joseph's Mission's chapel and village next spring.

Until we meet again,
Rye

On the first day out, the wagon train headed north toward the Platte River. A week later, they started their journey westward.

The plains seemed to go on forever. The terrain looked like nothing back in southwestern Ohio. Their guides advised the missionaries they would continue following the Platte River, heading toward a place they called Chimney Rock.

Once they passed Chimney Rock, the river split into north and south forks. They headed along the northern fork. Weeks later, they reached a trading post at the confluence of the Laramie and North Platt Rivers, named Fort John. There, they restocked their supply of bacon, beans, rice, coffee, and other necessities, as their next stop was weeks away.

When the fur traders learned John had served as a scout in Maryland during the Second War of Independence from Britain, they spent their evenings around the Wade's campfire exchanging stories.

The men were equally impressed when John talked of spending a season in Michigan trapping beaver. Even Rye told some of his trapping stories from Ohio and about the black bears he'd encountered. The trappers laughed and told Rye about the size of the grizzles who roamed out west.

"We're hoping to reach Independence Rock by 4 July," a Scottish fur trader named Hamish told the men. "It's a huge round granite rock where emigrants and missionaries heading west stop to carve their names."

True to Hamish's word, the wagon train stopped to camp overnight at the foot of Independence Rock on 4 July. Everyone carved their names and observed dozens of other names etched into the rock by previous travelers.

When they reached the Sweetwater River, there had been no breakdowns, and only a few travelers had become ill. They were careful to boil their drinking water, as they heard stories of several cholera cases among earlier emigrants.

"There is plenty of water and grass along the Sweetwater, but we must make nine passes across the river before we reach the South Pass through the Rockies," Hamish told Rye. "When we reach the South Pass, we should be halfway between the Mississippi and the Pacific."

Each pass across the Sweetwater River brought Cynthia to tears and much handwringing. At the South Pass, they entered a broad, nearly flat sagebrush prairie between two mountain ranges.

"We're headed to the Green River area, where we'll rendezvous with other mountain men and fur trappers," Hamish said. "From there, we go a short way south to a trading post to replenish our supplies. Then we'll start our final push northwest to Fort Hall, where you'll pick up your Salish guide, while we trappers drive west to the Columbia River Valley."

At Fort Hall, Rye found a man headed back East who agreed to take a letter and mail it from St. Louis. So Rye sat down to try to commit to paper their experiences over the past several months.

Saturday, 3 September 1842

Mr. Jacob Wade
The Wade Homestead
Christiansburg Highway
Christiansburg, Ohio

Dearest Family,

We made it to Fort Hall with few difficulties. One wagon broke an axletree when it dropped down to cross a small creek. We used the timber from a large nearby oak to make a new one. One man fell into one of the many rivers we crossed, but we pulled him out before he drowned. Fortunately, we traveled the whole distance without one broken wheel.

I can't begin to explain the majestic beauty of the West—from the plains and prairies of Nebraska country to the snowcapped mountains we see in the distance. We visited places called Chimney Rock and Independence Rock. We arrived at Independence Rock on 4 July, and we each carved our names and the date, as fellow emigrants had done before us.

At our ninth and final crossing of the Sweetwater River, we came to a small trading post where we purchased four large buffalo robes, as it has turned quite cold. A few snowflakes fell last night, but nothing we're not used to in Ohio.

The weather is cool and pleasant, with a dusting of snow all along the ravines bordering the crystal clear river, with an abundance of good grass for the oxen and cattle.

Mother tolerated all the trials with great fortitude. She had some apprehensions whenever we crossed a deep, rapid river. But she's never looked so healthy, with her rosy cheeks and clear blue eyes.

The fur traders are excellent guides. One in particular, a Scotsman named Hamish, continues to help us. They spend most evenings with us around our campfire while Father tells of his adventures trapping in Michigan. We make sure Grandfather Daniel and Mother have gone to bed and are fast asleep before the traders bring out their brandy keg.

We are told our Salish guide from the Flathead Tribe is already here, but we have not met him yet. He will take us the rest of the way to the Bitterroot Valley. It could be another month before we reach St. Mary's Mission. Our only worry is a possible raid from members of the Blackfoot Nation, as they and the Salish are cruel enemies.

If you want to write to us, give it to a parish member of St. Joseph's in Dayton. There might be more missionaries coming to Bitterroot soon. Grandfather, Mother, and Father all send their greetings, and we all pray our Ohio family is well.

Much love,
Rye

The missionaries' guide had reached Fort Hall two weeks earlier. To everyone's surprise, it was a young girl, probably no more than fourteen or fifteen years old.

"I'm not following a child into the wilderness," Rye told his father. "We may as well have brought Mary Jane."

"I am well acquainted with Matika and her extensive knowledge of the Bitterroot Valley," Hamish said. "Her father is Chief Shweabe; you need to be respectful of his only daughter."

Matika stood, at most, five feet tall. A small girl, she had dark skin and large dark brown eyes. Her black hair was plaited into two braids that hung past her waist and were wrapped in otter fur.

Rye had never seen such an exotic young girl. She wore a long woven dress, belted at the waist. On her feet were soft leather moccasins, perhaps deerskin. A colorful woven blanket was tossed around her shoulders. She had a feather stuck down into her belt and wore a loop necklace of colorful beads.

Matika called out to Rye, "Yellow Hair, where is the 'blackrobe' who leads your wagon train?"

Rye was surprised that, one, Matika spoke perfect English, and two, she was talking to him.

"My n–n–name is Emmett Ryker Wade," Rye said. "I will t–t–take you to Brother Daniel."

Why he stuttered and why he used his full name, he couldn't reasonably determine, but at that exact moment, he felt somewhat taken aback. He had never felt so intimidated by someone so young, and a girl at that. Rye appeared besotted.

The trip north along the Bitterroot River started out cold and rainy. The wagon covers did their job of keeping the missionaries and their supplies dry.

Matika changed into a deerskin dress decorated with porcupine quills. She wore a buffalo cloak to stay dry. Upon her head, she wore a small basket hat. She rode a small white pony with a long, fringed blanket thrown over it. She led a pack horse with her provisions and sleeping gear. Rye felt sorry for her, but she appeared to tolerate the weather better than those riding in semi-comfort.

That evening, Cynthia spoke to Matika about riding in her wagon.

"I so wish you would ride with my husband and me. It is so cold and rainy."

"I could not do the job given to me if I sat high in your wagon," Matika told Cynthia.

"Well, at least come to sleep in our wagon," Cynthia said. "My husband can sleep with my son."

"No, you should sleep with your husband," Matika replied. "I am comfortable sleeping under the trees with my woven blankets and buffalo hide shelter."

Fortunately, the rain lasted only two days. The morning of the third day, the bright sun quickly burned off the fog. The trip's final days were like typical autumn days in Ohio.

On Sunday, 24 September 1842, the travelers and missionaries from Ohio arrived at St. Mary's Mission. Father Nevels, several hundred Salish tribe members, and perhaps a dozen or so white men greeted the wagon train. Father Nevels explained that most former missionaries had gone south after building the chapel.

Because the Salish were nomadic, the Jesuit priests felt the best way to help them become part of a permanent village was to teach them farming. That explained why the wagon train was carrying so many farm implements and seeds for planting crops, as well as bringing two hundred oxen and cattle that followed behind the wagon train.

"As we planned, you shall be staying with us over the winter," Father Nevels told the group as they gathered in the chapel. "Once spring arrives, your assistance is needed to teach the Salish how to plant their crops. Finally, you'll travel north to build the new St. Joseph's chapel. I've assigned you newest arrivals the homes the last missionaries left vacant."

Their new home would be a traditional longhouse made from timber with a bark exterior. Two related families would share one house. Much to Cynthia's shock, there was an open hearth with a smoke hole in the roof.

"I didn't expect to see an open fire in the center of a single room," she complained. "I've cooked on an open fireplace, but this is primitive, with no separate rooms, just blankets hung over poles. I'm not sure I can stay two to three years if this is how we will live."

"Daughter!" her father scolded. "Remember your mission is for the glory of God."

"Cynthia, I promise to give you a proper home when we move on to St. Joseph's," John reassured her.

The days passed quickly. Winter soon arrived, and the air turned bitter cold. Because of Cynthia's kindness to Matika during the trip, the young girl brought fresh water almost daily and even helped Cynthia with the cooking and other daily chores.

One day, she brought the family three large trout and some blueberries she had picked and dried the previous season.

"Oh, Matika!" Cynthia exclaimed.

"I told my father about your kindness during our journey," Matika said. "He is allowing me to return your goodwill however I want."

"May I go with you the next time you go fishing?" Rye asked.

"Meet me in front of your lodge tomorrow before first light."

By early spring, Matika and Rye had become inseparable. She showed him the best places to hunt deer and elk. They fished for trout and foraged for berries, nuts, and honey.

Easter Sunday fell on 16 April 1843. As the family prepared to attend that morning's church services, Rye approached his father. "I'm in love with Matika," he said. "I want to marry her. Do you think I should ask Chief Shweabe this morning at Mass?"

"Let's ask Father Nevels what he thinks before you do something that is not their custom and perhaps embarrass Matika in the process," John said.

The next day, Rye and John approached Father Nevels for his advice.

"If Matika is willing, all they require is for you to state your intentions, then you must share your obligations and some gifts between the families, and they consider you married," Father Nevels said. "However, I feel strongly that we should also perform a traditional Catholic wedding ceremony here in the chapel. You understand this would be considered an intercultural union. You become as much a part of her clan as she becomes a part of yours."

Friday, 5 May 1843

Mr. Jacob Wade
The Wade Homestead
Christiansburg Highway
Christiansburg, Ohio

Dearest Family,

Today, I married Matika, a Salish maiden of the Flathead Tribe. She is exquisite, with long black hair and dark brown eyes. She is a small girl but capable of hunting and fishing in the wilderness, even on her own. Last year, she acted as our guide from Fort Hall to St. Mary's Mission. She is also the daughter of Chief Shweabe. We first exchanged gifts at her father's lodge, and then Father Nevels blessed our union with a brief ceremony at the chapel.

Mother gave me her gold wedding band to give Matika, with Father's approval. Matika made me a shirt she embellished with porcupine quills and shells. Chief Shweabe gave me a bow carved from cedar with rawhide string. The quiver is deer hide, and he attached turkey feathers to the shaft of twelve arrows. Some of the arrows he sharpened at the end, while some hold arrowheads made of flint. I hope you don't mind, Grandfather, but I gave Chief Shweabe the knife and sheath you gave me on my twentieth birthday. It is one of the most precious things I have ever owned, and her father's gift to me was so generous.

We finished the planting here at St. Mary's. Next week, we travel to the site where we plan to build the St. Joseph's Mission's chapel and village, where Father promised to build Mother a proper cabin. The longhouse we currently live in is very primitive.

Aunt Christina, we received your letter. It was so good to hear news from home. I was surprised to hear Susan Meijer and her family moved back to Maryland.

I hope to bring Matika home to meet you very soon. Please write again.

My love and affection to you all,
Rye

It had been two years since the Wades left Ohio with Brother Daniel and the other missionaries. They were close to completing the building of the mission at St. Joseph's. With Rye's help, John built Cynthia a small cabin with a proper stone fireplace. It was just big enough for the five of them, about the same size as their house back in Ohio. Cynthia seemed more content yet talked of returning to Ohio almost every day.

"What a pleasant spring we are having this year," Cynthia said. "Spring is the best time of year to bring a baby into the world. My babies were born during one of those cold February blizzards we occasionally have in Ohio."

Friday, 7 June 1844

Mr. Jacob Wade
The Wade Homestead
Christiansburg Highway
Christiansburg, Ohio

Dear Family,

I am so sorry it has taken over a year to send you another letter. We finally found a man headed back East who agreed to take our letters and post them when he reaches Chicago. You'll find three letters in this packet—one from each of us: me, Father, and Mother.

Four days ago, my beloved Matika gave birth to our first child. A healthy boy we named Jacob Emmett. Mother thinks he is small, but he arrived with a healthy cry and a full head of black hair. I love this baby and told Matika I hope we create a dozen more.

It is hard to believe my little Mary Jane turns ten on her next birthday. I hope you still plan to hold the family's annual festival. Next month the Salish have their 'Month of Celebration' to gather and trade goods. But they also conduct dance competitions, songs, games, and drumming. The drums can be heard miles away.

Last night, Father and Mother discussed when they might want to return to Ohio. I'll leave that for them to tell you. It probably won't be for at least another year. The missionaries want all the tribe members baptized and inoculated against smallpox before we leave. I'm not sure if Grandfather Daniel will return. He feels this has been his true calling. If he stays, what will Mother want to do? She is devoted to her father. I may return for a visit, but I love it here, and I believe Father does too; I only wish it was an easier journey. If they ever bring the railroad out this way, you should come and see this magnificent country for yourselves.

I'm taking Mother to the edge of our broad meadow today to pick blueberries. The blackberries should be ready in a few more weeks. Father and I fished an abundance of trout this spring. I was fortunate to land a large pike and a freshwater eel from a deeper part of the river. In addition to what we forage, we planted corn and various root vegetables. Last winter, Father appeared quite proud of himself for taking down a large elk with his bow and arrow. I've been able to hunt and obtain more duck and pheasant than we can eat, so we trade with others for different things, like herbs and foodstuffs.

Well, all this food talk is making me hungry. I miss your spice cake, Aunt Christina. I remember how Grandmother Marie and Aunt Margaret stored their spices in the old cupboard, which now sits in your library room. The few things we don't have here is an abundance of flour, sugar, nutmeg, cloves, or cinnamon. If we did, I'm sure Mother would make one for us.

Always and forever,
Rye

The winter of 1844 stayed bitterly cold. Over the long months, three deaths occurred among the tribe members. An elderly woman was the first person buried in the graveyard next to St. Joseph's chapel. Two men went missing after leaving on a hunting mission; the tribe believed they had perished. A party of Salish men ventured out to look for their bodies, but their search was unsuccessful.

The spring and summer found everyone busy planting, fishing, hunting, and preserving food in preparation for the possibility of another cold, snowy winter. Their fears came to fruition. The winter of 1845 was as bad, if not worse, than the year before. It started snowing in mid-October. By November, several feet of snow covered the ground with no hint of a thaw until late the next spring. On 5 November 1845, everyone in the Wade cabin came down with a severe case of the grippe. Brother Daniel and Cynthia were the sickest. It was several weeks before they each began feeling better, except for Cynthia.

Saturday, 6 December 1845

Mr. Jacob Wade
The Wade Homestead
Christiansburg Highway
Christiansburg, Ohio

Dearest Family,

It is with profound sorrow that I must inform you of the death of my dear, sweet mother. After contracting the grippe several weeks ago, she died early this morning. We tried everything to help quiet her cough and cool her fever. The Salish brought us herbs to burn, known for helping with breathing trouble. Nothing succeeded. Mother turned 49 in July and looked forward to helping us raise our Jacob.

Matika and her sister washed Mother and wrapped her in bright blankets. Father and Grandfather remain inconsolable. We cannot break through the frozen ground to bury her body. Several Salish men suggested we place her body high in an Alder, but Father would not consider it.

This letter is short, as there is no good news today. I hear Father outside working with a pickax and a shovel, attempting to dig Mother's grave. I must go now to help him. I plan to mail this letter as soon as possible, even if I must take it to Fort Hall myself.

My love to you all,
Rye

With the death of his daughter, Brother Daniel made the difficult decision to leave St. Joseph's Mission. He and a small group of missionaries wanted to help set up a new mission for the Shoshone-Bannock Tribe south of the Bitterroot Valley near the Snake River. Brother Daniel asked John to escort them as far as Fort Hall.

"When the new mission is built, I'll be back," Grandfather Daniel told Rye.

"Honestly, Grandfather," Rye said, "we may not be here much longer. We did not come here as missionaries, so our work is done. We might soon go back to Ohio."

"Once you decide to leave, please let someone here or at St. Mary's know where you are headed," Grandfather Daniel instructed Rye.

"I'll take your letter to Fort Hall," John told Rye. "I will be back before Matika delivers her baby."

On 24 July 1846, John, a handful of Salish men, and a small group of missionaries prepared to leave on a three-week trek.

The travelers made good time, and when they reached Fort Hall, John bid farewell to Brother Daniel. Each assured the other they would meet again, then John entered the trading post to barter for some much-needed supplies for the mission.

"You are John Wade from St. Joseph's Mission, are you not?" the owner of the trading post, Mr. Stanley, asked John.

"Yes, I'm John Wade."

"I must warn you—I've heard rumors the Blackfeet may be preparing a raid on your mission," Mr. Stanley said. "If you are interested, a man who lives west of here wishes to sell his farm and move farther west. You may be able to buy it from him for cheap. Oh, and here is a letter for you. It arrived last week."

The letter was from Christina; John opened it immediately.

Friday, 6 March 1846

Mr. John Wade
St. Joseph's Mission
c/o Fort Hall
Oregon Country

Dear John, Cynthia, Rye, and Brother Daniel,

I don't know when this letter will reach you—or if it ever will. I wanted to send letters in the past but have had little success finding a parish member heading out West. Today, I had the good fortune to find a group traveling to where you currently live.

John, I have unfortunate news concerning our dear father, Jacob. He passed away this morning. He fell ill Friday last and could not move or speak. Dr. Smith said the condition is called apoplexy, and he did not expect him to recover, given his age of 75 years. I do not think he suffered. Jamie and I were with him when he passed. He will be buried next to our dear mother and his loving wife, Sarah.

And now for some happy news. On 1 June 1844, I gave birth to George Edward O'Sullivan II, named after Jamie's Granduncle George. He is a dear boy whom we call Georgie.

More good news! On 24 May 1845, they established a school in honor of Uncle Philip Crane. It was built a few miles outside of Dayton, and they named it Crane Academy. Uncle Philip and Aunt Margaret would be so proud.

We hear from you so seldom, and we worry day and night. Your last letter arrived almost two years ago. Please write to let us know everyone is healthy and happy and that you will be coming home soon.

Much love to you all,
Christina, Jamie, Mary Jane, Lizzie, and Little Georgie

John was saddened to learn of his father's death and that the family had not yet received Rye's letter telling them of Cynthia's passing. But the good news was well received, and John couldn't wait to return to tell Rye about his new cousin, George, and the school named in Uncle Philip's honor.

Mr. Stanley had given John directions to the Wilson homestead. Seeing the beauty of the property, he was excited about the possibility of owning this Oregon Country treasure.

"For the last four years, my son and I helped open a mission in the Bitterroot Valley for the Salish tribe," he told Mr. Wilson—a young man who looked to be close to Rye's age. "The St. Joseph's Catholic Church in Dayton, Ohio, sponsored the trip, and the American Board of Commissioners for Foreign Missions was the investor. For our services, we received a handsome payout. We are more than capable of paying your very fair asking price. I'm headed back to Bitterroot to pick up my son and his wife and child. Their second child is due next month, so we may not return until later this fall, but definitely, before winter arrives."

After signing an agreement to purchase the land, John returned to Fort Hall, where Mr. Stanley summoned him again. "There's a young Shoshone girl who asked if she could go back with you to Bitterroot; the Lemhi Shoshone and the Bitterroot Flathead tribes are friendly," he said. "Her name is Dyani, and she knows Matika."

John learned from Mr. Stanley that Dyani had lost her entire family in a recent Blackfeet raid on her village.

When John and Dyani returned to St. Joseph's Mission, John told Rye about the agreement to purchase the farm near the Snake River. "I have seen it with my own eyes," John told him. "It is 200 acres of flat farmland a few hundred miles southwest of here. The house is a large white two-story farmhouse with several barns and outbuildings. Mr. Wilson promised to plant a crop of winter wheat, which should be ready for us to harvest in the spring. We shall be very happy there; with no threat from the Blackfeet."

John relayed the warning to Chief Shweabe that the Blackfeet planned to mount a raid.

"We Salish have been unhappy here for a long time," Chief Shweabe said. "We plan to abandon the missions and return to moving freely across the land. As soon as you leave, we will burn the missions, as is our practice."

John was not surprised when he heard the Chief's revelation.

Rye and Matika's second son, John Christian Wade II, was born on 14 August 1846. As soon as Matika was able they made ready for their journey. It was a tearful goodbye, but she knew she would see her father again. Before they left, John, with the help of several Salish men, placed a large stone at Cynthia's grave. John then chiseled on the rock, 'C. Wade 1796 –1845'.

"May we take Dyani with us?" Matika asked John. "She has no family."

"Yes, we will bring your friend to our homestead."

"When we reach our farm, we must send Christina and Jamie a letter letting them know we won't be returning to Ohio," Rye told his father.

SALLY ANN O'MALLEY
1850 – 1862

*"To you I shall say, as I have often said before,
Do not be in a hurry, the right man will come at last…"*

Jane Austen, *Jane Austen's Letters*

"Hurry up, Georgie," Christina called upstairs to her young son. "Your father is pulling the carriage up to the front porch. If you don't come down right now, we'll be late for Sally's birthday party."

It was July 4, 1850, and the O'Sullivans were invited to Sally O'Malley's fifth birthday party. Sally lived with her parents in Dayton, and from her very first birthday, the O'Sullivan family had always been invited to help Sally celebrate, along with America's birthday. In return, the O'Malley family came to Christiansburg for the annual harvest festival.

Simon and Ann O'Malley had been friends with Jamie and Christina O'Sullivan for over twenty years. They were neighbors when Jamie and Christina lived in Dayton and when Simon and Ann lost their son, John, to cholera. Days after John's death, Jamie and Christina lost their children, Sarah Jane and Little Jamie, to the same dreaded disease.

After their son John's death, a daughter was born to Simon and Ann, whom they named Virginia. Six years later, Sally was born.

After Sarah Jane and Little Jamie's deaths, Christina gave birth to four more children. Mary Jane was now fifteen, Lizzy was eleven, Georgie's sixth birthday had been the previous month, and Charlie turned one in April.

"I don't like going to the O'Malley's house," Georgie told his mother. "Sally is so quiet; she's no fun at all. The girls play with their dolls, and I'm left alone with nothing to do."

"There will be cake, punch, and games, and then we'll all go down by the river to watch the fireworks," Christina said. "We'll have lots of fun. Don't you like spending the night at Grandfather and Grandmother O'Sullivan's house?"

If you stood Sally and Georgie next to one another, you would think they were twins. Although Georgie was a few inches taller, they had the same reddish hair, tons of freckles, and light blue eyes.

"Hello, Georgie," Sally called out as the O'Sullivan's carriage pulled up. "Do you want to play jump rope with us?"

Sally, her sister, Ginny, and several friends stood on the sidewalk in front of the O'Malley's house.

"No thanks, I'd rather die."

"George Edward O'Sullivan!" his mother exclaimed. "If you don't behave, I'll send you to your grandfather's right now, and you will miss the birthday cake Mrs. O'Malley has baked."

"Come on, Georgie," his sister Mary Jane said. "We brought chalk. I'll draw a hopscotch design, and we all can play."

Sally was dressed in a bright yellow frock with a ruffled yoke. The dress appeared to set her long red curls, which her mother had tied with white ribbons, ablaze. She wore what looked like a brand-new pair of white boots. Sally's father, Simon, worked as the head salesman at a large dry goods store in downtown Dayton. Sally's mother, Ann, an excellent seamstress, sewed for many of Dayton's well-to-do women. She always dressed both her daughters like little princesses.

"Be careful," Sally's mother called out. "Don't let your new shoes get dirty."

It had become evident to everyone that Sally's mother remained overly protective of her daughters. They were not allowed to run or play too hard, and Ann called the doctor at the first sign of a sniffle.

"It is so good to see the O'Sullivan family back in town," Ann said as the two ladies sat in the parlor. "Have you heard from John or Rye lately, Christina?"

"Why yes," Christina replied. "They are still in Oregon Territory. In his last letter, John said he married Dyani last June. She is the Shoshone woman I told you about."

"The young girl who lived with them when they moved to the wheat farm four years ago?" Ann asked.

"From what Rye wrote me, she is nearly twenty-eight years younger than John," Christina whispered. "All Georgie talks about is going to visit his Uncle John. Yet he's never even met his Uncle John!"

"They announced at Mass last Sunday that Brother Daniel passed," Ann declared.

"I must send condolences to Rye on the passing of his grandfather," Christina said. "He lived with John and Rye for the past few years. He must have been close to eighty."

After Sally opened her gifts and Ann served cake, the families walked to Main Street to watch the parade. Later, they gathered at the riverbank to view Dayton's impressive fireworks display.

"Here, Georgie," Sally said. "Sit with me on my blanket."

"I'm sitting with my grandfather," Georgie replied. "Maybe my sisters will sit with you."

Sally started to cry and, once again, Georgie was in trouble with his mother.

"Georgie!" Christina exclaimed. "She asked you nicely, and you made her cry, and on her birthday. You both can sit with Grandfather O'Sullivan."

"Oh! Goodie!" Sally exclaimed.

"For heaven's sake," Georgie mumbled, ensuring his mother couldn't hear him.

In September of the following year, Emmanuel Catholic Church started teaching grades one through eight in its basement Sunday school classrooms. The new Emmanuel Parochial School was still under construction on West Second Street and wouldn't be completed until the next year. Emmanuel brought four Sisters of Notre Dame from Cincinnati to teach the forty-five enrolled students.

"You know we will need to pay tuition to send Ginny and Sally to this new school," Simon told his wife.

"I'll use my dressmaking money to pay for it," Ann said firmly. "I want my daughters to receive the very best education."

"What is it about little girls?" Sister Margaret muttered under her breath. She taught the first three grades at the new school. Stern but kind, Sister Margaret never used a ruler on students' knuckles or sat anyone in the corner as punishment. Twelve children squeezed into her tiny classroom. It was tight, but the three boys and nine girls were small.

The boys were always well-behaved. Surprisingly, the nine little girls gave her the most trouble. Their constant talking and laughing became quite disruptive. Almost every day, she needed to scold at least one or send someone to Sister Jean's office, except for one girl, Sally Ann O'Malley.

Sister Margaret noticed Sally had several close friends and appeared to play well with the others at recess, but she was quiet and shy in the classroom. She never raised her hand or spoke out. And she was the smallest child in the class. Sister Margaret made it her mission to pull Sally out of her shell.

By September of 1854, the children who had been in Sister Margaret's classroom for the past three years were being promoted into the fourth grade. Sister Margaret was surprised to learn that Sister Jean planned to move her from teaching the first three grades to teaching the fourth. She was pleased to know that she was moving with her pupils.

"Sally," Sister Margaret called out, "please read the next paragraph in the story."

It became evident to Sister Margaret that Sally loved reading. Surprisingly, she enjoyed reading aloud. It was the one thing that worked in helping Sally overcome her shyness.

Over the years, Sally's freckles all but disappeared. With her red curls, white porcelain skin, and deep blue eyes, Sally was the most delicate child Sister Margaret could remember teaching. Sally was still the smallest child in the class, and her mother dressed her like a little doll. Any other child might feel smug or superior because of her beauty, but Sally didn't notice how lovely she appeared. She had a delightful personality, and the other children liked her immensely.

Since 1810, except for the two years during the War of 1812, Christiansburg held its annual harvest festival every October 18, Christina's birthday. Many folks still called it the "Wade Harvest Festival."

Christiansburg had been named after Christina's grandfather, Christian Wade, who had always told her wonderful stories about their mill and home on the River Wey, and the annual harvest festival to celebrate the September equinox. All of Christina's family members who'd come from England had now passed, so no one alive today had attended those harvest festivals held in Alton, England.

"Christina turns fifty today," Ann said to her husband as they approached the homestead. "I hope she likes the quilt I stitched."

"I'm sure she will love it, because her best friend is the one who made it for her," Simon said. "I love that you embroidered her name and birthdate on the front, as well as your name."

Ann smiled. "That way, she won't forget who gave it to her."

As the O'Malley family turned up the lane, they noticed the sign at the end still read: *The Wade Homestead Est. 1810.* Christina was the last surviving Wade, and though the O'Sullivans now lived on the homestead, they planned never to change the sign out of respect for Christian Wade.

The festival had been going on since noon, and hundreds of people remained on the front lawn. The evening turned cold for mid-October in southern Ohio, so Jamie lit several bonfires around the property.

"I want to make an announcement," Jamie shouted to the crowd from his expansive front porch. "Davey Creager asked me for my daughter Mary Jane's hand in marriage, and she has accepted. These two children have known each other almost since the day they were born. They are planning to hold their wedding after Davey's ice cream saloon is up and running."

More than a decade earlier, Davey and his father started a dairy farm. That past summer, Davey acquired one of those new hand crank ice cream churns and began taking some of their cream to make small batches of ice cream to sell at Archer's Mercantile.

"I signed a lease on a building in Dayton," Davey revealed. "This winter, I'll cut ice from the river and deliver it via the canal to my new store, where I've built a large icehouse. I'll be able to sell my ice cream every day, all year long."

"I've asked my sister Lizzy and our friends, Ginny and Sally O'Malley, to walk with me down the aisle at my wedding," Mary Jane announced to the folks gathered on the lawn.

Sally Ann was ecstatic to be asked to participate in Mary Jane's wedding. Christina and Jamie hired Ann O'Malley to make Mary Jane's wedding dress. Ann also planned to make dresses for Lizzy, Ginny, and Sally. Mary Jane couldn't wait to start planning her wedding.

Once the last festival merrymaker left, Christina wrote in her journal as she had done almost every day since she turned twelve, just as her grandmother and uncle did before her.

Wednesday, October 18, 1854

Life goes by so quickly. It feels like we celebrated my Mary Jane's fifth birthday only yesterday, and now she is planning her wedding.

My house is full of family and friends tonight. I particularly miss John and Rye, but I did receive a lovely letter from each of them last week. It is wonderful to hear Rye's two boys, Jacob and John, are now ten and eight.

I was pleasantly surprised to see Sarah Vance and her family here from Indiana. Nancy and Russell Smith arrived early yesterday from Columbus. Liam and Finn traveled from Boston last week, and Molly Smith came up from Cincinnati. Of course, many local friends attended the festival. I must thank my dear daughters for making sure everyone was invited, though most know we hold the festival yearly on this date. Jamie's sister June came with Roger and Roger Jr. We are also delighted that Jamie's parents, James and Kiera, are healthy and happy, though well into their seventies.

Our farm manager, Henry Ames, his wife, Sharon, and their son, Tom, helped ensure everything for the festival was ready to go. Even their daughter, Sissy, assisted me in the kitchen preparing the food. Jamie and I couldn't have done it without all of them. Henry told us he read in the Farmers' Almanac that it should be a cool, dry day, which it was.

I was happy to see Dr. Jedediah Smith and his wife, Anne. Since his retirement, his son Matthew has taken over his practice. I was merely a small child when the Smiths arrived in Christiansburg. Their daughter, Molly, was one of my best friends, along with David Creager and the Vance boys. Now we are all grown, some

even with grown children. And now, my dear daughter Mary Jane,
is planning her wedding to her childhood friend, Davey Creager.

I love the quilt my dear friend Ann made for me; she is so talented.
I saw their daughter Sally and my Georgie conversing politely
in the library. She was reading one of the Jane Austen novels I
lovingly store in my grandmother's cupboard. If she finds my books
enjoyable, I must invite her over more often.

It's late, and I must be up early to feed all our guests.

CWO

David Peter Creager IV and Mary Jane O'Sullivan planned to be married on Saturday, February 2, 1856, at St. Paul's Lutheran Church in Dayton, Ohio.

"No lace or petticoats," Mary Jane said as she described the dress she envisioned to Ann. "I want a silk organza veil, but I don't want the veil to go over my face. I saw a picture in a magazine of a dress from Paris. It featured a long white fitted linen skirt with a demi train. The lower sleeves were long and fitted, but with enormous, puffed sleeves to the elbow. I want Sally in a short white silk organza dress with a satin underskirt and a violet-blue sash. Ginny and Lizzy will wear a dress similar to Sally's, but their dresses will reach their ankles. And of course, I'll be wearing the family's heirloom sapphire earrings. I want us all to carry blue violets. Mrs. Creager promised hers would be blooming by then. If not, I must send Father out to search the woods."

It snowed all night on February 1, 1856. When Sally awoke the following day, at least six inches of snow covered the ground. "How will I walk to the church without getting my shoes all wet?" she asked her mother.

"When your father dropped off the wedding announcement at the newspaper yesterday, he carried the dresses and shoes to the church, so your shoes will be fine."

"The people at the newspaper seemed impressed with the dress description; they were fascinated that it was a Paris design," Simon said.

"Are we allowed inside a Lutheran church?" Sally asked Ann.

"Don't be silly; I'm sure we will be allowed this one time," Ginny said to her sister.

Sally and Ginny couldn't be more different. While Sally was petite, Ginny was tall and curvy. Sally's hair was light reddish blond like her father's, while Ginny's was dark auburn, like her mother's. Six years apart, they shared little in common. While Sally liked to read quietly in her room, Ginny wanted to be out with her friends. Ginny mainly enjoyed going to the Creager's Ice Cream Shop; sometimes she allowed Sally to tag along.

"Your boyfriend, Georgie, will be at the wedding," Ginny teased her sister.

"He's not my boyfriend!"

"Okay, girls, it's time to leave for the church."

It was difficult for anyone to believe that Lizzy O'Sullivan would be planning her own wedding just one year later.

"I can't believe I'm going to be a bridesmaid at another wedding," Sally told her mother that evening as the O'Malley family sat at dinner.

"I hope our daughters wait until the perfect man comes along," Ann said to her husband. "I don't mean to gossip, but I don't like Josiah. He's from Virginia and doesn't seem to fit our circle."

"Just because he's a Southerner doesn't mean he's a bad person," Simon said. "Besides, he seems to love Lizzy."

At seventeen, Lizzy fell in love with a man seven years older than her. Josiah Ritcher was Davey Creager's business attorney, and Lizzy met him one day while visiting her sister at the ice cream shop. Josiah was your typical southern gentleman—soft spoken, refined and genteel. Jamie and Christina remained adamant that the couple wait until Lizzy turned eighteen, which meant a May wedding.

"I'd love to be part of your wedding party," Mary Jane told her sister. "However, our baby is due in July, and I would look like a big old whale in the dress you've chosen for your bridesmaids to wear."

Lizzy had asked Ginny and Sally to wear the dresses from Mary Jane's wedding, changing the sash from violet to dark blue.

But Lizzy wanted something different from what Ginny wore at her wedding. She wanted to wear her mother's light blue satin wedding dress. Tapering lower sleeves had covered Christina's hands but were puffed in an enormous billow from shoulder to elbow. Elaborate dark blue silk velvet and fanciful trim adorned the hem, sleeves, and bodice. It was thirty years old but looked unspoiled, as Christina kept it wrapped in tissue paper and stored in a trunk in the attic.

Instead of the turban Grand-aunt Margaret created that Lizzy's mother wore at her wedding, Lizzy asked to borrow her sister's veil. Grandfather O'Sullivan generously ordered an expensive coronet of orange blossoms for her hair. Of course, she intended to wear the Wade sapphire earrings. Lizzy prayed her mother's white peonies bloomed in time to make her a large and delightfully scented bouquet.

Elizabeth Marie O'Sullivan married Josiah Gibson Richter on Lizzy's birthday, May 23, 1857, at Christ Episcopal Church in Christiansburg, Ohio. They held a breakfast reception at the O'Sullivan's home.

The groom was from Lancaster County. Immediately following the reception, the young couple planned to visit his family in Virginia for a few weeks. Upon their return, they would move into their new home on Williams Street in Dayton, just a few blocks from her sister.

Josiah would move his law practice into the homes downstairs front parlor, as it had a separate entry.

"You look very pretty today, Sally," Georgie said.

"It's the same dress I wore last year, except Mother needed to let it out a little. I only wish I would grow taller; I am so short."

While most everyone was either in the dining room or sitting in the parlor, Georgie and Sally were alone in the library.

"I love coming to your house," Sally said. "I especially love looking at all the books in your mother's old cupboard."

"I've read a few of them, but I can't seem to grasp the Jane Austen books," Georgie admitted.

"I love the Jane Austen books," Sally said. "I guess they are more for girls to read than boys."

"Can I bring you some cake and punch?" Georgie asked.

"Why yes, that is very nice of you."

For Sally, the next few years rushed by in a blur, and everything seemed to be happening in her favorite month, July, including several birthday parties, a couple of babies born, and one remarkable wedding.

David Peter Creager V was born to Mary Jane and Davey on July 24, 1857. Twin boys, Karl and Klaus, were born to Lizzy and Josiah Richter on July 13, 1858.

On July 2, 1859, Sally's sister, Ginny, married Harry Lynch, a neighbor boy she had known all her life. Sally wore her very first long formal dress. It was a light-yellow satin dress with white lace sleeves and a white lace flounce over a bell-shaped skirt. Sally felt her sister looked like a queen in a dress her mother made, identical to the dress worn by Queen Victoria on her wedding day in 1840.

Two days after Ginny's wedding, Sally was turning fourteen. Her parents were hosting a party at the house, allowing her to invite several of her friends from school. Sally had finished her last year at

Emmanuel Parochial School and would enter her first year at Central High School in September.

"Are the O'Sullivans coming to my birthday party this year?" Sally asked her mother.

"I invited everyone, and Christina told me they were all coming," her mother responded.

July 4, 1859

This is my first entry into my new journal. It was a gift from the O'Sullivan family. My mother's friend, Christina, said she has written in her journal almost daily since she was twelve. She said her grandmother Marie and her uncle Philip also wrote daily in their journals.

It's a handsome leather-bound book with my name and "Volume One" embossed in gold letters on the front. It already contains enough pages to place entries for dozens of years if I write neatly, maybe until I'm thirty. I wonder what I'll be doing when I'm thirty.

Well, let me tell you about my birthday party. Three friends from school attended: Sally Evans, Susan Kane, and Daisy Martin. And of course, Georgie and Charlie O'Sullivan came, as they've attended my party every year since I can remember. Sister Ginny and her new husband, Harry, must have known I was receiving a journal as they gave me a fine new dip pen. Mother made me a dress from the leftover fabric from my sister's wedding dress.

Davey and Mary Jane Creager couldn't come because they were busy at their ice cream store. So after I opened my many presents from Mother and Father, we all walked down to the ice cream store for cake and strawberry ice cream. Mary Jane now sells her freshly baked cakes, which are delicious.

As is our tradition, we all watched the annual parade that afternoon and the fireworks down by the river that night. Georgie paid entirely too much attention to Daisy Martin. But by the end of the day, he sat with me at the fireworks display. It was a wonderful birthday.

SAO

May 31, 1861

Today was the last day of school. I'll be in the eleventh grade at Central next year. All Mother and Father talk about these days is the war and all the young boys volunteering to fight. We talked about it in history class. It has something to do with state's rights and slavery. It's hard to believe our country is being split apart. All the boys in my school say they will go and fight. I'm terrified!

SAO

July 4, 1861

It was the worst birthday ever. All the adults argued, even Georgie and Charlie. From what I could gather, Mr. O'Sullivan plans to enlist. Father and Mother tried to talk him out of it. What was he thinking at fifty-two? Mrs. O'Sullivan argued with her husband, saying that her mother died because of war, and Mr. O'Sullivan didn't know his grandparents because of war.

Georgie said he would enlist since he was now seventeen, but his father demanded he finish his last year at Crane Academy. Even

Charlie said he would fight, and he is only twelve. Davey said he would only go if they decided to draft men to fight, but he opposed the federal government's draft of men to serve in the Union military. He needs to help his father with the dairy and run his ice cream shop. Mrs. O'Sullivan told Davey he was being selfish.

Mr. Ritcher said he could never fight against his family, who still live in Virginia. He said if drafted, he would pay someone to take his place. Mr. Ritcher said he felt the federal government did not have the power to limit slavery's existence. Georgie's father told him to join the Confederacy.

No one watched the parade or the fireworks. I cried once everyone left for home.

SAO

October 18, 1861

There was no Wade Harvest Festival this year. Mother, Father, and I did ride out to visit Mrs. O'Sullivan because today was her birthday. Mr. O'Sullivan enlisted on September 30 and was already gone.

Georgie and I walked out to the apple orchard. It was a clear night, and the sky was full of stars. He clasped my hand and told me he planned to enlist as soon as he graduated. When I started to cry, he held me in his arms. He said he didn't want to see a friend he liked cry because of him. I certainly did not see that coming. I guess I like him too.

On the way home, Father told Mother Mr. O'Sullivan had joined the Illinois Volunteer Infantry Regiment as a sharpshooter.

Mother couldn't believe he didn't stay long enough to celebrate his wife's birthday. Mother said if he loved her, he would have stayed home.

SAO

May 18, 1862

Father, Mother, and I joined the O'Sullivan family to watch Georgie graduate from Crane Academy. After the graduation ceremony, they prayed for all the boys who enlisted and recited their names aloud. The sad part was that they named three boys when they said to pray for those who would not be coming home. I hope I never hear them call the name of someone I know who dies because of this stupid war.

SAO

October 18, 1862

Once again, we visited Mrs. O'Sullivan for her birthday. She mentioned to Mother and Father that she receives regular letters from Mr. O'Sullivan. He is currently in Corinth, Mississippi, and even participated in several battles. Once they started talking about death and dying, I left the room to find a book to read in the O'Sullivan's library.

Georgie came into the library to tell me he enlisted and was leaving in November. He joined Company C of the 63rd Ohio Infantry Regiment.

His mother once showed him a ring that belonged to his great-grandmother. When he told his parents he loved me, she gave him that ring to give to me. He called it a posey ring, engraved inside with "A Token of My Love." He felt that if I wore it while he was gone, he would be destined to return.

As he placed the ring on my finger, he asked if I would marry him as soon as he's home.

I told him I would.

SAO

GEORGE "GEORGIE" EDWARD O'SULLIVAN II
1862 – 1865

*"There was not one among the whole row of young men
who could be compared with him."*

Jane Austen, *Emma*

When Georgie turned eighteen on June 1, 1862, he immediately enlisted in the Union Army.

Georgie would be serving with the 63rd Ohio Volunteer Infantry Regiment. Established nearly a year earlier, the 63rd was stationed at Camp Davies in Mississippi. But it was November before he was called up. Before being sent to Camp Davies, he first needed to report for training at Camp Marietta, located at the confluence of the Muskingum and Ohio Rivers. It would be the farthest Georgie had ever been away from home.

Georgie's father, Jamie, had enlisted as a sharpshooter and served in the 66th Illinois Volunteer Infantry Regiment. In his last letter to the family, Jamie wrote that he'd participated in the siege of Corinth in May and several minor skirmishes. There had been another engagement in Corinth in October, and he was now stationed at Camp Davies. Georgie was pleased and somewhat relieved that he and his father would be stationed together. It had been over a year since Jamie left, and Georgie could not wait to see him.

Henry Ames, the O'Sullivan's farm manager, was asked to drive Georgie into Dayton so that he could catch the train to Springfield before traveling on to Marietta. Georgie had never seen his mother cry, so he tried putting on a brave face. It was difficult not to admit to his mother that he was terrified.

"Take care that Charlie doesn't do something stupid," Georgie whispered to his mother as he kissed her tear-stained cheek. "He told me last night he wanted to join in the fighting if he could convince someone he was older."

"How could anyone think a thirteen-year-old boy was old enough to enlist to fight in this war is beyond me," his mother said.

"Well, he is over five feet tall."

In Springfield, Georgie met other men traveling to Camp Marietta. After a short wait on the platform, the train gave a few blasts to warn them they needed to board. Adrenalin rushed through Georgie, sending shivers down his spine. He inhaled a few deep breaths and then boarded the train.

This was the first time Georgie had traveled on a train. He wondered if they might someday extend the railroad out West. Georgie's Uncle John and Cousin Rye had moved out West and lived in what was initially called Oregon Country. Now that Oregon was a state, their wheat farm was deemed to be in Washington Territory. His mother always read out loud to the family the letters she received from her brother and nephew. They'd left Christiansburg before Georgie was born, traveling west on the Oregon Trail.

Georgie found an open window seat beside a smartly dressed older gentleman, perhaps a few years younger than his father. As Georgie stared out the train window, he daydreamed he was not headed to war but headed west to meet his uncle and cousin.

"You seem deep in thought."

The voice of the older gentleman stirred Georgie out of his daydream.

"I was thinking how I would rather be going west to visit my uncle than on this train headed to Armageddon," Georgie told the older man.

"You must be traveling to Camp Marietta along with all these other fine fellows," the man said.

"Yes, I've enlisted into the 63rd Regiment of the Ohio Volunteer Infantry."

"How old are you, young man?"

"I turned eighteen in June," Georgie replied.

"How did your family feel about you enlisting at such a young age?"

"Well, my mother was not happy. She said I should wait until I was twenty to see if I might be drafted. My father enlisted last year. I think Mother is upset because she felt he should not have enlisted; he's fifty-two. He's currently stationed at Camp Davies, where I hope to go."

"Are you married or have a sweetheart?"

"I proposed to a pretty little blue-eyed lass just last month. I've practically known her since she was born, and I love her dearly."

"I loved my first wife dearly, but she died when our daughter was born. It was rough those first few years without her; she was so young. But I fell in love again, remarried, and now have five more children."

As the two men talked, Georgie felt more at ease. Talking with the older gentleman passed the time, and before long, they both realized they had arrived at the station in Marietta.

"I'm sorry, sir, I didn't introduce myself," Georgie said. "I'm Georgie O'Sullivan from Christiansburg, Ohio.

"It is good to meet you, Georgie. My name is John Sprague from Sandusky, Ohio. Perhaps we will meet again."

As Georgie stepped off the train, a young soldier approached him.

"Do you know who you sat with this entire trip?" the soldier asked. "That's Colonel Sprague, the head chap of the 63rd Ohio infantry. He was a prisoner of war and was only released in January in a prisoner exchange. He led our regiment at the Siege of Corinth."

Georgie spent several weeks at Camp Marietta marching and drilling with the other recruits.

As an enlisted soldier, he was issued the standard uniform. His knapsack contained one set of drawers, one shirt, and a pair of wool socks. Attached to the knapsack were a blanket and a half tent.

He held up his newly issued light blue wool trousers with braces. The high-top black leather brogans appeared a little tight. He figured they would loosen up with all the marching and drilling required of him the next few weeks. The dark blue sack coat boasted shiny brass buttons embossed with an eagle. Georgie knew little about style but felt the sack coat was somewhat old-fashioned. His lieutenant warned him he was required to keep the top button of his coat closed, or he would be charged a fine. He never did find out why. Finally, there was an overcoat with cape, a dark blue forage cap, and a square black neckcloth that he tied into a bow.

In addition to his uniform, he was issued a haversack for carrying food, a canteen, and a tin mucket for cooking, eating, or drinking. Georgie brought a copy of the New Testament, a comb, a dip pen, a Stillman wooden barrel traveling inkstand that his grandfather gave him, a journal, and a pocket knife. He arranged all these things neatly into his knapsack. He didn't bring anything for shaving as he planned to grow a beard and mustache; he already possessed long sideburns.

Lastly, Georgie was issued a cartridge box, a cap box, a bayonet, and a Springfield Model 1861 rifled musket.

After leaving Camp Marietta, the recruits traveled by train toward their destination, Corinth, Mississippi.

It took over a week to reach Corinth. In Corinth, the men hiked six miles before they reached Fort Davies. It was warm for December.

The men already at camp soon realized that dozens of new recruits and men recently returning from furlough had just arrived by train.

As the men stood outside their tents preparing supper, Jamie immediately saw his son walking toward him.

"Son, you are a sight for sore eyes."

"Father, you look like you must be eating well," Georgie teased him.

"If you have downtime, you should write a letter home to your mother and one to Sally. You can buy paper, envelopes, and stamps at the post office here in camp. I received a package from your mother last week. She sent soap, candles, two dollars, and the peppermint puffs you always liked. We will be here at Camp Davies all winter."

December 20, 1862

Mrs. Christina O'Sullivan
The Wade Homestead
Christiansburg Highway
Christiansburg, Ohio

Dear Mother,

Merry Christmas. I hope you and Charlie are well and Henry is taking good care of our homestead. I arrived at Camp Davies a few days ago and immediately found Father. He looks fine. We were told we would be here in Mississippi for the winter. Father may be coming home on furlough by next spring. There were two battles here in Corinth well before I arrived, in which any rebels in the area were defeated. I haven't seen any fighting yet. Hopefully, I won't for several months. I may be placed on post and garrison duty to protect the area around Camp Davies.

I thought about Uncle John and Cousin Rye while on the train to Marietta. It would be wonderful if the railroad went far enough that we could someday travel to visit them.

There was a man here taking photographs of the soldiers and the camp. He owns an odd-looking wagon we men call a 'Whattizit'. Father and I used some of the money you sent to sit for a portrait of us together, vignette style. It's remarkable. You will find it included in this packet. As you see, we are growing beards but keep them neatly trimmed. Mother, the next time you correspond with Uncle John, you should ask him and Rye to have their portrait taken and send it to you so I can see what they look like.

Please don't worry, Mother. Father survived all the fighting these last few months and looks quite fit. Tell Mary Jane, Lizzy, and Charlie Merry Christmas, and write when you can.

Your loving son,
Georgie

December 20, 1862

Miss Sally Ann O'Malley
14 Oak Street
Dayton, Ohio

My Darling Sally,

It has been over a month since we were together, and I miss you something awful. I arrived safely at Camp Davies, and I'm settled into my tent with many of the same men who came with me. I was given a firm cot and a heavy blanket, although it is very warm here for December.

I saw Father, and he looks quite fit. Much of the fighting happened before I arrived, so we are mainly here to protect the camp and the surrounding area. Tomorrow, we will be doing some repair work on the railroad.

I wish I were able to be with you this Christmas. Mother always does a fine job decorating the mantels with evergreen and holly boughs. I imagine you sitting with me in the library beside the fire. Perhaps you would read from one of the Jane Austen novels my mother keeps in her cupboard while I lay my head in your lap. Please write when you can and give my love to your mother and father. Merry Christmas.

Love,
Georgie

December 25, 1862

Mr. & Mrs. James O'Sullivan
25 East First Street
Dayton, Ohio

Dear Grandfather and Grandmother O'Sullivan,

Merry Christmas! Thank you for the inkstand. It comes in handy when I want to write letters home. I also take the time each night before bed to write a few words in my journal.

I have been engaged in some strenuous work on the railroad. It is arduous, but it is better than having latrine duty. Sometimes, I work in the officer's mess tent peeling potatoes or soaking and frying hardtack.

After I arrived here in Camp Davies, Father told me that Lizzy, Josiah, and the boys moved to Sidney, Ohio. Father and I both feel it must be because of the harsh words we all spoke to each other last July. In her last letter to Father, Mother said Lizzy was distraught and did not want to go, but Josiah threatened to take the boys if she stayed in Dayton. Father said he hoped never to see Josiah again. He told me he could not be held accountable for his actions if he did. I am hopeful that tempers will cool in the years to come. I do not want to lose my sister because of this horrible war.

I wish Father and I were home for Christmas. Nonetheless, I hope the weather is clear, and you can travel to Christiansburg for Mother's roast goose with stuffing. Please write me a good long letter so I don't become any more bored than I already am.

Your devoted grandson,
Georgie

As spring turned to summer, Georgie found himself headed to Tennessee. But before he left Mississippi, Georgie sadly watched his father leave for home. He was sad to no longer see him every day, but happy Jamie was going home to Georgie's mother. Jamie had fulfilled his duty to his country and promised Christina he would not re-enlist.

It was late September when Georgie was granted furlough. Perhaps the war would end, and he wouldn't need to return. He packed his gear, headed to the Nashville train station, and was in Christiansburg within the week.

On his first day home, Georgie came downstairs refreshed from having slept in his own bed, to find his father and mother in the kitchen eating breakfast.

"Georgie," his father said, "you should be glad you left Tennessee when you did. I read in today's newspaper that the Confederate army secured a decisive victory at Chickamauga. There were thousands of casualties, but the rebs could not reoccupy Chattanooga."

"Georgie, I am so happy you are home," his mother said. "I can't tell you how frantic I've been while you and your father were gone.

It reminded me so much of when I was a little girl. My father and brother left to fight the British in Maryland, leaving Mother and me alone. It killed my mother. But we aren't fighting the British; we are all Americans fighting each other. It is shameful."

"Mother, I must tell you that I was granted furlough only because I re-enlisted. When I re-enlisted, they promoted me to sergeant. I go back early next year."

"Jamie, did you know Georgie re-enlisted?" Christina demanded of her husband.

"Yes, Christina, I knew. He is here with us now, at least until the new year. Let's not dwell on his leaving but make the most of our time together."

"Wars have a cruel way of interrupting people's lives," Georgie said. "Therefore, I think we should hold our annual harvest festival this year. We'll invite the whole town and make it a grand affair with flags, singing, and patriotic speeches. It should help boost everyone's spirits. Let's invite Lizzy and Josiah; maybe it will bring our family back together."

Encouraged, Christina sent a letter to Lizzy inviting her, Josiah, and the twins to the festival. Still, she was disheartened when she received a letter from Josiah stating: *We must regretfully decline your kind invitation.*

"Lizzy will be attending your birthday celebration if I must ride up there to fetch her myself," Georgie told his mother when he heard the news.

A few days later, it was Georgie's Grandfather O'Sullivan who pulled up in front of the house. Georgie heard the carriage first and ran outside to welcome the unexpected visitor. Inside his grandfather's carriage, he saw Lizzy and the twins, Karl and Klaus.

"Mother, come quick," Georgie called. "It's Grandfather with Lizzy and the boys."

"Grandfather came up to Sidney and was quite persuasive in telling Josiah I should not miss my mother's fifty-ninth birthday," Lizzy sobbed. "He's allowed me to stay until Christmas. Grandfather wanted to surprise you. I hope we won't be any trouble."

"You know you are welcome here anytime," Christina said.

As soon as Christina settled Lizzy and the boys in their rooms, she spoke with Georgie and Jamie in the kitchen as she prepared the midday meal.

"Jamie, your father will be eighty on his next birthday," Christina whispered so James, who was sitting in the library, could not hear. "He has been so good to all of us; we need to plan a party for him."

"My parents married on my father's birthday in 1807," Jamie said. "They will be married fifty-six years on Christmas Eve, and I don't believe they have ever enjoyed a proper celebration."

"Then it's settled. Before you go back, Georgie, we will plan a surprise party for your grandparents," Christina announced.

October 18, 1863, started cool and clear. This should have been the fifty-third festival. But because no festival had been held in 1861 and 1862, or in 1813 and 1814, it was only the forty-ninth, which was still impressive for a small town like Christiansburg.

Jamie, Georgie, and Charlie, with the help of Henry Ames, hung red, white, and blue bunting from the balcony. They wrapped the pillars in festive red and blue garland. All different sizes of flags hung from every window and door.

By noon, buggies and riders arrived by the hundreds. Tables were set up on the lawn that would hold the food and drink each attendee brought to share. The Crane Academy military band played as their choir sang the "Battle Hymn of the Republic" and other patriotic songs. Children chased the ducks and geese; neighbors greeted neighbors they hadn't seen all summer. Georgie and Jamie each gave speeches greeted with much applause and loud shouts of "hooray." Not one person mentioned the war, and the celebration lasted well into the wee hours of the next day.

The O'Malleys, O'Sullivans, and Creagers traveled from Dayton, filling the house with love and laughter, and Christina did her best to find places for everyone to sleep. The evening was warm, so the men and boys slept outside on the porch. The women were lucky enough to enjoy the luxury of a soft down featherbed, while the younger girls slept on makeshift mattresses on the floor.

Before the ladies retired, Georgie and Sally finally managed to find some alone time. Hand in hand, they wandered through the apple orchard, neither one speaking a word. The night was clear, and the stars shone brightly. Each knew the time was coming when they would once again have to say goodbye. Neither knew what the future held once Georgie left to fight in a war now raging for over two years.

Little did Georgie, or any of the family, know that 1863 was the last year they would hold the Wade Harvest Festival.

A few weeks after the festival, Christina began planning James and Kiera's surprise birthday and anniversary party.

"Father," Lizzy said, "I received a letter from Josiah. He tells me he will pick up the boys and me after the party. Would he be welcome to attend? With his wife and sons gone these past few weeks, he had time to reflect on many things. He wants to apologize to you and the rest of the family for what happened last year."

"If it means we will see more of you and the boys, I'm willing to let bygones be bygones."

Jamie arranged with Mayor Ellis to hold his father and mother's party inside Dayton's Courthouse. Because James O'Sullivan had been a well-respected resident of Dayton for almost thirty-eight years, Dayton's mayor was more than happy to arrange the use of the building. Completed in 1850, it was one of the country's finest examples of Greek Revival architecture. It reminded Jamie of their house in Christiansburg, only on a much grander scale.

Georgie had been given the task of escorting his grandparents to the party and had finally convinced them to put on their finest suit and fanciest dress and walk with him to the courthouse. There, over one-hundred-and-fifty of James and Kiera's family and friends were already gathered, awaiting the guests of honor.

"Dayton is having a big Christmas Eve party for all the soldiers on furlough," Georgie told his grandparents as they bundled up for the short walk to the courthouse. "Mother, Father, and the rest of the family are already there."

"Four years ago we listened to our great president give a speech on these very steps. Just look at all the buggies parked in front of the courthouse tonight," James said. "This is going to be one heck of a party."

As the three walked up the limestone steps, past the six Ionic columns, under the portico, through the double iron doors, and into the main room, they immediately saw several hundred people, some standing on the grand spiral staircase. Hanging down from the ceiling was a banner with the words: *Happy Birthday, James and Happy Anniversary, James and Kiera.*

"Why Georgie, you lied to your old grandfather," James teased.

The party was a grand affair with a small orchestra; some attendees even attempted to dance among the large crowd. Mary Jane and Lizzy helped their mother create hundreds of canapés. Punch was served from a large silver bowl. Mary Jane baked a three-tiered vanilla cake, large enough to serve each guest, with plenty left over for everyone to take a small piece home.

Once the party was over, the family walked the few short blocks back to the O'Sullivan's home as a light snow started to fall.

Georgie was set to leave Dayton the day after Easter. He spent the entire week before Easter with the O'Malley family, having already said his goodbyes to his family and friends in Christiansburg.

While attending Mass with Sally and her parents at Emmanuel Catholic Church, Sally reminded Georgie that this was where she wanted to hold their wedding. Sally's church was like nothing Georgie had ever experienced. He was somewhat intimidated by the sheer size of Emmanuel. Still, Georgie would do anything to please Sally.

March 28, 1864, started warm and sunny, so Georgie and Sally walked the seven blocks to the train station. It was a difficult goodbye, with Sally weeping so hard she was almost inconsolable. By the time Georgie boarded the train, he, too, was near tears.

There wasn't an empty seat on the train; it was full of soldiers headed to Decatur, Alabama, after an almost six-month-long furlough. His regiment was now part of the Army of the Tennessee, under the command of General William T. Sherman.

Once in Decatur, Georgie found a buddy; they attached each of their half tents and sat down to write letters to their families. He wrote to Sally, his parents, grandparents, and sisters. He did not want his loved ones to worry if they did not hear from him for several months.

As often as he could manage, Georgie wrote in his journal.

May 9, 1864

We left Decatur, Alabama, on May 1, and marched some fifty miles a day, bivouacking each night after a long day of marching. On May 4, we rode the train, arriving in Chattanooga the following evening. The Union won the Battle of Chattanooga late last year, and the Johnny Rebs fled.

We marched seven more miles before arriving in Rossville, Georgia. The next day, we started marching south. We passed through several towns, marching another thirty to forty miles, before taking part in the reconnaissance in force near Resaca, Georgia, to determine the position and strength of our enemy. The Union Army is ready to chase the Confederate troops southward.

GEO

May 22, 1864

We formed a line of battle and took part in a fight near Resaca on May 13. We remained in position on May 14, skirmishing all day. Several men were wounded. By May 16, the enemy evacuated Resaca. We crossed the Oostanaula River at Tanner's Ferry and lay under arms all night. Marching another 30 miles, we arrived near Kingston, Georgia, on May 19, where we've remained in camp the past four nights.

GEO

June 9, 1864

After leaving Kingston, we marched another thirty to forty miles, forming a battle line near Dallas, Georgia. On May 27, we commenced skirmishing for five days. We reportedly lost a dozen men killed and half that many wounded. We worked our way toward Acworth, Georgia, where we have been encamped for the last five days.

GEO

July 2, 1864

Over the past month, I have had little time to write in my journal between marching and skirmishing. We are currently encamped near the foot of Kennesaw Mountain, Georgia, receiving orders to march at a moment's notice. Nearly a dozen men were wounded this month. We are very thankful the number killed is much less.

GEO

July 12, 1864

After the evacuation by the enemy at Kennesaw Mountain, we continued south. On July 4, we moved to the front, formed a line of battle, fortified our position, and supported the First Brigade in a charge, in which they were successful. On July 8, we skirmished with the enemy across the Chattahoochee River. We marched through Marietta and bivouacked on the road to Roswell. We are currently encamped on the south bank of the Chattahoochee River. Rumor has it we will stay here for several more days before we march toward Atlanta.

GEO

July 30, 1864

July 22, will forever be ingrained in my mind as the worst day of my life. I pray I will never experience another day as bad as that one. We were escorting 400 supply wagons near Decatur when we heard cannon fire.

In the early afternoon, the enemy opened fire upon our picket line from a wooded area as we were guarding the wagon train. They charged with such great superior strength that we were forced to fall back. Once we fell back, our regiment became somewhat disorganized, with men scattered everywhere. Captain Gilmore was shot, and the field doctor needed to amputate his leg. Lieutenant McCord was so severely wounded that he was removed from the field and died a few days later. When our banner bearer, Corporal Harris, was shot dead, Private Fouts from Company D lifted our banner and waved it over his head. He said he would rather die than have our banner fall into rebel hands. Surprisingly, we lost only two wagons and a few horses.

Colonel Sprague gave me and several others noticeable mention in the official record for unusual bravery, perseverance, and success in rallying disorganized portions of the regiment. Colonel Sprague has been promoted to brigadier general—he deserves a medal.

GEO

September 2, 1864

August 30, we marched all day, and it was midnight before we bivouacked near Macon railroad. September 1, several of us were on picket. Today, we were relieved from picket, marched south through Jonesborough, and received an official dispatch of the occupation of Atlanta by the Union Army.

GEO

Once Georgie's regiment arrived in Atlanta, one of the first things the men did was write letters back home. Because most of the railroads in Georgia had been destroyed by the Union Army, there was no good way to post the letters sent north. Fortunately, a wagon train was headed back to Chattanooga, and the passengers promised to put Georgie's letters on the next train to Ohio.

November 12, 1864

I've been selected, along with about 60,000 other men of the Army of the Tennessee and the Army of Georgia, to march with Sherman to Savannah. We leave in three days.

GEO

November 22, 1864

We marched into Georgia's capital today and met with little resistance. We destroyed some military buildings in Milledgeville but left the government buildings alone. The Confederate soldiers evacuated, and I don't think the city's residents are pleased to see us. Last year, President Lincoln proclaimed that the nation would celebrate an official annual Thanksgiving holiday on the last Thursday in November. We plan to spend Thanksgiving here before moving on to Savannah.

GEO

December 25, 1864

We arrived in Savannah three days ago. It doesn't seem like Christmas, but we are trying to make it as festive as possible by hanging pine branches inside our tent. I wrote letters home, but I don't know how they will get posted. Maybe we can mail them once we arrive in Raleigh.

GEO

February 17, 1865

We left Savannah on February 1, with plans to march through the Carolinas rather than take a steamer. We marched at least fifteen miles a day toward the capital of South Carolina. We captured Columbia today with little resistance and practically burned the city to the ground. As we marched, we destroyed almost everything in our path. We burned cotton fields, homes, and factories and destroyed the railroads. Some men are out foraging for food from local farms. It must be devastating to the citizens of Georgia and South Carolina.

GEO

March 24, 1865

After leaving Columbia, we advanced into North Carolina. We occupied Fayetteville on March 1, and reached Goldsboro yesterday.

GEO

April 18, 1865

We arrived in Raleigh on April 13. Rumors were confirmed that General Lee surrendered to General Grant on April 9, at Appomattox Court House, Virginia. We also learned that General Sherman went to Durham Station by train to meet with General Johnston to negotiate the terms of his surrender. While General Sherman was gone, news spread through camp that our great president, Mr. Lincoln, was assassinated three days ago. The men have nearly burned Raleigh to the ground, just as we did in Columbia.

GEO

April 30, 1865

General Sherman obtained Johnston's surrender, and we are now leaving Raleigh to march to Washington, D.C.

GEO

May 26, 1865

I am sitting in the train station in Washington, D.C., on my way to Louisville, Kentucky. We left Raleigh on April 30, marching toward Washington. We traveled through the battlefields of Virginia at a pace of some thirty miles each day. At that pace, several men died marching in this springtime heat. We received word that Confederate President Jefferson Davis was captured on May 10, and the war is now over. We arrived in Washington on May 24, and I marched with General Sherman, the Army of the Tennessee, and the Army of Georgia through the streets of Washington. They called it the Grand Review of the Armies, and hundreds of citizens cheered us along the route. We marched for over six hours. I saw President Johnson sitting on an exclusive reviewing stand with other personages. Following us walked hundreds of freed slaves. Following the former slaves, at the end of the parade, were dozens of cattle pilfered from the farms throughout the Carolinas. I'm anxious to go home.

GEO

Georgie mustered out of the army at Louisville, Kentucky, on June 20, 1865, and headed home to Christiansburg.

CHRISTINA ELIZABETH WADE O'SULLIVAN
1864 – 1879

"What a shame, for I dearly love to laugh."

Jane Austen, *Pride and Prejudice*

*G*eorgie had been gone nearly two years fighting a war that had been raging since April of 1861. He wrote home as often as he could…

As soon as the post arrived, Christina ran into the house to find Jamie and Charlie.

"A letter came from Georgie," Christina shouted. She tore the letter open, and began reading aloud:

September 7, 1864

Mr. and Mrs. James O'Sullivan
The Wade Homestead
Christiansburg Highway
Christiansburg, Ohio

Dearest Father, Mother, and Charlie,

I know you must be reading news of the war in the Dayton Daily Journal. Therefore, you won't need to forgive me for not writing sooner, as you must already know how busy I have been lately.

We arrived near Macon, Georgia, on August 31. September 1, I was on picket duty, part of a defensive line of men to warn of an enemy advance. Once I was relieved from picket, I marched with my regiment south through Jonesborough, when we received official word of the North's occupation of Atlanta.

Since leaving Chattanooga, we have marched over 350 miles and participated in the battles of Resaca, Dallas, Kennesaw Mountain, Decatur, and Jonesborough. My lieutenant advised us that our regiment lost 23 men killed, 88 wounded, 31 missing, and one captured. Of the 31 men missing, I sometimes wonder if some are deserters.

We reached Atlanta yesterday. Before the end of September, I should know if I stay here or continue with General Sherman's Army north to Virginia to assist General Grant. I saw many horrors during the Battle of Decatur, so I am content to stay here and finish the demolition of Atlanta. Unfortunately, it's not for me to decide whether I stay or go.

Charlie, you should be at ease knowing you are too young. Hopefully, this war will end soon, and you will not be obliged to fight.

I am passing this letter on to a company of wagon trains heading back to Chattanooga. I hope it's not too long before you receive it.

Your loving son and brother,
Georgie

"Charlie," his mother called, "your books and lunch are sitting on the table; you better get moving, or you will be late for school."

In 1864, thirty-five students attended Christiansburg Common School. Charlie was fifteen and starting the tenth grade. He wanted to stay with his many friends in Christiansburg, rather than attend Crane Academy like his brother. Claude Vance was still teaching at Christiansburg. This year would be his thirty-ninth year. Mr. Vance taught the upper grades, while Miss Williams and Miss Jones taught the primary grades.

Jamie and Christina remained hopeful that Charlie might be the first of their children to go on to college. Charlie expressed an interest in attending Ohio University. After graduation, he planned to read law with his brother-in-law, Josiah. Charlie and his best friend, Bud, intended to room together at college. Bud's given name was Matthew Smith Jr. He was the grandson of Dr. Jedediah Smith, Christiansburg's first doctor.

Christiansburg's current doctor was Bud's father. However, he'd enlisted in the Union Army and was stationed in Nashville, caring for thousands of sick and injured Union soldiers and a few hundred Confederate soldiers. A doctor from nearby Centreville had come to Christiansburg to manage Dr. Smith's practice while he was gone.

Dr. Smith's wife, Mary, told Christina she'd received a letter from her husband. In it, he explained there were dozens of hospitals in Nashville, some in private homes, treating nearly 14,000 sick or wounded soldiers.

That day, Charlie arrived home from school late, but Christina reasoned he had gone to the Mercantile with his friends.

Early the following morning, Christina called to Charlie. When he didn't answer, she climbed the stairs and knocked on his door but received no reply. When she entered his room, it appeared that his bed had not been slept in. Then she saw the note pinned to his pillow.

Dearest Father and Mother,

Bud Smith, Will Jones, Frank Rike, and I enlisted into the 179th Ohio Infantry Regiment, K Company, for one year. I took the liberty of pocketing two dollars I found inside the tin in Great-grandma Marie's old cupboard but will repay you when I receive my first pay. I also pilfered some bread and cheese from the larder.

Our train leaves Dayton early this morning for Camp Chase in Columbus. We will be gone before you wake. Our regiment will be attached to the Post of Nashville. So by early October, we will be with Bud's father. Please don't worry. I will write as soon as we arrive in camp.

Your loving son,
Charles

Jamie left early that morning to discuss business with his father in Dayton, so he wasn't home to hear Christina's scream. As soon as she gathered her wits, Christina ran to find Henry Ames. She explained the situation and asked him to drive her to Dayton.

Once in Dayton, Christina rushed into her father-in-law's house. Kiera was startled when she saw her daughter-in-law. "Christina, what on earth is the matter? Is it Georgie?"

"No, it's Charlie! He enlisted! Read the note he left!"

"The men are at the sawmill ordering materials for the new house on Tecumseh Street," Kiera said. "They should be back for lunch. Please sit down. Would you like some tea?"

"No, there's no time!" Christina exclaimed. "I'll ask Henry to drive me to the sawmill."

At the sawmill, she saw the two men as they left the office. Christina fell into Jamie's arms, sobbing. He barely made out what she was trying to say. Thus, Henry stepped in and delivered the news.

Back at the elder O'Sullivan's home, Christina lay on the chaise by the front window while the others discussed their next steps.

"Do you think the Army will release Charlie and Bud since they're only fifteen?" Jamie asked his father.

"Let's go to the recruitment office to see if we can get some answers."

The recruiter explained that he could do nothing. Charlie had joined legitimately by signing up for a noncombat position. "Those four boys came in yesterday to enlist," the recruiter told them. "Two of the boys had their fathers' permission. They will probably be put on garrison duty or assigned to help in one of the hospitals. They should be safe, as Nashville has been under Union control since 1862. The war is about over anyways, what with the Union now occupying Atlanta."

The two men returned home with no good news to impart. Jamie knew his wife would be distraught; he wished he knew how to repair her spirit.

Arriving back in Christiansburg, Jamie and Christina rode to Dr. Smith's house to talk to Bud's mother, Mary.

"Yes, Bud left me a note too," Mary told them. "He said he was going to Nashville to find his father. I wrote to Matthew, but he may not receive it for several weeks. I don't know what else to do until I hear from either Matthew or Bud."

Finally, a letter arrived from Charlie.

October 10, 1864

Mr. and Mrs. James O'Sullivan
The Wade Homestead
Christiansburg Highway
Christiansburg, Ohio

Dearest Father and Mother,

First of all, please don't be mad. Bud and I arrived on October 8, and are working with Dr. Smith. Bud and I share a small room right here in the hospital. We also eat our meals here, so we aren't going hungry. I haven't seen Will or Frank; they might be on garrison duty.

I work mainly on a cleaning crew. We wash down beds, floors, walls, everything. Sometimes, I work in the laundry. You name it, Bud and I clean it. Yesterday, I was sent to someone's house where ten wounded Confederate soldiers were staying, all in pretty bad shape. The lady who owned the house was a Confederate. She was polite to me, probably because I helped to clean her house. Many wounded men I see have developed gangrene, and almost all have dysentery.

I'm anxious to receive your letters. Address your letter to Nashville General Hospital #3, Nashville, Tennessee, and I should receive it pretty quickly. Don't worry about me; unlike Georgie, I won't see battle.

Mother, I'm so sorry I will miss your birthday this year and probably all the holidays after, at least until this war ends. You will find enclosed the two dollars I pocketed the day I left.

Much love to you both,
Charlie

The days passed slowly for Christina. While Jamie stayed in Dayton to start a new construction project, Christina spent much of her day in the Ames's cabin visiting with Henry and his wife, Sharon. Henry was getting on in years, so his son Tom was doing most of the farm work for the O'Sullivans. The Ames's daughter, Sissy, was married and living in Christiansburg, but she often stopped by, bringing the Ames's grandchildren. Christina heard from Charlie at least once a week; she wrote to him almost twice that.

In early November, Christina received a letter from Georgie. He said his superiors had selected him, along with nearly 60,000 men, to participate in what he identified as the Savannah campaign. The plan was to leave Atlanta in a few weeks. They hoped to capture Savannah before Christmas.

On a mild day in mid-December, Christina was out in her garden picking the last of the Brussels sprouts when she noticed Mary Smith's carriage coming up the lane.

"Hello, Mary," Christina called. "Come inside, and I'll make some tea. Have you heard from Matthew?"

"Yes," Mary said. "Is Jamie home?"

"Jamie," Christina called. "Mary is here, and she brought news from Nashville. Let's sit in the parlor."

Jamie and Christina immediately knew it was bad news by the look on Mary's face. "My dearest friends," Mary started. "The simplest way to tell you is to say it straight out. Charlie has died. In late November, Charlie became very ill. He died from typhoid fever on December 10. They did everything they could, but he was just too sick."

Christina was in shock and couldn't speak.

Jamie asked, "When will they be bringing our boy home?"

"The Confederates attempted to take Nashville a few days after Charlie died, but before the battle, the Army was able to give Charlie a proper burial. It may be another month before they return his body to Christiansburg."

That night, Christina wrote in her journal, *Today was one of the most distressing days of my life, nearly as ghastly as when my first two babies died in my arms.*

"I wasn't able to tell Charlie goodbye," Christina told Jamie as they rode to church that Sunday. "I've now lost my grandparents, parents, aunt and uncle, sister, and three of our children. My only brother and nephew moved thousands of miles away, and I doubt we will ever see them again. I am afraid we might lose Georgie, too."

Charlie's sisters Mary Jane and Lizzy and their families, came home for Christmas, but there was no joy at the Wade Homestead. The pain and sorrow of losing Charlie and not hearing from Georgie for over a month remained unbearable for everyone. Christina now understood how her mother felt and why she became so sick when Christina's father and brother left home in 1813 to fight the British in Maryland.

After the start of the new year, a letter finally arrived from Georgie. He was in Savannah and found a way to get his letters posted. He wrote that they first captured Fort McAllister then stormed and captured the Port of Savannah on December 21. General Sherman offered Savannah to President Lincoln as an early Christmas gift. They planned to rest there for a month before marching to Raleigh.

Though the letter was a welcome relief, and for now, it seemed that Georgie was well, it did little to lift Christina's mood. Charlie's death was too great a burden to bear. Unlike when Sarah Jane and

Little Jamie died nearly thirty-two years before, Christina had gone on to have four more babies to love and care for.

On January 31, Jamie, accompanied by Henry Ames, drove the hay wagon to Dayton's Union Station to claim Charlie's body.

Charles Eugene O'Sullivan was laid to rest on February 1, 1865. Beside Charlie lay Sarah Jane and Little Jamie. Three young siblings gone because of diseases for which there was no cure.

By the time they left the graveyard, it had started to sleet. It was a miserable day for everyone. Unbeknownst to any of the mourners, Georgie left Savannah the very same day. Christina thought to herself, *Parents should never have to bury their children. I don't know if I will ever laugh again.*

Two months after they laid Charlie to rest, word reached Christiansburg that Lee had surrendered to Grant. Sadly, three days later, Kiera passed away at age eighty.

"She was fine the day before," James cried. "The doctor thinks it was probably her heart. I can't believe she is gone."

"Father," Jamie said, "I think it best if you sold the house here in Dayton and move in with us back in Christiansburg."

"Yes," James said. "I agree."

Jamie's mother was buried in Christiansburg on April 14. After the funeral, the family gathered at the farm for a luncheon that Sharon Ames and her daughter Sissy prepared. Exhausted, the O'Sullivans went to bed early.

The following day, as they sat on their porch, they saw one of the Rike boys riding toward their house.

"Have you heard the news!" young Adam Rike exclaimed. "President Abraham Lincoln was assassinated last night and died early this morning."

The war was entering its fourth year, and Christina didn't think she could take another piece of bad news. At eight years old,

Christina couldn't understand how her mother could die because she was unhappy. For a time, she despised her mother for leaving her, a mere child. Now she better understood how her mother must have felt and was angry at herself for hating her.

Jamie's sister June and her husband Roger traveled from their home in Lima, Ohio, and stayed with their father in Dayton for a few days, along with their son, Chip, and his wife, Marion. Chip had served with the 25th Ohio Volunteer Infantry Regiment. He'd been severely injured at the Battle of Gettysburg and was sent home before the end of the war. He now walked with a cane and looked much older than his twenty-nine years.

Several weeks later they received a letter from Georgie. He was unaware of his grandmother's recent death or the death of his brother. In his letter, Georgie wrote that they entered Raleigh on April 13. As soon as Sherman could obtain Johnston's surrender, they would leave Raleigh and march to Washington, D.C. to celebrate their victory.

It wasn't until May 11, while Jamie and Christina were out by the barn readying their kitchen garden for planting that they heard the postman call out. "Union troops captured Confederate President Jefferson Davis yesterday; the war is over!"

"Georgie will be coming home," Jamie told Christina; they held each other and cried happy tears.

Georgie entered Washington on May 24, 1865. As soon as the Grand Review of the Armies was over, he walked to the train station. The Army confirmed that he would muster out at Louisville on June 20. Soon after, he would return home and be surrounded by family and friends. Hopefully, he thought, before Charlie left for college. Georgie was anxious to marry Sally and start his own family.

Georgie was the happiest he'd been in more than three years. He would be back in time for Sally's birthday, along with the Fourth of July parade and fireworks he loved so much. He couldn't wait to spend the evening with his grandparents at their home in Dayton or taste his sister Mary Jane's cake and ice cream.

He would be home in time to help Tom with the harvest and even help organize the Wade Family Festival. His father also promised to take him into the O'Sullivan and Sons Building Company family business, which meant something to Georgie now.

Unfortunately, Georgie was unprepared for the grief and sorrow awaiting him in Christiansburg.

With Georgie finally home, James and Jamie followed through with their plan to donate a small parcel of land near the town center for a park, naming it the *Charles Eugene O'Sullivan Memorial Park*. They planned to build a large gazebo and an equally large bandshell to be enjoyed by all the citizens of Christiansburg.

On July 4, 1865, Christiansburg held a sunrise service to dedicate the new park. A large monument was placed near the park's center with a plaque bearing Charlie's name. The plaque was also inscribed with the names of five other men from Christiansburg who died during the war. Boys from the Christiansburg Common School raised the American flag, and a young boy played taps on his bugle. It was a somber and moving ceremony.

Later that day, they would travel to the O'Malley's for a much happier celebration: Sally was turning twenty. Dayton officials had asked Jamie and Georgie to wear their uniforms and march in a parade the city had planned for the first Fourth of July celebration since the end of the war Northerners called the War of the Great Rebellion. Most Southerners still called it the War for Southern Independence or The War of Northern Aggression.

Also marching with the O'Sullivans was Jamie's nephew Chip Taylor, or Roger as he preferred to be called now. Roger and his wife, Marion, recently made his Grandfather James a great-grandfather for the fourth time. Their son, Roger III, was now one year old.

"Hurry, boys," Christina called. "We need to be in Dayton before the parade starts so you can find your places."

Liam and Finn came from Boston to watch Jamie, Georgie, and Chip march in the parade. Because of the war, they'd been unable to travel to attend their mother's funeral, but they were here now, along with their wives and children.

It was a day full of mixed emotions. Christina felt both sadness and happiness, wishing Charlie and Kiera were still alive to witness this joyful occasion.

Much to everyone's delight, Liam and Finn left Boston to open a law office in Dayton. Liam bought his father James's house with all its furnishings. Finn had Jamie build a new home on fashionable Plum Street for him and his young family.

James moved into Charlie's old room once Jamie and Georgie moved Charlie's things into the attic. Christina hoped the spare bedroom would someday become a nursery for Georgie and Sally's future babies. She was excited to one day have four generations under one roof. Christina knew it was selfish, but she hoped Georgie and Sally would never leave the homestead.

In the meantime, when Sally wasn't busy with wedding plans, her father drove her to Christiansburg to lend a hand in redecorating Georgie's room into something more suitable for a new bride.

Christina rode into Dayton several times that summer to help Ann and Sally with the wedding plans. Ann and Sally were grateful for her help; they remembered Christina's two daughters' weddings were well organized.

All this activity helped Christina cope with her grief over Charlie's untimely death.

The anniversary of Charlie's death fell on a Sunday in 1865. Christiansburg Episcopal was overflowing with citizens anxious to express their condolences to the O'Sullivans. The family laid a wreath at Charlie's grave and another at the monument in the park they named after their son and brother. Later that day, Jamie and Georgie trudged through the woods to find and cut the perfect Christmas tree.

After Sunday dinner, the entire O'Sullivan family was on hand to decorate the tree. The children made colorful paper chains and strung popcorn and cranberry garlands. Christina had yet to count how many people seemed to fill almost every corner of her large house. Georgie caught her smiling at a story Klaus was telling his grandfather. He hoped his mother was on the road to recovery from her long period of mourning over Charlie.

Georgie and Sally's marriage took place on the evening of December 23, 1865. It was held at Emmanuel Catholic Church in Dayton, Ohio.

Outside the front door was a small nativity scene on the church's lawn, and two wreaths festooned with bright red ribbons were hung on the church's white double doors. Six finely embellished Christmas trees decorated the nave, while boughs of evergreens adorned each windowsill. Candlesticks were placed at the end of each pew along the center aisle.

A lavish reception was held in the church's large social hall following the candlelight ceremony. Along with many friends and family, Sister Margaret, Sally's first teacher, was one of their honored guests.

It was a nice warm day in early June when Christina and Sally decided to relax on the front porch after breakfast. Soon after they sat down, Sally told her mother-in-law she was expecting a baby in mid-December.

"Have you told anyone else?" Christina asked.

"No, we saw Dr. Smith only yesterday, and he confirmed our hunch," Sally said. "Wouldn't it be splendid if the baby was born on Christmas Day?"

Christina loved all her grandchildren, but she sensed this grandchild might well become someone extraordinary.

The months passed quickly, and it was an unusually warm evening in November when Christina saw the O'Malley's carriage coming up the driveway. They had been invited to help celebrate the nationwide holiday then President Lincoln had declared three years earlier, to be observed on the last Thursday of every November as a day of thanksgiving, praise, and prayer.

Sally was returning from visiting her parents in Dayton, and as the O'Malleys were walking up the front steps, Christina noticed Sally's hands looked extremely swollen. When Sally went inside, Christina motioned her good friend, Ann, to a rocker on the porch.

"Sally's hands seem swollen. Are her feet as swollen as her hands?"

"Yes," Ann replied. "We stopped to see Dr. Smith on the way here. He advised her to refrain from eating anything salty, like bacon or ham; she should eat only vegetables, fruit, and drink plenty of fresh milk. The baby isn't due for several weeks, but he wants Sally to rest and forgo anything strenuous. He plans to come over and perform a bloodletting after the holiday. Dr. Smith believes it's just the unseasonably warm weather causing the swelling."

"The spare room is ready for you and Simon. Come inside, and I'll put supper on the table."

Just then, Georgie came running down the stairs. "Sally is complaining of a severe headache. Is it time for the baby?"

"It's weeks before her time, and I hate to disturb Dr. Smith on Thanksgiving Eve. I think we can wait," Christina said.

"I'll go up and pour some cool water into her wash basin to sponge her face," Ann said.

The next morning, Sally ate a small bowl of porridge and drank a cup of chamomile tea. She no longer complained of a headache, so Christina felt the incident had passed. Due to Sally's condition, Thanksgiving would be a quiet affair, with only the O'Malleys in attendance.

It was the last day of November, and Sally was experiencing what appeared to be early labor pains.

"Georgie, it is fortunate that you stayed home today," Christina said. "I suggest you ride to fetch Dr. Smith."

December 1, 1866, a daughter was born to Sally and Georgie. The baby seemed in good health. But because she was several weeks early she was very tiny.

Dr. Smith had stayed at the homestead all night and was sitting in the kitchen with Christina as she baked soda biscuits and brewed a pot of good strong coffee. Suddenly, the calm was broken by a scream.

"Dr. Smith, come quickly; something is wrong with Sally Ann!" screamed her mother.

Entering Sally's room, Dr. Smith found Sally convulsing; her eyes rolled back into her head. She was thrashing about, and her back was severely arched. Dr. Smith tried his best to revive Sally, but in minutes she had collapsed into a coma.

Christina rushed out to the barn to find Georgie. By the time he ran upstairs, Sally had passed. Georgie collapsed beside Sally's bed sobbing uncontrollably. Christina held her good friend, Ann, in her arms. Sally's father, Simon, leaned against the wall softly crying. Everyone was in a state of shock.

Sally's funeral Mass was held at Emmanuel Catholic Church in Dayton, where Sally and Georgie had been married less than one year earlier. As Sally's coffin was being caried from the church, Jamie needed to support his son. Georgie's grief was so unbearable he was unable to walk by himself. As everyone left the church, Georgie noticed Sister Margaret sitting in the back row. Her head was bowed, and tears were flowing down her cheeks.

They buried Sally beside her little brother, John.

Georgie and Sally had already discussed names for their baby. If it was a boy, they planned to name him Simon, after Sally's father. If it was a girl, they wanted to name her Christina, after Georgie's mother.

So on Christmas Day, 1866, Christina Elizabeth O'Sullivan was baptized at Christ Episcopal Church. There was no sadness that day.

After church, the family gathered around the large dining table to enjoy Christina's roast turkey, chestnut stuffing, and all the usual trimmings. The meal was finished with a large slice of pumpkin pie. Mary Jane brought a cake she had baked expressly for her grandfather's birthday celebration.

With a slight chuckle, Jamie asked, "When I call for Christina, who will come?"

"When I was a young girl back in Maryland, our farm manager's wife, Mrs. Swadener, called me Tina," Christina mused.

"That's perfect," Georgie said. "From this day forward, my baby will be known as Tina."

"Georgie?" Christina asked. "Bring me the Wade Bible from the old cupboard in the library so I may record Tina's birth."

Christina also chose this time to note Sally Ann's death.

"Jamie?" Christina asked. "How do you feel about me going back to teaching? Miss Williams might want my help with the primary grades. Claude has retired, and Miss Jones is teaching the older children."

"Is this so you can stay close to Tina?" Jamie asked. "You turn sixty-eight in October; don't you want just to relax and enjoy our time together? Georgie oversees our building company, Sissy comes over daily to help in the main house, and Tom now manages the farm. We should sit back and let the young people run this world. We've earned it."

James, sitting in the library reading the paper, overheard the conversation. "You should let Christina go back to teaching," James said. "The older I get, the more I understand how important it is to follow your heart's desire before you're too old to enjoy it. Now that Tina is entering the first grade, she would love her grandmother with her at school."

"Are you being facetious?" Christina asked her father-in-law.

"No, not at all," James said. "But maybe you should ask Tina."

"Well, I'll ask Tina, and then I'll go to the school board president," Christina said.

Jamie laughed. "That would be me."

In early September 1878, James passed away in his sleep. He would have turned ninety-five on his birthday in December. He was laid to rest beside his beloved wife, Kiera, in the graveyard next to Christ Episcopal Church.

James, Kiera, and Jamie had come to Christiansburg with the original wagon train in 1810. Although James and Kiera came from Ireland and had been raised Catholic, they had converted to Episcopalian soon after arriving in Christiansburg. Most of the early pioneers who came to Christiansburg were gone. Only the children who accompanied their parents were alive today.

"Well, I am glad I decided not to return to teaching," Christina told Jamie that evening as they waited in the library for Tina and Georgie.

"I hope you are as happy with your decision as I am," Jamie responded. "These last seven years have been wonderful, with both of us being home together."

Tina turned twelve in 1878. As she did every year, she spent the summer with her grandparents in Dayton. Today, her father was bringing her home to Christiansburg. As they walked into the library they overheard the conversation between Christina and Jamie.

"Well, I would have loved you to have been my teacher," Tina announced. "School starts in a few days. You could always change your mind, Grandmother."

"No, I'm content just helping with your homework."

After Tina went to bed, Georgie spoke with his parents in the library. "While I was in Dayton today, I stopped by to see Mary Jane and Davey at their ice cream shop. We discussed traveling to Idaho Territory to visit Uncle John and Cousin Rye. Davey needs to stay to take care of the store, but Mary Jane is excited about going. I want to take Tina out of school early next year so she can go with us, and I was hoping you could come as well, Mother. That is, if it's okay with Father."

"I'm almost seventy-five years old!" Christina exclaimed.

"Please, Mother, we'll take good care of you," Georgie implored her. "We will make sure we don't have any building projects pending next spring, and Liam and Finn said they will help Father if anything comes up while we are gone."

"How will you travel?" Jamie asked.

"We'll start on a paddle steamer from Cincinnati down the Ohio River. Another steamer will take us up the Mississippi. Finally, we will travel on the Missouri River to Council Bluffs, Iowa," Georgie explained. "In Council Bluffs we will pick up the train to Ogden. From there, we take a smaller train to Boise through Pocatello. Rye could pick us up in Boise. We will be traveling first class all the way."

"I remember taking a steamer with Uncle Philip from Cincinnati to my first teaching assignment in Madison, Indiana," Christina said.

"It was quite an adventure for a young girl of eighteen. I still remember the lavish red and gold dining room as if it were yesterday. You realize, Georgie, that Ryker's sons are your age. In fact, you are only two days older than Ryker's oldest son, Jacob. While there, we must help organize a birthday celebration for you both."

"Today, Mary Jane told me she remembered receiving new shoes from Grandpa and Grandma O'Sullivan on her fifth birthday," Georgie said. "I don't know how she remembers Grandpa's words from forty years ago, but he told her that since she was given new shoes, she was all set to go on an adventure. I guess we will all need to purchase new shoes!"

The four O'Sullivans traveled on river boats for over two weeks before arriving in Council Bluffs. They hired a buggy to take them into town, where they rented rooms at the Pacific Hotel for one night.

After breakfast in the hotel's restaurant, they traveled to Union Station, where they boarded the train for their journey on the Transcontinental Railway to Ogden.

Their first-class accommodations were opulent, with velvet cushions and gilded mirrors. They feasted on antelope and trout. The Pulman sleeping cars were converted to regular seats during the day. It required just three days to travel from Council Bluffs to Ogden. In comparison, John and Rye had spent months traveling west by wagon train. They transferred to a second train in Ogden bound for Boise.

When the four travelers exited the train in Boise, they noticed a handsome young man standing next to a buggy. "Hello, I'm Jacob Wade," he said. "You must be the O'Sullivans. My father, Ryker, asked me to meet you here in Boise and take you to our homestead. We live just a few miles west of the small town of Mountain Home. We should be there within the hour."

Christina and Mary Jane immediately saw the resemblance to Ryker, excepting that young Jacob wore his dark hair in two long braids.

In Ohio, they mainly grew corn. As they drove through vast wheat fields, Christina recalled vague memories of the wheat fields in Frederick, Maryland.

"As a very young girl, before we moved to Ohio, we lived in a large water mill in Maryland," Christina told her granddaughter. "My father and my brother John grew wheat and rye. I was a naughty little girl who often ran through the wheat to hide from my brother. Our farm manager, Mr. Swadener, was unhappy about me running through the wheat, so I would hide behind Mrs. Swadener as he scolded me. Do you know Mrs. Swadener called me Tina?"

"How old were you when you came to Ohio?" Tina asked.

"I turned six the year we moved to Ohio."

"This wheat looks ready to harvest," Georgie addressed Jacob.

"Yes, you came at the right time, Georgie," Jacob jested.

"It won't be the first time I've helped with a harvest," Georgie replied. "Is it like cutting hay?"

"We just bought one of those new grain binders," Jacob replied. "You can be the first to try it."

Georgie laughed. "I'll watch you first. Have you sown your spring wheat?"

"Yes, last month."

"Jacob?" Christina asked. "Did you know you and Georgie share a birthday?"

"Yes, by two days," Jacob responded. "Mother is planning a big party. It isn't often two men from the same family turn thirty-five."

As they turned up the lane toward John's house, Christina saw a sign that read: *The Wade Homestead Est. 1846.* Tears sprang to her eyes as she anticipated seeing her brother and nephew after almost forty years. She was anxious to see them but also hesitant. They'd all been so young when they last saw each other; she was an old woman now.

Christina noticed two smaller houses to the left as they neared the large white farmhouse. Now grown men, Rye's sons had families of their own. Then she saw them, John and Ryker. Mary Jane jumped from the buggy and ran into Ryker's waiting arms. Although the anticipation felt unbearable, Christina waited until the buggy stopped and John helped her down.

"It's been a few years since I helped you down from a carriage," John said, with tears streaming down his cheeks.

Georgie and Tina stood a few steps away, patiently waiting for their relatives' reunion to conclude.

"Oh, forgive me," Christina said. "Let me introduce you to Georgie, my son, and Tina, my granddaughter."

John then introduced his wife, Dyani, and Rye introduced his wife, Matika. Jacob introduced his wife, Aponi, and John introduced his wife, Maria. Standing among the adults stood six little boys and one little girl. Jacob was blessed with four sons: Jacob, Matthew, Mark, and Luke. Young John had welcomed one daughter and two sons: Matika, John, and Ryker.

Much to Tina's delight, Matika was also twelve.

"They call me Tika," she told Tina. "You have such bright red curls. Do you want to see my dolls?"

The two little girls ran hand in hand into Tika's charming blue bungalow. The rest of the family entered the big house, and Dyani began preparing lunch. It was a feast: Bison pot roast with potatoes, frybread topped with beans and a fried egg, freshly caught whole trout on rice sprinkled with the roe, and mashed sweet potatoes.

"My goodness!" Christina exclaimed. "You and Matika must have a very substantial garden; maybe you can show it to me later."

Sunday, the entire clan traveled to Mountain Home to attend church. To accommodate everyone, they needed several wagons and buggies. It appeared as if they were part of a small wagon train.

That day, the pastor arranged for a photographer from Boise to take portraits of all the church attendees. After the service, each family was given a turn at posing in front of the church. It was well past noon before the Wades and O'Sullivans could take their turn. Difficult as it was, the photographer guaranteed he could squeeze all nineteen in the frame. He succeeded, despite having six rambunctious little boys to corral.

Afterward, the congregation met in the meadow behind the church to partake of a substantial carry-in lunch. Dyani and Makita brought their frybread topped with blueberries.

The boys played tug-of-war and ran foot races. The girls even entered the fun when the boys started a game of tag—until it got a little rough.

Everyone was tired and dirty when they returned to the farm. Since the children were still in school, they needed baths and were sent immediately to bed. The children had invited Tina as their special guest to attend their school the next day.

Not wanting to overstay their welcome, the O'Sullivans planned to return home after just two weeks. Before they left, Georgie had to try his hand at harvesting wheat.

John hitched three horses to the front of the grain binder and started off. It looked extremely easy to Georgie until he tried. He not only had to control three horses but maintain a straight line. The sight had everyone in stitches. The boys were rolling on the ground; they laughed so hard their stomachs hurt.

"Please stop, Pa," Tina urged. "You're scaring me."

"It was easier carrying my gear and marching in a straight line during the war!" Georgie exclaimed. "I think I'll stick with building houses."

Georgie's comment left Christina with a tear running down her cheek as she remembered her dear, sweet Charlie.

The goodbyes were difficult at the end of two weeks, but the memories would last until they could all be together again.

CHRISTINA "TINA" ELIZABETH O'SULLIVAN MURPHY
1879 – 1934

"You must be the best judge of your own happiness."

Jane Austen, *Emma*

*A*fter Tina returned from the trip to Idaho Territory, several weeks remained before the start of the new school year. So her father escorted her to Dayton for her annual summer visit with her grandparents, Simon and Ann O'Malley.

The O'Malleys lived on a lovely street lined on both sides with large American elm trees. Tina enjoyed jumping rope, playing hopscotch, and roller skating down Oak Street's wide sidewalk under those large, shady trees. Sometimes she would walk downtown to gaze through the windows of the many fine shops along Main Street or take the streetcar to visit her Aunt Mary Jane's ice cream parlor.

And of course, there was the Fourth of July. Every year on the Fourth, Tina, her father, grandparents, and Aunt Virginia visited the small graveyard next to the old Catholic church to place flowers on Tina's mother's grave and also on her Uncle John's. Tina's Christiansburg grandparents, Christina and Jamie, always attended the annual parade. Twenty or more O'Sullivans stood along the parade route. That year, Tina was dressed in a pink summer frock Grandmother Ann O'Malley had designed and sewed for her.

Grandmother Ann often took Tina to visit Susan Wright, one of her grandmother's neighbors. Mrs. Wright was also a fine dressmaker. They would exchange ideas or ask each other for help with an exceptionally complicated design.

It was during the summer of 1874 (the year Tina would turn eight), Susan Wright gave birth to a little girl named Katharine. In addition to Bishop Wright, Mrs. Wright, and baby Katharine, the Wright family included two older sons. One son was a few months younger than Tina, the other about five years younger. Tina loved baby Katharine, but Orville and Wilbur Wright paid little attention to Tina, which was fine with her.

When the Bishop was away, Mrs. Wright allowed Tina to lie on the floor in the Bishop's study to look through one of the large encyclopedia volumes or read something by Sir Walter Scott she discovered in the Wright family's extensive library.

By summer's end of 1879, Ann taught Tina how to make a pattern, cut the fabric, and stitch the sides together.

"Next summer, I will teach you how to fit a dress and add embellishments, like buttons and bows," Ann told her granddaughter.

Now that Grandfather Jamie was slowing down, Tina's father ran most of the day-to-day business activities of O'Sullivan and Sons Building Company.

Tina adored her father, Georgie. Unfortunately, her father moved his Dayton Sales Office into a larger building with a small apartment on the second floor. Most weeks, Tina's father spent his time in Dayton, only coming home for church on Sunday. With her father gone, Tina kept busy visiting neighbors with her grandmother and grandfather or helping to entertain the many guests who visited the homestead.

The Ames family had moved out of the homestead's small log cabins several years earlier into a house on Front Street in Christiansburg.

However, they came daily to manage and work the O'Sullivan's large farm. Tom Ames was now in his early fifties and appreciated help from his two young sons. Sissy, Tom's sister, came several days a week to help Tina's grandmother with the cleaning and laundry.

Tina kept her large sewing basket in Grandmother Christina's old cupboard in the library. The sewing basket originally belonged to her great-great-grandmother Marie, and it still contained skeins of Marie's old embroidery yarn.

Tom's father, Henry, had died several years before, but Henry's wife, Sharon, still visited Tina and her grandmother at the homestead. A few days before Thanksgiving, during one of Sharon's visits, Tina was showing Mrs. Ames her latest sewing project when the mail arrived. Christina came into the library holding a letter that she proceeded to read aloud.

November 5, 1882

Mrs. Christina O'Sullivan
The Wade Homestead
Christiansburg Highway
Christiansburg, Ohio

Dear Aunt Christina,

I am writing to inform you of your brother John's passing. My grandfather was eighty-eight years old. His wife, Dyani, found him early this morning when she tried to wake him for breakfast.

He was a good man who lived a long life. His family never tired of hearing his stories of when he was a young boy working at the family's mill in Maryland or when he was a soldier or a fur trapper. Please know it was a peaceful passing. He will be sorely missed.

Respectfully,
Jacob Wade

Christina was sad to hear of her brother's passing but very thankful Georgie had talked her into traveling out west to see him one last time three short years earlier.

By Christmas, Tina noticed Grandfather Jamie had a nagging dry cough. He also complained about stomach pain, so Tina's grandmother suggested he see Dr. Smith.

"It looks like you may have developed an ulcer," Dr. Smith told him. "Make sure you take a spoonful of bicarbonate of soda in a glass of water right before bed."

By early summer, Jamie was in severe pain. Dr. Smith sent Jamie to a specialist in Dayton, who confirmed Dr. Smith's newest suspicion: Jamie had developed advanced stomach cancer and had only a few months to live. Christina was devastated.

Georgie returned to the homestead more often to be with his father and help his mother. Aunt Mary Jane and Aunt Lizzy also came to stay. Jamie spent most of his last days resting on the couch in the library as he looked out over the homestead, watching the men work the fields.

Jamie died the evening of September 3, 1883; he was seventy-four years old. Jamie's last words were, "What a beautiful sunset."

Tina turned seventeen in December, with plans to graduate from Christiansburg Common School the following May. Tina had always contemplated becoming a teacher like her grandmother. She hoped someday to teach Latin or English literature at Crane Academy. So her father was allowing her to attend Oberlin College the next September.

It was the summer of 1884. Tina and Grandmother O'Malley made several new dresses for Tina to take with her to Oberlin. Katharine Wright would be ten in August and loved spending time with Tina.

"I adore the white dress you are sewing," Katharine told Tina on one of her rare visits to the O'Malleys. "I can't wait until I'm old enough to go to college and wear lovely dresses like these."

"Do you want to be a teacher, Katharine?"

"Yes, and I have decided I want to go to Oberlin College, just like you, when I am older."

The four years Tina spent at Oberlin were extraordinary. All of Tina's professors appeared open to having the students hold discussions on any topic. They regularly discussed political issues or economic concerns. Tina excelled at mathematics and Latin but enjoyed her English literature classes the most.

With Grandfather Simon now passed on, Grandmother O'Malley wanted Tina to live with her when she graduated and perhaps teach at Central High School in Dayton. Then again, Tina had always hoped to teach at Crane Academy. This desire was almost like an obligation—or a calling Tina couldn't ignore.

Crane Academy was an all-boys private school named after Philip Crane, Christiansburg's first schoolmaster. Philip was Tina's great-granduncle through his marriage to Margaret Wade, the daughter of the founder of Christiansburg. Philip had studied the classics at Winchester College in Winchester, England, and had given hundreds of books to the Wades. Some of these books now held prominence on the shelves of the old elm cupboard in the O'Sullivan's library.

In May 1888, with both of Tina's grandfathers deceased, her father was the only family member to attend her graduation from Oberlin College. Grandmother Christina was eighty-three, and Grandmother Ann was almost seventy-eight. Neither lady felt up to making the nearly seven hour train journey, but they planned a large party upon Tina's return home.

The Crane Academy administrators seemed delighted to interview such an educated and articulate young lady and hired Tina to teach Latin for the 1888–1889 school year.

Tina's first year of teaching went by quickly. Soon it was summer break. During a sweltering week in mid-June, Tina could tell that Grandmother Christina was unwell. She was becoming more and more frail and thin, and Tina wanted to be near her. Instead of spending the summer in Dayton, as she usually did, Tina remained in Christiansburg.

On August 12, 1889, Christina Elizabeth Wade O'Sullivan's heart gave out, and she died in her son's arms. She was buried next to Jamie, her loving husband of fifty-six years. Christina had loved Jamie from the first day she saw him, when he was one and she was five. They'd traveled with their parents on a wagon train led by Christina's father, Jacob, during their move from Maryland to Ohio.

The last of the Ohio Wades was gone. Tina wrote to Ryker Wade in Idaho to tell him that his Aunt Christina had passed.

After her grandmother's death, Tina started using her given name, Christina. Family members still called her Tina, but she was Christina to her contemporaries at Crane Academy.

One evening, as Christina returned from school, she noticed her father talking with three young men outside one of the old log cabins. Christina pulled her runabout buggy into the barn, gave her horse hay and water, and went into the house.

"Father," Christina called, "who are those three men I saw go into the old log cabin?"

"Three brothers come from Boston looking for work," Georgie replied. "Their parents came to America from Ireland many years ago—from Cork. Unfortunately, their parents are dead, and they heard there might be opportunities in Ohio for skilled carpenters. They came by the office today with no place to stay. I'm allowing the boys to stay in the old log cabin, and on Monday I will have Liam help them find a place to live in Dayton. Liam owns a boarding house with some rooms available. I've asked them in for dinner."

Sean, Rowan, and Brandon Murphy appeared to be in their early twenties. Christina laid out bread, butter, ham, and cheese from the larder. She roasted potatoes and carrots and brewed a large pot of hot coffee; it was a cold night for early October.

"Because of the dire poverty and the famine in Ireland, our parents came to America almost thirty years ago," Sean said. "We lived in an old tenement building in Boston infested with rats. Our mother died from the white plague, and our father soon followed her with the same illness. We heard Ohio possessed fresh air and opportunities to live a long life."

"I am so sorry to hear of your parents' passing," Christina said. "I've never heard of the white plague?"

"I think its proper name is tuberculosis," Rowan answered.

"Well, thank you again for supper. We've taken up enough of your time, and we must be getting to bed," Sean said. "I think we might be having a busy day tomorrow."

As the three men prepared to return to the log cabin Brandon spied an old fiddle hanging in the entry hall. "What a handsome old fiddle," Brandon said.

"It belonged to my great-grandfather, James O'Sullivan," Christina replied. "He was born in Dublin."

"Sean plays the fiddle," Bandon said.

"That fiddle hasn't been played in years," Georgie declared. "Will you play for us, Sean?"

"I have my flute in my knapsack," Brandon added.

As Christina and her father sat on the porch, the three men played and sang well into the night. Young Rowan even entertained the group with a cracking Irish jig.

"You men are more than welcome to come and play for us anytime," Georgie said. "Now, let me fetch you some blankets. There's wood behind the shed for a fire."

As Christina prepared for bed, she sat down at her desk to write in her journal. The journal was very special to Christina; it was the one the O'Sullivans gave to Christina's mother, Sally, on Sally's fourteenth birthday.

October 20, 1889

Three red-headed Irish men are now sleeping in farm manager Tom's old log cabin. I have never served dinner to three strange men, but they were very polite and well-spoken. After dinner, we sat on the porch and they entertained us with some lively Irish music. It's been over ten years since I heard someone play Greatgrandfather O'Sullivan's fiddle. I believe grandfather played it for me on my birthday the year I turned eleven. I hope these three young men do not take advantage of my old softy. Sometimes, Father is too benevolent.

CEO

Before daybreak, Georgie carried a tray of corn muffins and mugs of strong coffee out to the log cabin.

The men asked to be given some work to help pay for their food and lodging, even though they planned to stay for just a few days. When the farm manager, Tom Ames, arrived, he put the men to work fixing the fence near the pond.

Later, Christina fixed a breakfast of poached eggs, fried ham, biscuits with red-eye gravy, and skillet potatoes. The men sat around the kitchen table, talking and laughing. Other than a kind *thank you* spoken to Christina, the men barely seemed to notice she was in the room, or so Christina thought.

The O'Sullivans attended church at Emmanuel Catholic in Dayton only on the six holy days of obligation. So Christina and Georgie planned to attend Christ Episcopal in Christiansburg that Sunday morning and invited their three guests.

However, the men chose to muck out the barn and stables, so Christina promised them a hearty Sunday dinner.

"The men seem to be hard workers," Christina told her father later that evening as she reached for a book of poems.

As Christina prepared for school the following day, she noticed the men had already left for Dayton. When she entered the kitchen, she found a note on the kitchen table.

Miss Tina,

We don't want to appear ungrateful, but the last few years have been challenging. We don't often find such kind people, so sometimes we forget our manners and do not adequately thank those who help us. Therefore, I hope this brief note is enough to express how much my brothers and I genuinely appreciate your hospitality over the last few days. I hope we will cross paths again.

Sean Murphy

Despite suggesting he was a poor orphan, it appeared to Tina that Sean Murphy was well educated.

Every year, Georgie, Liam, and Finn held a large Christmas party for the employees at Liam and Finn's law firm, the men at O'Sullivan and Sons Building Company, and their families. It wasn't a large affair, as the two small companies employed only two office managers, one secretary, and six laborers.

Christina and her aunts, Mary Jane and Lizzie, always helped as hostesses. The party was held at Liam's home in Dayton, with food and drink from the White Horse Tavern. They hired an older gentleman to dress as Kris Kringle and pass out gifts to the workers' children.

As Christina sat on the large sofa next to the front window, she saw Sean Murphy walking toward her.

"May I fetch you a glass of punch, Miss Tina?" Sean asked.

"Oh, no, thank you, Sean," she responded. "But please, sit with me. It has been a while since you visited our homestead in Christiansburg. How are you finding Dayton and working for my father?"

"It has been the best experience of my life so far."

One cold and very snowy morning a few days before Christina started the next term at Crane Academy, she was enjoying her free time sitting alone in the library with a cup of tea.

The O'Sullivans didn't receive much mail. Seeing the mail carrier struggle to ride up the lane seemed unusual to Christina, particularly on such a day. She greeted the man on the front porch.

"A letter for you, Miss Christina," he said. "From Idaho Territory."

"Why thank you, Mr. Thompson. Please come in and warm up before you head back out."

"No, I must be on my way."

January 6, 1890

Mr. Georgie O'Sullivan and Miss Tina O'Sullivan
The Wade Homestead
Christiansburg Highway
Christiansburg, Ohio

Dear Georgie and Miss Tina,

With deep sadness, I write to inform you that my father, Rye, and mother, Matika, have both died, having been sick since well before Christmas. The doctor told us they suffered from influenza. Father died on 2 January, and Mother died on 4 January. They now rest next to each other in the graveyard of our church in Mountain Home.

Dyani, my brother John, and I, along with our children and grandchildren, pray that your family is well.

With fond regards,
Jacob Wade

"I'll write a letter tonight, sending our condolences to the Wades," Tina told her father at supper that evening.

Nonetheless, after they received Jacob's letter, the O'Sullivans never heard from any of the Idaho Wades again. Tina's recollection of her family in Idaho faded as the years passed.

Christina stayed in Dayton with Grandmother Ann O'Malley, the same as she had every summer since she was young. Grandmother Ann was now seventy-nine and still living very happily on her own.

One warm Sunday, after church, Christina walked to her aunt and uncle's ice cream parlor, where she noticed Sean sitting alone.

"Good afternoon, Sean," Christina said. "I see you like my aunt's strawberry ice cream."

"Please sit with me, Christina."

"Are you ready for Dayton's Fourth of July celebration?" she asked.

"Yes, I was wondering if I could escort you to the parade," Sean said.

"I would be honored. Please bring your brothers and be prepared to meet dozens of my family members."

When Christina returned home, she told her grandmother about meeting Sean at the ice cream parlor.

"Sean has asked to take me to the Fourth of July parade, Christina said. "We want you to come with us."

"As you know, our young friend Susan Wright died last year on the fourth; she was only fifty-eight," Ann reminded Christina. "Your mother would have been thirty-four this year if she had lived."

"All the more reason to come with us to the parade," Christina said. "We can visit Mother's grave early that morning with Father."

For the next several weeks, Sean and Christina spent most evenings together. He came to the house, they strolled along the river after church, or enjoyed dinner at one of the local taverns.

"Are you and Sean courting?" Grandmother Ann asked Christina one night after Sean had returned to his room at the boarding house.

"Yes, Grandmother. I may be in love with Sean Murphy."

It was a Saturday morning in early September, when Christina hurried down to her aunt's ice cream and bakery shop. Then she stopped at her father's sales office. Christina had been planning a surprise birthday party for her grandmother, who was turning eighty that day.

"I just picked up grandmother's birthday cake, Christina told her father. "When will the workers from the telephone company be at the house to install her new telephone?"

When the telephone came to Dayton in 1884, Georgie installed one in his sales office. Liam and Finn also installed a telephone at their law office. Even Christina's Aunt Mary Jane had one in her ice cream shop. The exchange included almost two hundred customers.

"The party starts at noon, and they should be there this morning to surprise Ann with her birthday present," Georgie said.

Christina laughed. "I'd better get back before they arrive, or Grandmother will be befuddled."

Christina invited all her grandmother's customers and friends. Ann O'Malley had remained a friend of Christina's grandparents for over sixty years, and all the O'Sullivan family dearly loved her, so Christina's aunts, uncles, and cousins were also invited.

Nearly all the guests had left by early evening except for Georgie, Christina, and Sean. They sat in Ann's living room, enjoying the last of the cake.

"Did you invite everyone in to see your new telephone?" Christina teased her grandmother.

"I've never received such a marvelous gift in all my life; I just had to show it off."

There was a slight breeze, so Christina wrapped a shawl around her shoulders as she and Sean stepped outside to clear the backyard of all the birthday bits and pieces.

"What an absolutely lovely party," Christina said. "I'm so pleased you came, Sean."

Suddenly, Sean grasped Christina's hand. "Christina O'Sullivan, please make me a happy man and become my wife?" He held out a gold ring with a small dark blue sapphire.

"Why that's Grandmother Ann's ring; my grandfather gave her on her birthday when he proposed."

"Yes, your grandmother gave it to me to give to you tonight, exactly sixty-four years after your Grandfather Simon gave it to her."

Of course, Christina said yes. They decided to marry the following September, giving Christina time to finish her contract with Crane Academy.

"Next year, I will be a married lady and retire from teaching," Christina told her grandmother that evening after Sean had left and the two ladies prepared for bed.

The following summer, Christina and Ann started to work on Christina's wedding dress.

The dress was to be made of ivory Duchess Satin. The puffed and ruched sleeves would cup her shoulders, then taper down to her wrists. The dress was designed with a fully fitted bodice, a high neckline swathed with chiffon, and a straight skirt. There would be no large bustle or hooped petticoats, just a slight bustle in the back. By sewing the dress straighter at the front and sides and tighter around the hips, it would show off Christina's tiny waist.

Christina's grandmother sewed celluloid pearls and glass beads in a leaf design down the back of the three-foot train. The bodice was covered in cotton lace and many pearls. Her cathedral-length veil was made of silk tulle and extended beyond the length of Christina's train. There was also a short blusher veil to cover her face.

On September 26, 1891, Miss Christina Elizabeth O'Sullivan married Mr. Sean Patrick Murphy at Emmanuel Catholic Church in Dayton, Ohio. She wore the traditional orange blossom chaplet wreath in her hair and carried a bouquet of orange blossoms, snowdrops, and white camellias.

Sean slipped his mother's exquisite gold ring onto Christina's finger next to Grandmother Ann's sapphire ring. It was a traditional Irish wedding band with a detailed pattern of Celtic swirls and triskeles engraved on the sides. Christina vowed never to take it off for as long as she lived.

Sean and Christina moved to the homestead in Christiansburg after the wedding. But when Christina realized she was expecting her first child in late July, she and Sean moved to Dayton to live with Grandmother Ann. Sean felt it best for Christina to be in Dayton, near a telephone and the small hospital on Main Street.

Christina worried about her father all alone in the big house in Christiansburg. Georgie was still a young man, not quite fifty. He assured Christina he enjoyed being a gentleman farmer, spending most of his days on his porch watching the spring planting, as he was spending less time at his sales office in Dayton. He had already turned over much of the day-to-day operations of O'Sullivan and Sons Building Company to his new son-in-law, Sean.

On June 17, 1892, Sean left for work after breakfast, giving Christina a quick kiss goodbye. She was expecting Sean home for lunch when she received a telephone call from Sean's brother, Rowan.

"There has been an accident. Sean fell off the roof of the house we are building. They carried him to your Uncle Liam's home. Come right away!"

Christina was unaware that Sean had broken his neck and died instantly. When she arrived at her uncle's home, she saw from the faces of her loved ones that she would never see Sean alive again. She was heartbroken but had little time to properly grieve.

On July 22, 1892, John Patrick Murphy was born. As much as Grandmother Ann wanted Christina to stay in Dayton, three months after John's birth, Christina moved back to Christiansburg to raise her son.

When John was ready to start school, Christina returned to teaching. She was hired to teach English Literature and Latin at Christiansburg Public School. She continued to teach until John graduated high school.

On December 31, 1899, Georgie, Christina, and John gathered with hundreds of Christiansburg residents at the Charles Eugene O'Sullivan Memorial Park, named after Christina's Uncle Charlie, to mark the turn of the century. There was music by the local school orchestra, food booths, and an extravagant fireworks display at midnight.

Early in 1900, Georgie was instrumental in bringing a new telephone exchange to Christiansburg. The business rented space on the second floor of the old Crane Mercantile building on Front Street. The first floor would remain O'Brian's Bicycle Emporium, which had opened three years earlier, after Danny O'Brian bought the building from John Archer.

Over the next decade, Christina documented six deaths in the old Wade Bible.

23 April 1901	– Liam O'Sullivan, 85, Natural causes
17 August 1902	– David "Davey" Creager IV, 68, Buggy accident
13 June 1905	– Ann O'Malley, 95, Natural causes
18 December 1905	– Finn O'Sullivan, 90, Natural causes
20 February 1905	– Elizabeth "Lizzy" O'Sullivan Richter, 65, Breast cancer
4 August 1909	– Karl Richter, 51, Heart attack

Christina's family had expanded so widely that she planned to stop posting all the marriages, births, and deaths in the Wade Bible, except for those within her immediate family.

In 1911, Georgie commissioned the Dayton Electric Light Company to bring electricity to Christiansburg. He then assigned two of his best workers to wire his entire house for electric lights. The years were passing quickly.

On March 21, 1913, Georgie planned to drive Christina and John into Dayton for Good Friday services at Emmanuel. They had driven just a few miles when they encountered a sudden, intense rainstorm with high winds and were forced to turn back.

"Father, I am so glad we returned home. The wind and pouring rain were frightful; I thought we would be blown off the road," Christina said. "With the ground already saturated, will the levees hold in Dayton?"

"My mother had an expression, 'It shall rain dogs and polecats,'" Georgie replied, as he parked the automobile in the barn. "It's merely an early spring rainstorm; it should stop soon. Just look at my new Model T; it's covered in mud."

"I'll help you wash it," John said. "I want it good and clean when we go to Dayton on Sunday."

Saturday, March 22, 1913, started cold but sunny. Then came a second rainstorm. On March 23, Easter Sunday, a third storm added more water to the already swollen Great Miami River.

"It doesn't look like we will be attending church in Dayton today. I've phoned as many workers as have telephones and advised them to pass the word to stay home tomorrow," Georgie told Christina. "Luckily, most live in East Dayton, a good distance from downtown and the river."

"I'm worried for Aunt Mary Jane," Christina said.

"I telephoned your cousin. David said it looks bad and he doesn't think the levees can hold back all the water flowing into the river. If the river overflows, he and his family plan to shelter on their building's top floor. He assures me that he will look after your aunt," Georgie said, attempting to calm his daughter's fears.

On March 24, the river continued to rise. The levees failed on March 25, and flooding began along the city's streets.

On March 26, downtown Dayton was flooded with nearly twenty feet of water. Fires broke out, destroying homes and businesses.

The city was in ruins. The news reported that over one hundred people lost their lives. Fortunately, Georgie's office and the Creager's ice cream shop survived the devastation.

Soon after the disastrous flooding in Dayton, Mary Jane was diagnosed with breast cancer and died eight months later. Coincidently, Mary Jane's sister, Lizzy, had died from the same dreaded condition.

At her aunt's funeral, Christina noticed her son, John, sitting with Susanna Barr, a young girl they knew from church.

After what Christina deemed a short courtship, John married Susanna on June 13, 1914. The wedding was held at Emmanuel Catholic Church, where the two young lovers first met. Susanna was a lovely girl of nineteen. John was a handsome young man who would turn twenty-two the next month.

Susanna Barr was the adopted daughter of Mr. and Mrs. Becker, the owners of the Barr-Becker Brewery. Their wedding was considered Dayton's most important social event of 1914, as Susanna's family was very wealthy.

The Beckers invited dozens of Dayton's most prominent political and social figures. In addition to his mother and grandfather, dozens of John's relatives sat on his side of the aisle.

The happy young couple moved into the house in Christiansburg with Georgie and Christina. As a wedding gift, Mr. Becker paid for a cook and a housekeeper for one year, hoping it would help Susanna learn to become a good homemaker. Christina supportively allowed Susanna to take over the running of the household.

Several months after the wedding, Georgie installed a proper plumbing system and a dedicated bathroom in their home and ran electricity and water into the old washhouse. He ordered a brand-new electric Hurley Thor washing machine from the Hurley Electric Laundry Equipment Company located in Chicago, so no more toting water from the well out back to the washhouse or carrying buckets of water into the house to bathe or wash dishes.

The ladies were ecstatic when Georgie ordered a new steel gas-coal stove from Sears Roebuck & Co. to replace the old cast-iron wood-burning cookstove monstrosity that had stood in the kitchen since 1880.

One hot summer day in 1914, Christina received a telephone call from her old friend Katharine Wright, who invited her to join the Woman's Suffrage Party of Montgomery County.

With her days free to pursue her own interests, Christina began attending suppers, speeches, and luncheons with Katharine and several other well-known Daytonian socialites. In early October, the group made plans for a suffrage parade to be held later that month in support of the amendment on the November ballot.

On October 24, a group of marchers descended on Main Street in downtown Dayton. Marching with Christina were Georgie and John. Hundreds of respectful spectators lined the sidewalks. The ladies wore matching white dresses and straw hats, carried large bouquets, and waved Dayton pennants. Christina was proud to be marching with her childhood friend, Katharine Wright, Katharine's father, Bishop Wright, and Katherine's brother Orville. Unfortunately, despite their efforts, the measure granting women the right to vote failed once again.

Susanna suffered a miscarriage in early 1915, which devastated the family.

Miraculously, on May 1, 1916, a son was born to John and Susanna at the small hospital in Dayton. Susanna's father was adamant that she give birth at the hospital, and no one could argue with Mr. Becker. Little John weighed only five pounds at birth, so John and Susanna called him their miracle baby.

John Sr. was now a married man with a child. Since Georgie was seventy-two and slowing down physically, he felt his grandson was ready to take over most of the everyday business dealings at their building company.

Because John's father, Sean, had died before he was born, his grandfather was the only father figure John ever knew. Georgie had taught John how to run a successful business from the time John was young. Now John was growing the O'Sullivan and Sons Building Company, doubling the number of workers and more than doubling the number of new building projects.

On April 6, 1917, the United States officially entered the war in Europe by declaring war on Germany.

John was twenty-five, but because he and his family owned a large farm, he received an exemption. Unfortunately, several of his young cousins were not so lucky.

"I feel so inadequate," John told his family as they gathered in the library one evening after supper. "I should not have received an exemption."

Susanna had put the baby to bed and was reading a book. John and Georgie were playing checkers. "I don't care," Susanna said. "You are needed here with us."

"You should consider providing food to your country as your contribution to the war effort," Christina added. "You should never feel inadequate for doing something your government feels is your duty."

The next ten years passed quickly as the O'Sullivan and Murphy families lived harmoniously, watching young John grow into a fine young lad.

Christina's father passed away on a frigid day, January 22, 1928. Georgie was eighty-three and had been in poor health for several months; the doctor said it was likely his heart. Though his wife, Sally Ann, was buried in the Catholic graveyard next to Emmanuel in Dayton, Georgie always said he wanted to be buried in Christiansburg when his time came.

Georgie's daughter, Christina, was in her sixties, his grandson, John, was thirty-six, and his great-grandson was eleven. After the funeral, John found his mother sitting alone in her father's bedroom. He could tell that his mother had been crying.

"What should we do with my father's medals and memorabilia he kept from the Civil War?" Christina asked her son.

"There's his old trunk in the attic; I say we store everything there," John replied. "And we should probably burn the old confederate flag he captured; that battle is over."

"You are probably right."

"Mother," John began, "I'm planning to change the name of our company from O'Sullivan and Sons Building Company to Murphy Construction Company. Several months ago, I discussed it with grandfather, who was okay with the change. Of course, Uncle Rowan, our current sales manager, and Uncle Brandon, our foreman, will continue to play a significant role in the company's future. The name change will also honor my late father, Sean.

"You have my blessing," Christina said.

The turn of the century brought many changes, from electric lights and telephones to indoor plumbing, and from automobiles to women receiving the right to vote. Christina was amazed at how things had changed since she was a young student at Oberlin College fifty years earlier. She wondered what the next fifty years would bring.

In September 1934, John Jr. started his first year at the University of Dayton. The family envisioned him obtaining his law degree and eventually taking over the Murphy Construction Company.

VIRGINIA "GINNY" MARIE NIELSEN MURPHY
1938 – 1944

"We live at home, quiet, confined, and our feelings prey upon us."

Jane Austen, *Persuasion*

Virginia Marie Nielsen was born on March 29, 1923, in Sandusky, Ohio, to William Eugene Nielsen and Hannah Marie Kraus. Virginia's father, William, was born in Brooklyn, New York, in 1895 to Johan and Sofia Nielsen. Virginia's mother, Hannah, was born in Vienna in 1900 to Henri and Margarite Kraus.

The Nielsen family were farmers from Denmark's Schleswig region. Virginia's great-grandfather was killed in 1865 while fighting in the Second Schleswig War. After the Germans defeated the Danes, the area became part of the German Confederation.

Because of the ethnic strife between the Danes and the Germans, Virginia's paternal grandfather, Johan, came to America with his widowed mother, aunt, uncle, and four older cousins when he was six years old. The Nielsens purchased one hundred acres of farmland in the area early Dutch immigrants called *Lange Eylandt* (now Long Island) from a Mister Van Dijk.

When Johan turned sixteen, he and his cousin Lars moved from the farm to the more populated Brooklyn, New York, area. The young men rented a room in a large boarding house owned by the Jensen family. The Jensens emigrated from Denmark at about the same time as the Nielsens. Almost immediately after arriving in Brooklyn, Johan and Lars were lucky enough to be accepted into a two-year apprenticeship program with a local company that manufactured cast brass handles for serving trays, cabinets, and drawers.

Morten and Freja Jensen owned the large boarding house. Freja always prepared the finest Danish dishes for her boarders. On any night, she might serve plenty of *frikadeller* with boiled potatoes and pickled beet salad, or her *hutspot met klapstuk*, with *appeltaart* for dessert.

Morten and Freja's daughter, Sofia, was a child when Johan moved in with the Jensen family. By the time Sofia turned seventeen, Johan was taken by her delicate beauty and grace. A year later, they married; Johan was twenty-five. A daughter, Edith, blessed their union two years later. It would be another eight years before their son, Virginia's father, William, was born.

Johan had long since completed his apprenticeship and earned a good wage, but he dreamed of owning his own factory. He heard stories about the city of Sandusky, Ohio, located directly on Lake Erie. It had a thriving industrial area, and goods could be transported either by ship through the port or by rail.

Johan and Sofia made the difficult decision to leave their family and move to Ohio with young William. Edith stayed behind in New York with Grandmother Freja. Once Johan, Sofia, and William arrived in Sandusky, Johan used most of his savings to acquire a building and manufacturing equipment, opening the Nielsen Handle Factory in 1905.

A month after the assassination of Archduke Ferdinand in 1914, the Austro-Hungarian government declared war on Serbia, and political tensions in the area became disquieting to those living in the region.

Being of Jewish descent, Virginia's maternal grandfather, Henri Kraus, felt less and less safe in Europe. Therefore, he intended to immigrate to America. He sold his jewelry business to a friend, Mister Baum, and with some difficulty secured travel vouchers for himself, his wife, Margarite, and their daughter, Hannah. The family would take a train from Vienna to Trieste, Italy. At the Port of Trieste, they would sail aboard the SS *Linz* to New York. Sadly, a month before they were to leave for America, Margarite contracted scarlet fever and died.

After his wife's death, Henri decided to keep to his original plan. On Hannah's fourteenth birthday, she and her father boarded the SS *Linz* and sailed for America. Once they arrived in New York, Henri began to look for work. A man told him about a handle factory in Ohio; it was looking for artists who could design and fabricate brass handles and pulls.

Henri wrote to the owner, Johan Nielsen, explaining he was a skilled jewelry designer and goldsmith who had owned a jewelry store in Vienna. Mr. Nielsen was impressed with Henri's background and offered him the position as his new head designer. Henri and Hannah immediately packed their belongings and traveled by train to Ohio.

They stayed in a local hotel for several days until they could find a permanent place to live. They eventually rented an apartment in a sizeable four-family house on Erie Street, a quiet tree-lined street conveniently located near the factory and Hannah's school. It was a small furnished apartment on the ground floor, just big enough for the two of them.

The Nielsens would often invite Henri and Hannah to their home for Sunday dinner. This was how Virginia's mother, Hannah Kraus, became acquainted with William Nielsen; Virginia's father.

Sofia had learned the art of Danish cooking from her mother and intended her meals to be more festive events than mere suppers. To help Hannah and her father feel at home, Sofia often made veal wiener schnitzel with lemon and parsley garnish, boiled beef in broth, served with a mix of minced apples and horseradish called *tafelspitz*, or sauerbraten with potato dumplings. By all accounts, William's mother was an excellent cook.

In return, Henri invited the Nielsens for long, leisurely lunches on Saturdays. After blessing the challah bread (baked with raisins and honey) Hannah had baked the day before, and then the wine, Hannah served her guests a unique meal of gefilte fish and a savory stew called *cholent*. William especially loved the chocolate cake she often served for dessert: a rich cake with a dark chocolate coating and apricot jam spread between the layers, served with unsweetened whipped cream. It was a recipe from Hannah's mother, Margarite. After lunch, the families often enjoyed a relaxing walk along the Sandusky River. (Years later, after a long work week, William missed those Shabbat lunches with Henri and Hannah.)

After courting for several years, Hannah and William were married on a lovely Saturday in June 1921. Because they were of two different faiths, they participated in two marriage ceremonies. The first was held in the morning at Grace Evangelical Lutheran. The second took place after sundown at Temple Israel. Hannah was dressed in a white wedding dress of silk and lace. On her head, she wore the small diamond tiara that Hannah's father had designed and crafted when he owned his jewelry store in Vienna. On his wedding day, he had gifted it to his wife, Margarite. Now this stunning tiara belonged to Hannah.

Once married, Hannah moved into the Nielsen's large Victorian house with William and her father-in-law, Johan. Hannah immediately became the "lady of the house," as William's mother,

Sofia, had died two years earlier after suffering a ruptured appendix. Sofia's death had been devastating for William and Johan, and the old house on Oak Street was wrapped in sorrow until Hannah arrived. More joy entered the Nielsen home when Virginia was born two years later.

Sadly, the happiness of a new baby did not last. In the summer of 1925, Johan was crushed by a load of lumber and instantly killed as he unloaded a truck at work. William became the sole owner of the Nielsen Handle Factory at the young age of thirty.

The following winter, tragedy struck again when both Hannah and Henri contracted influenza. Their illness turned into pneumonia, and they died a week apart. Virginia was only three years old when her mother and grandfather died.

A few days after the funerals, William wrote to Edith. He knew it was a selfish request, but he hoped his sister would consider leaving the only home she had ever known and move to Sandusky to help him rear his young daughter. When her parents moved to Sandusky, Edith stayed in Brooklyn to help Grandmother Jensen run the boarding house. She'd never married and now felt obligated to help her brother and his young daughter. So she boarded a train with just a few items of clothing in a small suitcase and moved to Sandusky.

It was March 28, 1938, Virginia's fifteenth birthday. Virginia's father and her aunt planned a party and invited three of Virginia's closest girlfriends.

Sitting on a crystal stand was an impressive white cake iced in pink buttercream Aunt Edith had baked. On top of the cake, she placed tiny white roses made of sugar paste. While Aunt Edith ladled punch from a silver punch bowl into shiny silver cups, Virginia's father scooped home-made vanilla ice cream into delicate crystal champagne coupe glasses.

The dining room was decorated with balloons and streamers, and Virginia was opening her many birthday gifts wrapped in bright tissue. Her favorite was the five-year diary her father gave her, along with a fancy blue pearl fountain pen. The diary came with a lock, and Virginia put the key on a chain to wear around her neck.

"Oh, Ginny!" her friend Marta exclaimed. "I love the dress and matching hat your Aunt Edith gave you. You will look so pretty in yellow with your lovely blond hair and blue eyes."

Virginia had inherited her father's fair hair and complexion, while Virginia's mother had been an attractive brunette with dark brown eyes.

"I'm going to save it to wear for the Easter Parade, with my new white gloves and clutch purse you, Emma, and Polly gave me. Papa is taking me to Kuebler's for a new pair of white t-straps."

"You will look grand!" Polly exclaimed.

Before Virginia knew it, school was out, and she, her father, and Aunt Edith moved to their cottage at Lakeside Chautauqua for the summer. William had bought the house in 1926, just after the death of his father.

Their place was like a mini mansion: a large three-story house on Park Row with a waterfront view of Lake Erie, two sleeping porches, and four bedrooms. Occasionally, Papa allowed Virginia to invite one or two of her girlfriends to stay over.

She was ready for the cool breezes off Lake Erie, the Methodist revivals, or maybe a picture show or concert at Hoover Auditorium. But best of all, Virginia loved Cedar Point Amusement Park.

June 15, 1938

Dear Diary,

Polly, Emma, Marta, and I spent the entire day at Cedar Point. As I settled into my seat on the Cyclone, I noticed the cutest, tall, red-haired boy. He was operating the ride, and when he put the gate down over my lap, he smiled and winked at me. I'm in love!

Ginny

Every day, Virginia wrote in her diary about the red-haired boy until, one day, he asked for her name.

"You come here almost every day," John said. "Aren't you tired of riding this old roller coaster? I'm John Murphy. What's your name?"

What chance did Virginia have against kismet?

July 4, 1938

Dear Diary,

His name is John Murphy, and he's a college man. He has worked at Cedar Point every summer since 1935, starting the summer after his freshman year at the University of Dayton. He is 22! I introduced him to Papa, and he invited John to dinner on Sunday. I hope he likes pea soup because Aunt Edith will likely make her gule ærter.

Ginny

September 1, 1938

Dear Diary,

John came to the cottage today to say goodbye. We've seen each other almost daily, or as often as Papa would drive me to the ferry. I don't know how I'll survive with him gone. He promised to return next summer and asked me to be his pen pal. I plan to write to him every day. I hope he writes back.

Ginny

During the following school year, Virginia and John corresponded at least once a week, writing letters back and forth.

John returned the next two summers, and Hannah's father offered him a room at their cottage at Lakeside. John was no longer running the Cyclone roller coaster, as he was promoted to a position in the park's front office.

The summer of 1940 would be John's last summer working at Cedar Point because he was graduating from law school in June. At the end of the summer, John was going back to Dayton to work with his father in the family's construction business, and Virginia needed to complete one more year of high school. She was afraid she might never see John again.

Later that same year, the U.S. government asked William if he would retool his machines to manufacture munitions for England. Although Germany now occupied William's father's homeland of Denmark, Johan had ingrained the horrors of war in William. Johan's views about war influenced his young son so much that William refused the government's request.

As time went on, the materials needed to make his metal handles were becoming more difficult to procure. As a result, his business suffered.

September 20, 1940

Mr. John Murphy Jr.
3110 Christiansburg Highway
Christiansburg, Ohio

Dear Johnny,

I'm a senior, but I guess you already knew that. I was chosen as the literary editor for our school paper. Neither Polly nor Marta decided to return to school this year, and I will miss them greatly. Emma and I plan to room together at Ohio Wesleyan next year. I think I'll study to become a teacher.

I'm worried about Papa's factory. He told Aunt Edith he must lay off some workers. We acquired a boarder last week. She graduated from college in May and now teaches the sixth grade. Emma told me her brother enlisted. I hope we don't go to war in Europe.

I trust your father isn't working you too hard and you remain well. I will write again soon,

Your Pen Pal,
Ginny Nielsen

Over the next three months, Virginia and John wrote letters to each other almost every week. Virginia wrote about school, and John told her about the houses he and his dad were building.

December 24, 1940

Mr. John Murphy Jr.
3110 Christiansburg Highway
Christiansburg, Ohio

Dearest Johnny,

I received the lace handkerchiefs today, and I love them; thank you so much. I hope you received the scarf I sent you, and that the navy blue looks good with your gray overcoat. As you can see, Aunt Edith taught me to knit.

Papa is closing the factory at the end of this year. He wants me to stay in school so I can graduate, but he won't be able to send me to college.

I'll be eighteen next March and plan to start looking for a job.

Aunt Edith took in two more boarders, so they moved my bedroom downstairs, into the solarium.

I'm so glad you miss me because I miss you too.

Merry Christmas!
Ginny

It was becoming evident to everyone who knew them that Virginia and John were more than pen pals; they had fallen in love.

March 20, 1941

Mr. John Murphy Jr.
3110 Christiansburg Highway
Christiansburg, Ohio

Dear John,

I was so excited to receive your letter. In only eight more days, you will be here in Sandusky. Can you believe I'll be eighteen? One of our boarders moved out last week, so Aunt Edith has a room ready for you. Papa sold the cottage on the lake and was finally able to sell the factory building and all the machinery. It helped him immensely with the bills.

I'm curious to see the surprise you mentioned in your last letter. Papa said he thinks you bought me a pony. We laughed when we tried to imagine Aunt Edith shooing a pony out of her petunias. Anyway, I hope it's not a pony.

Love,
Virginia

March 28, 1941

Dear Diary,

I know it's been awhile since I last wrote to you. Today is my eighteenth birthday, and I have such fantastic news; I must tell someone.

When I got home from school today, John had already arrived from Dayton. He asked me to wear my nicest dress as he made reservations for dinner at Dominick's Restaurant ... just the two of us. Once the host sat us at our table, John explained how his father offered my father the bookkeeper

*position at Murphy Construction, and Papa accepted! Diary, we
will be moving to Dayton!*

*But best of all, Diary, John said that he asked Papa for permission to
marry me. He got down on one knee right in the middle of Dominick's
Restaurant and presented me with the most sparkly diamond ring. Diary, I
almost flipped my wig, but I said yes! I'm so giddy I can't sleep, but I must
sign off for tonight because tomorrow will be a glorious new day!*

Ginny

Virginia was set to graduate from Sandusky High School on May 24, 1941, and John and his family planned to come up from Dayton for the celebration. John's family had come to Sandusky several times to visit him during the summers he worked at Cedar Point, so the Murphys and the Nielsens were well acquainted.

The day after the graduation ceremony, everyone gathered at Washington Park for the city's annual end-of-year school festival. There were carnival rides, game booths, and food tents, and the school band played at the gazebo. John received a medal for winning the sack race, and Virginia's father won her a Kewpie doll at the duck shoot. John's mother wasn't feeling well, so she and John's grandmother left the festivities early and returned to their hotel.

 John's father, John Sr., was a big burly man with dark reddish hair, while his mother, Susanna, was delicate and petite with fair hair. She suffered from migraines and needed to rest almost every afternoon because of severe fatigue.

At seventy-five years old, John's grandmother Christina was a feisty, outspoken woman who wore her hair in a little bun at the nape of her neck. She usually dressed in all black, except that day she wore a beige skirt and jacket she made just for the occasion.

Later that day, as the couple walked along the river, John told Virginia that when his grandmother Christina turned seventeen, her father sent her to Oberlin College, where she studied to become a teacher.

"My grandmother taught school for several years but retired after she married my grandfather Sean. My grandfather died at twenty-six years old, a month before my father was born. My grandmother returned to teaching once my father was older."

"I notice she still wears her wedding band next to another gold ring with a small dark blue sapphire," Virginia said. "She must have loved your grandfather very much."

"She did. And here's another interesting anecdote about my grandmother: she was part of the suffrage movement," John revealed. "My grandmother was one the organizers for the first Dayton Suffrage Parade held on October 24, 1914, marching with her childhood friends Katherine and Orville Wright."

"What a truly amazing woman!" Virginia exclaimed.

The annual end-of-year school festival always finished with magical fireworks—an impressive grand finale. That year's extravaganza did not disappoint.

Virginia's father had already moved to Dayton to work with the Murphys. He signed the house in Sandusky over to his sister, and she prepared to continue taking in boarders to help with expenses. As she had lived there for over fifteen years and made many friends, Aunt Edith was pleased to stay in Sandusky even though she would miss her brother and niece very much. She had no desire to move back to New York or to Dayton.

Murphy Construction Company's sales office was in a blue-collar community south of Dayton. The Murphys purchased a large plot of land, and over the previous two years, they built new houses in a small neighborhood of over thirty homes in Van Buren Township.

With money left over from the sale of his company, William bought one of those new houses. It was a two-up, two-down, with one small bathroom.

Virginia found the small community of newer homes quite different from the large old Victorian houses on the tree-lined streets back in Sandusky.

Decoration Day was always held on May 30. That year, the Murphys planned to host a picnic at their home in Christiansburg where John lived with his parents and grandmother. They invited relatives who lived nearby, the entire crew from Murphy Construction and their families.

Virginia had heard so much about the farm and was excited because today would be her first time visiting the "homestead," as John called it.

Virginia saw a sign as they neared the house that read: *The Wade Homestead Est. 1810.* As her father drove up the long lane toward the house, she spotted several horses grazing in a pasture surrounded by a white fence and a large pond with ducks and geese.

Near the house stood a black barn. Behind the barn, she caught a glimpse of a small apple orchard of perhaps six trees. She'd been told there were also woods behind the house with two old log homes, which she was excited to explore.

The Murphys owned almost two thousand acres, and there was newly planted corn surrounding the house as far as the eye could see. John later explained to Virginia that in between building houses, he and his dad farmed the land with help from several local young men. Some years, they rented parcels of land to local farmers for grazing sheep or cows.

Virginia met dozens of John's cousins. Some were named Creager, O'Sullivan, Richter, Lynch, and Taylor, but no one named Wade.

"The last Wade to live in this house was my grandmother Christina Elizabeth Wade O'Sullivan," Christina told Virginia. "She died in 1889, three years before my John was born."

Virginia was sitting on the front porch of her new home when her neighbor called out from next door.

"Hello, I'm Maxine. You look like you're all moved in."

Maxine looked to be about Virginia's age.

"Hi, I'm Ginny. I moved in last month. How long have you lived here?"

"Because it's so close to work, my parents purchased the first home the Murphys built," Maxine replied.

"My dad also moved here because it's close to his office," Ginny said. "He works for Murphy Construction. Where does your dad work?"

"My father, mother, and I all work at Delco Products," Maxine said. "Do you need a job?"

"I do!" Virginia exclaimed. "I'm being married next April and need to earn money for my wedding dress."

Because there were over a million men in the army in 1941, companies needed workers and started hiring women to fill the void. Maxine's dad secured Virginia an interview the following Monday. Virginia was hired on the spot and started working on the assembly line, for fifty cents an hour, the very next day.

Delco was a division of General Motors, and Virginia was putting together shocks and struts for trucks and cars. The plant was close, but Virginia bought a bus pass and commuted to work with Maxine.

Although the United States wasn't at war, many parts that Virginia assembled were for army trucks, gun carriages, tank destroyers, and other armored vehicles. She knew how opposed her father was to war, so she was extremely nervous about telling him about the duties of her new job.

It wasn't long before summer turned to autumn. The weather was beginning to turn cold. When John and Virginia had some free time, they attended Halloween parties, hayrides, bonfires, and scavenger hunts.

The Murphys invited William and Virginia for Thanksgiving and asked if Aunt Edith could come down from Sandusky. Virginia asked if she could also invite her school chum, Emma, so that Aunt Edith wouldn't have to travel alone. The Saturday before Thanksgiving, Emma telephoned.

"Wow, Virginia, I'm so excited to come for Thanksgiving. Dad said I could drive his new Chevrolet Coupe. I miss you so much; catching up and seeing your new abode will be great. I'll pick up your Aunt Edith extra early next Thursday, and we should be there by noon."

Virginia was upstairs putting clean sheets on her bed for Aunt Edith when she saw Emma pull up in front of the house. Aunt Edith would stay in Virginia's room, and the two girls planned to sleep on the hide-a-bed in the living room.

"They're here," Virginia called down to her dad.

Virginia made two pumpkin and two apple pies. She ran down the stairs to the kitchen and packed the pies into two picnic hampers. They quickly hugged and greeted everyone to avoid getting to the Murphy's late. The four piled into Emma's car and headed to Christiansburg.

John set a platter containing a large turkey before his dad for him to carve. Virginia and Emma helped John, carrying a large ham and all the traditional Thanksgiving trimmings: stuffing, mashed potatoes, candied sweet potatoes, gravy, cranberry relish, and succotash. After Susanna said grace and everyone filled their plates, John's dad opened a bottle of Burgundy wine and gave the toast.

"I am honored to be your host for this bountiful feast prepared with love by my precious wife and dear mother. Thank you to Virginia for bringing the pies; they look delicious. Mother, Susanna, John, and I are grateful to share Thanksgiving with you fine folks today. Cheers!"

Grandma Christina had started work on Virginia's wedding dress a few weeks before, so she invited the ladies upstairs after Thanksgiving dinner to see her progress. Christina's grandmother Ann O'Malley had taught Christina to sew during her summer visits with her grandparents in Dayton.

"Christina, you are a true artist. Virginia's dress is so lovely!" Aunt Edith exclaimed. "Nothing is more stunning than a wedding dress made from white *peau de soie* taffeta."

"I love the sleeves," Emma said. "Especially how they come down to a point over your hand."

Virginia's dress was designed with a fit-and-flare silhouette, and Christina added a long detachable train and off-the-shoulder netting. She was also making a long veil from silk tulle. Christina showed everyone the Wade sapphire earrings as Virginia's "something blue," and Aunt Edith described the Kraus tiara Virginia would wear as her "something old."

For Virginia's bridesmaids, Maxine and Emma, Christina made matching gowns of light pink satin. Emma tried hers on while she was there, and it fit perfectly.

The morning of Sunday, December 7, 1941, started fair and cold. When Virginia and her dad walked to church, the temperature was in the mid-30s, so they bundled up against a light breeze.

They were often invited to the Murphy's for Sunday dinner. That day, they brought a chocolate cake Virginia baked that morning from a recipe in her mother Hannah's old recipe box. It was her father's favorite cake and had been passed down from Virginia's grandmother Margarite. It was called "The Sacher-Torte," after a cake created in Vienna in 1832. Luckily for Virginia, her mother had translated it from Austrian German into English. Confident John's mother and grandmother would appreciate the recipe, Virginia typed a copy to give them.

The Sacher-Torte

1. Preheat the oven to 350 degrees and grease and flour all over a 9" by 2" round cake pan or line the bottom with waxed paper.

2. Over low heat, melt eight squares of semi-sweet chocolate.

3. In a small bowl, lightly beat eight egg yolks (save the whites). Add the melted chocolate, eight tablespoons of melted unsalted butter, and one teaspoon of vanilla extract. Blend until smooth and satiny.

4. In a separate bowl, using an eggbeater, beat eight egg whites with a pinch of salt until foamy. Slowly add three-fourths cup of superfine sugar and beat until the whites hold a stiff peak but are still glossy.

5. Mix one-third of the egg whites into the chocolate/yolk mixture. Now, pour that mixture into the bowl with the rest of the whites. Fold gently, using 20 to 30 strokes.

6. Sprinkle one cup of unbleached cake flour over the chocolate batter and fold gently until no egg white remains.

7. Pour the batter into the pan. Bake until the cake is puffed and dry-looking on top, about 40–45 minutes. Cool in the pan for ten minutes before turning out onto a wire rack.

8. Split the cake in half and spread one-half cup of strained apricot jam between the two layers.

Chocolate Glaze

1. Place eight squares of semi-sweet chocolate into a pan over medium-low heat with one-half cup of boiling water and one cup of granulated sugar. Cook, stirring frequently, for about 4 to 5 minutes.

2. As soon as the glaze is smooth, immediately pour it over the cooled cake and let set at room temperature for a few hours before serving. This cake is best served the same day it is made, accompanied by a dollop of unsweetened whipped cream.

After dinner, William exclaimed, "The food was superb! I can't thank you enough for inviting Virginia and me for such a lovely meal."

John's mother, Susanna, excused herself and went upstairs to rest.

"Let's go into the living room and turn on the radio," John's father suggested. "I want to listen to 'World Today'; I think it comes on at two-thirty."

"The New York Philharmonic is live on the radio this afternoon, playing a concert at Carnegie Hall," Grandma Christina said. "I'll listen in my room. Good afternoon, all."

John's father built a roaring fire in the large stone fireplace in the living room. Then, John and his father lit their Meerschaum pipes. They smoked a unique blend of tobacco and Virginia loved the aroma, or the "room note," as John called it.

But one of the things Virginia enjoyed the most whenever she visited was searching through the old cupboard in the library to find a good book to read.

"The old elm cupboard is a family heirloom," John had explained to Virginia the first time she visited the homestead. "It was built in England and brought to America by an early ancestor, Christian Wade. Our little town is named after Mr. Wade. I believe his father-in-law was the builder of the cupboard."

An embroidered piece hanging on the wall next to the cupboard showed an angel leaning against a willow tree. In the background, someone had painted a river with a watermill. On the table next to the cupboard was a dollhouse covered by a glass display case. It was a replica of the mill depicted in the embroidered piece. A larger dollhouse sat on the central table. It was almost a mirror image of the Murphy's present house and looked as if some small child had very much loved it. Virginia needed to ask John if he knew the story behind the embroidered piece and the two dollhouses.

She found a book of poems by William Wordsworth and Samuel Taylor Coleridge. It was titled *Lyrical Ballads with a Few Other Poems,* published in 1798, and she wanted to read "The Rime of the

Ancyent Marinere" by Coleridge. Virginia brought her book into the living room and quietly read while the men listened to the radio.

Suddenly, radio host John Daly broke into the program to announce that Pearl Harbor had been attacked, and war with Japan was inevitable.

Everyone was in a state of shock. Grandma Christina came out of her upstairs bedroom to ask if they had heard the announcement. "What does this mean, John?" she asked her son.

"They said President Roosevelt will be meeting with his cabinet tonight. I think we will know more tomorrow. Let's stay positive, but I believe this means we are again at war."

John Sr. had been twenty-five when the United States declared war on Germany in 1917. Because his family owned a large farm, he'd received an exemption and was not required to serve.

Virginia's father, William, was twenty-two when America entered World War I. He applied for a deferment based on his personal beliefs, but it was denied. Fortunately, the war was over once he was trained and ready to be deployed.

America had enjoyed twenty-four short years of peace and was again at war. Virginia worried if her John would be drafted or if he could receive an exemption like his father. Virginia remembered the poem she had been reading when she heard the announcement and wondered, *Although I've done nothing wrong, will this war become the albatross around my neck?*

The following day, Virginia awoke to the grim reality that America was at war with Japan. Three days later, Germany and Italy declared war on the United States. John told Virginia and his family that he was anxious to volunteer for the Army Air Corps. Virginia worried that her April wedding might be called off, but John assured her they would marry before he left.

Delco organized a Christmas party that year for its workers. The dinner dance was to be held in the ballroom of the Biltmore Hotel in downtown Dayton.

Virginia and her girlfriends planned on being "dressed to the nines." Virginia decided to wear her favorite black tea dress from several years before—the one with the sweetheart neckline and thick shoulder pads. To compliment her outfit, she intended to wear her black peep-toe slingback platform shoes, her black velvet hat with the red bow and veil, and black lace gloves.

Maxine drove a 1934 Plymouth sedan and had volunteered to drive Virginia and several of their friends to the party.

"Hi-de-ho, Virginia," Maxine called. "Are you about ready? The gals are waiting in the car."

"Come on up," Virginia called down from her bedroom. "I'm almost ready."

Maxine climbed the stairs and exclaimed, "Gosh, you look able, Grable! Your 'gams' look great too. Are those real nylons? I went out to buy some, but they're hard to find. I couldn't find them in any of our local stores. Dad said they might start rationing food and clothes. It's going to be awful. I tried to repair the 'ladders' on mine, but they were too far gone. My mom helped me draw a 'seam' down my legs with my black eyebrow pencil."

"Wow! Maxine, your red dress is simply too perfect!"

"This was last year's prom dress, and Mom shortened it for me," Maxine explained. "Come on, Virginia. We need to push off if we're going to arrive at this shindig on time."

The ballroom was decorated with dozens of white-flocked Christmas trees. Wreaths made from ivy and pine garland gave off a wonderful Christmassy smell. The only light in the room came from the multi-colored lights on the Christmas trees, along with the candles placed on every table nestled among huge arrangements of red poinsettias.

Handsome waiters wearing white coats and gloves served a turkey dinner with all the trimmings. After dinner, everyone danced while the band played all the popular tunes of the day. No one talked about the uncertainty of the coming months or what next Christmas might bring. Instead, they relaxed, laughed, and danced until almost midnight.

As they left the hotel, delicate light snow was falling. Driving home, the girls "oohed" and "aahed" over all the Christmas lights shining brightly on the houses and businesses. They didn't seem to have a care in the world.

Virginia and John's wedding was set for Saturday, April 11, 1942, at St. Paul's Lutheran Church. Thankfully, after John enlisted, it was several months before he was accepted as an aviation cadet, so there was no need to change the date.

A few days before the wedding, Aunt Edith and Virginia went shopping.

As they rode the bus downtown to Rike's department store to buy Virginia her going-away outfit. Aunt Edith explained, "I want you to pick out whatever you want. You need to look exceptional on your wedding day."

Aunt Edith had gifted Virginia a sweet yellow dress for her fifteenth birthday, so the pale-yellow suit she chose brought back happy memories. Since the jacket was trimmed in navy blue, Virginia chose navy gloves and a small navy pill-box hat with a snood to cover her blond curls. Virginia's favorite purchase was a pair of navy leather pumps, to which she added a detachable bow clip.

"Thank you for everything, Aunt Edith. I especially love my new shoes."

"A girl can't go on an adventure without a pair of shiny new shoes," Edith claimed.

"Let's have them deliver our packages; I'll treat you to lunch upstairs at the Coin Room," Virginia told her aunt. "I've been craving one of their famous Sloppy Joe sandwiches and a cherry phosphate."

"Afterward, I want to walk through the book department," Edith replied. "I'd like to find a good book to read next week on the train home."

"We promised Dad we would bring home something to cook for dinner," Virginia said. "On our way to the Arcade, I need to stop at Gallaher's drug store."

The wedding day arrived cool and clear. Virginia was upstairs in Christina's room, preparing to slip into her wedding gown, when Aunt Edith, Maxine, and Emma entered.

"Maxine, can you fix my hair into an updo with 'Victory rolls' on either side and a chignon in the back?" Virginia asked.

"I am honored to fix your hair on your wedding day."

After she dressed, Aunt Edith placed the Kraus tiara onto Virginia's expertly styled hair.

Virginia and her father arrived at St. Paul's Lutheran Church, and her quiet demeanor helped to calm her father's nerves. Maxine handed Virginia a bouquet of white calla lilies.

A small reception was held at the church with cake and punch. Afterward, the family drove back to the house so John and Virginia could change out of their wedding clothes. As they left the house, they were met with a flurry of rice and well-wishes. John borrowed his father's 1939 Mercury. The newly wedded Mr. & Mrs. John Patrick Murphy, Jr. were off on their honeymoon to Niagara Falls.

After leaving Officer Candidate School in Miami, John was sent to Texas to start his flying instruction.

After several months, John finished his training in Texas among the top of this class and was commissioned as a second lieutenant. The family traveled to Texas to watch as John received his wings. It was July 1942.

"John, I can't tell you how proud I am!" his mother exclaimed.

He looked so handsome in his dress uniform with its brass buttons and patches. Virginia was proud, too, but she was more worried than she let on. She knew she must be cheerful for all their sakes, but it became more challenging each day John was away training.

John returned to Ohio with the family, as he had been given a few days of furlough before leaving for additional training in Boise, Idaho.

"Wow, Texas was sure hot, but it's hot and humid here in Ohio, too," John said. "Let's go for a swim in the pond."

"Thanks, but I think I'll stay on terra firma and maybe drink a nice glass of lemonade," Virginia announced with a smile.

John was tanner than she had ever seen him. His red hair was now a shade more like strawberry blond. Virginia always thought John very handsome, but he appeared to have grown more handsome since joining the Army. Maybe it was the uniform, or perhaps it was just that she missed him so badly when he was away. While John was home on leave, Virginia worked hard not to show how worried she was. However, after he left for Idaho, she became so distraught that she couldn't eat or sleep for several days.

Sunday, August 22, 1943

Lt. John P. Murphy Jr.
US Army Pocatello Airbase
453rd Heavy Bombardment Group
735th Bomb Squadron
Pocatello, Idaho

Dear John,

I was so happy to receive your letter today! You just returned from Florida and they immediately transferred you from Boise to Pocatello. Wow! You have seen more of this great country than I will see in my lifetime. Since you seem to be moving around so much, I hope you receive our letters. I sure wish the Army had stationed you here at Wright Field. Wouldn't that be wonderful?

Speaking of Wright Field, your dad has a friend who works there. He told us all about the airplane you are learning to pilot, the B-24 Liberator. He explained that it was a very large plane. It must take a lot of skill to fly.

Your crew sounds interesting; you have men from all across the country. They seem so very young, some just nineteen years old. The responsibility you feel for their safety must be overwhelming.

Well, I'm signing off for now. I'm a working girl, and a working girl needs her beauty sleep!

Love, as always!
Ginny

In early September of 1943, John received a two-week furlough. The weather was still warm in southwestern Ohio. By mid-October, the maples and oaks would become the gorgeous shades of red and gold Virginia loved. Though she was born in March and her wedding was in April, autumn was Virginia's favorite time of year.

She and John spent as much time together as they could, enjoying each other's company and trying not to dwell on the future. In just a few months John would be sent overseas, and Virginia was becoming increasingly worried. She didn't know how she would go on if anything happened to him.

A few weeks after John left Ohio, Virginia received a letter from him, saying he'd arrived safely at March Field in Riverside, California. She was happy when she saw the letter in her mailbox but slightly annoyed that he wrote about men dying while training before going to war. This caused her to worry that much more.

With John's busy training schedule and Virginia working so many hours, they found it challenging to find the time to write. But each was adamant they would attempt to send at least one letter a week. On November 21, John wrote to say he'd received orders to depart for Europe and didn't know if he could write again until after he landed. This holiday season was going to be rough on everyone.

It wasn't until mid-January that Virginia received John's letter telling her he was stationed somewhere in the British Isles. Because all military mail was censored, he was not allowed to say precisely where he was.

Every day, she worried more and more about his safety. He said he was eating well and was starting to receive her letters, some postmarked as late as November. He wrote that he had not received the

Christmas packages she mentioned in her letters but felt they should arrive soon.

Because John knew his letters were being read by ranking officers, he never wrote about any missions he was assigned to fly or the dangers he faced. The letters from John came sporadically, and it was torture for Virginia when there was no letter in the box for days, sometimes weeks.

Spring arrived early in 1944. The redbud trees were the first to show their blossoms, followed closely by the yellow of the forsythia and the daffodils.

Unfortunately, the mood was somber in both the Murphy and Nielsen homes. Virginia was still working at the factory, so after John left for basic training, she moved back in with her father.

Easter was on April 9, and Virginia and her dad started the day by attending church at St Paul's. The Murphys invited the Nielsens for Easter dinner, and even though gas was now rationed, and Virginia and William could have taken the bus, they instead drove the short distance to Christiansburg.

Grandmother Christina had obtained a canned ham with her ration coupons; the meal was delicious and plentiful. Unfortunately, no one was in the mood to celebrate, so Virginia and her dad left to return home by early afternoon.

"John's mother looked very weak today," Virginia said as she and her dad drove home. "Her complexion appeared gray, and the lines on her face seemed more pronounced."

"I wasn't too surprised when she excused herself immediately after dinner," William responded. "She'd hardly eaten anything on her plate. Did you notice she appeared to be having problems with her balance?"

"I think her headaches are becoming more painful, too," Virginia added.

Three days later, Susanna Lillie Barr Murphy died from a cerebral aneurysm at just forty-nine.

Susanna's parents had immigrated from Scotland to Northumberland, Pennsylvania, where Susanna was born. The family moved to Dayton when Susanna was three years old.

Susanna's father co-owned a beer brewery with Mr. Becker. The Barr-Becker Brewery was located along the Great Miami River with access to plenty of water and the Miami-Erie canal for shipping their product.

Unfortunately, both of Susanna's parents had died in a car accident in 1911. The Barr family was out for a Sunday drive in their brand-new Stoddard-Dayton when their car hit a rut in the road. Mr. Barr lost control and crashed into a tree. Because she was sitting in the back seat, only sixteen-year-old Susanna survived.

Mr. and Mrs. Becker had no children of their own. So after the death of Susanna's parents, the Beckers adopted and raised Susanna and loved her as if she were their daughter. They ensured she wore the finest clothes and sent her to the prestigious private Catholic secondary school for girls in Dayton, Notre Dame Academy.

The Beckers and the Murphys both attended Emmanuel Catholic Church; it was there that Susanna met her husband and where Susanna's funeral Mass was held. She was buried in the Barr-Becker family plot in Dayton's Woodlawn Cemetery.

John's father was devastated by the death of his loving wife. It was difficult, but the family decided to spare young John the grief of learning that his mother died while he was away fighting a war, so they didn't inform him.

JOHN PATRICK MURPHY JR.
1942 – 1947

"It isn't what we say or think that defines us, but what we do."

Jane Austen, *Sense and Sensibility*

*I*t was shortly before his marriage to Virginia that John enlisted in the U.S. Army Air Forces. He soon became an aviation cadet, starting his training in Florida less than a month after their wedding.

May 3, 1942

Mrs. Virginia Murphy
3110 Christiansburg Highway
Christiansburg, Ohio

Dear Virginia,

I just "landed" in sunny Miami Beach at the Air Forces Technical Training Command. The train ride down was long and boring. We are barracked in one of the newer hotels here, and it's really classy: an innerspring mattress and a private bath with a shower. About seventy-five yards across from our barracks is the massive Atlantic Ocean.

I received two more shots with four more to go; boy, are my arms sore. I picked up a small shell on the beach yesterday; you'll find it enclosed with this letter.

Please let me know if you plan to move back home with your father.

Love,
John

John was sent to Kelly Field in San Antonio, Texas, at the end of May for flying training. He left the rank of Aviation Cadet on July 20, 1942, and was commissioned as a Second Lieutenant.

He was relaxing on his bunk before "lights out." Some of his buddies wrote letters, while others started a lively poker game. John was talking with Bill Stewart, a fellow pilot in training from Boston.

"My parents, my wife, my grandmother, and my father-in-law are all coming down from Ohio this weekend to watch us receive our wings next Monday," John said. "I can't wait to see my girl!"

"I bet she's a knockout," Bill responded.

"The cutest little blond, blue-eyed beauty you will ever meet."

John Sr., Susanna, Virginia, Christina, and William traveled by train from Cincinnati to San Antonio to attend the pinning ceremony. John was so proud that his family made the trip down to Texas, and they seemed equally proud of his accomplishments. The next day, he traveled with his family to Christiansburg for a short furlough before being sent to Boise, Idaho.

While they prepared for bed his first night home, John cradled Virginia in his arms.

"I'm giving you a pair of gold wings," John explained. "The story goes that whoever wears this pin for a full day and then presents it to his mom or wife to wear will be followed by 'Dame Fortune' wherever he goes. It's a silly superstition, but I hope you wear them every day."

In Boise, John learned he would be part of the 453rd Heavy Bombardment Group, 735th Bomb Squadron training on the B-24 Liberator.

His crew of ten men were assembled, as they went through three more phases of aircrew training.

From Boise, John spent some time training back in Florida and was then transferred to Pocatello, Idaho. The entire time John was in Idaho, he was unaware he had distant cousins living nearby.

At twenty-five years of age, John was the pilot and the oldest crew member. The other nine men were: co-pilot Bob Jones; navigator Jack Kirby; bombardier Smitty Carson; radio operator/waist gunner Harry Dawson; nose turret Jerry Williamson; tail turret Jim Wright; ball turret Barry Neely; top turret Ed Weiss; and engineer/waist gunner Benji Wilson.

The ten men started as strangers from ten different areas of the country. They soon formed what they hoped would become a lasting brotherhood. The men shared many of the same experiences of growing up poor during the Great Depression and now facing war together.

John found the big four-engine, heavy bomber extremely difficult to fly with its stiff and heavy control. Because of its single exit, it could quickly turn into a death trap. The B-24 earned the nickname by its crews as the "Flying Coffin."

In early September, John received a much-deserved two-week furlough. Before he left for home, John received a letter from Virginia telling him the weather in Ohio was still hot and humid. She also told him the Murphys planned to hold their annual Labor Day picnic a week after Labor Day to coincide with John's time off. This year's celebration would be extra special because John would be home.

After John's furlough, he left for additional aircrew training at March Field in Riverside, California.

October 1, 1943

Mrs. Virginia Murphy
129 Gladstone Street
Dayton, Ohio

My Darling Virginia,

I arrived safely in California. But I must tell you that seeing you for those two glorious weeks was just what I needed to keep going.

I'm enclosing a picture of my crew. I don't think I could find a better bunch of boys. The ship, part of which you can see, is the "old standby" of the 735th. It's endured a lot of hard knocks, but she always comes back for more. This won't be the one we take to war, but she's a honey.

We've had awful weather; the fog is so thick you could cut it with a knife. When the field is closed for weather, they send the ships to an emergency field. Mine was sitting in a desert in Nevada while I was on furlough.

You remember Bill Stewart. Well, his plane went missing while I was in Ohio. Bill and his crew left from an emergency field near here with a two-hour gas supply, but command never heard from it after takeoff. They kept planes in the air, continuously looking for them. They finally located it yesterday. It crashed head-on onto a mountain and burned. Bill and his entire crew were lost. He was a good friend. It's hard to believe he's gone.

Tomorrow's mission calls for high-altitude training, which means we'll fly about 20,000 feet or nearly four miles straight up. Our aircraft is not pressurized, has no heat, and you should see what we wear for our flights. Everything is lined with sheepskin, and to make things even more uncomfortable, we wear bulky oxygen masks at high altitudes.

Sometimes our plane can be exposed to temperatures from minus thirty to minus fifty degrees. But actually, we stay pretty warm. My pants have a cord that plugs into the plane's power supply, and my jacket and boots connect to the pants.

The B-24 is considered a strategic bomber, and once we reach our final destination, we will conduct bombing raids on specific targets (I hope that passes the censors). Don't worry! I've promised my entire crew that I'll do everything possible to bring us all home safely.

Give my love to all,
John

December 10, 1943

Mrs. Virginia Murphy
129 Gladstone Street
Dayton, Ohio

Dearest Ginny,

I received a letter from Grandma Christina today, thanking me for the birthday letter I sent to her. It sounds like it arrived right on time. She told me about the party you all gave her; I sure wish I had been there. Was she seventy-seven this year?

I received my new plane today, and it is nice! They flew it in from a manufacturing facility in Detroit. The only bad thing is that it still has a few bugs. Those will need to be flown out, much like a new car. We tried for days, racking our brains to find a name for our ship. After much discussion, the guys agreed to let me name her "Little Ginny."

I'm writing this letter with the new pen I snapped up yesterday. It was a gift to myself for Christmas. It's one of those brand-new Parker Vacumatics. It hasn't improved the scrawl, but it writes mighty fine.

We will leave here in a few days, traveling by train to San Francisco. I'm anxious to see the things I've only seen from the air, like the Golden Gate Bridge, Chinatown, and Treasure Island.

You should see me in my complete outfit, with weapons and all. Each crew member wears a long knife and a pistol in a shoulder holster… rather a formidable outfit. I'm not as good a shot as your dad. I remember how good he was at the duck shoot at the festival in Sandusky! I probably couldn't hit a barn with the pistol, and more than likely will never get close enough to the enemy to have to use the knife.

Please don't send any more letters to March Field; use my A.P.O. address instead. It will reach me much faster. I haven't heard from any of the gang for quite a while, so if you see any of them, give them the address and ask them to drop a line now and then. There is no need to say I will be slow in answering because I always am anyway, and they all know it.

Well, my love, it's time to say goodnight and that I love you and miss you very much.

Love,
John

From San Francisco, John flew to Palm Springs, California, where he spent Christmas.

December 25, 1943

Mrs. Virginia Murphy
129 Gladstone Street
Dayton, Ohio

Merry Christmas, My Darling Virginia,

We are on the move, so I'll make this brief. Please don't send any more letters or packages until I know I have reached my final destination. We are spending Christmas here in California, and I just returned from chow. I am stuffed to my ears with oyster cocktail, green pea soup (not as good as Aunt Edith's), and roast turkey with all the fixings. The Waldorf salad was new to me, and the fruit cake was actually pretty tasty. I also ate a piece of apple pie topped with a slice of cheddar cheese.

They sent us back to the barracks with a box of hard-tack candy and a tin of assorted nuts. They plan to keep the mess hall open all day, leaving us free to help ourselves to anything and everything in sight.

I'd planned on calling you Christmas Eve, but censorship restrictions forbid us to use the phone, so that was out. The Christmas holiday was as good as expected, but I miss the good times of former years.

We'll probably be flying out of here in a few days, so you may not receive any letters for several weeks, but don't worry. I will close this letter by wishing you a very Happy New Year.

Love as Always,
John

On December 28, John flew to Midland, Texas, and then to Memphis, Tennessee, where he spent New Year's Eve. In Tennessee, he was so close to home that it was maddening. They left Tennessee and flew to Puerto Rico, Trinidad, Brazil, and West Africa.

January 9, 1944

Mrs. Virginia Murphy
129 Gladstone Street
Dayton, Ohio USA

Dear Virginia,

We've been on the move for several weeks, and I now know my final destination, and I'm pretty pleased. I'm getting three square meals every day and have gained six pounds. I can't tell you where I am at this writing, but it's stranger than any place I've ever seen. Since we've been moving, I've met two boys I knew from home. It was a treat to talk about old times.

The C.Q. is turning the lights out, so I must stop writing. Tell everyone hello, and write as soon as you can. The mail will pile up, and I'll have a lot to read at one time. I'll write again when I reach the last stop.

Give my love to all,
John

When they left West Africa, they flew to Wales and arrived in England on January 11, 1944. John was stationed at the RAF Old Buckenham Airfield, or "Old Buck" as the men affectionately called it. It was one hundred miles from London and fifteen miles from Norwich, England.

January 12, 1944

Mrs. Virginia Murphy
129 Gladstone Street
Dayton, Ohio USA

Dear Virginia,

I am at a Bomber Base somewhere in the British Isles. I'm well pleased with the country, even though it is cold. My ancestors, the Wades, came from near here, if that tells you anything. I haven't met any local people yet, but from what some of the boys say, they're very friendly.

I've seen quite a chunk of the world, and by now, I have quite a cross-sectional view of how the other half lives. You can bet that there's no place like home.

This is a rather noisy place to write a letter. There's a card game going on here in the hut. It's centered around the stove and by my bunk. They're playing with English money, so there's a big discussion about how much each is worth. Card playing is the easiest way to learn about English money, and it helps fill in the leisure time.

There is very little of life's luxuries, such as cigarettes and chewing gum. They have some, but the supply is limited. Only so much per day per man. If you find it convenient, can you add some Lucky Strikes and a few packs of Beeman's gum in your next package? I also just learned that we are only allowed two weekly razor blades. You mentioned having to carry so many ration books. You're not alone, as they require us to carry one too.

While not the finest I've ever eaten, the food is pretty good. At any rate, I'm getting enough and not losing any weight.

The temptation is too great; I've got to get into this card game. So, in closing, give my best to all, and I'll write again soon.

Love,
John

April 9, 1944

Mrs. Virginia Murphy
129 Gladstone Street
Dayton, Ohio USA

Dear Virginia,

Happy Easter, my love! I'm hopeful you and William could attend church today and perhaps spend the day at Mom and Dad's. Was Grandma Christina able to find a nice ham for dinner?

I'm so glad you and Mom could celebrate your birthdays together. I'm missing so many family events. I received a long letter from my mother last week saying she loved the Jane Austin book I sent her. The cake Grandma baked for the two of you sounds scrumptious; she sure can cook! It's just another thing I miss. I sure hope we'll be able to celebrate your next birthday together.

It's been a while since I've attended church; probably the last time was our wedding. However, I attended Mass this morning, which was uplifting. After Mass, they served us a fine dinner here on base.

If this letter seems messy, it's because I'm writing by candlelight. The power has been off…again…for several hours. Any news is pretty scarce, and anything I might want to tell you would be censored. So until such time when I will be able to tell you some of those stories, this idle chatter will have to do.

Now, I say to you with love and best wishes.

Goodnight,
John

P.S. If you can send my dark garrison cap with the emblem, I might just as well get some use out of it. J

John could not know that his mother would be dead three days after he wrote this letter.

John's first few missions were relatively easy compared with the ones he might fly later over Germany. They called those early missions over France "milk runs."

After every mission, the men were debriefed before heading to chow and returning to their huts. John mostly slept between missions; every man was exhausted. They awoke early and they went to bed late.

On the morning of May 8, eighteen B-24s departed from Old Buck. It was John's tenth mission, and they were scheduled to bomb a German aircraft factory. As they neared their target, they encountered a Focke-Wulf pack, a dozen or more German fighter planes coming in for the kill. They were hammered with flak and gunfire from all sides, yet Smitty dropped all eight of the one-thousand-pound bombs right on target.

As John turned to head back to base, flak hit both the nose and ball turrets. John knew it must have shattered the Plexiglass. He reasoned that Jerry, Barry, and Smitty were dead—if not by the hit, by the exposure to a blast of minus fifty-degree air at 200 mph. The propeller on their number two engine was no longer spinning, and oil was splattered on the windshield.

His co-pilot, Bob, called out over the intercom, hopeful for a report on the rest of the crew but didn't hear back from the nose or ball turret gunners, navigator, or bombardier. There was so much black smoke that it was difficult to see where they were going. Once the smoke cleared, John was able to stabilize the severely damaged plane and fly by sight, guided by landmarks below. He followed a winding river but had no idea where it might take them.

With no help from the navigator, John was unaware that he'd wandered nearly three hundred miles off course. He and Bob soon found themselves alone in the sky, somewhere over what they thought was France. With a crippled plane and realizing they had no more than ten minutes of fuel left, John knew there was no way they'd make it back to base. Once again, Bob called out over the intercom to any crew members who might still be alive to prepare for an emergency landing.

"John and I are going to attempt to land this baby in the field ahead," Bob said. "Those of you who are able should parachute now, or you can prepare yourselves for an emergency landing and ride it out with us."

Flying low over a wheat field, they could see three farmers below them with two large plow horses. John and Bob decided to land their massive beast on the tiny field below. As they came down, trying desperately not to kill innocent civilians, the landing gear hit a ditch pitching the plane forward. It broke into pieces and caught fire.

It was a chilly evening in early May, and Virginia and William had just sat down for dinner when there was a knock on the door. William opened the door, and Virginia saw a young boy who looked about fifteen years old. She realized he was a Western Union messenger. The blood drained from her face, and she slumped back into her chair. Once she regained her composure, William read the telegram to her.

TELEGRAM

WASHINGTON D.C.
MAY 10, 1944

MRS. JOHN P MURPHY JR 129 GLADSTONE ST VAN BUREN
TOWNSHIP OHIO

THE SECRETARY OF WAR DESIRES ME TO EXPRESS HIS DEEPEST
REGRET THAT YOUR HUSBAND SECOND LIEUTENANT JOHN
P. MURPHY JR HAS BEEN REPORTED MISSING IN ACTION SINCE
8 MAY ON MISSION TO GERMANY PERIOD .

IF FURTHER DETAILS OR OTHER INFORMATION ARE RECEIVED YOU
WILL BE PROMPTLY NOTIFIED PERIOD .

"If he's been taken prisoner, we will hear from him through the Red Cross," William explained, trying to ease Virginia's fears.

When John regained consciousness, he was in a small bed in an unfamiliar room. He heard a conversation in French between two people. A woman was angry and was shouting. Although John had studied French in school, there was little he could easily understand. He did hear her say again and again, *"L'Américain ne peut pas être ici."* John interpreted this with his limited French as "The American can't be here."

John had suffered a concussion and was in and out of consciousness for several days. During one of his lucid moments, the farmer who rescued John spoke to him in perfect English. "My sons and I pulled you away from your airplane. No one can know you are here. We never know who might be a Nazi sympathizer, and my wife is very afraid," he told John. "But I couldn't let you die in our field along with your comrades. You suffered a broken leg and a broken arm, which we placed in splints, but I fear you experienced other injuries we cannot fix. You are safe for a time in my house."

"Where exactly am I?" John asked.

"You landed in Belgium, about five kilometers north of Liege. My name is Noah Peeters, and my sons and I brought you into my house. I live with my wife, Ella, and my two sons, Adam and Lucas. I have grim news: none of your crew survived. My sons helped me bury the men in our orchard. We buried your uniform in a tenth 'grave' so the Germans wouldn't suspect anyone had escaped."

The sadness was more overwhelming than the pain, and for days, John mourned the loss of his crew.

John's plane was still smoldering in Noah's field when several neighbors came to the house to warn the Peeters that German soldiers had been seen in the town square asking about the crash and if anyone found any survivors. Noah showed his neighbors the ten graves behind the house.

"If the Germans want to dig up the graves, they will find ten bodies," Noah lied.

It was nearly four months before John could stand for more than a few minutes. On a warm day in early September, Noah and John were sitting on the porch when they heard what sounded like tanks coming up the road toward the farm.

"Lucas, go and see if it's the Germans," Noah told his son. "If they are German tanks, you and Adam must help me hide John in the woods."

It was over an hour before Lucas returned.

"Father, they are British tanks headed to Brussels!" Lucas happily exclaimed. "I told the man who looked to be in charge that we have been hiding an American flyer who crashed his plane on our farm. They will be sending a truck to get him."

Early on September 3, 1944, John was picked up by an ambulance traveling with the British Second Army. A British corporal pulled up in front of the Peeter's farm and said, "Hey mate, you must be the American pilot I've been ordered to pick up. Gather your gear. Do you need help?"

"I feel fine. May I ride up front with you? Unfortunately, I've nothing to bring but these nine dog tags."

John said farewell to the family who risked their lives to save his and gingerly climbed into the front of the ambulance. "Someday, I hope to return to thank you for your kindness and generosity properly. I will inform my government where my nine brothers are buried."

By late that evening, they entered Brussels. The Germans had already fled the city, but before they left they set fire to several buildings in an attempt to destroy documents.

The next day, the Belgian forces made a victorious entry into Brussels alongside British soldiers. Thousands of civilians cheered the troops as they paraded through the streets. Some even climbed aboard the tanks as they rolled through town. The people of Brussels were euphoric as they celebrated their liberation from German occupation.

It was several more days before John could find someone to take him to Calais, France, where he was told he might secure transportation back to London.

It had been five months since John was declared missing in action. Although the family had not been officially notified, Virginia began to accept that John might not return.

The morning of September 24, Virginia awoke to the sun streaming through her window, falling warm across her face. Her father turned the radio on downstairs, and Virginia heard it reporting warm temperatures and sunny skies. Suddenly, a feeling of peace washed over her. Was it a premonition of something good to happen today?

"Dad, the phone is ringing," Virginia called. "I'm upstairs getting dressed for church. Can you answer it, please?"

"Hello? What? I can't hear you! Who? John? John! Virginia, come down quickly; it's your John calling from London!"

Virginia ran down the steps and collapsed into her father's arms, weeping for joy.

While recuperating in a London hospital, John learned he had broken his back, pelvis, left leg, left arm, and several ribs and suffered a severe concussion. The doctors in London told John he was lucky to have survived. John knew he owed Mr. and Mrs. Peeters and their sons an enormous debt of gratitude. (After the war, John corresponded with Noah regularly. Ten years after the war ended, John learned Noah's wife was ill. He now knew exactly how he could settle his debt. Ella was sent to a hospital in Zurich, and John paid all her medical expenses.)

A few days after he arrived in London, the Red Cross arranged for John's father to call his son to tell him about his mother's death.

John cried. "I feel that Mom's death is partly my fault," he said through his tears. "I know there wasn't anything I could have done, but I'm sure having me gone placed a great deal of pressure and stress on her, with me so far away."

John was released from the hospital on October 3, 1944. With his back injury and concussion, he was no longer fit to fly. He was sent back to Old Buck, where he was put in charge of debriefing returning pilots.

October 5, 1944

Mrs. Virginia Murphy
129 Gladstone Street
Dayton, Ohio USA

My darling Ginny,

I was released from the hospital and returned to my base here in Britain. Because of my back, I'm no longer flying, so they put me behind a desk. It's not a bad job, and it's helping me decompress and reflect on what's important in life.

We are going to enjoy a wonderful, long life, I promise. Take care, my love, and I hope to see you soon,

Love,
Johnny

It was October 10, 1945, and John was finally going home. He was one of almost fifteen thousand who were being sent home on the RMS *Queen Mary*.

The ship played an integral part during the war, transporting troops back and forth between England, the United States, and Canada. The entire structure had been painted navy gray, so she was dubbed the "Grey Ghost" during the war.

John arrived in New York on October 17. As soon as he found a phone booth, he called Virginia to say he was in New York and was taking a train to Cincinnati. His train was scheduled to arrive the afternoon of October 19.

A rowdy homecoming party met John as dozens of family and friends greeted him at the train station. There were hugs, tears, and hearty slaps on the back. John looked thin and was walking with a slight limp.

The next day, John and his father drove to Emmanuel Catholic Church to visit Susanna's grave. Years ago, she planted red roses in front of the house in Christiansburg. So, before they left, the two men picked a large bouquet, as autumn would soon see the last of the roses gone for the year. They left them at the base of her monument.

Several months after John returned to Christiansburg, he and his father decided to develop some of their farmland to build expensive, modern-style homes, naming the neighborhood "Wade Estates."

Christiansburg now comprised over five thousand residents, and after nearly one hundred and forty years, it was no longer a village, or even a small town, but a thriving city.

John suggested that they upgrade their construction company from a small family-owned business and start a corporation; they formed Murphy Construction, Inc.

John Sr. secured the position of president and loan officer. John Jr. was elected vice president and secretary and managed their marketing and sales, hiring two sales agents to work with him.

They asked William, Virginia's father, to join their partnership as treasurer and finance director. They then added a director of architecture and design and a construction foreman.

Murphy Construction had a stellar reputation for building top-quality homes. They were highly sought-after for their workmanship and innovative modern design. They treated their workers fairly, and their honesty was well-known by anyone who did business with them. As their company grew, they found other projects, acquiring more land and developing other neighborhoods.

In the years ahead, the company prospered. The Murphy family was considered wealthy, but they always remembered their humble roots.

On July 12, 1947, John and Virginia welcomed a little girl into the Murphy family. She had dark red hair like her grandpa. They named her Carol Ann. Living with her parents, grandfather, and great-grandmother, Carol never knew anything but love and affection.

EPILOGUE

*"From all that I can collect by your manner of talking,
you must be two of the silliest girls in the country.
I have suspected it some time, but I am now convinced."*

Jane Austen, *Pride and Prejudice*

After Lizzy read the stories that her great-grandpa John wrote, she and her grandma Carol left for Europe. But before they did, Carol gave Lizzy a handsome leather-bound journal to document the journey—and beyond.

August 9, 2018

There is so much to see and do in Paris. Here are my favorites: Notre-Dame de Paris (awe-inspiring); la Tour Eiffel (breathtaking); Le Louvre (Mona Lisa); Le Musée d'Orsay (Monet); Le Petit Palais (Rembrandt and Reubens); Church of Saint-Sulpice (magnificent pipe organ); Le Train Bleu (favorite restaurant).

Lizzy

August 12, 2018

OMG! The Orient Express was awesome! Grandma Carol and I each wore one of our new cocktail dresses for dinner. I felt like an heiress! I should have brought the family tiara! We saw castles, rivers, lakes, and mountains in France, Switzerland, Austria, and Italy.

Lizzy

August 17, 2018

Venice is so romantic, from gelato to the singing gondoliers to the Peach Bellini (yes, Grandma let me take a sip). Our gondolier was handsome with his striped shirt, straw hat, and neckerchief. I'm coming back someday with my husband…if I ever get married.

Lizzy

August 20, 2018

Grandma Carol and I rode the high-speed train to Vienna and are staying at Hotel Sacher. We shared a piece of the legendary Sacher-Torte, just like Great-grandma Virginia used to bake. I'm glad Grandma and I added Vienna to our itinerary. We must look for Mr. Baum's jewelry store.

Lizzy

August 24, 2018

I love Vienna. We toured the Hofburg Imperial Palace and ate at the Palmenhaus; then we attended a Mozart & Strauss concert in the Orangery at the Schönbrunn Palace. The highlight was a performance of the famous Lipizzaner horses at the Spanish Riding School.

Lizzy

August 27, 2018

Driving on the left side of these narrow Irish roads is scary, especially through the roundabouts. We haven't met one O'Sullivan, but we've seen some astonishing sights. They say Ireland is comprised of forty shades of green. I believe it!

Lizzy

August 30, 2018

I'm getting the hang of driving on the left! We visited Cork and had dinner at Murphy's Fish & Chip Shop. I wonder if they could be related to our Murphys. Grandma was dizzy the rest of the day after leaning backward to kiss the Blarney Stone!

Lizzy

September 1, 2018

Grandma Carol and I checked into our London flat today in Kensington. We walked to Marks & Spencer for groceries, and later we rode the Tube to Covent Garden, where we ate dinner at Rock & Sole Plaice, London's oldest fish & chips restaurant. The mushy peas are not something I'd want to eat every day. Tomorrow we will try and find Mr. Thomas Bailey's furniture store.

Lizzy

September 17, 2018

We commissioned a tour of London on a double-decker bus. I think Grandma and I have done all the touristy things and seen everything there is to see here in London. Yesterday, we rode to the Ritz for afternoon tea in one of London's iconic taxis. I LOVE Victoria Sponge Cake! Tomorrow we're taking the train to Windsor, to tour Windsor Castle.

Lizzy

September 24, 2018

We went to the theatre last night and saw the musical Wicked! It really was "wicked." LOL! Sadly, we couldn't find Mr. Bailey's furniture store or Mrs. Ashburn's China Shop. Next week we are going to Bath.

Lizzy

October 1, 2018

We stayed two nights in Bath, in the B&B that was Jane Austen's home. We stayed in the Lizzy Bennet suite. Since my name is Christina Elizabeth, I've decided I want to be called Christina; the name has such a great family history. Though I love Jane Austen, I think I've outgrown being called Lizzy.

Christina

October 8, 2018

We are in Alton and found the Alton Grammar School, where Philip Crane was the schoolmaster. There is a small B&B nearby; Grandma is sure it's where Philip and Margaret Crane lived. We visited the Church of St Lawrence where Philip and Margaret were married in 1790.

Christina

October 9, 2018

A local explained how to find the old mill site on the River Wey just outside Alton. The mill wheel is lying in a wooded area near the river. The millhouse and the house are in ruins. I snapped many pictures.

Christina

October 11, 2018

Grandma and I visited the Chawton House Library. It is a large Elizabethan manor house, centuries old! It was one of the homes of Edward Austen Knight but is now open to the public.

Christina

October 12, 2018

Chawton is lovely! The Bailey family still owns the Bailey Estate—a grand Elizabethan manor house now open to the public for tours and events. Grandma and I met the estate's manager. After hearing our story he introduced us to the current owners. They were very friendly and, believe it or not, invited us in for tea. We also visited St Nicholas Church, where Christian and Marie Wade were married in 1766.

Christina

October 15, 2018

Grandma and I are back in London and packing for home. We sail tomorrow for New York on the Queen Mary. We are taking a side trip to Maryland before we return home. We fly into O'Hare on October 27th.

Christina

October 24, 2018

We reached Frederick, Maryland, and found the site where the Wade's mill sat along Carroll Creek. Of course the mill is gone, but there is an old abandoned stone house; perhaps the Swadener's house. We visited Mount Olivet Cemetery, where we discovered the graves of Lydia Wade and Francis Scott Key. This area is charming, with lots of farms and rolling hills. Maybe someday I'll return and hike the Appalachian Trail; Grandma said it wouldn't be with her!

Christina

October 27, 2018

Grandma Carol and I returned from Europe the same two people but somehow changed. Each of us looked at the experience from a different perspective. Grandma connected with her past while I planned my future.

Grandma wanted to show me the family history through the eyes of my great-grandfather, John Murphy. She accomplished this to the best of her ability. I'm certain her father would be pleased with the results.

My given name is Christina and my middle name is Elizabeth. I love the family history behind both my names, but I've been called Lizzy from the day I was born. While on our European tour, I decided that at eighteen I've outgrown this nickname. I now want everyone to know me as Christina. I jokingly told Grandma that we should have brought the family tiara on our trip for me to wear because I am now Christina III.

The places we visited were awe-inspiring, and the trip gave me a much greater appreciation for the stories that my great-grandfather worked so hard on for so many years. But I don't want to look only at the past; I'm ready to focus on my future.

Christina

November 1, 2018

The last seven days of our trip were spent crossing the Atlantic back to America aboard the Queen Mary, relaxing and planning our next adventure. Together, Grandma Carol and I made a huge decision and knew we needed to discuss it with my parents. Once back in Chicago, Grandma helped me lay out my plan.

My parents know how much I love them and Chicago, but my mom knows just how special Christiansburg is to me. I explained that I wanted to live there with Grandma Carol—with their blessing of course—and apply to the University of Dayton, Great-grandpa John's alma mater. Instead of Culinary School, I want to study English Literature and perhaps teach someday at a college or university.

I explained to my parents that I enjoy cooking, but for my life's work, I want to become an educator like Philip Crane—and even Christina I and Christina II. I reminded them of how much I loved going to Christiansburg in the summers and spending time in Grandma's library reading the old books I found in her cupboard, particularly books by my favorite English author, Jane Austen.

Another idea Grandma and I discussed with Mom and Dad was to convert the two log cabins in the woods. One would become a wedding chapel while the other would be a tearoom and gift shop. With Grandma's marketing skills, I know we could make both venues work, plus it will give Grandma something to occupy her time. We even discussed reimagining the barn and holding fall festivals every year, selling pumpkins and apple butter and offering hayrides with Great-grandpa John's old tractor; maybe even selling antiques and bric-a-bracs. We listed out the pros and cons, and in my opinion, the pros definitely outweigh the cons. Mom and Dad gave their blessing for me to attend UD in the spring.

Christina

January 14, 2019

The week I started classes, work began on renovating the two log cabins.

First, a small parking lot was created next to the barn. The plans call for meandering paths with lights along the paved trails. Grandma has commissioned a company to add landscaping and flowers around the cottages to create the look of an old English garden.

The exteriors of each cabin will be carefully covered in white clapboard, so as to not damage the logs. At a local store selling vintage hardware, we found beautiful old chandeliers.

The first log cabin is being converted into the wedding chapel, with stained glass fitted into the existing windows. A steeple will be built and placed on top of the chapel. We acquired pews from an old church and an antique spinet piano. Lastly, a sign is being commissioned to be placed out front welcoming everyone to the "Little Chapel-In-The-Woods." Our wedding chapel will be open just in time for the summer wedding season.

The second log home will be turned into a quaint tearoom, made to look like an old English country cottage. We even found a company to thatch the roof.

Red climbing roses have been planted and trained onto white trellises on either side of the freshly painted red front door. Tea, teapots, cups, and other tea-related items will be available for sale. The pastel colors, white tables, and white café chairs take a cue from Grandma's shabby chic morning room.

We named the tearoom "Red Rose Cottage Tea Room" after Margaret and Philip Crane's cottage in Alton, England.

Christina

May 12, 2020

It has been almost two years since Grandma Carol and I returned from Europe, and the tearoom and wedding chapel are successfully up and running.

Our plan now is to organize a harvest festival to be held at the Wade Homestead on Friday, October 18. It will be the 50th Wade Harvest Festival, one hundred and fifty-six years after the last one was held in 1863.

We sent invitations to aunts, uncles, cousins, parents, grandparents, godparents, college, high school, and work friends. Fifteen distant cousins from Idaho are planning to come, and a young couple from England named James and Mary Bailey sent their RSVP.

We will decorate the house, barn, chapel, and tearoom with fall embellishments and trimmings, including pumpkins, hay bales, and dozens of potted mums in various colors. White twinkle lights will cover the trees, and a large white tent will sit on the front lawn. A pig roast with all the trimmings is being catered, and we hired a local country band. And, just like back in the 1800s, we expect almost everyone to stay until well after midnight.

Christina

May 4, 2024

Today I will proudly graduate with my Master of Science in Education from the University of Dayton.

Many changes have occurred over the past three-hundred and sixty-one years since my ancestors built their mill in Alton, England, in 1663.

No one can predict the future, and the many changes in just one lifetime only compound over a dozen generations. But one thing for my family that has never changed is still standing in the library of the old house in Christiansburg, where I live with Grandma Carol.

It was built in 1766 from the wood of a Wych elm tree, and that one thing is—Christina's Cupboard.

Christina

The Beginning

WADE BIBLE ENTRIES

Christian Henry Wade
Son of Samuel and Mary Ann Wade
Birth: 27 February 1747 Alton in Hampshire, England
Mill Owner and Farmer
Death: 3 March 1831 Christiansburg Ohio
84 years – Angina
Married: 6 September 1766 St Nicholas Church
Chawton in Hampshire, England
Wife: Marie Elizabeth Bailey
Daughter of Thomas and Mary Bailey
Birth: 14 June 1749 Hawthorne Hall, Chawton in Hampshire, England
Death: 15 January 1828 Christiansburg Ohio
79 years – Dropsy

Margaret Marie Wade
Daughter of Christian and Marie Wade
Birth: 14 August 1767 Alton in Hampshire, England
Milliner, Seamstress, and Mercantile Owner
Death: 25 September 1838 Christiansburg Ohio
71 years – Diphtheria
Married: 10 July 1790 Church of St Lawrence
Alton in Hampshire, England
Husband: Philip Alistair Crane
Son of Martin and Lucy Crane
Birth: 4 May 1767 Deane in Hampshire, England
Schoolmaster, Carpenter, Builder, Farmer, Mercantile Owner, and Master Beekeeper
Death: 27 September 1838 Christiansburg Ohio
71 years – Diphtheria

Jacob Henry Wade
Son of Christian and Marie Wade
Birth: 23 September 1772 Alton in Hampshire, England
Mill Owner, Farmer, and Soldier
Fought in The War of 1812: 16th Regiment – Maryland Militia
Death: 6 March 1846 Christiansburg Ohio
75 years – Apoplexy
Married: 5 May 1791 St Andrews Church
Farnham in Surrey, England
Wife: Sarah Jane Langley
Daughter of John and Martha Langley
Birth: 2 October 1775 Farnham in Surrey, England
Death: 24 September 1813 Christiansburg Ohio
39 years – Melancholy

John Christian Wade
Son of Jacob and Sarah Wade
Birth: 2 April 1794 Frederick Town Maryland
Farmer, Trapper, Fur Trader, and Soldier
Fought in The War of 1812: 16th Regiment – Maryland Militia
Death: 5 November 1882 Grangeville Idaho
88 years – Natural Cause (died in his sleep)
Married 1st Wife: 9 September 1815 St Joseph's Catholic Church
Dayton Ohio
Married 2nd Wife: 10 June 1849
Oregon Territory
1st Wife: Cynthia Jane Daniel
Daughter of William and Ruth Daniel
Birth: 8 July 1796 Philadelphia Pennsylvania
Jesuit Missionary
Death: 6 December 1845 St Joseph's Mission
Oregon Territory
49 years – Grippe
2nd Wife: Dyani – Lemhi Shoshone Akaitikka
Birth: Abt. 1822
Death: Unknown

Emmett Ryker "Rye" Wade
Son of John and Cynthia Wade
Birth: 2 February 1820 Christiansburg Ohio
Trapper and Wheat Farmer
Death: 2 January 1890 Grangeville Idaho
70 years – Influenza
Married: 5 May 1843 St Mary's Mission, Oregon Territory
Wife: Matika – Bitterroot Salish – Flathead Tribe
Birth: Abt. 1828
Death: 4 January 1890 Grangeville Idaho
Abt. 62 years – Influenza

> **Jacob Emmett Wade**
> **Son of Emmett and Matika Wade**
> Birth: 3 June 1844 St Joseph's Mission
> Oregon Territory
> Death: Unknown

> **John Christian Wade II**
> **Son of Emmett and Matika Wade**
> Birth: 14 August 1846 St Joseph's Mission
> Oregon Territory
> Death: Unknown

Emma Marie Wade
Daughter of John and Cynthia Wade
Birth: 2 February 1820 Christiansburg Ohio
Death: 2 February 1820 Christiansburg Ohio
Infant – Stillborn

Lydia Marie Wade
Daughter of Jacob and Sarah Wade
Birth: 20 September 1797 Frederick Town Maryland
Death: 25 December 1809 Frederick Town Maryland
12 years – Consumption

Christina Elizabeth Wade
Daughter of Jacob and Sarah Wade
Birth: 18 October 1804 Frederick Town Maryland
Schoolmistress
Death: 12 August 1889 Christiansburg Ohio
84 years – Heart Disease
Married: 18 October 1827 Christ Episcopal Church
Christiansburg Ohio
Husband: James Kean "Jamie" O'Sullivan III
Son of James II and Kiera O'Sullivan
Birth: 21 May 1809 Cumberland Maryland
Carpenter, Builder, and Soldier
Fought in the War of the Rebellion – Sharpshooter
Private – Co. G 66th Illinois Infantry Regiment (Reed's Sharpshooters)
Death: 3 September 1883 Christiansburg Ohio
74 years – Stomach Cancer

> **Sarah Jane O'Sullivan**
> **Daughter of James III and Christina Wade O'Sullivan**
> Birth: 16 August 1829 Dayton Ohio
> Death: 15 August 1833 Dayton Ohio
> 3 years 11 months – Cholera
>
> **James Kean "Little Jamie" O'Sullivan IV**
> **Son of James III and Christina Wade O'Sullivan**
> Birth: 27 February 1831 Dayton Ohio
> Death: 14 August 1833 Dayton Ohio
> 2 years 6 months – Cholera
>
> **Mary Jane O'Sullivan**
> **Daughter of James III and Christina Wade O'Sullivan**
> Birth: 10 November 1834 Dayton Ohio
> Owner – Creager Ice Cream Parlor and Bakery Shop
> Death: 23 November 1913 Dayton Ohio
> 79 years – Breast Cancer
> Married: 2 February 1856 St Paul's Lutheran Church
> Dayton Ohio

Husband: David "Davey" Peter Creager IV
Son of David III and Laura Creager
Birth: 10 February 1834 Christiansburg Ohio
Owner – Creager Ice Cream Parlor and Bakery Shop
Death: 17 August 1902 Dayton Ohio
68 years – Buggy Accident

> **David Peter Creager V**
> **Son of David IV and Mary Jane Creager**
> Birth: 24 July 1857 Dayton Ohio
> Owner – Creager Ice Cream Parlor and Bakery Shop
> Death: 29 October 1925 Dayton Ohio
> 68 years – Heart Attack

Elizabeth "Lizzy" Marie O'Sullivan
Daughter of James III and Christina Wade O'Sullivan
Birth: 23 May 1839 Dayton Ohio
Death: 20 February 1905 Dayton Ohio
65 years – Breast Cancer
Married: 23 May 1857 Christ Episcopal Church
Christiansburg Ohio
Husband: Josiah Gibson Richter
Son of Joseph and Ellen Richter
Birth: 2 April 1832 Lancaster County Virginia Attorney
Death: 4 July 1907 Dayton Ohio
75 years – Infection (tooth extraction)

> **Karl Richter**
> **Son of Josiah and Elizabeth Richer**
> Birth: 15 July 1858 Dayton Ohio
> Death: 4 August 1909 Dayton Ohio
> 51 years – Heart Attack

> **Klaus Richter**
> **Son of Josiah and Elizabeth Richter**
> Birth: 15 July 1858 Dayton Ohio
> Death: 19 May 1938 Dayton Ohio
> 79 years – Heart Attack

George "Georgie" Edward O'Sullivan II
Son of James III and Christina Wade O'Sullivan
Birth: 1 June 1844 Christiansburg Ohio
Carpenter, Builder, and Soldier
Fought in the War of the Rebellion
Sergeant – Co. C 63rd Ohio Infantry Regiment
Death: 22 January 1928 Christiansburg Ohio
83 years – Age-Related Heart Disease
Married: 23 December 1865 Emmanuel Catholic Church
Dayton Ohio
Wife: Sally Ann O'Malley
Daughter of Simon and Ann O'Malley
Birth: 4 July 1845 Dayton Ohio
Death: 1 December 1866 Christiansburg Ohio
21 years – Eclampsia Convulsions (childbirth complications)

Charles "Charlie" Eugene O'Sullivan
Son of James III and Christina Wade O'Sullivan
Birth: 21 April 1849 Christiansburg Ohio
Gave his life for our Country during the War of the Rebellion
Private – Co. K 179th Ohio Infantry
Death: 10 December 1864 Nashville Tennessee
15 years – Typhoid Fever

> **Christina "Tina" Elizabeth O'Sullivan**
> **Daughter of George and Sally Ann O'Sullivan**
> Birth: 1 December 1866 Christiansburg Ohio
> Teacher – Graduate of Oberlin College, May 1888
> Death: 25 November 1958 Christiansburg Ohio
> 92 years – Stroke
> Married: 26 September 1891 Emmanuel Catholic Church
> Dayton Ohio
> **Husband: Sean Patrick Murphy**
> **Son of Jack and Emma Murphy**
> Birth: 19 June 1865 Boston Massachusetts
> Carpenter and Builder
> Dayton/Christiansburg Ohio
> Death: 17 June 1892 Dayton Ohio
> 26 years – Broken Neck (work accident)

John Patrick Murphy Sr
Son of Sean and Christina O'Sullivan Murphy
Birth: 22 July 1892 Dayton Ohio
Land Owner/Developer and General Contractor
Dayton/Christiansburg Ohio
Death: 15 August 1967 Christiansburg Ohio
75 years – Myocardial Infarction (broken hip and surgery)
Married: 13 June 1914 Emmanuel Catholic Church
Dayton Ohio
Wife: Susanna Lillie Barr
Daughter of Claude and Goldie Barr
Birth: 14 March 1895 Northumberland Pennsylvania
Death: 12 April 1944 Christiansburg Ohio
49 years – Brain Aneurysm

John Patrick Murphy Jr
Son of John Sr and Susanna Murphy
Birth: 1 May 1916 Dayton Ohio
Land Owner/Developer and General Contractor
Dayton/Christiansburg Ohio
Fought in The Second World War
Pilot B-24 Liberator 735th Bomb Squadron
Death: 15 July 2012 Christiansburg Ohio
96 years – Natural Causes
Married: 11 April 1942 St Paul's Lutheran Church
Dayton Ohio
Wife: Virginia "Ginny" Marie Nielsen
Daughter of William and Hannah Nielsen
Birth: 28 March 1923 Sandusky Ohio
Death: 4 June 2018 Christiansburg Ohio
95 years – Intracerebral Hemorrhage

Carol Ann Murphy
Daughter of John Jr and Virginia Murphy
Birth: 12 July 1947 Dayton Ohio
Advertising Executive – Chicago Illinois
Married: 6 September 1969
St Paul's Lutheran Church Dayton Ohio
Divorced: 10 June 1980
1ˢᵗ Husband: David Alan Edwards
Son of Raymond and Ginger Edwards
Birth: 19 May 1946 Columbus Ohio
Attorney – Cleveland Ohio
Carol Ann Murphy Edwards Married: 19 May 2002 Palm Beach
2ⁿᵈ Husband: Gary Michael Davis
Son of Robert and Shirley Davis
Birth: 31 December 1942 Milwaukee Wisconsin
Advertising Executive – Chicago Illinois
Death: 25 January 2010 Palm Beach Florida
68 years – Pancreatic Cancer

> **Jenny Kristine Edwards**
> **Daughter of David and Carol Edwards**
> Birth: 26 May 1972 Cleveland Ohio
> Restaurant Owner – LaSalle Chop House
> Chicago Illinois
> Married: 19 September 1998
> Grace Cathedral Chicago Illinois
> **Husband: Brian Michael Peters**
> **Son of Miles and Brenda Peters**
> Birth: 24 July 1972 Chicago Illinois
> Cardiologist – Chicago Illinois

> > **Christina Elizabeth "Lizzy" Peters**
> > **Daughter of Brian and Jenny Peters**
> > Birth: 25 March 2000 Chicago Illinois

I hope you enjoyed this book. Would you do me a favor?

Like all authors, I rely on online reviews to encourage future sales. Your opinion is invaluable. Would you take a few moments now to share your assessment of my book at the review site of your choice? Your opinion will help the book marketplace become more transparent and useful to all.

Thank you very much!